# HASHTAG HOLIDATE

## LUCY LENNOX

ISBN: 978-1-954857-69-8



**Cover Design:** Najla Qamber | Qamber Designs
**Cover Illustration:** LIS Artworks
**Editing:** One Love Editing
**Proofreading:** Jodi Duggan

# HASHTAG HOLIDATE

I came to Legacy, Montana, to sell a fantasy—twelve Insta-ready #Holidates of Christmas. One career-making brand deal. Zero drama.

Then my videographer bailed, and in walked Maddox Sullivan.

Grumpy. Gorgeous. Growly. A mountain man with zero chill and even less tolerance for influencers like me. He agrees to film my content—off-camera only—but when my first date cancels, guess who ends up in front of the lens?

Cue the fireworks.

Our chemistry is instant. My followers are obsessed. #TeamMaddrian starts trending. Suddenly, all my dates are mysteriously dropping out, and Maddox is reluctantly starring in every single holidate—sleigh rides, snowball fights, cocoa by the fire, kisses under the mistletoe.

And I... I'm starting to forget this was ever supposed to be pretend.

Because every time Maddox looks at me, I feel something real.
Something lasting. Something terrifying.

I came here for curated content. Now, I'm dreaming of a life I
never thought I wanted—with a man I never saw coming.
But am I falling for the picture-perfect holiday fantasy? Or could
this be the start of my real-life happily ever after?

# 1

# #LUXURYMEETSLEGACY

## ADRIAN

I STARED out the rental car window at the weathered timber sign.

*Legacy, Montana. Population 8,743.*

In other words, too small for a good wine bar. They probably had domestic beer on draft and antlers on the walls of their one roadhouse.

My phone buzzed with another notification. I didn't bother looking, not only because I was driving, but also because I already knew what it would say. Three thousand followers lost this week. The comment under a recent post had summed it up: *Getting boring, Adrian. Same old luxury hotels. Yawn.*

Which was exactly why I was here, of course, freezing my ass off in twenty-eight-degree weather instead of lounging poolside in LA. My latest sponsor, Nordique luxury après-ski wear, wanted "true holiday magic"—the kind of wholesome Christmas content I'd never done. But if I pulled this off, it could mean a full-time brand ambassador deal. The kind of eye-popping money that would keep me from crawling back to Connecticut to work for my father's insurance company.

I'd spent five years building a brand, and Adrian Hayes—the luxury lifestyle personality and digital nomad—wasn't known for small towns. I thrived in cosmopolitan cities and exclusive resorts, places where the lighting was perfect and the backdrops were designed to be photographed. Not... I looked around at the rustic town of Legacy and sighed. Hunter McShotgun's Wilderness Outpost.

But maybe rustic could work. Maybe the small-town vibe would give me exactly the kind of authenticity and relatability I'd been missing in recent posts. At least I really freaking hoped it did because the project with Nordique had the potential for much more.

When I'd first pulled up the company's social media tags on my laptop, I'd winced. "Looks like their target demographic is forty- to fifty-year-olds," I'd protested to my manager, moving to my phone to scroll through my own posts—rooftop cocktails in Miami, a celebrity chef's restaurant opening in New York, a carefully curated beach day in Malibu. I squinted at the monitor to see if there were any visible signs of aging. "What the hell do they want with *me*? Do I look fifteen years older than I am?"

"Of course not, babe. But Nordique wants a spokesmodel who's aspirational, not actually old as shit," Vic had countered with the brutal honesty that made him both an excellent manager and a terrifying human being. "Every gay man with a jawline and a ring light would suck Old Man Winter's you-know-what for this client. Stop whining and say yes. You'll make it elegant and unique. You always do."

*Elegant and unique.* That phrase had echoed in my head for days after I'd agreed to take the job.

In the influencer world, you had to give people the same but different. They wanted a consistent personality but not the same old repeated content. I'd built my following by being aspirational but approachable, luxurious but attainable. For the women, I was the gay best friend they wished they had, with a life they wished they could afford. For the gays, I was the man they dreamed of and sent their lurid fantasies (and pics) to. For the straight men, I was the account they loved to hate and the person who set their wife's bar hella fucking high.

I was also known for being a little bit different. A little bit unpredictable. Take the time I did a skincare tutorial using glacier runoff in Iceland. Or the time I turned my broken umbrella into a prop on a Scottish Highlands tour and got reposted by *Vogue*.

Which was why I was low-key panicking now. Unpredictable wasn't easy to plan on short notice.

After scrambling for a concept that would combine "dressing to impress" with celebrating the holidays, I'd finally landed on "The Twelve Dates of Christmas." Twelve videos of me experiencing holiday traditions while modeling Nordique's winter collection.

When I'd hinted at the upcoming series and asked for location recommendations, my followers had suggested too many places to count. But one had stood out as the perfect choice. Nordique's tagline was "Where luxury meets legacy," which meant Legacy, Montana, with its single ski slope and its small but growing reputation as a hidden gem for LGBTQ+ travelers was a clear winner.

Hopefully, a town this small, maybe with the help of its tourist population, would be able to provide a dozen potential "romances" with small-town guys for my followers to get invested in, too.

All I needed was a videographer since my usual cameraman's emergency appendectomy had left me hanging.

But first, I needed a small vat of coffee to combat the effects of my early morning flight.

When I parked and stepped out of the car, the cold air immediately bit at my face, and my breath formed little clouds in front of me. I zipped my jacket higher and said a silent apology to my beautiful Prada winter boots—which had never seen actual snow until today—as I crunched down the icy street.

I had to admit, the place was cute, if you liked this sort of aesthetic. The main street looked like a Christmas card—timber storefronts draped in lights, snow underfoot, the scent of pine and woodsmoke in the air, so different from LA's perpetual mix of exhaust fumes and distant ocean.

I slowed as I passed the hardware store, its windows filled with an elaborate vintage Christmas display featuring mechanical elves and miniature trains circling through snow-covered villages. An actual, old-school hardware store, not some hipster interpretation with $500 hammers and artisanal nails. How refreshingly... *authentic*. I was starting to feel more positive about this place already.

An art gallery window display caught my eye—large-format photographs of what appeared to be last year's Starlight Ski Spectacular—the most famous of Legacy's holiday traditions, according to my research. Unlike the typical tourist shots I'd seen, though, these images captured something raw and emotional— skiers silhouetted against thousands of twinkling lights, faces illuminated with genuine joy, the sensation of movement so vivid I could almost feel the powder spray.

I stepped closer, intrigued. These weren't the posed, oversaturated pictures that dominated Instagram. They were so real I could practically feel the cold air and hear the laughter. One photo in particular held my attention—two women embracing at the bottom of the slope, rainbow light necklaces glowing against the snow, their faces a perfect balance of exhaustion, affection, and elation.

The placard read simply "Winter Light Series by Maddox Sullivan."

I pulled out my phone and found the man's Instagram. He was a Legacy local. Modest follower count, but his feed was compelling—natural landscapes, candid portraits, moments captured rather than created. It was the complete opposite of my carefully curated feed.

Then I hit his self-portrait, and my thumb froze on the screen.

Maddox Sullivan wasn't the aging hippie or tweedy academic I'd expected. He was probably close to my thirty-two years, with broad shoulders, tousled dark hair, and rugged features that radiated quiet confidence and made my stomach do a little swoop. No filters, no angles—just messy, magnetic reality.

The contrast between his realness and my curated content hit me like a slap. But it also sparked an idea.

What if I could combine luxury with real? What if "The Twelve Dates of Christmas" featured someone who embodied everything my brand *wasn't*—someone authentic, unpolished, and rooted in this place?

I needed Maddox Sullivan behind my camera.

And maybe, if I was lucky, I could get him in front of it, too.

I pushed open the gallery door, the bell jingling merrily as I entered. The space was smaller than expected but beautiful, with exposed brick walls and polished hardwood floors that creaked pleasantly underfoot. Local art filled the walls—not just Maddox Sullivan's photography but paintings, sculptures, and mixed-media pieces that collectively told the story of the town and its surroundings.

The woman behind the counter looked up with a smile. She appeared to be in her early thirties, with a messy auburn bun on top of her head and big-framed glasses perched on her freckled nose. She wore a red turtleneck sweater under a well-worn pair of denim overalls, complete with telltale paint splotches on them. In a nearby portable crib-thingy slept a baby with cherubic cheeks and perfect red lips.

"Welcome to the Hart Gallery. I'm Avery. Anything I can help you find today?"

I flashed my most charming smile, the one that consistently garnered the most engagement on my selfies. "Actually, yes. I'm looking for information about Maddox Sullivan. The photographer?"

"Oh, Maddox!" Her eyes lit up with recognition. "Those winter shots are something special, aren't they? He's not in today, but his studio's just upstairs. He does commercial work and videography, too, if that's what you're looking for."

I glanced up at the ceiling as if I could see through it to the studio above. "Commercial work," I murmured, feeling my shoulders relax in relief.

Avery nodded. "He's very talented. Been capturing Legacy since he was a teenager with his first camera. That's his hardware store you probably passed on your way in."

"Oh, right," I said, remembering the charming Christmas display. I was momentarily surprised she clocked me as a new arrival, but I supposed in a place like this, anything new stuck out. "He's a photographer, *and* he runs the hardware store?"

"The Sullivan family's run the store for four generations. Though I think Maddox himself has more interest in cameras than hammers." She shrugged.

I smiled politely. "Do you know the best way to get in contact with him? Should I just stop by the store?"

"Not sure if he's working today." She reached beneath the counter and produced a simple but elegant business card on heavy stock. Sullivan & Lens, it read, with a website and a small logo that combined a camera aperture with a mountain silhouette.

"He's probably slammed right now because of the holiday, but you can shoot him a text or email."

"Appreciate it," I said with a final smile, tucking the card into my wallet.

I left the gallery feeling more optimistic than I had all day. Finding a skilled videographer in Legacy had seemed like an impossible task, but now I had a lead—and from what I'd seen of his work, Maddox Sullivan might be exactly what I needed to make "The Twelve Dates of Christmas" the viral success that would help me land Nordique as a permanent sponsor.

I grabbed a coffee at a small local shop and pulled out my phone as I walked back to my car, opening my email app to compose a message to him. I needed to strike the right tone— professional but enticing, acknowledging the short notice but emphasizing the opportunity. I hoped he'd recognize what a fantastic situation this could be for him. My platform could bring his work to a much wider audience.

I hesitated before hitting Send, rereading what I'd written.

*Hi, my name is Adrian Hayes (@realadrianhayes), and I'm a digital content creator filming a holiday content series for Nordique in and around Legacy over the next three weeks. I'm looking for a videographer since my usual guy had a medical emergency and when I saw your work at the Hart Gallery, particularly the Winter Light Series, I thought your eye for winter scenes was amazing and would really elevate the project.*

*Let me know if you're interested and we can talk numbers, but I do think this could be a great opportunity for you to grow your plat-form. (I have 1.2 million followers.)*

*Talk soon,*
*Adrian Hayes*

I hit Send before I could overthink it further, then started my car and programmed my nav app for the rental cabin I'd be calling home for the next few weeks. As I pulled away from the gallery, I realized I was already mentally rearranging my content calendar, imagining shots of Legacy's Christmas lights, the "famous" ski spectacle, and the charming small-town holiday celebrations—all with the ruggedly handsome Maddox Sullivan behind the camera.

If he agreed, of course.

Why wouldn't he, though? The money was excellent, the exposure real, the opportunity substantial.

But by the following morning, there was no response from Maddox Sullivan.

So I took the bull by the horns, as they probably said in places like this, and made my way into town in search of the man.

The hardware store smelled like sawdust and cinnamon, a combination that made no sense but somehow worked. I spotted him immediately—broad shoulders in a faded gray thermal, dark jeans worn just right, and a messy shock of hair that looked like it had never seen a styling product in its life.

*Hot. Annoyingly so.*

I adjusted my cashmere scarf and strolled toward the counter, flashing my best charming-but-not-trying-too-hard smile. "Maddox Sullivan?"

He turned, giving me a slow, assessing look. His eyes—storm-cloud gray, because of course they were—landed on my perfectly curated winter ensemble before flicking back up.

"Who's asking?" His smooth and slightly dismissive voice caught me off guard, sending an unexpected ripple of warmth through my chest. I covered it with my most practiced professional smile.

I wasn't sure whether to be offended or intrigued. "Adrian Hayes. I'm the one who emailed you about a videography job."

Maddox blinked, then pulled his phone from his back pocket. He thumbed through his messages for all of three seconds before snorting. "Oh. Right." He locked the screen and slid the phone back, as if the conversation was already over.

I frowned. "I assume you realize it's a paid opportunity?"

"Yep." He reached for a screwdriver from a nearby shelf, inspecting it with far too much interest for someone who wasn't actively fixing something.

"And?"

He set the screwdriver down with a quiet clink and finally—*finally*—looked at me again. "Not interested."

I blinked. "I— Are you serious?"

"Yep." His mouth quirked in something that wasn't quite a smile. "I don't do influencer gigs."

A couple passing by with a shopping cart slowed to eavesdrop, exchanging glances when they heard his response. My cheeks warmed—I wasn't used to rejection, especially not with an audience.

I stared at him, waiting for the punchline. He wasn't joking.

An older woman at the cashier stand nearby must have heard us because she said, "He also doesn't do vacations, sick days, or anything remotely fun since—" She angled a fond but stern glance at him. "Since forever, basically. But he's the best photographer in three counties when he's not being a complete grouch."

Maddox's jaw tightened. "Thank you, Bonnie. Isn't it time for your break?"

"My shift started twenty minutes ago."

But a nearby customer asked for her help finding something, leaving an awkward silence between the grouch and me.

"Like she said—" I gestured vaguely toward the gallery down the street. "—you're a photographer. And a videographer. And people pay you to take pictures. That's what I'm trying to do here."

He crossed his arms, those strong forearms flexing against his sleeves in a way I refused to acknowledge. "You run a content farm. I don't work on farms."

I huffed out a breath, willing patience into my voice. "You don't understand. This wouldn't just be 'content.' It's a high-production-value brand deal with authentic—"

"I'm thinking *you* don't understand," he interrupted. "I don't do scripted moments. I don't do posed perfection. And I sure as hell don't do Christmas campaigns for luxury après-ski brands."

Part of me—the part of me that suffered from debilitating FOMO—admired his ability to say "no" so decisively.

But unfortunately for Maddox Sullivan, the rest of me was competitive as fuck. This guy was the best Legacy had to offer... and I wasn't the type to take no for an answer.

#ProjectHotAndGrumpy #IrresistibleForceVsImmovableFlannelShirt #MaddoxOrBust #ChallengeAccepted

**2**

# #THANKYOUNEXT

## MADDOX

"You told him *what*?" Maya's voice hit a pitch that made me wince.

"I told him no." As she sat on the counter kicking her feet, I continued stacking the winter emergency kits by the front register, preparing for the annual rush of tourists who'd inevitably get themselves stuck in snow drifts come December. The familiar weight of the kits in my hands was grounding—four generations of Sullivans had prepared Legacy for winter emergencies, and I wasn't about to break the chain.

"Back up. *The* Adrian Hayes—who has over a million followers and works with luxury brands even I've heard of—came to see you yesterday... and you told him you don't work on 'content farms'?" Though I wasn't looking directly at her, I could *hear* her eye roll.

"That's exactly what I said." I adjusted the display of hand-crank flashlights that wouldn't die when the batteries inevitably froze. These were the flashlights Dad had insisted on stocking after that blizzard in '08 had left half the town without power for three days. "Real tools for real problems," he'd always said—a

Sullivan Hardware motto that didn't exactly mesh with influencer aesthetics.

"Maddox. Seriously?" My seventeen-year-old sister sounded more like forty-seven sometimes. "You do realize that was an opportunity, right? The kind that pays actual money?"

I grunted, tucking a pack of hand warmers into a kit. "I have a job. Two, in fact." *Three, if we count parenting a seventeen-year-old.*

"A job that requires you to arrange emergency kits in a hardware store that's been slowly declining in revenue since Mom and Dad died. And your other job is *literally what he's trying to hire you for!*"

I stopped mid-motion, the familiar pang hitting my chest at the mention of our father. Three years, and it still felt raw. "Helping run the family business isn't something I need to apologize for. And my photography schedule is already packed with family portraits and Santa stuff. You know that."

I ran my hand along the worn edge of the counter—the same counter where Dad had taught me to count change, where Mom had set up her Christmas cookie station every December, where I'd developed my first roll of film in the back room because I couldn't afford proper equipment. This wasn't just a failing business; it was the physical embodiment of our family history.

"Your photography could have a much bigger audience if you didn't have the marketing instincts of a particularly antisocial brick," Maya replied. "Look, I appreciate everything you've done—taking care of me, keeping the store going—but I'm months away from college. You need to think about what's next for you."

"I'm thinking about what's next for *us*," I corrected, moving toward the window display to check that the vintage mechanical elves Dad had insisted on setting up every year were still working properly. "After you're at school, I'll have plenty of time to—"

Maya hopped off the counter and followed me. "To what? Take

more wedding photos of people who can barely afford your already too-low rates? Turn down opportunities that could actually put Sullivan & Lens on the map?"

I rolled my eyes. "Tell me how you really feel, Maya."

"Maddie," she said more softly, using the childhood nickname that always made me pay attention. "I've seen how you look at the brochure for the documentary workshop in Denver. The one you keep hiding in your desk drawer. You've been putting your dreams on hold, and I get why. But you can't keep using me as an excuse."

I fiddled with one of the elves, avoiding her too-perceptive gaze. The workshop was a pipe dream—five thousand dollars I didn't have, a week away from the store I couldn't afford. But she was right that I'd been using her and the store as convenient shields against taking risks with my art.

"Also?" she added, returning to her usual snarky tone. "Avery texted me that he came by the gallery asking about your work. She said Adrian was *hot*. Having seen his Instagram, I agree."

I adjusted an elf that had tilted precariously. "Avery thinks the UPS guy is hot." I didn't mention that Avery was still under the influence of pregnancy and postpartum hormones or that she only pointed out hot men to tease her wife.

"The UPS guy *is* hot. Stop avoiding the question." She pressed between me and the window display, forcing me to meet her eyes. "Was Adrian Hayes cute or not?"

I sighed, silently cursing small towns and their efficient gossip networks. The last "influencer" who'd breezed through town had captured Legacy's "quaint mountain charm" for his travel vlog, completely missing the actual heart of the place while using our town as nothing more than a picturesque backdrop. He'd even tried to convince Becca Gorham to reschedule the annual Moose Trot 5K so he could get better lighting for his sponsorship with some energy drink company.

"Objectively? He was fine. He looks like he's been assembled in a laboratory to appeal to the maximum number of people. Symmetrical features, perfect teeth—well, almost." The truth was, he had one adorably crooked canine that made him look impossibly more attractive because it lent a little realness to his otherwise perfect look. I shook my head and continued. "Blond hair that somehow looks both casual and styled."

"You actually noticed his hair. *In-ter-es-ting*." She skipped back to the register.

"What's interesting is how quickly you're latching onto this nonstory," I said, moving back behind the counter. "The guy came in, I said no, that's the end."

She made a considering noise. "Avery said he looked determined when he left the gallery."

"Determined to do what? Force me to film his selfie campaign?"

"Maybe. You're the best photographer in three counties, and you know it."

I couldn't deny the tiny spark of professional pride her words kindled. My Winter Light Series hanging in the gallery had been a labor of love—three freezing nights on Slingshot Mountain with nothing but my camera and a pack of hand warmers, capturing the raw emotion of the Starlight Ski Spectacular. Photos that told the real story of Legacy, not some glossy, manufactured version of it.

"Flattery won't make me change my mind, Maya. You didn't read his email. The guy was a pain in the ass," I said, trying not to think of his actual ass. Which was arguably the one good part about him. I cleared my throat. "Trust me on this."

"Nothing changes your mind once it's made up. You're more stubborn than Dad was." She paused, and I heard her shifting gears. "So... what's this guy's plan now? Find someone else?"

"Don't know, don't care." Which wasn't exactly true. I cared… even if I didn't want to. Adrian Hayes didn't interest me, but the "paid position" he'd offered did.

"No one around here can do what you do. Maybe—"

"Maya, stop. I already said no."

"Too bad." She sighed dramatically. "A gig like that could've helped fund the new darkroom equipment you've been saving for. And expand the portrait business. It even could've helped with my tuition next fall…"

I hated that her wheedling was also factually accurate. Maya was brilliant—top of her class with scholarship offers already rolling in—but none of the scholarships covered everything. And despite what people assumed about the Sullivans, the hardware store barely broke even these days.

The quarterly financial statements spread across my desk in the back room told a story that kept me awake at night. Property tax increases, competition from the big-box stores in Billings, and rising supplier costs had combined into a perfect storm. We'd make it through winter, but next year was looking bleak unless something changed.

"I'm not selling out for new camera gear," I said, my resolve obviously wavering.

"You're a videographer. Taking videos is what you do."

That Maya's words were an echo of Adrian's was particularly annoying.

"Because those are *real* moments," I argued. "Real people. Real emotions. Not some manufactured holiday fantasy to sell over-priced sweaters."

The memory of my last gallery showing flashed through my mind—the way people had stood silent before my images, some with tears in their eyes. I'd captured something honest in those moments—the jubilation on Jenny Ringold's face when she proposed to her longtime girlfriend at last year's festival, the quiet determination of Mrs. Hoffman's grandson completing his first full run despite his prosthetic leg. Those were the stories that mattered, not whatever artificial holiday fantasy Adrian Hayes wanted to construct.

Maya sighed. "Fine. Die on your artistic integrity hill. Just don't act surprised when that guy finds someone else and you're kicking yourself for missing the opportunity. And the cash."

"Don't you have an exam to study for?" I demanded.

Maya treated me to another epic eye roll before disappearing into the back room and out the back door.

I took a deep breath and let it go. The conversation was moot since I'd already sent the guy packing. Adrian Hayes was no longer my problem.

A few minutes later, the bell above the door jingled, proving me wrong.

I looked up to see the man himself stride in, this time wearing a camel coat that probably cost more than my monthly income and, I had to admit, hugged his body just right. He'd paired it with a purply-blue scarf that complemented his eyes, and when he paused in front of the window, the soft winter light caught in his golden hair like he'd choreographed it that way.

For a single charged moment, I couldn't tear my gaze away.

"Mr. Sullivan," he said, placing both hands on the counter and leaning forward slightly. "I think we got off on the wrong foot."

His emphasis on the *Mr. Sullivan* made me want to laugh, but I restrained it.

"I don't think we did... *Mr. Hayes*," I replied evenly. "I understood what you wanted. I said no. Seems pretty straightforward."

His smile didn't waver, but something flashed in his eyes—determination or frustration, I couldn't tell. "Let me buy you a coffee. Or lunch. Ten minutes of your time, that's all I'm asking."

He leaned in a little more—close enough for the faint scent of something spicy and expensive to reach me.

"So you can try to convince me that your project isn't nonsense and fluff?"

Adrian straightened, assessing me with more calculation than I expected. "You know what? I think you're afraid."

*Clickbait. Don't fall for it.*

I gritted my teeth and ignored my own brain. "Excuse me?"

"I think you're afraid that if you work with me, you might actually enjoy it." He smiled again, but this one seemed more genuine, with a touch of challenge. "You've got this whole 'authentic artist' persona going on, and you're terrified that working on a commercial project might undermine that."

His words hit uncomfortably close to home. I had built walls around my work, standards that kept me "pure" but also, if I was being honest, safely insulated from criticism beyond my small pond. Was there a part of me that was afraid of what exposure to a bigger audience might reveal—that maybe I wasn't as good as Legacy thought I was?

I felt heat rising in my neck. "You don't know the first thing about me."

"And you don't know me either," he countered, which was annoyingly true.

"Here's my offer," Adrian continued, apparently taking my silence as permission. "If you think my work is manufactured fluff, then help me create something *authentic*. While I'm wearing Nordique clothes, of course. You maintain creative control over how we shoot, and if you hate what we're doing at any point, you can walk away with a week's pay as severance."

I crossed my arms, studying him. Part of me—a very small, probably delusional part—actually believed he might be sincere about letting me have my way with the shoot. The rest of me remembered all the wannabe influencers who'd treated our home like a quaint backdrop for their personal brand ever since the Marian family had started putting Legacy on the map.

Like that travel TikTokker last spring who'd staged a "spontaneous" picnic in Lennon Marian's private field without permission, trampling his sister's prized wildflowers. Or the fitness influencer who'd blocked the trail to Pronghorn Ridge for two hours while filming workout routines, forcing actual hikers to wait or turn back.

To them, Legacy wasn't a real place with real people—it was just aesthetically pleasing scenery to boost their metrics.

The door jingled again as Mrs. Hoffman entered, shaking snow from her boots.

"Morning, Maddox!" she called cheerfully. "Got that ice melt I called about?"

"Set aside behind the counter," I replied, glad for the interruption. "Need help carrying it out?"

"My granddaughter's in the car. She'll come get it." She approached the counter, eyeing Adrian with undisguised curiosity. "Don't think I've seen you around before."

Adrian turned on the charm, extending his hand. "Adrian Hayes. Just visiting for the holidays."

"Evelyn Hoffman." She shook his hand, then looked between us. "Am I interrupting something?"

"Mr. Hayes was just leaving," I said firmly.

Adrian's smile didn't falter. "Actually, I was hoping to convince Maddox to join me for lunch at..." He paused, glancing at Mrs. Hoffman. "Where would you recommend for the best lunch in town?"

Mrs. Hoffman brightened. "Oh, Timber, without question! Alex just revamped the menu last month, and the butternut squash soup is a must-try."

I suppressed a groan. Of course she'd suggest Timber. It was the best damn restaurant in town.

"Sounds perfect," Adrian said, turning back to me with triumphant eyes. "Timber at noon? Ten minutes of your time."

I could practically see the town gossip network lighting up like a Christmas tree. By nightfall, half of Legacy would be speculating about me and the handsome stranger with the pretty face. The other half would already be planning our wedding. In a town where everyone knew your business before you did, this lunch would be headline news—exactly the kind of attention I'd spent years avoiding.

I wanted to argue that he'd had more than ten minutes of my time already, but since Mrs. Hoffman was watching our exchange with the avid interest of someone who would definitely be sharing this story at her next book club meeting, if not sooner, I refrained.

"Fine," I relented, if only to end the conversation before half the town heard about it. "Noon. But only ten minutes."

Adrian's genuine smile was annoyingly appealing. "Excellent. Looking forward to it." He nodded politely to Mrs. Hoffman. "Lovely meeting you, ma'am."

As he strode out of the hardware store, designer boots crunching in the light dusting of snow outside, Mrs. Hoffman turned to me with raised eyebrows.

"Handsome fellow," she observed. "Friend of yours?"

"No," I said firmly, reaching for her bag of ice melt. "Just someone passing through."

"Hmm," she hummed, clearly unconvinced. "Well, he seems nice. And Timber does sharing plates..."

I sighed, already regretting my decision. This lunch was just delaying the inevitable rejection, but ten minutes of my time seemed a small price to pay to get Adrian Hayes out of my life for good. Ten minutes to definitively explain why I didn't do influencer gigs, didn't manufacture moments, didn't compromise my principles for follower counts or sponsor dollars.

"Don't get any ideas," I warned her. "I can already see you scheming. I don't want or need any of your 'sharing plates.'"

She grinned at me. "Maddox, I was born scheming. And you *do* need a man warming your bed and helping you out around here. 'S'not my fault if killing two birds with one handsome stone makes the most sense."

I glared at her, making sure she saw how serious I was. "Stand down, Evelyn. I will not be making babies with that city boy. This is not Hallmark, and he isn't returning to his hometown looking for love. This is real life, and he's as deep as a sheet of sandpaper, even if he's a thousand times smoother."

"Mmf. We'll see." She turned to leave.

"We won't see!" I called after her.

As soon as Mrs. Hoffman disappeared out the door, I pulled out my phone and texted Maya.

> I'm meeting him for lunch. DON'T start planning the wedding, regardless of what you hear around town.

Her response was immediate.

MAYA

> Too late. Rosie Marian already texted to say she heard from Mrs. Hoffman that the two of you were flirting at the cash register. Tell me everything. A Christmas wedding isn't possible at this late date, but there's always New Year's...

How the fuck was that possible? Mrs. Hoffman had barely hit the sidewalk. I let out a growl and slipped my phone back into my pocket, regretting everything.

TIMBER WAS busy as always during lunch. The restaurant occupied the ground floor of a converted timber lodge that had worn many hats over the years: the town's first hotel, then a kind of pub, and later, its first gay bar. Alex Marian had managed to preserve Timber's rustic character with rough-hewn ceiling beams and a massive stone fireplace, while adding modern touches that gave a nod to its LGBTQ history, like subtle rainbow accents, an expanded outdoor patio for use in summer, and a recently renovated kitchen that served some of the best food in three counties.

The familiar scent of applewood smoke and rosemary hit me as I pushed through the door. Dad and I used to come here every Saturday—"man time," he'd call it, though it was really just an excuse to let Mom have some peace. Back then, a big-screen television that played college football had dominated the space, and Rick Longleaf had snuck me soda refills all afternoon for free. Though Alex had renovated and modernized it, the worn patch in the hardwood near the bar marked where generations of Sullivan men had propped their boots while nursing a beer.

I spotted Adrian immediately—he stood out like the sunrise in a room full of night skies. He'd snagged a small table near the fireplace and was scrolling through his phone, occasionally pausing to take a sip from a coffee mug. Several people were sneaking glances his way, clearly wondering who the attractive stranger was.

Alex caught my eye from behind the bar and raised an eyebrow in question, but I shook my head slightly—a signal that I'd explain later—and made my way toward Adrian's table.

As I approached, Adrian looked up and smiled, slipping his phone into his pocket.

"Thanks for coming," he said, gesturing to the chair across from him. "I ordered you a coffee. Black, right?"

I raised an eyebrow as I sat. "Lucky guess."

"Not really. You strike me as a no-nonsense kind of guy."

"And you strike me as someone who probably drinks complicated coffee with Italian names."

Adrian laughed, lifting his mug. "Guilty. But in my defense, they were out of oat milk, so I had to settle for regular."

"The tragic struggles of life in small-town America."

"I'm adaptable," he said with a shrug. "Part of the job."

"Speaking of which," I said, checking my watch. "I'm pretty sure you've already given me your pitch."

"And you're still determined not to take it?"

I opened my mouth to respond but hesitated. Creative control was seductive. So was the money he promised.

An image flashed through my mind—Maya's college acceptance letter to the University of Washington that she'd shown me last week, her face alight with excitement even as worry creased her brow when she mentioned the housing costs. Then another image—the stack of unpaid supplier invoices in my desk drawer, the leak in the store's roof I'd been patching instead of properly fixing, the darkroom equipment I'd been coveting that would let me expand beyond basic portraiture.

Adrian's eyes lit up like he sensed weakness, and he pressed his case. "You choose the locations," he reminded me. "You direct the shoots. We'll feature real Legacy residents, not models. And we tell the Legacy story you want to tell."

"And where do you fit in?"

"I'm the outsider experiencing Legacy for the first time." He gestured around the bar. "Places like this. Real. Authentic."

I nearly choked on my coffee. "You keep using that word. I do not think it means what you think it means."

He grinned, then grew serious. "Look, I get your skepticism. My world is curated and filtered, and yours... isn't. But that's exactly why I need you. This project needs to feel genuine, not staged. Nordique wants to associate their brand with traditions, with moments that matter. I think you can help me find them." He leaned back, studying me. "Your photos don't lie. That's the magic I need."

Something in his phrasing caught me by surprise. Not "your pictures are pretty" or "your aesthetic matches our brand"—but "your photos don't lie." Despite myself, I felt a flicker of professional pride that this man, who garnered over a million followers with his polished content, had recognized the honesty in my work.

I drummed my fingers on the table, thinking. He was saying all of the things I wanted to hear. I didn't know if I could trust him, but the money would solve several problems. Maya was right— with her leaving for college next year, I needed to think about expanding my photography business. And although I had several Christmas photo shoots on my calendar in the next few weeks, the busyness wouldn't last. Bookings were always slower in winter.

"A couple of rules," I said finally.

Adrian's expression brightened. "Name them."

"First, the creative control needs to be in writing. If I think something's cheesy or fake, we don't do it."

"Agreed."

"Second, we feature real Legacy traditions and events, but *your* participation needs to be real, too. No manufactured moments."

Adrian hesitated. "The, ah... let's call it a *concept* for this series is... well, dates. As in, 'The Twelve Dates of Christmas.' Where I and, hopefully, a dozen local gentlemen take my followers on a special holidate. Get it, *holi*date?"

"You..." I paused. "You want to film yourself on dates with local guys?"

"*Holi*dates," he repeated. "You know, like, ice skating and drinking cocoa. Christmas tree decorating. Sleigh rides. That kind of thing. So, as far as my participation being real goes, I will definitely be there... but I will not actually be looking for love with twelve different men." He chuckled uncomfortably.

I pictured a parade of Legacy's eligible bachelors being trotted out for Adrian's enjoyment, each one performing "spontaneous" holiday activities while the viewing public cooed over their charming mountain-town romance. It wasn't necessarily offensive, but something about it felt hollow—like staging wedding photos before you've even fallen in love.

I stared at him for a long moment. He wasn't the only one who was suddenly uncomfortable. "Are you single?"

He frowned. "Yes, of course. Or else I'd have my partner here going on these dates with me."

For some reason, picturing him with a partner made me more unsettled. But then I realized the opportunity this presented.

"I have a third rule," I said abruptly.

It was Adrian's turn to blink. "Okay...?"

"Have you thought about how you're going to find these twelve unsuspecting gentlemen?"

Adrian frowned. "I mean, not really? Grindr or something. In the grand tradition. Isn't there a search and rescue training program in town?" He smiled, and his eyelids dropped into a deliberately sultry pose. "Finding a date's never been a problem for me in the past."

An inconvenient, utterly unwanted bolt of lust whipped through me, just as he'd intended. I resisted the urge to laugh out loud... or punch him.

"Yeah, no," I said, my voice deeper than I'd meant it to be. "That's not gonna work here. I will source you a dozen gay men."

He grinned and opened his mouth to make a joke, but before he could, I continued.

"Legacy's a small town, Hayes. And do you know what the prime directive of small towns is?"

He shook his head.

"Matchmaking. There is nothing that gets them more excited than a single man or woman. Right now, they are trying to make *me* their mission, and any single man in town is fair game."

Adrian chuckled uncomfortably. "But... I've only been here two days. No one even knows me—"

"Yes," I agreed.

As if on cue, my phone buzzed with another text. I didn't need to check it to know it was probably Avery Marian, or Mrs. Hoffman, or any of the self-appointed matchmakers who'd been trying to set me up since I came out at sixteen. The same well-meaning busybodies who'd arranged five "accidental" meetings with eligible men at the Fall Festival, who still invited me to dinner and "coincidentally" had their nephew/grandson/family friend visiting from out of town.

"Since they saw you talking to me at the hardware store earlier," I continued, "at least a dozen people have started planning our wedding. And I mean that literally. Did you have a preference between a Christmas or New Year's ceremony, by the by?"

Adrian swallowed hard, and I nodded grimly.

"Exactly. I need this town to lay off making matches for me. The best way to do that is to make you my sacrificial lamb and get them to matchmake for you instead. After all, you'll be going home as soon as this project is done. So... you and me, not a thing. You and *other* eligible men, not a problem. That's rule three. Got it?"

He snorted a soft laugh. "Ah. You seem to be playing fast and loose with my love life."

"Take it or leave it."

"I believe we both know I'm going to take it." Adrian's smile was radiant, and though I knew it was probably practiced and perfectly calibrated, it was still annoyingly effective. "When can you start?"

"Tomorrow morning. I'll need today to rearrange some things at the store, grab my equipment... and find some poor schmuck to set you up with."

He ignored my jab. "Perfect. Should we meet at—"

"We'll meet at the Pinecone at seven," I interrupted. "If you're serious about experiencing Legacy, we start with breakfast where the locals eat."

The Pinecone had been serving the same menu since I was a kid—chicken-fried steak and eggs that could cure any hangover, sourdough pancakes that put IHOP to shame, and coffee strong enough to strip paint. If Adrian wanted authentic Legacy experiences, we'd start with food that hadn't been styled for Instagram.

Adrian looked like he was about to protest the early hour but caught himself. "Seven it is."

I stood, having made my decision faster than I'd planned. "Dress warmly. We'll be outside early."

He rose as well, extending his hand. "Looking forward to it."

I shook it briefly, ignoring the solid warmth of his grip, and let go. "Don't make me regret this, Hayes."

"I won't," he promised, eyes bright with something that looked dangerously like smug satisfaction. "This is going to be great."

Despite all my misgivings, I couldn't deny the spark of excitement I felt. Yes, I needed the money. Yes, Maya would be insufferable when she found out I'd changed my mind. But there was something else, too—a professional curiosity about what it would be like to step outside my comfort zone, to have my work seen by more than just the regular Legacy crowd. Maybe, just maybe, this project could be a bridge to something bigger—not just for Adrian, but for me.

As I headed for the door, Alex waved me over to the bar.

"New friend?" he asked, mixing something that smelled of citrus and lime.

"New client," I corrected. "Short-term project."

Alex raised an eyebrow. "The guy's practically glowing. You sure that's all it is?"

I glanced back at Adrian, who was now on his phone, probably updating his agent or sponsor. "Positive. In fact... I need a favor."

After pinning a reluctant Alex down as my first video date victim, my phone buzzed with a text from my sister.

> **MAYA**
>
> Well? How'd it go?

I typed back quickly.

> I said yes. Don't be an asshole.

Her response came immediately.

> **MAYA**
>
> Did you know champagne consumption at New Year's weddings nearly doubles that of weddings on any other night? So maybe a Valentine's wedding would be more practical...

I pocketed my phone without replying, already mentally cataloging equipment I'd need for tomorrow. One thing was certain—working with Adrian Hayes would be anything but boring.

Whether that was good or bad remained to be seen.

#ADozenGayMen #SacrificialCityBoy #TwelveDatesOfTorture #ThisBetterBeWorthIt

3

# #SEVENAMSHOWDOWN

ADRIAN

SEVEN IN THE morning in Montana was an entirely different beast than seven in the morning in Los Angeles. I figured that was, at least in part, because it was so cold.

I was used to LA, where the city would already be humming—delivery trucks rumbling, coffee shops churning out espressos, the subways and busses packed with exhausted commuters. I'd always been a morning person, a trait that had served me well in capturing that perfect morning golden hour content when most influencers were still asleep.

But in Legacy, 7:00 a.m. meant crystalline air that hurt to breathe, a sky still clinging to the last stars, and silence so profound it felt like the world was holding its breath.

As I trudged from my rental car toward the Pinecone Café, each footstep crunching in the fresh dusting of snow, I revised my assessment. It wasn't just cold here; it was cold as *fuck.*

The kind of cold that didn't just nip at your exposed skin but seemed to seep right through designer wool and find every vulnerable spot.

The kind of cold that made a man seriously question his life choices.

Not just agreeing to meet at this ungodly hour—though that was certainly part of it—but the entire concept. "Twelve Dates of Christmas" had seemed brilliant yesterday. This morning, with my face stinging and my rental cabin's unfamiliar coffee still not hitting my system, the project felt as precarious as my overpriced boots on the icy sidewalk.

Overnight, my manager had sent a flurry of excited texts about the project. "Love the teaser!" Vic had enthused. "The luxury-meets-rustic angle is chef's kiss. Nordique is already thrilled with the initial concept. Don't fuck it up."

I was trying very hard not to.

The Pinecone Café was exactly what I'd expected—a small clapboard building with a green-painted door, windows foggy with condensation, and a handful of pickup trucks in the parking lot. The sign was hand-carved wood with pine tree accents. Quaint. Cottage-y. Exhaustingly on-brand for a small mountain town.

I paused outside to compose myself, checking my reflection in the window. My camel coat from yesterday had been swapped for Nordique's signature navy parka with subtle gold accents—warm enough for Montana mornings but still photogenic. My indigo-blue cashmere scarf remained, adding a pop of color for my early morning Instagram story.

I'd already posted a teaser about the project, and my engagement numbers had spiked overnight. People loved a Christmas concept, and the idea of me—known for luxury hotels and cosmopolitan settings—roughing it in the wilderness had novelty appeal. Apparently. If I could just pull off these twelve dates without completely destroying my brand positioning, Nordique would be thrilled.

The bell jingled cheerfully as I stepped inside and experienced a wave of sensory overload—the sizzle of bacon on a griddle, the scrape of forks against plates, the low murmur of conversations that momentarily paused as the door opened.

Several heads turned, locals briefly assessing the newcomer before returning to their conversations and plates of food. I spotted Maddox immediately, nursing a mug at a corner table, his broad shoulders hunched slightly as he scrolled through his phone.

He looked up as I approached, his expression unreadable. "You're late."

I checked my phone. "It's 7:02."

"Around here, on time is late." He gestured to the chair across from him. "Coffee's ordered."

I slipped into the seat and unwound my scarf. "You been here long?"

"Long enough to go through the shot list for today." He pushed a handwritten page across the table. "I've scheduled your first date —Alexander Marian at the Marian Lodge for their annual hot chocolate tasting at ten. Should give us an hour to get the establishing shots of town before that. I have a tentative schedule set for the rest of your 'dates,' too."

I scanned the list, impressed despite myself. "You work fast."

"Small town. Easy to arrange things." Maddox took a sip of his coffee, eyes fixed on me over the rim. "Plus, Alex owes me a favor."

"The owner of Timber is your first victim?" I raised an eyebrow, remembering the friendly, attractive man behind the bar. "He seems nice."

"He is nice. Also gay, single, and photogenic as fuck."

I lifted an eyebrow. "Why aren't you dating the guy?"

Maddox shrugged but failed to answer the question. "You wanted authentic Legacy experiences, and everyone loves Alex.

Trust me, the local matchmaking network would have paired you with him eventually anyway."

A server appeared with my coffee and two plates of what appeared to be breakfast—golden waffles topped with berries and a side of bacon for me and a towering stack of pancakes for Maddox.

"I didn't order—" I began.

"I did. Sadie's waffles are the best in three counties." Maddox nodded at the server. "Consider it your first authentic Legacy experience."

The woman grinned, and when she spoke, it was in a soft Texas drawl. "You boys let me know if you need anything else."

"I don't suppose you have... oat milk creamer?" I asked, gesturing at my coffee.

When she frowned apologetically, I waved it off and gave her a friendly smile. "Never mind. This is great! Thank you."

When she left, I sighed. "If only the Wild West had oats."

Maddox snorted.

I eyed my plate suspiciously. "I usually just have a protein shake in the mornings."

"And I usually don't start filming self-absorbed social media campaigns at dawn, yet here we are, adapting." He pushed the plate closer to me. "Eat. We've got a long day ahead."

I took a bite of waffle, if only to stop myself from responding with something equally cutting. The flavor caught me off guard— butter melted into every crevice, and the berries carried a tart sweetness that obviously didn't come from a can. It was annoy- ingly, undeniably delicious.

"Okay," I admitted after swallowing. "It's... passable."

A ghost of a smile crossed his face as I scarfed another bite. "Told you."

We ate in surprisingly comfortable silence for a few minutes. I used the opportunity to study him more carefully. In the warm light of the café, Maddox Sullivan was even more attractive than I'd initially registered. His dark hair was sleep-mussed, his jaw shadowed with stubble, and his gray eyes focused entirely on his food. He wore a simple flannel shirt beneath a worn wool coat, practical jeans, and boots that had clearly seen years of actual mountain use rather than fashion runways.

He was the antithesis of the men I usually featured in my content—polished models and influencers who knew their angles and how to pose without direction. Maddox radiated genuineness in a way that made me simultaneously intrigued and jealous.

It was annoying as fuck that I'd taken twenty minutes getting camera-ready, and he'd managed to roll out of bed looking like a lumberjack thirst trap.

"You're staring," he said without looking up.

"I'm assessing," I corrected, looking away. "You'll be behind the camera, but you're also my local guide. Your style will reflect on the project."

He snorted. "My 'style' is functional and warm. Which yours should be, too, by the way." He gestured to my outfit with his fork. "That fancy parka might look good, but it won't cut it if we're shooting outdoors all day."

"It's a Nordique Alpine Explorer," I replied defensively. "Designed for extreme winter conditions."

"Uh-huh. And those boots?"

I glanced down at my footwear—sleek, designer, and admittedly more suited to Milan Fashion Week than Montana wilderness. "They're... transitional."

Maddox rolled his eyes. "We'll stop by the hardware store after breakfast. Get you some real boots."

"I have plenty of—"

"Real. Boots." He fixed me with a stare that brooked no argument. "I'm not dragging you out of a snowdrift when those glorified dress shoes fail you."

"Fine." I took another bite of waffle to hide my irritation. "But anything I wear needs to feature Nordique prominently. That's literally the point of this campaign." I couldn't bring myself to admit Nordique didn't sell winter boots. I'd even tried to order the ones they used in their catalog shots but couldn't find them on the boot brand's website.

"Hence why I said we'd stop by the store. We sell fancy boots, but practical ones." At my surprised look, he added, "Small town, remember? Sullivan Hardware has evolved. We carry everything from nails to high-end outdoor gear."

He must have caught me staring at a man who'd just walked in wearing faded jeans, worn cowboy boots, and a cowboy hat because he grumbled, "And cowboy hats like that, if it's what has you drooling."

I blinked back at Maddox. "I was drooling over the pancakes, thank you very much. Just not sure I've seen an actual cowboy hat worn unironically before. That guy seems legit."

He nodded. "Lennon Marian, cattle rancher. Owns a couple thousand acres outside of town. He's Alex's cousin. Stay for any amount of time in Legacy these days, and you'll trip over a Marian."

"So," I said, forking another bite of pancake. "Tell me about Alex. What should I know before our date?"

Maddox's expression shifted subtly, becoming more detached and professional. "Alexander Marian. Moved here from California wine country a few years ago after his family started investing in Legacy. He runs Timber, which he renovated into a wine bar and gourmet pizza place a few years ago. He's smart, friendly, loves the outdoors, makes the best wine pairings you'd never think of, and has an annoying habit of quoting obscure poetry when he drinks."

"Perfect," I said, jotting notes. "Any topics to avoid?"

Maddox's professional facade cracked, and a genuine smile appeared. "Hmm. Our local fire chief and his random fire inspections? But I'm sure that won't come up." He took a last bite of his breakfast. "Other than that, he's an open book. Just be yourself." He paused, reconsidering. "Actually, be a better version of yourself. The one that isn't constantly thinking about camera angles and hashtags."

I ignored the jab. "And the hot chocolate tasting? What should I expect?"

"It's a holiday meet-and-greet event put on by Alex's family. The Marians bought the old Legacy Lodge and Inn about twenty years ago. It was historically significant to the town, but the town couldn't afford to keep it up."

He sat back and took a sip of coffee before continuing. "As a gesture of goodwill, the family periodically opens up the main lodge for locals and tourists to visit, including offering these holiday hot cocoa flights. Over the years, the cocoa tasting has become a Legacy holiday tradition." Maddox wiped his mouth with a napkin and stood. "Ready? We should get those establishing shots while the light's still good."

The next two hours passed in a blur of activity. True to his word, Maddox first dragged me to Sullivan Hardware, where he outfitted me with proper winter boots that, to my surprise, were actually the ones I'd tried to find. They were perfect—rugged but stylish enough to work on camera.

"These aren't on their website," I murmured, noticing they were more comfortable and warmer than they appeared.

"Limited distribution," Maddox explained. "They test certain lines in specialty mountain shops before wider release."

"That's actually perfect for the campaign. Exclusive access is always good content. You could get some online orders if you have a shop set up."

He didn't bother responding with more than a huff of frustration, presumably due to the fact that I dared imply his business wasn't fully modernized.

Properly equipped, we spent the morning capturing footage around town—the Christmas decorations along Founder's Row, the historic buildings with their fresh blanket of snow, locals going about their morning routines. Maddox's instincts as a photographer were undeniable. Where I would have staged carefully posed shots of quaint storefronts, he captured a pair of elderly men playing chess through a steamy café window, their weathered hands moving pieces with deliberate precision. When I suggested a standard shot of the town's Christmas tree, he instead directed me to a low angle that framed it against the mountains, making it appear to touch the sky.

Maddox was surprisingly skilled, catching moments I would have missed, finding angles that showcased Legacy's charm without veering into cliché.

By nine thirty, we'd amassed enough B-roll to establish the setting, and I was feeling optimistic about the day ahead. We returned to my rental car to stow some equipment and check our phones before heading to the lodge for my first official date.

None of my messages or missed calls were urgent, but Maddox frowned at his screen.

"Problem?" I asked.

"Little bit." He typed something quickly, then pocketed his phone and glanced back at me. "Alex can't make it. We're short one date for your date video."

I felt a beat of disappointment before feeling unexpected excitement come over me like the Grinch's slow grin.

"I know where we can find a stand-in. He's grumpy as hell, but he'll look good in front of the camera despite the scowl."

Maddox's eyes widened before narrowing again. The narrowing did something to his whole face—made it sharper, more dangerous... and unfairly hot. The scowl in question was present and accounted for. "Not on your life. Remember rule three?"

I smiled brilliantly. "Rules were meant to be broken, Maddox."

#FuckRule3 #GrumpyButCute #HotCocoaHotWater

# 4

# #RULESCHMULE

## MADDOX

AFTER ARGUING with Adrian the entire drive to the lodge, I was *this close* to telling him to forget the whole thing. The only thing that kept me from pulling over and tossing him into the snowbank was remembering the stack of invoices on my desk.

I needed this money. Badly.

"I'll call around," I told him. "Find someone who can stand in. You go inside and scope out... whatever. Just give me a few minutes."

I could tell Adrian wanted to roll his eyes at me and accuse me, yet again, of being a stubborn pain in the ass. A "creative purist" who wasn't able to shift on the fly.

But that wasn't why I didn't want to be in front of the cameras with him. The real reason was simple—I wanted to be seen as the videographer, not the date. I didn't want to be the recipient of his charming smile and pithy comments. I wanted to take the best damned images and video possible and use it to bring as many eyes onto my work as I could.

Without getting caught up in a silly fantasy.

"Yeah, Maddox, what's up?" Nate Lewis's warm voice rumbled over the other end of the line.

"I need a favor. I've got a guy—"

"Heard all about your guy," he said with a laugh. "Everyone in town's talking about it."

"We need someone to be his date today for a video shoot. I was hoping you could—"

I could hear him talk to someone in the background before coming back to the line. "Definitely can't today, but put me down for a sleigh ride with the guy. Maybe Sunday, yeah? Be good publicity for us. Sorry, Maddox. Gotta go."

The call was over before I could say thanks.

I quickly dialed several other people. If they did say yes, it was the same as with Nate. They'd be happy to help, but not today.

After exhausting the list of contacts in my phone, I blew out a frustrated breath and dialed one more number.

"Sullivan Hardware, this is Maya."

"I need your help with something."

After hopping out of Adrian's rental car, I walked to the lodge's entrance to find the man and update him on the plan. I held the door for two teenage girls who were racing to catch up with their parents, but when they stepped inside, I heard one of them take a sharp inhale.

"Holy shit, Brynn. That's *Adrian Hayes*!"

"No!" the other girl hissed, grabbing her friend's arm. "No freaking way."

"My parents are going to lose it. He changed my life. He seriously... omigod. How... how am I going to talk to him without acting like a complete cringe-fest? I have to say something to him, but what? And what if I burst into tears?"

Since they were basically blocking the door anyway, I didn't feel bad eavesdropping.

Brynn nodded, eyes like lasers honed in on the beautiful idiot across the room. "Like, remember his post about his parents? And how he was so there for everyone in his comments. Hashtag 'family complications' went viral for days after that."

The other girl closed her eyes for a beat. "He was so real for that. Like, so, so real."

"And when he talked about burnout? I made my mom watch it with me. It was the first time she actually listened when I said I needed a break."

Not-Brynn shoved her hand in her coat pocket, most likely looking for her phone. "That one got shared by, like, every teacher at my school. My counselor said it made the rounds on the staff Slack or whatever."

"Ugh, he's even hotter in person," the original girl whispered. "He's like the perfect guy, pretty and kind. I hate that he's gay! It's so unfair."

They moved deeper into the lodge, giggling excitedly as they scurried toward a table off to the side where their parents were being seated.

I stood rooted to the spot, their words still echoing in my head.

*Changed my life? Shared by teachers? So real?*

It wasn't that I didn't think Adrian had fans—obviously, he did. But I'd assumed they liked him for curated photos, luxury travel tips, and whatever cashmere-scarf brand he was hawking that week. Not... *this.*

Not for talking about burnout. Or complicated family stuff. Or giving a damn about anyone's comments.

I shoved my hands into my pockets, teeth gritted against the cold still coming in through the doorway behind me. The girls might've seen something in Adrian Hayes I hadn't. Or maybe I hadn't wanted to.

Didn't mean I was wrong about him, though.

But maybe—maybe—I wasn't entirely right either. Maybe there was more to his posts than I'd given him credit for.

"Did you find someone?"

I blinked at Adrian. He'd approached me while I stood there staring into space and was now looking at me with a little divot of concern between his eyes.

"Uh, no," I said.

"You're freezing. Come sit by the fire." He pulled me away from the door and guided me to a table against the wall on the far side of the giant stone fireplace.

Thankfully, he didn't pressure me to be his date or say something obnoxious about my rules. Instead, he took the seat opposite me at the small table and waited patiently for me to speak.

I swallowed. "So... obviously, it's very last-minute. And the good news is..." I closed my eyes and cracked my neck from side to side before opening them again and meeting his expectant expression. "I've lined up plenty of dates for you this week."

"Pretty sure I can guess the bad news from that chiropractic routine you just did," he pointed out. "Spit it out, Sullivan."

"No luck on finding you a date for today."

He lifted one perfectly shaped eyebrow but didn't say anything. His patience routine was unnerving.

I ground my back teeth together. "So I will do it on three conditions."

His second eyebrow shot up to join the first, and the edges of his lips curved in satisfaction. "Oh, goody. More rules."

"One, that you keep your smug bullshit to yourself. Second, that this is the only time. Rule three has a onetime exception only.

Third, see those teenage girls over there trying hard not to stare and point at you?"

Adrian's eyes dipped in confusion as he turned to scan the room. "Uh, yeah?"

"They're apparently fans of yours and would really like to take a photo with you," I admitted reluctantly. "And since we're waiting on my sister to show up to help us with the filming, now that I can't hold the camera, you have time."

He stared at me with incredulity. "You want me to go greet my fans while you sit here and watch?"

I flicked out my fingers and examined my nails as casually as I could. "Your adoring crowd awaits. And if you think I'll be watching you instead of catching up on work via my phone, you're sadly mistaken. I have a photo shoot to confirm for tomorrow and a million emails to return." I waggled my fingers in a "get out of here" motion. "Now, shoo."

He let out a breath and stood. Within microseconds, he was sporting his toothpaste smile and setting off to charm his fans.

I pulled out my phone to check my email and account balances, but when I heard twin gasps of surprise coming from the family with the girls, I couldn't help but look up to appreciate how excited they were and pat myself on the back for helping them out.

Adrian introduced himself politely to everyone and chatted for a few minutes, but I was surprised that it was actually the mother and father who stood up and asked if they could give him a hug.

I stared at the scene. What the actual fuck? Were they as starstruck as the teens? This guy wasn't a psychologist sharing healthy communication habits or a philosopher posting moralistic platitudes. He was a luxury lifestyle persona. His job was literally to sell the fantasy of a richer lifestyle, of wealth and opulence.

Of greed and privilege.

The mother wiped a tear away with a laugh as she took the girls' phones to take a few pictures.

I couldn't look away. Who the fuck was Adrian Hayes that he'd had this kind of effect on a random family of tourists in Legacy, Montana?

"For real?" Maya asked with a laugh. I blinked and looked up at her.

"You're here," I said stupidly.

"And Mom used to say I was the smart one in the family," she teased.

I shook my head to clear it. "Thank you for coming. I was, uh... lost in thought about some work stuff."

Maya looked over at Adrian and back at me, her eyes dancing with mischief. "Work stuff. Right."

As I scrubbed my face with my hands to keep from snapping at her, she leaned to the side to watch Adrian as he finished up with his adoring fan club.

"God, he's even cuter in person, isn't he?" she said on a sigh. "Remember that time I asked you to help me make sugar cookies for Rosie after her favorite horse died?"

I blinked at her, confused about the rapid subject change. "Uh, yeah?"

"I got the idea from a post Adrian did about having a terrible day. Anyway, never mind. Where do you need me?"

Keeping up with the conversational pace of a teenager wasn't easy at the best of times, and now was definitely not the best of times. I tried to set aside her fangirling and get to work.

And tried not to picture Adrian Hayes having a terrible day.

Or someone comforting him with sugar cookies.

#NeedMoreMen #GossipGirls #IgnoreTheDepth #SoldierOn

**5**

# #FIRSTDATE

ADRIAN

THE INTERIOR of the lodge was warm and inviting, with a fire already crackling in the stone fireplace, the scent of chocolate and spices filling the air, and a few groups of people scattered throughout the large area enjoying their treat.

As I returned to my table after talking to the nice family from Virginia, I took another appreciative look around our setting for today's shoot. The Marian Lodge was unexpectedly breathtaking with its massive antler chandelier hanging from exposed wooden beams, plush leather furniture worn to a butter-soft patina, and vintage ski equipment mounted on the walls as decoration. The place felt like it had a century of stories embedded in its timbers. This wasn't the manufactured coziness of boutique hotels I usually featured; this was the real deal, with patches of uneven flooring and the occasional draft that spoke of authentic history.

Maddox had nailed the selection of this place for our first shoot. It was perfect.

When my eyes landed back on the table, I noticed he'd been joined by a teenager I assumed was his sister, Maya. She had his dark hair and something of his features, but where he radiated tension, she practically bounced with enthusiasm.

"Hi," she announced, grinning widely as she approached me. "This is the best thing to happen all year."

Maddox sighed. "Maya, this is Adrian Hayes. Adrian, my sister, Maya."

"*The* Adrian Hayes," Maya corrected, shaking my hand. "I follow your Instagram. Your Amalfi Coast series last summer was incredible."

I smiled, instantly warming to her. "Thank you. It's an amazing place."

"Don't encourage her," Maddox warned. "She's already way too excited about this."

Maya rolled her eyes. "Ignore him. He's allergic to social media. And fun." She shrugged off her coat, revealing a Sullivan Hardware sweatshirt beneath. "So I'm all yours for two hours, then I'm meeting up with a study group. What's the plan?"

Rebecca Marian, the owner of the lodge who'd originally shown me to a table, approached us wearing a dark red apron and a reindeer antler headband. "Welcome, Sullivans, we're so glad to have you."

As she confirmed everything with Maddox and apologized for Alex's cancellation, I assessed the table she'd set up for us by the fireplace.

The lighting was excellent—natural illumination from the windows, combined with the warm glow of the fire. The rustic wooden table against the stone fireplace would frame the scene beautifully, and the colorful hot chocolate station nearby provided visual interest.

"This looks great," I assured her. "Thank you so much."

"No problem. Just let us know what you need. I'll be out with the first round in just a moment."

After Maya took off after her in search of the ladies' room, I glanced over at Maddox. He was nose down in setting up a tripod for the best angle, and it currently looked like he wanted to murder it.

"Sure you're okay with this?" I asked.

"What? It's fine."

"Fine. Yes. Great." I eyed him up and down. While strikingly attractive—and let's be honest, doing a lot of things for me personally—the man's current look was hardly date-appropriate. "Should we, ah, do something about what you're wearing?"

"Yes," he said, stopping his adjustments and locking eyes with me. "We should be grateful for it, in the way of beggars not being choosers."

I opened my mouth to argue when I realized maybe his haphazard "I woke up and threw on the shit in the corner of my room" look might make the Nordique clothes I had on appear even better than usual by comparison.

"Solid plan," I said with a nod. "Now, let's go over what we're going to discuss on camera."

Maddox looked pained. "Can't we just... talk? Like normal people?"

"Normal people don't have a million followers analyzing their every word," I countered. "We need themes, talking points, organic but strategic conversation starters."

"This is why I hate—" He caught himself, exhaling slowly. "Fine. What were you going to discuss with Alex?"

"This historic lodge, his bar and restaurant, how Legacy became an LGBTQ+ friendly destination..." I flipped through my notes. "Perfect segue to highlight Nordique's commitment to inclusive luxury."

"Sounds rehearsed," Maddox observed.

"It's not rehearsed; it's prepared. There's a difference."

"Not to viewers, there isn't." He crossed his arms. "If you want authentic, you need to be willing to go off-script."

His words hit a nerve. The most successful content of my career had always been the unplanned moments—a luxury hotel's rooftop infinity pool where I'd genuinely gasped at the sunset view, an unscripted interaction with an elderly Italian chef who'd insisted on teaching me his great-aunt's pasta technique. Those rare glimpses of real emotion had garnered more engagement than any carefully choreographed campaign. But they were also terrifying—uncontrolled, unpredictable, impossible to replicate.

"I'm not proposing a script. It's like you're deliberately trying to paint me into a box of your own making," I said, trying not to snap.

Thankfully, his sister returned, all smiles. "We ready? Mrs. Marian is on her way out with the hot cocoa." She looked back and forth between us. "I'm going to channel my inner *Bachelor* film crew, right?"

"Not exactly," Maddox interjected with an obvious attempt at remaining calm. "Less reality TV and more like two people having a normal conversation over hot chocolate."

"While at least one of us is wearing carefully selected apparel and trying to be engaging," I added, raising an eyebrow.

Maya glanced between us, amusement dancing in her eyes. "This is going to be amazing." She stepped behind the camera. "Let's do this."

We took our seats at the table by the fire. Mrs. Marian approached with the first round of hot chocolates—classic milk chocolate in handmade mugs, topped with house-made whipped cream and dusted with cinnamon.

"And we're rolling," Maya called.

I shifted into content creator mode, offering the camera my practiced smile as I introduced the concept.

"Welcome to the first of our 'Twelve Dates of Christmas.' Today, I'm in Legacy, Montana, celebrating the season with Maddox Sullivan. Maddox is a local photographer and the owner of Sullivan Hardware here in Legacy. Who better to show me the ropes for my very first date here than a Legacy native?"

I smiled at Maddox, who looked like he'd rather be performing his own root canal with rusty pliers. His jaw was clenched so tight I was surprised his perfect teeth weren't cracking.

Instead of prompting him to say hello, I continued speaking in hopes he'd chill the fuck out. "Today, we're exploring one of the popular local holiday traditions, which is a hot chocolate tasting here at this historic lodge."

I turned to Maddox again and said a silent prayer that his good looks would distract my audience from his dismal attitude. "Maddox, why don't you tell us about the lodge and its significance to the town?"

Maddox shifted in his seat. "Yeah, uh... it's a lodge. Been here since the 1800s. Used to be an old inn until the Marian family bought it and renovated it."

I waited for him to continue, but he simply reached for his hot chocolate.

"And," I prompted, feeling like I was trying to extract blood from a particularly stubborn stone. "How did they end up hosting an event like this?"

Maddox seemed to consider the question seriously. A tiny dot of whipped cream clung to the tip of his nose, making him look simultaneously ridiculous and adorable. Like if Grumpy Cat wore a Santa hat.

"Since purchasing the lodge, which used to be called Legacy Lodge and Inn, the Marians have gone out of their way to preserve the town's history," he said finally, his voice deepening with unexpected conviction. "Inviting locals to see the renovations and to feel like the lodge was still a part of our collective story. As the family has continued to invest in Legacy, they've always made a point of doing it mindfully. Projects like this lodge's historic preservation have helped Legacy retain its past with dignity and honor as we move into the future. The Marian family's annual hot cocoa mornings give us a chance to come together and honor our past and our future. We're all very grateful."

Even though he sounded a little like he was representing the Chamber of Commerce, there was something in his tone—a genuine pride and affection—that caught my attention. For a moment, I glimpsed the man behind the grump, someone who cared deeply about his community.

"That's... really well put," I said, momentarily forgetting the camera as I reached across to wipe the whipped cream off his nose.

The instant my fingertips brushed his skin, I realized my mistake. The touch was too familiar, too intimate for a first meeting—something I'd have done with a longtime friend or a lover, not a reluctant business associate. But there was no taking it back now. His skin was warm beneath my touch, and for a heartbeat, our eyes locked in mutual surprise at the casual contact.

Maddox's eyes widened, and his cheeks turned pink faster than a sunset timelapse. "Even a broken clock is right twice a day," he murmured.

"And even a grumpy photographer can be eloquent once per lunar cycle," I countered with a wink. "So which one are we tasting first?" I segued smoothly, lifting my mug. "Mrs. Marian, tell us what flavors you have for us today."

We both took sips as Mrs. Marian stood next to us, explaining the hot chocolate flight and telling us a little bit more about her family's lodge. The chocolate in this first selection was rich and velvety, the homemade whipped cream melting slowly into the warm liquid. I made the appropriate appreciative noises, describing the flavor profile for the viewers.

"It's like drinking a warm hug wrapped in cashmere," I enthused. "The way the vanilla notes complement the richness of the chocolate is absolutely—"

Maddox set down his mug with a decisive thunk. "Let's not get carried away. It's good, but I remain steadfastly loyal to my grandmother's own recipe. No offense, Mrs. Marian."

She laughed warmly. "None taken. Your grandmother's Christmas open house was the inspiration for our hot cocoa mornings."

As she wandered off to grab our next round, I focused back on Maddox. "Was this an open house at the hardware store?"

"Another annual tradition featuring the Sullivan family recipe. Been served at the hardware store's Christmas open house for over fifty years." He wiped his lips carefully, checking for more rogue whipped cream. "She used real dark chocolate and a pinch of cayenne pepper for depth."

"Sounds delicious. Tell me about it."

His expression softened slightly. "It was my favorite day of the year growing up. The store would be transformed—lights everywhere, pine garlands on the counters, Mr. Peterson—the *elder* Mr. Peterson—dressed as Santa. And my grandmother standing behind a giant pot of hot chocolate, making sure every kid in town got a candy cane and a full mug."

I could picture it vividly—the hardware store transformed into a winter wonderland, young Maddox wide-eyed at the magic of it all. For a moment, I felt a pang of something like envy. My own childhood Christmases had been elegant, formal affairs with catered food and professionally wrapped presents. The kind of Christmases that photographed beautifully but rarely featured in any stories I told. Nothing as messy or warm as what Maddox described.

The warmth in his voice was captivating. I found myself genuinely interested, the practiced conversation topics forgotten.

"And you still do it?"

His smile faded a little. "We try. It's not the same without my parents, but Maya and I keep it going. Tradition matters, you know?"

I nodded, unsure how to respond to the unexpected vulnerability. The casual mention of his parents' absence hung in the air between us. I wanted to ask what had happened but sensed it wasn't the right moment. He struck me as someone who wouldn't want to reveal too much on camera.

Before I could formulate a reply, Mrs. Marian arrived with the second round of hot chocolates—these topped with homemade marshmallows and chocolate shavings.

"Mexican chocolate," she announced. "Cinnamon, vanilla, and a hint of chili."

The moment broken, we returned to the tasting. As we progressed through the flight, Maddox gradually relaxed, his commentary becoming less grudging and more animated. He had strong opinions about the white chocolate peppermint (too sweet), enthusiastic praise for the dark chocolate orange (surprisingly complex), and outright skepticism about the final offering—a lavender-infused concoction with gold-dusted marshmallows.

"Fair warning," Mrs. Marian teased before leaving us to the final tasting. "This one's a little out-there, but it was a special request sent in via my granddaughter's social media account by several fans of the tasting."

After she'd moved far enough away to be out of earshot, Maddox made a face.

"This," he declared, eyeing the purple-tinted drink like it had personally insulted his heritage, "is exactly what's wrong with Instagram culture. Nobody needs edible gold or flowers in their hot chocolate. It's pretentious nonsense."

I laughed despite myself. "Not a fan of the nontraditional aesthetic?"

"It's hot chocolate, not a fashion statement. It should taste good, not just look good in photos."

"You know," I said, leaning closer, "for someone who claims to hate social media, you seem to have a lot of opinions about it."

"I have opinions about everything," he retorted. "Ask anyone in town."

"Oh, I plan to. I'm making a spreadsheet of 'Maddox Sullivan's Grumpy Opinions' as we speak. I'm guessing by the end of our twelve dates, I'll have enough material for a coffee table book."

His lips twitched, fighting a smile. "Your dates," he corrected. "Not our dates."

"Our dates since you will definitely be there," I corrected with a grin. "And if you thought I was implying something more than that, don't flatter yourself, Sullivan."

"Like I'd date someone who needs outdoor wear with fancy labels when the weather's barely below freezing," he shot back.

"Says the man who's been checking out my fancy-labeled ass since yesterday."

Maddox choked on his hot chocolate. "I have not—"

"Let's circle back to this pretentious hot chocolate," I interrupted, taking pity on him as his face turned crimson. "Is your objection to lavender specifically or all flowers in beverages? What's your stance on chamomile tea? Discuss."

"Don't try to distract me with tea politics," he growled, but I could see the humor in his eyes now.

Something about the banter felt easy, natural, as if we'd known each other longer than the mere day it had been. I found myself forgetting we were on camera, forgetting the carefully constructed talking points, forgetting everything except the way his eyes crinkled at the corners when he was trying not to smile.

I sat back and tapped the side of my mug, which seemed to be hand-thrown pottery, similar to a few pieces I'd seen at the gallery the other day. "There's nothing wrong with making ordinary things beautiful. That's what photography does, isn't it? Finds the beauty in the everyday?"

Maddox studied me for a moment, his expression unreadable. "There's a difference between finding beauty and manufacturing it."

"Is there? Or is it just snobbery in reverse—looking down on something because it's polished rather than raw?"

He opened his mouth to respond, then closed it again, genuinely considering the question. "Maybe," he admitted finally. "Maybe my issue is more with showing the sunshiny, filtered version of something instead of making the effort to find the true beauty below the surface. Real authenticity as opposed to..." He hesitated. "*Hashtag* authenticity."

"Authentic. There's that word again," I murmured, holding his gaze. His smoky eyes offered more temptation than any of the hot chocolate varieties had. I tried to stay focused. "What is authentic, really? If I genuinely enjoy this ridiculous, overly complex, lavender hot chocolate, isn't that authentic? Even if I also think it would look great in a filtered photo on my Instagram?"

"The problem isn't enjoying it," he said slowly. "It's changing the entire experience to make it photographable. It's the difference between capturing life and staging it."

"So you've never repositioned a subject for better light? Never asked someone to move slightly to improve composition?" I raised an eyebrow. "Because that sounds an awful lot like staging to me."

Maddox smiled—a real smile that reached his eyes and transformed his face from merely handsome to devastating. My heart did a stupid triple-thunk before stuttering back to a normal rhythm.

"Touché, Hayes. Maybe you're not completely superficial after all."

"High praise indeed." I returned his smile, surprised by how good it felt to crack through his defenses. "And maybe you're not a completely judgmental asshole."

"Don't bet on it," he warned, but the warmth in his eyes belied the gruffness of his tone. "I still have eleven more 'dates' to prove you wrong." His finger quotes drew my attention to his strong hands. The kind of hands that snuck unbidden images into my head. Things he could do to me with those hands if given the chance.

I cleared my throat. "Eleven more dates to change your mind about me, you mean," I corrected, raising my mug in a toast.

Maddox clinked his mug against mine. "We'll see who converts whom."

Maya cleared her throat loudly. "Um, guys? We about done, or do you want to keep doing... whatever this is?"

The sound of other conversations and clinking mugs nearby seemed to burst the strange bubble we'd been in. I'd completely forgotten about the camera or the hot chocolate tasting.

Judging by Maddox's startled expression, so had he.

"Right." I straightened, professional mask sliding back into place. "So that concludes our tour of the Marian family's famous hot chocolate flight, the perfect holiday indulgence for visitors to Legacy, Montana. Stay tuned for my next 'Twelve Dates of Christmas' adventure! And a special thanks to Nordique for hooking me up with their delicious merino Selwyn trousers and what has to be the softest cashmere sweater I've ever worn." I held out my arm to show the sweater off to the lens.

Maddox surprised me by reaching over to run a hand up my forearm. "That is nice," he said, his voice a deep rumble. "My father had a Nordique fisherman's sweater passed down from his father. It didn't feel like this, though."

I swallowed. "It's, ah... it's the Calden crewneck," I said, trying to take advantage of the unexpected product-focused moment. "It also comes in a gorgeous mossy-green color."

He blinked at me and stood up, scraping his chair against the wooden floor. "Cut. That's... that's good. Got what we needed. I should check in on Alex, make sure he's okay." He pulled out his phone, avoiding eye contact. "Maya, can you help pack up while I make this call?"

Without waiting for a response, he strode toward the door, already dialing as he went.

Maya watched him go, then turned to me with a raised eyebrow. "So that was..."

"A good start to the series," I finished professionally, despite my confusion over Maddox's behavior. "Your brother has a natural camera presence. Once he takes the stick out of his ass."

"Uh-huh." Her tone was heavy with implication. "That's one thought. Another is that what the two of you just shot was the most chemistry I've seen my brother have with anyone since... well, ever."

I felt heat rising in my cheeks and blamed it on the fire. "We were playing to the camera. That's what content creation is— manufacturing moments that resonate."

"You know he still has that sweater," she said in a softer tone. "He keeps it in his desk at the store like a lucky charm. I didn't realize it was Nordique. That's kind of cool."

Before I could respond, Maddox returned, his expression thunderous. "Alex isn't answering. But Ella just texted to check how the shoot went, which is interesting, considering she was the one supposedly going over to nurse Alex."

Maya suddenly became very interested in packing up the camera equipment.

"What are you saying?" I asked.

Maddox's eyes narrowed. "I'm saying something is fishy about his last-minute cancellation." He turned to his sister. "Maya, do you know anything about this?"

"Me?" She blinked innocently. "Why would *I* know anything?"

"Because you and Rosie Marian have been known to pull... shenanigans."

"That's ridiculous," Maya protested, though her cheeks flushed tellingly. "Maybe Alex really is sick. Or maybe he got a better offer. Or maybe the universe just wanted you two to have hot chocolate together. Cosmic alignment. Serendipity. Whatever. Don't blame your adorable sister or her beloved former babysitter."

Maddox looked unconvinced. "You have five minutes to strengthen your defenses against a detailed interrogation," he promised his sister before turning back to me. "I promise I'll arrange a backup plan for your next date."

I blinked. "What kind of backup plan?"

"In case we have another mysterious cancellation."

"Don't be ridiculous. I'm sure the guy was just under the weather. Besides—" I gestured between us. "—this worked well. The footage will be good—honest reactions, genuine conversation. If tomorrow's date falls through, we could always—"

"No," Maddox said firmly. "Absolutely not. Today was a onetime emergency solution."

"But—"

"No buts. I'm the videographer, not the date. That was the deal. Rule number three, remember? And today's rule about only allowing *one* exception to that rule?"

I raised my hands in surrender. "Fine. Just trying to keep things simple."

Maya coughed something that sounded suspiciously like "missed opportunity."

Maddox ignored her. "We'll meet Wednesday at nine at the Pinecone to coordinate. Emerson's Christmas Tree Farm opens at ten, and your date—a local firefighter named Marco—will meet us there." He emphasized the name as if daring the universe to interfere again. "I'll confirm again before I go to bed tonight."

"Sounds perfect," I said, gathering my things while trying not to think of Maddox Sullivan in bed. "Nine it is."

As we left the lodge, Maya fell into step beside me while Maddox walked ahead, texting furiously—presumably still trying to reach Alex.

"For what it's worth," she said quietly, "I think your followers are going to love what we got."

"Thanks." And that was my only purpose here, so nothing else mattered anyway. At least, that's what I told myself as I tried unsuccessfully to tear my gaze away from Maddox's retreating figure.

I watched Maddox's ass as he leaned over to put his equipment into their truck and found myself replaying our conversation by the fire—the unexpected depth beneath Maddox's gruff exterior, the way his eyes had lit up when talking about his grandmother's hot chocolate.

For the first time since arriving in Legacy, I felt myself relax a little. Even when things went wrong, they seemed to work out okay. So far, we'd managed to avert a crisis at every turn.

And averting a crisis with Maddox Sullivan wasn't so bad. In fact, spending time staring at him across the table while his face softened into memory or tightened in challenge had actually been pretty amazing.

I quickly pushed that thought aside. *You're here for content, Adrian. Nordique. Career trajectory, remember? Not about gawping over pretty assholes. Remember what Vic said, and don't fuck this up.*

But as I watched Maddox help Maya into the passenger seat, his strong hands moving with surprising gentleness, I couldn't help but wonder if Legacy, Montana, might offer me more than pretty pictures after all.

#WhippedCreamOnTheNose #ReluctantlyAuthentic #TouchTheCashmereAgain #EyeCrinkleKryptonite

# 6

# #UNPLANNEDCHEMISTRY
## MADDOX

How was it possible to be both proud of your work product and also horrified by it?

I sat in my studio above the gallery, rewatching the reels I'd sent Adrian for the fourth time, ignoring the morning light that filtered through the large windows and the usual clutter in my crowded workspace. Photos lined the walls, mostly candid shots from around Legacy: Ravi Menon teaching his wife to ski, Jade Cleary and her prized tomatoes in the summer sun, Maya laughing at last year's Christmas parade.

But right now, my attention was fixed on my monitor where Adrian Hayes sat bathed in firelight, his perfect face animated as he described the "notes of complexity" in the orange and dark chocolate cocoa. The way the light caught his features was almost unfair—all elegant angles and warm shadows that made him look like he'd been designed specifically for cameras to love him.

There'd also been moments I hadn't noticed until I'd gone through the footage. Like the odd little moment in which he tugged nervously at his sleeve cuff after I'd mentioned family tradition or the curious way he'd stared at my eyes when he'd mentioned the specific mossy-green option for the sweater.

"Fuck," I muttered, replaying it to analyze our interaction again.

The chemistry was undeniable. Even through the lens, you could see the spark between us—the way our banter flowed naturally, how his polished persona cracked whenever I managed to genuinely surprise him, the brief moments when his mask slipped to reveal something more real.

Like when he'd reached out to wipe that damn whipped cream off my nose.

I paused the footage on that moment, cursing under my breath. His expression had been completely unguarded then— warm, amused, almost tender. It was the kind of authentic moment he claimed to want... and exactly the kind of footage that would have our small town's matchmakers working overtime.

My phone buzzed with another text from Maya:

> MAYA
>
> You're seeing it, right? Holy shit, Maddie.
> You two look amazing together. The way
> you smiled when he—

I didn't bother reading the rest. My sister had been insufferable since yesterday, alternating between teasing me about Adrian and asking if she could come to our next date—er, *shoot*.

My phone buzzed again before I could set it down.

> MAYA
>
> You can't ignore me forever. I saw those
> lingering looks. The TENSION. Even Rosie
> says—

I switched my phone to silent and tossed it onto my desk. The last thing I needed was the Legacy gossip network analyzing every interaction between Adrian and me. Since shortly after Mom and Dad died, they'd been convinced I needed someone to "take care of." As if I hadn't had my hands full taking care of Maya and myself. And the store. And my photography career.

As if I needed one more damned thing to take care of.

I grumbled and turned back to the footage with the intention of organizing the files and closing out of the program. Focus on the files, shithead. Not the way Adrian's eyes crinkled when he laughed or how they glinted when I managed to ruffle him.

I cursed again as I picked up my phone to check Instagram.

The door downstairs chimed, scaring the fuck out of me.

Alex Marian called up the stairs. "Maddox? You here?"

"Yeah," I called back, dropping my phone and quickly minimizing the computer window showing Adrian's face. "Come on up."

Alex appeared at the top of the stairs, looking suspiciously hale for someone who'd been "violently ill" yesterday morning. He carried two coffees from the Pinecone.

"Peace offering?" He held out one of the cups.

"Depends." I accepted the coffee but fixed him with a hard stare. "Want to tell me what really happened yesterday?"

Alex had the grace to look sheepish. "Would you believe food poisoning?"

"No. And if you insist on it, I'm going to question your role as a restauranteur..."

He winced. "Fair enough. Migraine?"

"Try again."

He sighed, dropping into the spare chair. "Fine. My cousin may have convinced me to cancel."

I narrowed my eyes at him. "Lennon?" The gruff rancher wasn't the type to meddle or matchmake, so that was surprising.

He shook his head. "Rosie."

"Ahh." I rolled my eyes. Lennon's sister had been Maya's babysitter once, but she'd become more like Maya's unofficial big sister since our parents' deaths. The two were thick as thieves... and just as cunning when they got an idea in their heads.

"It wasn't for the reason you think—"

"Sure," I interrupted, sarcasm present and accounted for. "It's too bad, you know. Because this guy is totally your type."

His eyebrows winged up. "Model-pretty, charming as hell, and looks good in fancy sweaters?" Alex continued with a teasing grin. "Nah. I don't deserve such riches. You, though..."

I held up a hand. "Don't jump on the matchmaking bandwagon. This guy's going straight back to LA where he came from."

Alex studied me with his usual calm demeanor. "The post I saw on Insta was fire."

I turned back to my monitor, trying to hide my reaction. "The post shows two people drinking hot chocolate, nothing more."

"Right. Because everyone looks at their videographer like they want to devour them instead of the lodge's famous cocoa flight." Alex leaned forward to watch the screen. "Come on, Maddox. When's the last time you sparked with someone like that?"

"Sparks aren't always a good thing," I reminded him, though the lie felt hollow even to me. "They cause forest fires, you know."

"Uh-huh. It was some kind of fire alright. How'd the date really go? Deny it all you want, but just know there were witnesses to that fire, my friend. Everyone who saw you two together said there was something there."

"Not a date," I corrected, jabbing the keyboard a little harder than necessary to close the editing program. "A shoot. And even if there was... a... spark... it doesn't matter. I'm not interested in being anyone's vacation fling before they fuck back off to their real life and leave Legacy far behind."

Alex's expression softened. "Not everyone leaves, Maddox."

The words hit closer to home than I wanted to admit. Mom and Dad hadn't meant to leave either, but that hadn't stopped the black ice that had taken them both in one horrible moment. Or the man I'd been dating at the time who'd quickly taken a job back in his hometown of Seattle to escape the weight of my grief. Since then, I'd focused on what I could control—the store, Maya's future, my photography. Getting involved with someone like Adrian Hayes, whose entire life was built around moving on to the next perfect location, was asking for heartbreak. Not to mention frustration.

"What was the real reason you canceled on me?" I said, running a hand through my hair. "Because I'd love to stop talking about Adrian Hayes for a solid five minutes if at all possible."

Alex hesitated, then shrugged and grinned a little self-consciously. "My life is complicated enough right now without throwing this high-profile fake-dating thing into the mix."

I opened my mouth to ask what was so complicated when my phone buzzed again. This time, it was a text from Marco about tomorrow's scheduled date. *Shoot.*

MARCO

Hey man, really sorry but I got called for a last-minute training thing at the station. Rain check on the Christmas tree thing?

"You've got to be fucking kidding me," I growled. "Fucking fire chief is ruining my plans for tomorrow's shoot."

Alex's eyes widened in horror. "You were sending Adrian on a date with Chief Kincaid?"

I frowned at him. "No. I don't have a death wish. Although, now that I think of it... I should see if he's available. Kincaid wouldn't put up with any fancy-pants flirtation bullshit. He'd put Adrian Hayes in his place."

"Don't do that to Adrian," Alex said, nostrils flaring. "No one deserves to be set up with Chief Bullshit-Fire-Code-Infractions."

At the reminder of Alex's ongoing feud with the fastidious fire chief and his no-nonsense fire inspections at Timber, I let the subject go.

"You're on the hook, I'm afraid. A little tree chopping never hurt anyone."

"Not it," Alex said cheerfully. "Seriously, I can't. I have a large group coming in for a holiday lunch. Why not just admit you're attracted to the guy and save us all a lot of trouble?"

"I'm not—" But the lie died in my throat as I glanced at my monitor, where I'd minimized the video. Even the thumbnail showed Adrian mid-laugh, his head thrown back, completely unguarded. Beautiful.

I gritted my teeth. *Fuck.*

"The guy flaunts his pretty feathers for a living," I said instead. "He's empty as a pocket. And he's leaving in three weeks. I have milk in the fridge that will last longer than this guy."

"Wasn't suggesting a marriage, Maddox." Alex stood, clapping me on the shoulder. "Fuck him and get out from under this funk."

Before I could squawk in indignation, Maya burst through the door, practically vibrating with excitement.

"Maddox!" Her cheeks were pink, and her eyes sparkled. "Have you seen the numbers? Your hot chocolate date is going viral!"

Maya thrust her phone in my face before I could respond. The screen showed Adrian's Instagram story—clips from our "date" set to some trendy song, with the caption "When your videographer becomes your emergency date... #LegacyMontana #TwelveDates-OfChristmas"

The view count was astronomical.

"Twenty thousand views in the first hour," she announced triumphantly. "And the comments are gold. Everyone's shipping you two."

"Shipping isn't a real thing," I muttered, though my stomach did an annoying flip at seeing one of Adrian's responses to a comment asking if he had a new boyfriend...

*Just friends. He's definitely talented right?"* he'd written with a winky emoji, followed by a fire emoji.

The fire emoji made my face heat, and I forced myself *not* to think about what it implied.

"Tell that to the Operation Maddrian group chat," Alex chimed in helpfully.

"Operation Maddrian? No. You're making that up." I quickly searched the comments.

Maya commandeered my computer mouse. "Stop scrolling and actually read some of these! 'The tension!' 'The way the grumpy one softens when the pretty one laughs!' 'This is better than Hallmark!'"

My face flooded with even more heat until the fire emoji began to look downright frigid compared to my face. "He gets to be the pretty one, and I'm the grumpy one? Says who? I'm not fucking grumpy."

"Are, too," the two of them said at the same time before breaking into laughter.

I dropped my head into my hands. "Don't you both have literally anywhere else to be?"

"Not when this is happening." Maya scrolled through more comments. "Oh my god, someone made a compilation of every time you almost smile at him. It's set to 'Can't Fight This Feeling.'"

I groaned. "That's it. I'm moving to Alaska."

"Alaska has influencers, too," Alex pointed out helpfully. "And probably worse internet for uploading your obvious sexual tension with them."

I threw a lens cap at his head. He caught it, laughing.

"I hate both of you," I announced, standing up. "And I'm going to the store, where at least the power tools don't try to make something out of nothing."

"Oh, I don't know," Maya said cheerfully. "I'm sure the screwdrivers and drills could—"

"Stop now, I beg of you!" I cried, stopping her from making whatever raunchy insinuation she was going for. "You're my baby sister, for crying out loud. Jesus."

I grabbed my jacket, pointedly ignoring them both. "I have actual work to do. A business to run. Bills to pay. A Christmas photo shoot for the McClures and their dogs tonight. You know, real-life stuff that doesn't involve shipping or viral videos or—"

*Pretty boys.*

My phone buzzed. Again.

ADRIAN

Hey. So Marco had to cancel. Any chance you're free to...?

"Don't even think about it," I muttered to my phone before sending him a single-word response. *No.*

"Was that Adrian?" Maya asked, her tone far too innocent. "Because I heard there was a, um, *thing* scheduled at the firehouse, so—"

"No." I pointed at her. "Absolutely not. Rule number three exists for a reason."

"Yeah, because you're scared," she shot back. "Scared of actually letting someone see past your grumpy shell. Scared of admitting that maybe, just maybe, the universe is trying to tell you something."

"The universe isn't trying to tell me anything," I argued. "Just because we're both gay doesn't mean we somehow belong together, Maya. Don't be that guy. Girl. Whatever."

Her smile dropped, and she glared at me. "Unfair hit below the belt."

I closed my eyes and inhaled while Alex, thankfully, stayed quiet. "Sorry. You're right. Sorry."

Maya reached out and touched my arm. "I just think it's time for you to live a little, Maddie. Stop taking everything so seriously. Go on a date. Let yourself have a little fun."

"It's not fun, it's a job," I reminded her, but my heart wasn't in it. I was tired. Tired from working, tired from trying so hard to keep all the balls in the air. Tired of being the grumpy one.

Tired of being alone.

I remembered the way Adrian's fingers had felt brushing my nose, how his laugh had sounded when it was genuine, how his eyes had sparkled when challenging my opinions on lavender hot chocolate.

My phone buzzed again.

ADRIAN

You can't deny the on-screen chemistry was great. C'mon. It'll be quick. In and out. You said the tree farm opens at 10, we can be done by 11:30. Professional. Painless.

"Fuck," I muttered, letting my head thunk against the doorframe.

Because he wasn't wrong. The chemistry had been great. The footage was compelling. And something about trading barbs with Adrian Hayes had made me feel more alive than I'd felt in years.

Which was exactly why it was dangerous.

"I'm going to the store," I announced. "To do actual work. You two can keep scrolling social media all you want."

As I descended the stairs, I heard Maya call after me, "Don't forget to dress cute for your second date!"

I slammed the gallery door harder than necessary, the bell jingling in protest. The crisp winter air hit my face, helping clear my head as I trudged toward the hardware store. I needed to focus on real problems—like the stack of still-unpaid invoices in my desk drawer, or the leak in the stockroom roof, or the fact that our heating bill had nearly doubled this month.

Not Adrian Hayes and his perfect face and his surprisingly genuine laugh and—

"Maddox! Just the man I was hoping to see!"

I suppressed a groan as Evelyn Hoffman emerged from the drugstore, practically vibrating with enthusiasm. The woman had been trying to set me up for fifteen years. The fact that she now had social media ammunition was clearly too exciting for her to contain.

"Hi, Mrs. Hoffman. Kind of in a hurry—"

"Oh, I just wanted to say how lovely that video was! Such chemistry with that handsome fellow. You know, my nephew's coming to visit next week, but perhaps I should cancel since you and Adrian seem so—"

"We don't seem anything," I cut her off, probably more sharply than the sweet woman deserved. "It's a business arrangement. That's all." I didn't remind her that she'd already forced poor Nelson and me into a date together, and it had been a complete disaster. In addition to being a "menswear specialist" at a department store—his words, not mine—he was also a lighting designer for a theater over in Spokane and felt that my career and I would benefit tremendously from his lighting expertise.

I had not-so-politely disagreed.

"Sorry to run off," I said, waving toward the hardware store as if gesturing to someone very important inside. "Have a great day, Mrs. Hoffman!"

As I entered the store, I breathed in the familiar scent of sawdust and metal. The morning light streamed through the front windows, catching the Christmas display Dad had meticulously arranged every year. Now, Maya did most of the decorating while I handled inventory and bills.

I headed back to my office, determined to focus on actual work instead of viral videos and meddling townspeople. The bills wouldn't pay themselves, no matter how many views Adrian's post got.

My hand brushed against something soft as I reached for the paperwork—Dad's old Nordique sweater, carefully folded in the corner of the drawer. I consistently forgot I'd stashed it there after finding it draped over Dad's office chair in the weeks after his death, and every time I "found" it again was a bittersweet reminder. The wool was still impossibly soft, the cable-knit pattern intricate and beautiful despite its age.

"Your grandfather gave me this the day I took over the store," Dad had told me once. "Said a Sullivan man needed a proper sweater for Montana winters."

I ran my fingers over the soft knit, remembering Adrian's genuine surprise when I'd touched his sweater yesterday. The way his blue eyes had widened, how his practiced smile had softened, that crooked canine had emerged, and it had turned into something real.

My phone buzzed again in my pocket.

ADRIAN

> Not to push, but the tree farm would be
> perfect for showing off Nordique's new
> winter collection. And since you already
> know the equipment…

My hands shook with nerves that I would cave and agree to anything he asked. It was tempting to take everyone's advice. To live a little. But I knew myself better than they did.

I didn't do casual very well. Especially not with someone who… sparked… with me the way Adrian did.

> Just find another date! I thought you had
> your Grindr app primed for this.

ADRIAN

> I'm trying! But someone told me not to
> bother finding my own dates, remember?
> Wasn't that Rule 1? And you have to
> admit we had good chemistry.

I stared at his message, fingers hovering over the screen. Because he wasn't wrong—we did have chemistry. The kind that made my chest tight and my skin warm. The kind that was hazardous for someone who couldn't afford distractions.

The kind that made me want things I couldn't have.

I shoved the phone back in my pocket without responding, but the damage was done. Now, all I could think about was Adrian Hayes in a pine forest, snowflakes catching in his perfect hair, that genuine laugh echoing between the trees…

"Fuck," I muttered, dropping into my chair. "Get it together, Sullivan."

But even as I tried to focus on the invoices, I couldn't shake the feeling that somehow, in less than forty-eight hours, Adrian Hayes had managed to get under my skin in a way no one had in years.

A soft knock interrupted my brooding. Maya stood in the doorway, her expression unusually serious.

"Before you yell at me," she said, holding up her hands, "I came to apologize. I shouldn't have teased you about Adrian. I know how hard you work to keep everything going here, and I wasn't being fair."

I deflated slightly. "Come here, squirt."

I stood up as she stepped into my open arms, squeezing me just as tightly as I did her. "Thank you," I murmured into her hair.

She pulled back and perched on the edge of my desk, idly picking up a scattered paperclip from the desk as I took my seat again. "I just... I see how tired you are sometimes. How much you gave up to take care of me and the store. And when I saw you actually laughing with him yesterday—"

"Maya—"

"No, let me finish." She met my eyes. "You deserve good things, Maddie. Even temporary ones. Even if they're wearing stupid-expensive sweaters and have too many Instagram followers."

I reached for Dad's sweater, running my thumb over the worn wool. "Life isn't about what we deserve. It's about what we can handle. And I can't handle—" I gestured vaguely, encompassing Adrian, the viral video, the whole mess. "All of that."

"Can't? Or won't?" She held up her phone with one of the reels playing on a loop.

For a moment, I let myself imagine what it would be like to capture Adrian's laugh again. To be the reason for it.

"It doesn't matter," I said firmly. "Two and a half more weeks and he's gone. Better to keep things professional."

Maya hopped off the desk with an exaggerated sigh. "Fine. Be stubborn. But when he shows up with some random date who acts like a doofus and looks like shit on your camera, don't come crying to me."

I swiveled my chair back to face the invoices. "I won't. Because I'm calling Fannin Linwood. He owes me a favor. And he's amazing in front of the lens."

She rolled her eyes and sighed. "Never mind, then. Those two will for sure hook up, and then your window of opportunity will close forever."

As she headed back out to the front of the store, I stared after her. She was right. Fannin was known for enjoying time with pretty men. He'd gotten a reputation on the snowboard circuit as a total player. He'd seduce Adrian in a hot minute, and Adrian would probably thank him for the opportunity.

*Fuck. Fucking fuck.*

My phone buzzed again.

> ADRIAN
>
> I might have a lead on a guy. Alex Marian suggested I call Fannin something. He's a ski instructor, I think. You know him? Think he'd look good cutting down Christmas trees?

My jaw ached from grinding my back teeth together.

I stared at the message, picturing Adrian among the pines with Fannin fucking Linwood, snowflakes catching in his golden hair, that genuine laugh pointed at Fannin's model-pretty face and broad shoulders, while Fannin's large hand spanned Adrian's lower back.

The two of them together would make for beautiful footage. Professional, artistic footage that could help the store and Maya's college fund.

But the idea pissed me off. For professional reasons, obviously. What if Fannin spent the entire time flirting? We'd be there all day. And what if Adrian stood out in the cold too long? His red cheeks might read splotchy and weird on-screen.

No. It would be better if I did it. For the sake of the finished product.

We could always use Fannin on a different shoot. *Date.* Maybe one in which he taught Adrian how to ski or snowboard.

My stomach twisted. That was a stupid idea for all the reasons I'd just said, wasn't it?

I picked up my phone again and banged out a text.

> I'll do it. But this is the last time.

His response was immediate.

ADRIAN

> Methinks we don't like the ski instructor.

> Remember we're meeting at the Pinecone at 9. Don't be late.

ADRIAN

> There's my grumpy mountain man. See you at 10. Just kidding.

And then he sent a kissy-face emoji.

I dropped my phone like it had burned me, but the damage was done. My traitorous heart was already racing at the thought of talking to him again. Of flirting with him again. Of being his... date.

*Pretend* date.

It was a stupid idea, and I was stupider for being the one to agree to it.

"Be easier this way, though," I muttered, turning back to the invoices. "Quicker. Less bullshit to deal with."

But even I didn't believe that blatant lie.

#DenyDenyDeny #SparkShmark #FuckingEmojis #NoFannin

7

# #MADDRIANFANFICNOWAVAILABLE

ADRIAN

SOMETHING warm and perilously close to excitement fluttered in my chest as I lay in my bed at the rental cabin and read Maddox's response for the tenth time.

> MADDOX
>
> I'll do it. But this is the last time.

I tried tamping the feeling down. This was business. Content creation. A professional arrangement, nothing more. But I couldn't stop grinning over how quickly he'd backed off his precious Rule Three.

I had plenty of other things to grin about, too, obviously.

The numbers I'd woken up to had been staggering. Views: 223K and climbing. Comments: over 8,000. Shares: nearly 15,000. These weren't just *good* metrics—they were *viral* metrics, the kind that could make or break a sponsored campaign.

Vic clearly agreed, based on the quick succession of voice messages he sent.

*"You're on fire,"* he said breathlessly in the first. *"Nordique is*

*obsessed. Obsessed, babe. They're talking long-term brand ambassador. Exclusive contract. Multiple campaigns across next year's product lines. As in a private jet to Chamonix in January and a branded capsule collection next fall!"*

This was followed quickly by, *"They want to see sustained engagement and 'emotional storytelling.' And whatever that spark is between you and Mountain Man? They want more of it. Fast."*

And then, slightly more concerningly, *"But don't get soft on me. You're selling the fantasy, not falling for it."*

I dropped my phone on the bed and stared at the ceiling.

An exclusive deal with Nordique was the dream. It would lock in everything I'd spent the last five years building. But that last line from Vic, about *selling the fantasy, not falling for it*, echoed in my head.

Why did it feel like I was doing both?

I picked up the phone and stared at the Instagram posts again. I'd known the reels would do well, but I hadn't expected just how much my followers would engage. Even as I watched, the comments kept pouring in.

> OMG the tension between these two!! You could cut it with a knife! 🔥

> That grumpy mountain man is HOT. Does he have an Instagram??

> The way he looks at you when you're not looking at him... I CANT 😵

> Is this scripted? Because if not... get married immediately

> #Maddrian #MountainManHottie #HolidayLoveStory

I choked on my own spit.

*Maddrian?* Seriously?

I continued scrolling, my cheeks heating inexplicably when I got to an actual frame-by-frame breakdown of our "intimate moments"—everything from when I'd wiped whipped cream off his nose to our heated debate about lavender hot chocolate.

They weren't falling for Nordique, or Legacy, or even my cute dating idea. They were falling for the idea of a romance between me and Maddox. A romance that didn't exist.

And if I didn't already have the feeling that was a problem, I definitely did when I slid into a booth at the Pinecone for a late breakfast.

"Morning, handsome!" Sadie called cheerfully. "Coffee's already brewing. Your usual?"

"Uh. I don't know what that is, but sure." I smiled, shrugging off my coat and draping it carefully over the back of the chair.

She set a coffee and a tiny pitcher in front of me. "Oat milk creamer," she said proudly.

"Oh. Wow. Thank you," I said, inexplicably touched.

"No trouble. Anything for a friend of Maddox's. You two looked mighty fine over at the Marian place yesterday," she tossed out at full volume before disappearing to the kitchen.

Her words seemed to be a signal all the other diners in the place were waiting for. My breakfast quickly became a whirlwind of whispered comments from people sitting nearby, pointed glances from others, and actual conversations with the people brave enough to walk up and speak to me.

"It's so nice to see Maddox smile again," an older woman said wistfully. "You know he lost a little of his sparkle when he lost his parents, may they rest in peace."

Another guy narrowed his eyes at me. "Don't you go distracting Maddox from his job now, you hear? Sullivan Hardware's been our local go-to longer than you've been alive."

It was small-town trial by fire, and by the time I finished my waffles—apparently, they were my "usual" now—I felt like I'd been run through a gauntlet.

It only got worse when I got back to the cabin and answered Vic's call.

"Adrian! My sweet moneymaking angel!" His voice was so loud I had to hold the phone away from my ear. "Have you seen the numbers? *Have you seen the numbers*?"

"You messaged me about them before dawn." I switched to speaker so I could open my laptop on the coffee table. The numbers had only multiplied since breakfast. They were too big to fully wrap my head around. "They're... impressive."

"*Impressive*? Darling, they're fucking spectacular. I've never seen engagement like this on your account. Ever. Not even that time you 'accidentally' fell in the pool at the Santorini shoot."

I winced at the memory. That "accidental" fall had been meticulously planned, right down to the specific white linen shirt that would become perfectly translucent when wet.

"The comments are giving me *life*," Vic continued. "Everyone's shipping you and Mountain Man. You've created a monster, baby, and everyone loves a monster, especially a hot, grumpy one."

"I didn't create anything," I protested, ignoring the twinge of annoyance at Vic's reference to Maddox. "Maddox is a photographer and videographer. A talented one. And a good guy. When my original date got sick, he stepped in as an emergency solution—"

"Well, that emergency solution is now your golden ticket! Nordique is thrilled. Just got a call from their marketing director—the *director*, babe—raving about you. This is exactly what they were hoping for."

I sucked in a breath. "They said that?"

"Yes, with the small caveat that you need to 'stay luxe,' whatever the fuck that means. I'm assuming they want you to keep featuring their fancy shit while exchanging smoldering glances with Lumberjack Ken—"

"His name is Maddox," I corrected automatically, then immediately regretted it when Vic made a knowing "mmhmm" sound.

"Listen," he said, suddenly serious. "This is a gift. The algorithm gods have smiled upon you. Lean into it."

"Lean into what, exactly?" I asked, already pretty sure I knew.

"The chemistry, darling," he said, confirming my suspicion. "The unexpected romance angle. The luxury-meets-rustic narrative. It's fresh, it's engaging, and most importantly, it's *selling*."

I pinched the bridge of my nose. "There is no romance angle, Vic. Maddox is the videographer. That's all. He didn't sign up for any of this other stuff."

Vic was quiet for a moment, then made a disapproving noise. "That's a shame. But you're on with a firefighter today, right? See if you can spark some flames with him, and then everyone will forget about Maddrian. Let's make hay while the sun shines."

I didn't inform him the firefighter had canceled and Maddox had already agreed to stand in. That would only add fuel to Vic's fire.

"I'll try my best. In the meantime, see if you can start lining something up for January. A tropical haven, preferably. I wasn't meant to live in a place like this. I'm wearing two pairs of socks, Vic. *Two*."

After ending the call with Vic, I flopped back against the sofa pillows and stared at the ceiling. The analytics on my phone continued to update, numbers climbing in real time.

I should have been thrilled. I *was* thrilled. This kind of organic viral momentum was what every influencer dreamed about and could convince Nordique to offer me a permanent contract.

But I was also conflicted because my success had come from

the one element I hadn't planned or controlled—Maddox Sullivan.

Grumpy, refreshingly real, frustratingly attractive Maddox, who clearly wanted nothing to do with me or my "content farm." Who'd agreed to help me so the town matchmakers would lay off him and had been thrown from the frying pan into the fire.

I switched from Instagram back to my text window and scrolled up to our earlier exchange, the one in which I'd suggested a local ski instructor could step in.

It had taken a surprisingly short time for his response.

Was it wrong that I wanted to read something into it? Like, maybe Maddox didn't mind stepping in as much as he claimed? That he'd had as much fun as I had? How was it that the Maddrian hashtag and the uptick in Legacy matchmaking enthusiasm hadn't turned him off?

I closed my messaging app and blew out a breath. *Sell the fantasy, don't fall for it*, I reminded myself.

I forced myself to work for a few hours, checking in with other sponsors, responding to comments and DMs, and posting more content from our day yesterday. But every time I looked at one of our reels, it was impossible not to focus on the dark-haired man across from me at the hot chocolate table.

Finally, I couldn't stand it anymore. I pulled out my phone and texted him.

> Are you seeing this? The reaction to our videos?

MADDOX

> No. Some of us have actual work to do.

> For some of us, this *is* the work. Don't be a job snob.

MADDOX

He's a poet, ladies and gentlemen.

I tried to relax my cheeks, which were already sore from grinning like a fool. He was so fun to provoke.

The comments are going INSANE. Apparently you have "mountain daddy energy"

MADDOX

What the hell does that even mean?

It means half my followers want to climb you like a tree. The other half want to adopt you and feed you soup.

MADDOX

Disturbing. All of it.

Oh come on, don't tell me you haven't looked at the comments. "The way he looks at Adrian when Adrian's not looking" has 500 likes.

MADDOX

I don't look at you any particular way.

Sure, Sullivan. And I don't spend twenty minutes styling my hair to look "effortlessly tousled"

MADDOX

Twenty minutes? For hair that looks like you stuck your finger in an electrical socket?

HEY. This is premium chaos. It takes skill to look this accidentally perfect.

MADDOX

"Accidentally perfect"

Was that… was that an emoji? From the man who probably still has a flip phone?

MADDOX

I'll have you know I WOULD still have a flip phone if Maya hadn't upgraded my phone against my will. Also she's reading over my shoulder right now and says to tell you she's team #Maddrian

Not sure our ship name should be so… Maddox-central.

MADDOX

It's better than #Adriox

Okay that one sounds like a cleaning product. Fine. Maddrian it is.

MADDOX

There is no Maddrian. It's a made-up word for a made-up thing.

Sure, but tell that to the 847 people who used the hashtag in the last hour.

MADDOX

I'm turning my phone off now.

Wait! Before you go full hermit mode… for tomorrow's Christmas tree cutting, remember to dress warm. And maybe try to look less like you're attending your own execution?

MADDOX

I enjoy a lecture on warm clothing from someone who owns more Speedos than sweaters.

How do you know about my Speedos… has someone been scrolling social media incognito? 😼

There was a pause, and I wondered if I'd annoyed him or embarrassed him. Or both. But a few minutes later, I got a response.

MADDOX

Of course I checked you out before agreeing to do business with you.

Checked me out. I like the sound of that, Sullivan.

MADDOX

Your *account*. And since it seems you can't go a week without posting a cheesecake thirst trap shot, I've had my eyeballs seared by several images of you wearing nothing but dick mittens.

I... don't even know how to respond to that. Dick mittens?

MADDOX

"Budgie smugglers" seemed too complimentary. Like you had something live and worthwhile in there.

Are you fishing for a... budgie pic? 🦤

MADDOX

This conversation has gone in a horrific direction. If you send me a pic of your... budgie... I will print it out and post it on the bulletin board at the hardware store. Which reminds me, I have work to do. Goodbye, Hayes.

Wait! One more thing...

MADDOX

What?

> Tomorrow when we're cutting down trees and being all ruggedly authentic… try to remember you're supposed to be the grumpy one. I have a reputation to maintain.

MADDOX

> Trust me. My grumpiness is very authentic. Especially at 9 AM.

> Perfect. See you tomorrow, mountain daddy.

MADDOX

> I'm blocking your number.

> No you're not 

MADDOX

> *sigh* No I'm not.

My cheeks continued to hurt the rest of the afternoon and evening. When I ran back to town to grab takeout for dinner at Timber, I ended up meeting several locals who all welcomed me and congratulated me on the success of the first posts.

While I enjoyed my time meeting new people, the way I usually did, I was low-key disappointed the place seemed to be missing one ornery photographer.

I checked my phone off and on all evening in hopes of seeing more of his snarky texts, but there weren't any. For the first time in a very long time, I hurried to bed early.

Morning couldn't come fast enough.

WHEN MY ALARM WENT OFF, I showered and dressed carefully, selecting pieces from Nordique's premium collection—brown wool trousers, the exquisite cream Maribel sweater that came up high on my neck, and the camel overcoat that had prompted an unexpectedly heated stare from Maddox the day he'd agreed to be my videographer.

A look that had lingered just long enough to make me think about it later. In the shower.

I added the scarf and my new boots and styled my hair with less product than usual, going for a more touchable look that would work with the casual vibe of a Christmas tree farm.

"Stay luxe," I reminded myself with a mental eye roll. Nordique's unnecessary instruction echoed in my mind as I assessed the final look in the mirror. The outfit walked the line perfectly—upscale enough for the brand positioning but practical enough for a winter outing.

The Pinecone was already bustling when I arrived at 8:55. I'd intentionally come early, partly to avoid another "you're late" lecture from Maddox, but mostly to prepare myself mentally for spending the day with him. I needed coffee and a game plan.

Sadie spotted me as soon as I walked in and waved me to "my" table—apparently, I now had a designated spot as well as a "usual" breakfast. Small towns were weird.

She returned moments later with a steaming mug of coffee, oat milk creamer, and, to my surprise, a plate covered in an omelette with a side of fruit. "Figured you'd want something a little lighter today. Your special someone likes his eggs over medium. Should I get that going?"

I nearly choked on my first sip of coffee. "My— Sadie, I'm afraid you've got the wrong idea. Maddox isn't my 'special someone.' We're colleagues. Working together."

Sadie's knowing smile didn't falter. "Sure, honey."

I didn't know how to respond to that but was saved by the bell —literally—as the door jingled and Maddox himself walked in.

His expression darkened considerably when he noticed how many people were watching him walk toward me.

"Morning," he said tersely, yanking off his coat.

"Welcome to the gauntlet," I murmured. "Maybe we should have met somewhere else."

"Everywhere would have been the same." Maddox dropped into the chair across from me. "This town's gossip network works faster than Instagram's algorithm."

As he settled in his seat, he eyed my outfit with a critical gaze that lingered just long enough to make my skin warm. "That's what you're wearing to cut down a Christmas tree?"

I glanced down at my carefully chosen ensemble. "What's wrong with it?"

"Nothing, if you're attending a board meeting in Aspen. Everything, if you're actually planning to drag a tree through the snow." His tone was mocking, but his eyes traveled up and down my sweater again before he picked up his coffee.

"It's Nordique's premium collection," I explained. "The whole point is luxury that functions in winter settings. 'Where luxury meets legacy,' remember?"

His eyes rolled so hard I was surprised they didn't get stuck. "Don't come crying to me when you get sap on your thousand-dollar pants."

"They're only four hundred," I corrected, then immediately regretted it when his eyebrows shot up.

"Only four hundred," he repeated flatly. "For pants. That you're wearing to a tree farm."

"I didn't pay for them, Maddox. But it's my job to make them look good in rugged settings," I defended. "That's literally why I'm here."

Something flashed in his eyes—maybe annoyance, maybe something else—before he looked away. "You might have considered warning your date this was a *luxury* tree-cutting adventure."

"My date can dress himself however he likes," I shot back, unable to resist a small smirk. "Unless you'd like me to dress you, Maddox?"

"Fucking Christ," he muttered under his breath. His voice dropped low on the curse, and it hit me in the solar plexus.

Was a grumpiness kink a thing?

As Sadie approached with a tray, Maddox's face lit up. "Morning, Sadie. I could kiss you right now for that."

Sadie set down his coffee and breakfast—eggs over medium, as predicted, with sourdough toast and a side of bacon. Then she glanced back and forth between us with a knowing look that made Maddox's ears turn pink. "Kiss *me*? I don't think so."

"Uh. I think we're good here for now," I said quickly before Maddox simply got up and stormed out.

She sighed happily. "You sure are. You two enjoy," she said with meaning so thick you could spread it on toast. "Take your time."

As she walked away, Maddox stabbed a piece of egg with unnecessary force. "Great. By dinner, half the town will think we're engaged."

"Would that be so terrible?" I asked lightly, trying to keep the conversation from derailing into his usual grumpiness. "Being engaged?"

His fork paused halfway to his mouth, eyes locking with mine in a way that made my breath catch. For a moment—just a moment—something vulnerable and yearning crossed his face.

Then it was gone, replaced by a teasing eye roll. "Engaged in general? Not terrible at all. Engaged to a man who wears budgie smugglers for a living? Terrible doesn't begin to cover it."

I laughed, putting a hand to my chest in mock offense. "You

wound me, Sullivan. And here I thought we had something special. My business manager thinks so, too, not to mention half the damned internet."

"Ah, and people on the internet are always right," he retorted, but the corner of his mouth twitched in what might have been the ghost of a smile.

"Where's Maya?" I asked, changing the subject. "I thought she was helping with the camera work."

"AP Calculus test," he replied, taking a bite of toast. "Just you, me, and the tripod today."

The implications of being alone together hung in the air between us. Yesterday, Maya had been our buffer, the third presence that kept things professional and distanced.

Sort of.

I tucked into my meal, not particularly worried that we'd have to manage the filming on our own, but something about it must have concerned Maddox because he seemed to feel like he needed to reassure me.

"Don't worry. I can handle it on my own as long as you're willing to get creative with me on the angles and shots. I'll walk you through it."

"Gee, thanks, oh Wise One. Show me the ways of shooting video without a cameraman," I said, unable to avoid sarcasm. "You do know I've been creating content on my own for five years, right?"

"Content," he said with a sniff of disdain. "Well, today we're creating footage with actual substance."

"Right. As opposed to my usual empty, soulless nonsense?" I leaned forward slightly in challenge.

Maddox met my gaze steadily. "Your words, not mine."

"You know, for someone who claims to value *authenticity*, you're awfully quick to judge work you haven't even seen."

"I've seen your social media," he countered. "Rooftop pools. Celebrity chef openings. Designer outfits in perfectly lit settings. It's well executed, yes. But it's also..."

"What?" I pressed when he hesitated.

His eyes darted away, then back to mine. "Safe. Controlled. Everything in its perfect place. No real moments." He shrugged and took another bite of food.

The assessment stung, partly because it echoed my own doubts in quiet, late-night moments.

But it was one thing for *me* to think it and another for him to judge. "And you're an expert on real moments?"

"I know them when I see them." His voice softened unexpectedly. "Like when you laughed yesterday. Not the perfect Instagram laugh—the real one, when you forgot you were being filmed."

As we finished up the remaining bites of breakfast, I suddenly felt exposed, as if he'd seen something I'd worked hard to keep hidden. The careful construction of Adrian Hayes, Luxury Lifestyle Influencer, had cracks—and somehow, in less than two days, Maddox Sullivan had found them.

"We should go," I said, signing the receipt Sadie had brought and reaching for my coat. "Don't want to be late for our tree date."

"Not a date," he corrected, standing while taking a final sip of coffee.

"Right," I agreed, trying to ignore the inexplicable disappointment that flared at his insistence. "Just work. Rule Three—you and me... not a thing. I get it."

As we headed for the door, I noticed several patrons watching us, whispering behind menus and coffee mugs. Maddox noticed, too, his shoulders tensing as he pushed through the exit.

Outside, the morning air was crisp and cold, biting at my cheeks and nose. Maddox's truck was parked nearby—an older-model Ford that somehow suited him perfectly: practical, sturdy, no-nonsense.

The inside of his truck was surprisingly clean, with worn but well-maintained leather seats. A small photo was tucked into the visor—Maddox, a younger Maya, and two smiling adults who had to be their parents. They looked happy, the kind of genuine happiness that hadn't been a part of my own family life.

"That's a great photo," I said softly as Maddox started the engine.

He glanced up, and his expression turned wistful for an instant when he realized what I was looking at. "Thanks," he said gruffly and left it at that.

We drove in silence for a while, the town giving way to snow-dusted fields and then dense pine forest. I watched out the window as the landscape transformed, more beautiful and wilder than any backdrop I'd used for content before.

"Oh, wow! It's snowing!" I said excitedly as delicate flakes began to drift down. I traveled to cold-weather destinations plenty, but snow was one of the few things I missed from my childhood in Connecticut.

"Just flurries," Maddox said, but his tone had lost some of its edge. "Supposed to pick up later."

I pressed my face closer to the window, watching the snowflakes dance in the morning light. "It's beautiful."

"You act like you've never seen snow before," he remarked, glancing at me curiously.

"Not much since I was a kid," I admitted. "LA snow is just sad rain that got ambitious."

A sound escaped him—something between a snort and a chuckle. When I looked over, his face had gone soft again, his eyes crinkling slightly at the corners.

"What?" I asked.

"Nothing." He shook his head, but the almost-smile lingered. "Just... sad rain that got ambitious. That's actually pretty funny."

"I have my moments," I replied, unreasonably pleased at having made him laugh. "I'm not just a pretty face in expensive pants."

His eyes flicked to me, then quickly back to the road. "Never said you were."

The acknowledgment hung in the air between us, neither of us quite brave enough to address it directly. Instead, we lapsed into silence as the truck wound its way up the mountain road, the snowfall gradually intensifying around us.

By the time we reached the Christmas tree farm, a light blanket of white covered the ground, transforming the landscape into something magical—like a scene from a holiday movie, but better because it was real.

And inexplicably, I found myself more excited about spending the day cutting down a Christmas tree with grumpy Maddox Sullivan than I had been about any carefully planned content shoot in recent memory.

Which was very, very good for the project.

And very, very bad for my professional detachment.

#ChemistryAsContent #NoFannin #YourUsual #Maddrian #TwoMenAndATripod

8

# #BIGWOOD
## MADDOX

"No, no, not that one either. The branches are too sparse on the left side," Adrian insisted as we rounded yet another row of trees.

I bit the inside of my cheek to keep from saying something I'd regret. We'd been trudging through Emerson's Christmas Tree Farm for nearly forty minutes, and Adrian had rejected at least a dozen perfectly good trees. The light snowfall that had seemed so picturesque when we'd arrived was now coming down harder, and the temperature was dropping faster than my patience.

"It's a real-life Christmas tree, not a photoshopped image," I pointed out, readjusting the camera bag on my shoulder. "They're supposed to have character."

Adrian turned to face me, snowflakes catching in his hair and on the shoulders of his camel coat.

He had no business looking that good while being so annoying.

"Character is fine. Baldness on one side is not." He gestured dramatically at the offending pine. "Would you hang ornaments on a tree that looks like it's been through fraternity hazing?"

I snorted despite myself and adjusted my woolen hat over my ears. "That's awful."

"So's that tree," he countered, already moving deeper into the row of pines.

I followed, my boots crunching through several inches of fresh powder. I hadn't worried this morning, when I saw the weather report mentioned a potential storm moving in this afternoon. But I also hadn't counted on Adrian being determined to find the mythical "perfect tree" regardless of the warnings.

"You know," I called after him, "most people just grab the first decent-looking tree they see, tie it to their car, and go home to drink eggnog."

"Most people aren't filming content for their sponsor," he replied without turning around. "Nordique clients don't buy 'decent-looking' trees. They buy perfect ones."

"And Nordique clients cut down their own trees in eight-hundred-dollar pants?" I asked, eyeing his impeccable outfit that somehow still looked runway-ready despite our trek through the tree farm.

Adrian glanced back with a smirk. "Let's be honest. Nordique clients don't cut down their own trees. But they still expect their hired help to find the perfect one."

"I take it I'm the hired help in this scenario?"

"I mean, technically, I hired you..." he teased with a wink that did something irritating to my stomach. "And you are helping. Actually, you're better than hired help. Not only do you seem to know how to cut down a tree, but you're also photogenic enough to look good while doing it in these videos. Win-win."

I rolled my eyes, hoping the cold air explained the heat rising in my cheeks. "Your flattery needs work, Hayes."

He shot me a teasing look. "I don't know, your blushing says otherwise."

"Don't flatter yourself. My red cheeks are from the cold," I lied.

My cheeks continued to burn as I tried to focus on the technical aspects of our shoot. The clearing we were approaching would actually provide decent lighting—what photographers call "God rays" were streaming through the pine branches as the snowflakes danced in the beams of light. Despite my aggravation, my brain automatically began composing the shots I wanted.

"We should set up the tripod here," I said, changing the subject. "The light's good, and there's enough space to get the full tree-cutting sequence without having to move the equipment."

Adrian nodded, looking around with a more professional eye. "The background is nice, too. No distractions, just trees and snow."

For a moment, we were in sync—two professionals evaluating the same scene. I'd learned over the past couple of days that beneath his carefully curated exterior, Adrian Hayes actually knew his shit when it came to visual composition. He might not have approached photography the same way I did, but his eye was undeniably good.

I began unlocking the tripod legs, my fingers already stiff from the cold.

"We should work quickly," I said, nodding toward the darkening sky to the northwest. "That doesn't look friendly."

Adrian followed my gaze, his expression momentarily concerned before the professional mask slipped back into place. "All the more reason to find the perfect tree immediately."

"We've seen at least three perfect trees already," I reminded him.

"Those were adequate trees," he corrected, stepping carefully through the snow in his designer boots. "I'll know the perfect one when I see it."

I finished setting up the tripod, my breath forming clouds in the increasingly frigid air. Adrian wandered a few yards away, examining pines with the critical eye of a diamond appraiser. Even from behind, his silhouette against the snowy backdrop was striking—the tailored coat emphasizing his broad shoulders tapering to a narrow waist, blond hair catching the weak streaks of sun in a way that warmed the scene.

I caught myself staring and quickly looked away. This was exactly the problem with our so-called "chemistry" that everyone in town was gossiping about. Adrian Hayes was objectively attractive, and I'd have to be dead not to notice. But noticing and acting were different things. And I had no intention of becoming another chapter in the Adrian Hayes Travelogue of Temporary Flings.

"Maddox!" His excited voice broke through my thoughts. "This is it. This is the one!"

I turned to see him standing beside an enormous blue spruce, at least eight feet tall and nearly as wide. It was, I had to admit, a spectacular specimen—full and symmetrical, with the perfect conical shape of a Christmas tree straight out of a storybook.

"Of course you'd pick the biggest tree in the lot," I called back, unable to keep the amusement from my voice. "Compensating for something, Hayes? Your poor little budgie, perhaps?"

His delighted grin only widened. "Trying to represent my enormous Christmas spirit," he replied, spreading his arms as if to embrace the massive tree. "What do you think? Is she a beauty or what?"

I approached, taking a few quick snapshots before assessing the tree with a critical eye. "It's too big for your rental cabin," I pointed out practically. "The ceilings are only eight feet. You'd have to cut the top off."

"How dare you suggest mutilation," he gasped, placing a protective hand on the tree's branches. "We'll make it work. Every perfect tree deserves the perfect home."

"And who's going to drag this monster back to the truck? It weighs at least a hundred pounds."

Adrian raised an eyebrow. "Isn't that what I have you for, mountain man? To do all the manly lifting while I stand here and look pretty?"

"You're hilarious," I said, even though I was already moving my tripod closer. The tree was a showstopper, and the footage would look amazing. "Just remember this conversation when you're covered in sap and pine needles."

"I'll consider it a rustic spa treatment," he quipped, brushing snow off a branch. "Pine-scented exfoliation. Very on-brand for Nordique. It'll be all the rage once I mention it. You'll see."

I couldn't stop the laugh that escaped me. For all his polished exterior, Adrian's humor had a way of catching me off guard—little glimpses of a real person beneath the influencer facade.

As I set up the camera angle, I watched him circle the tree, genuine excitement lighting up his face. There was something almost childlike in his enthusiasm that made it difficult to maintain my irritation. Maybe that was the real danger of Adrian Hayes —not just the perfect face or the sharp wit, but those flashes of authenticity that made me wonder which version was the real him.

"Alright, Hayes," I said, adjusting the focus. "You found your perfect tree. Now comes the fun part."

He turned to me with a brilliant smile. "Posing majestically beside it?"

"Cutting it down." I reached for the axe I'd brought, holding it up with a challenging grin. "Unless you'd prefer to use your credit card?"

His expression faltered slightly, eyes widening as he stared at the axe in my hand. "I, uh... hadn't exactly planned that part out."

"You mean you've never cut down a Christmas tree before?" I asked in mock surprise, already knowing the answer.

Adrian's perfect confidence slipped just a fraction. "Not personally, no."

"Well then," I said, unable to suppress a slightly wicked smile as I held out the axe. "You're about to have another authentic Legacy Christmas experience, influencer boy."

The mixture of alarm and determination that crossed his face was almost worth the entire frigid trek through the woods. Almost.

Adrian stared at the axe in my hand like I was offering him a live snake. "That's... *very* rustic. Possibly *too* rustic."

"That's the whole point of this shoot, isn't it?" I challenged. "Real alpine experiences in rugged but luxurious couture?"

He squared his shoulders, the momentary uncertainty quickly covered up with a cocky facade. "Of course. This won't be the first time I've tackled a new challenge for my followers. It also won't be the first time I've put myself in harm's way to impress a date."

I blinked at him. "Impress me?"

He tilted his head at my camera. "Not you specifically."

Of course. The fake date. The project concept. Not me. Him. *Us.*

"Right," I said quickly, clearing my throat and fiddling with my camera settings. "The more cringe you make it, the more video shares you'll get, so feel free to be your full awkward self. Hell, if you accidentally injure yourself with the blade, it would probably get shared even more."

Adrian stared at me in shock before barking out a laugh of disbelief. "You're the one who'd have to carry my bloody carcass out of here. Be careful what you wish for."

I hid a smile as I positioned the camera to capture a wide shot of the tree with Adrian beside it. Once the shot was set, I began recording and walked over to where he stood self-consciously holding the axe.

"First, you need to check which way the tree is likely to fall." I demonstrated how to assess the tree's natural lean. "You want it to come down away from you, obviously."

"Obviously," he echoed, eyeing the massive spruce with newfound respect.

"Then you need the right stance." I planted my feet shoulder-width apart. "Stable but flexible. You don't want to be caught off-balance when it starts to go."

Adrian mirrored my position, looking more like he was posing for a lumberjack calendar than preparing to chop down a tree. His new boots sank deeper into the snow as he shifted his weight.

"Now what?" he asked, gripping the axe a little too tightly.

I moved behind him without thinking, reaching around to adjust his hands on the handle. "Left hand here, right hand here. You want a firm grip but not a death grip."

The moment my chest pressed against Adrian's back, I realized my mistake. The faint scent of that cologne I'd caught a few days ago—something expensive and subtle—filled my senses. I was suddenly acutely aware of how perfectly my height matched his, how easily my arms fit around him.

"Like this?" Adrian asked, his voice oddly tight.

"Yeah," I managed, forcing myself to focus on the task. "Now, when you swing, it's all in the hips and shoulders. Let the weight of the axe do the work."

I guided him through a practice swing, my hands still covering his on the wooden handle. He was warm despite the cold and more solid than I expected. His body moved with mine through the arc of the swing... and his ass rubbed against my dick.

Even through forty-seven layers of outerwear, I felt it... and, god help me, I responded. A flicker of heat flared in my core, and all the blood in my body rushed south.

"I, uh... I think I've got it," Adrian said quickly, stepping away.

"Yeah." I took a deliberate step back, too, grateful for the cold air on my warm face. "No, yeah, absolutely. Just, ah, remember to aim for the same spot each time. You're creating a notch, not randomly hacking at it."

Adrian nodded, focused now on the tree rather than our uncomfortable proximity. He took a deep breath, raised the axe, and swung.

The blade connected with the trunk with a dull thud, barely sinking in before bouncing off.

"That was... pitiful," I said, unable to hold back a laugh.

His eyes narrowed. "Test swing."

Three more swings, three more underwhelming results. I bit my tongue but couldn't keep from saying, "Not sure you need this many test swings."

He bit out a curse and made a fourth attempt. This time, the blade finally bit into the bark with a satisfying thunk. Adrian's face lit up with triumph, making my breath catch a little in the thin air.

"There you go," I said. "Turns out, you just needed to be needled a little."

"Fuck off," he said with a laugh before hauling the axe back for another attempt.

I stepped behind the camera, adjusting the frame to capture his increasingly confident swings. Despite the ridiculous contrast of his luxury outfit against the rugged activity, he looked good. Natural, even. The determination on his face, the way his body had quickly adapted to the rhythm of the work—it made for compelling footage.

After about ten minutes of steady chopping, sweat glistened on his forehead despite the cold. He'd removed his camel coat and scarf, working in just the cream sweater that hugged his torso like a second skin. I tried not to notice how the physical exertion had brought a flush to his cheeks or how his hair had fallen across his forehead in a way that was frustratingly attractive.

"How much longer?" he asked, pausing to catch his breath. "This tree is tougher than it looks."

"Welcome to real work," I teased. "Not everything can be accomplished in a ninety-second clip."

He shot me a look. "I'll have you know I've done plenty of hard work in my life."

"Lifting a pitcher of margaritas on a yacht doesn't count."

Adrian's flushed cheeks darkened, which, of course, only made him more attractive. "Neither does being an ass, yet here you are, excelling at it."

I grinned, enjoying our back-and-forth more than I should. "Keep chopping, city boy. You're about halfway."

Adrian rolled his shoulders and resumed his attack on the tree with renewed vigor. I captured his efforts on camera, occasionally offering guidance on his technique. The snow continued to fall more heavily around us, the light taking on that peculiar quality that comes before a serious storm.

"I'm creating a notch on this side," Adrian said, gesturing to the wedge he'd cut. "Don't we need to chop from the other side, too?"

I raised an eyebrow, impressed. "You've been watching lumberjack videos on YouTube."

"I prepare for my shoots," he replied with dignity. "Even the ones with emergency-substitute grumpy photographers."

"You're right," I admitted, walking over to inspect his work. "Cut a bit higher on the opposite side, and the tree will fall in this direction." I pointed away from where we were standing.

He nodded and moved to the other side of the trunk. His technique had improved considerably, each swing now landing with purpose. I found myself watching his movements rather than focusing on the camera—the flex of muscle beneath that ridiculously expensive sweater, the determination in his expression, the competence he'd developed in just minutes.

The tree began to creak ominously after several more powerful blows. Adrian paused, looking to me for guidance.

"A few more should do it," I advised. "But be ready to move when it starts to go."

He nodded, bracing himself for the final cuts. The tree swayed slightly with each impact, the cracking sounds growing louder. Adrian's face was a study in concentration, completely focused on the task.

"It's going!" I called out as the massive spruce began to tilt.

But something was wrong. Instead of falling in the direction we'd planned, the tree was leaning toward Adrian. He was still too close, still focused on his chopping, not realizing the danger.

"Adrian, move!" I shouted, already lunging toward him.

His head snapped up, eyes widening as he saw the tree tipping. He froze for a split second too long, and I didn't hesitate—I dove forward, tackling him around the waist and sending us both tumbling into the deep snow several feet away.

The tree crashed down with a thunderous sound, branches brushing my back as we rolled clear of its path. When we finally stopped moving, I found myself on top of Adrian, my hands braced in the snow on either side of his head, our faces inches apart.

Time seemed to stop. Snowflakes fell around us in silent slow motion as we stared at each other, breathing hard. His eyes were wide, pupils dilated, lips parted slightly in surprise. My heart hammered against my ribs, and I couldn't tell if it was from the adrenaline of the near miss or from the sudden, overwhelming proximity of him beneath me.

"Thank you," he said, his voice a little shaky and his breath forming a small cloud between us. "That's not how Hallmark movies portray this shit. Homicide by Christmas tree."

"The tree wasn't going to kill you," I replied, my voice rougher than I intended. "Maybe just maim you a little."

He laughed, the sound vibrating through his chest and into mine where our bodies pressed together. "You can't let me have my dramatic moment, can you?"

I should have moved. Should have rolled off him, made a joke, maintained the professional distance I'd been so determined to keep. But I couldn't seem to make my body cooperate. His eyes held mine, something unspoken passing between us as the snow continued to fall, insulating us in our own private world.

Our bodies were pressed together, knees to chest—and every delicious thing in between—and I felt the warm, solid muscle of him against me.

Adrian's gaze dropped to my mouth for a fraction of a second, and my breath caught. The air between us felt charged, electric. Without conscious thought, I found myself leaning even closer, drawn by some invisible force I didn't want to name.

His hand came up to brush snow from my hair, his fingers lingering against my temple. "Maddox," he whispered, and my name on his lips sounded like a question I desperately wanted to answer.

Adrian's heartbeat raced beneath my palm, which had somehow found its way to his chest. The rational part of my brain was screaming warnings, reminding me of all the reasons this was a terrible idea, but it was being drowned out by the roaring in my ears and the heat spreading through my body despite the snow seeping into my clothes.

His head tilted up slightly, eliminating another inch of the space between us. I could feel his breath on my lips now, warm and inviting. My eyes began to close of their own accord.

A violent shiver ran through Adrian's body, breaking the spell. His teeth actually chattered as another shudder shook him.

"You're freezing," I said, clarity rushing back as I noticed the snow melting into his sweater, the pallor beneath his flushed cheeks.

"I've had men call me hot before, but never cold," he replied with a weak attempt at his usual charm, but his continued shivering betrayed him.

I rolled off him and stood quickly, offering my hand to pull him up. "Come on. We need to get you warmed up."

He took my hand, rising unsteadily to his feet. His designer clothes were soaked through from our tumble in the snow, his expensive sweater now clinging to him in a way that would have been distracting if I wasn't worried about hypothermia.

I shrugged out of my jacket and wrapped it around his shoulders. It was lined with shearling wool and would provide more warmth than the designer coat he'd left in a snowdrift.

"I can't take your coat," he protested weakly.

"I'm not offering options here. Besides, I'm used to the cold." I settled it over him despite his objections. "And you're soaking wet."

He pulled the coat tighter around himself, looking surprisingly vulnerable in my well-worn outerwear. "Thanks," he said quietly.

I returned to the camera equipment, quickly dismantling the tripod and packing everything away. The sky had darkened considerably, the snow falling faster now. We needed to get back to the truck before the weather worsened any further.

"So," Adrian said as I finished packing up. "All we need to do is drag a hundred-pound tree back to your truck through increasingly deep snow while a blizzard descends upon us?"

"That about sums it up," I agreed, shouldering the equipment bag. "Unless you want to leave your perfect tree behind?"

"Never," he declared with such conviction I had to smile. "But... I don't suppose you have a tree stand at your store?"

I raised an eyebrow. "Of course we do. It's a hardware store, for god's sake. We actually sell Emerson trees there, too."

"Good." He hesitated, looking uncharacteristically uncertain. "Because I just realized I have no way to set this up in my cabin, and I... kind of really want to. Will you help me?"

The request hung in the air between us, carrying more weight than its simple words suggested. Going to his cabin. Extending our time together. Continuing whatever had almost happened in the snow.

Every instinct told me to refuse. To maintain boundaries. To remember that in less than three weeks, Adrian Hayes would be gone, back to his perfectly curated life in LA, while I remained in Legacy with my responsibilities and reality.

But as I looked at him standing there in my coat, snow and sweat turning the edges of his hair dark, I found myself nodding. "Okay."

What the fuck was I thinking? There was a storm coming, and if I went to Adrian's cabin, I'd end up spending the night there. That was not acceptable. Everyone had seen that movie, for god's sake, and knew how it ended: with only one bed.

I quickly added, "But, uh... not today. We'll unload it at the cabin, and then I've got to head back into town and check on Maya. I'll bring a stand out tomorrow and help you get it inside before your next da—ah, *shoot*."

The smile that broke across his face was like sunrise after a long night—warm, bright, and devastatingly beautiful.

"Perfect," he said, raising a teasing eyebrow. "Just like this tree."

I groaned and forced myself to turn away and focus on figuring out how to drag the massive spruce through the deepening snow. "Let's get moving before we become the only people on Earth who've died from hypothermia at a Christmas tree farm."

As we began the laborious process of hauling the tree, I tried to convince myself that I was just being a good business owner—securing a customer's satisfaction, ensuring the shoot could be completed properly.

But the memory of Adrian beneath me in the snow, his eyes darkening as he looked at my lips, made it impossible to believe my own lies.

I was in dicey territory, and the storm brewing around us was nothing compared to the one taking shape inside me.

BY THE TIME I arrived home that evening, every muscle in my body ached. Hauling Adrian's ridiculously large tree through the snow, securing it to my truck, and then leaning it up against the porch of his rental cabin had been a workout even by my standards. But that wasn't what had me pacing the floor of our apartment above the hardware store, a forgotten mug of coffee cooling on the kitchen counter.

It was what had happened—or almost happened—in the snow.

I'd nearly kissed Adrian Hayes. And worse, I'd wanted to. Badly.

The realization hit me like a sledgehammer as I replayed the moment for the hundredth time. The weight of my body against his. The softness in his eyes. The way my name had sounded on his lips. If he hadn't shivered from the cold, would I have closed that final distance between us?

"Fuck," I muttered, running a hand through my hair as I crossed to the window.

Snow continued to fall outside, muting and softening Founder's Row. Even though the storm hadn't intensified as predicted, I'd still raced away from Adrian's cabin like my ass was on fire. He'd invited me in for a drink, but I'd made excuses about needing to check on the store before the storm worsened.

The truth was more complicated. I hadn't trusted myself to stay, not with the memory of our almost-kiss still pulsing between us. I'd felt something real out there among the trees—something that scared me more than I wanted to admit. Every accidental brush of our hands afterward had sent electricity through me, a current I wasn't prepared to handle.

I picked up my forgotten coffee and grimaced as I took a sip of the cold liquid. The chill reminded me of Adrian's violent shiver, how quickly I'd shed my own jacket for him. How natural it had felt to protect him.

My phone buzzed on the counter. I knew without looking that it was probably Adrian, asking about footage from today or perhaps ideas for tomorrow's shoot. I should check it. Should maintain professional communication.

Instead, I walked to my desk and woke up my computer. The footage from today's shoot was already uploaded, waiting to be edited. I hesitated before clicking Play, knowing exactly what I'd see.

Adrian's face filled the screen, his expression transforming from concentration to triumph as the axe bit into the tree. The camera had captured everything—his determination, his unexpected competence, the genuine joy when he'd succeeded. There was nothing rehearsed or artificial about these moments. They were raw, real. Beautiful.

I let the footage continue playing, watching our interactions from the objective eye of the camera. The ease of our banter. The way his expression softened when he thought I wasn't looking. The tension visible in both our body language as I positioned his hands on the axe.

Anyone watching would see it instantly. The chemistry everyone in town was gossiping about was right there in high definition, impossible to deny.

I paused on a frame where we were both in shot, Adrian looking at me with an expression I hadn't caught in the moment—something warm and curious and far too genuine for my comfort.

Maya's voice echoed in my head. *"When's the last time you sparked with someone like that?"*

The truth was, I couldn't remember ever feeling this kind of immediate connection with anyone. Not even with Michael, the guy I'd been dating when my parents died. The one who'd left because he "couldn't handle" the weight of my grief and the responsibilities I'd inherited. The relationship I'd convinced myself had been serious... until it had proven to be anything but.

My fingers hovered over the keyboard, unsure whether to continue editing or just close the program altogether. The footage was undeniably good—exactly the authentic moments Adrian had been hired to capture—but something about watching it made me restless.

I closed the video and leaned back in my chair, exhaling slowly. This thing with Adrian—whatever it was—scared me more than I wanted to admit. Because for some reason, it felt like Michael's departure had been a paper cut compared to what Adrian's inevitable exit would be.

Before the month was over, Adrian Hayes would return to Los

Angeles. Back to his influencer life of luxury hotels and designer clothes and carefully manufactured moments. Legacy, Montana, would become nothing more than a successful content series in his portfolio, a stepping stone to bigger sponsorships.

And I'd still be here. Running the store. Worrying about Maya's college tuition, the leak in the stockroom roof, and the suppliers demanding payment.

My phone buzzed again, more insistently this time. Reluctantly, I crossed the room to check it.

Two messages from Adrian.

ADRIAN

> Thanks again for today. Tree looks amazing. The footage even better.

> Hoping the storm doesn't mess with our shooting schedule tomorrow at the reservoir. Weather app says it might clear by mid-morning. Fingers crossed we'll still be a go for ice fishing with your friend Reid.

So professional. So proper. No mention of what had almost happened between us.

No reference to the moment when everything had shifted.

Maybe I'd imagined it. Maybe for him, it had just been an adrenaline response, a momentary connection without deeper meaning.

The thought should have been comforting. Instead, it left a hollow feeling in my chest.

I typed back a brief, equally professional response:

> Footage looks good. Let's touch base in the morning about weather. Rest up.

My thumb hovered over the Send button before I added:

> Tree really is perfect. Good choice.

It was the closest I could come to acknowledging what had happened between us. A small olive branch extending into the chasm of what remained unsaid.

His response came almost immediately:

> ADRIAN
>
> High praise from my grumpy mountain man. I'll take it.

His use of the word "my" hit me funny. It was both annoying and sweet. I hated that I liked it.

Another text came in a moment later.

> ADRIAN
>
> Going to study some ice fishing videos on YouTube. Have to impress my date tomorrow. ;)

The wink emoticon was so perfectly, irritatingly Adrian that I couldn't help but smile. Even through text, he managed to be both charming and infuriating.

I set the phone down without responding, knowing anything I said would only encourage him. Instead, I returned to my computer and pulled up the contract he'd sent over before our first shoot—the one outlining exactly how many videos we needed to complete, the payment schedule, the deliverables.

Business. This was business. A short-term project with a clear end date.

I needed to remember that, to hold on to that reality like a lifeline. Because the alternative—admitting that Adrian Hayes was getting under my skin, that I was attracted to him in a way that went beyond the physical, that I actually enjoyed his company when he wasn't being performative—that alternative led nowhere good.

Tomorrow, I would be professional. I would maintain appropriate boundaries. I would not think about how he'd looked lying in the snow beneath me, snowflakes catching on his eyelashes, lips parted in invitation.

I would not wonder what would have happened if he hadn't shivered.

I would not imagine how those lips might have felt against mine.

I closed my eyes, willing away the images that refused to fade. When that didn't work, I shut down my computer and headed for the shower, turning the water to cold in a desperate attempt to clear my head.

The project was partway done. Ten more days of filming. Then Adrian would leave, and everything would return to normal.

I just had to keep my head. And my heart. And remember that some trees, no matter how perfect they appeared, were never meant to be brought home.

#AlmostKiss  #IveSeenThisMovie  #UnplannedSnowAngels #PineExfoliation #TenMoreDates

**9**

# #ORNAMENTALCOMBAT

ADRIAN

Sleep had been impossible.

I'd spent half the night staring at the ceiling, replaying that moment in the snow—the weight of Maddox's body on mine, the way his gray eyes had darkened, how his breath had ghosted across my lips just before my damned shiver broke the spell.

The other half of the night I'd spent pacing, wondering if he was lying awake, too, cursing himself for almost kissing me.

By dawn, I'd given up on rest altogether. The massive spruce leaned against the porch of my rental cabin like a silent, sappy sentinel casting long shadows across the fresh snow, and I couldn't stop replaying the almost-kiss with Maddox or the way he'd practically fled afterward, making excuses about checking on the store.

Maybe he'd been right.

*Professional.* That's what we needed to be. Nothing more.

As I'd waited for my coffee to brew, I got a text notification from today's scheduled "date."

REID BULLOCK

> Sorry, man. Can't do the video thing at the reservoir today. Something came up.

I closed my eyes and groaned before sucking in a breath as another text came in. This time, it was from the grump.

MADDOX

> Storm now expected within a few hours.

I gritted my teeth, imagining being stuck in this small cabin all day by myself.

> Any chance I can run into town to grab the stand and some lights and decorations?

Wasn't sure how I'd get the tree in the stand and into the cabin alone, but apparently, I'd have plenty of time to try.

MADDOX

> I'm already on my way with everything.

I blinked and reread the message before responding.

> You're bringing the stuff here? Now?

MADDOX

> Told you I would.

The coffee maker gurgled as I watched dark clouds gathering strength on the horizon. My phone chimed with a weather alert. I was just beginning to wonder if Maddox should turn back home when his truck appeared in my driveway, tires crunching through fresh powder.

My heart did a stupid flip in my chest. I took a steadying breath and opened the door before he could knock.

"You didn't need to come," I said by way of greeting.

Maddox held up the tree stand and grunted, "Couldn't leave you hanging after I made you a promise." His eyes met mine for a split second before darting away, a muscle in his jaw twitching.

There was an awkward moment as he stepped past me into the cabin, his body angling carefully to avoid any accidental contact, like I might burn him if we touched. The air between us felt charged, like the static before lightning strikes.

"Coffee?" I offered, my voice sounding too loud in the sudden silence.

"Sure." His eyes swept over the interior of the cabin, lingering on the rumpled throw blanket on the couch where I'd spent my sleepless night before returning to me. "Where do you want this?"

"Uh, what do you think about here, in front of the window? It'll be nice to see the lights through the window as you drive up."

After a few minutes, we fell into a comfortable rhythm, discussing placement options. It was casual. Safe. No mention of the destruction of his vaunted Rule Three, yesterday's body-to-body tackle, or the heated moment in the snow that followed.

Wrangling the enormous tree inside was another story.

"On three," Maddox instructed, gripping his end of the trunk. "One, two—" The tree caught on the doorframe, sending a shower of needles cascading over us both. "Shit!"

I couldn't help laughing as pine needles decorated his hair like nature's own confetti. "Very festive," I teased, reaching out to brush some from his shoulder before catching myself. My hand froze midair, and we both pretended not to notice.

By the time we had it upright in the stand, we were both breathing hard, pine needles clinging to our clothes and hair.

"Hold it steady," Maddox instructed, dropping to his knees to tighten the bolts on the stand.

I gripped the trunk, acutely aware of him positioned beneath the tree, his capable hands working quickly. The domesticity of the moment—us decorating a tree together like a couple—made my chest tighten with a longing I hadn't expected.

A sliver of bare skin caught my attention above the waistband of his jeans and below the T-shirt that had ridden up his back. Muscles moved under his skin, drawing my eyes until I felt the sudden shift from domesticity to something altogether different.

"You can let go now," he said, looking up. A pine needle was caught in his stubble, right at the corner of his mouth.

Our eyes met, and for a heartbeat, I was back in the snow, feeling the weight of his body against mine. I released the tree abruptly, taking a step back.

"Perfect," I said, wincing at my breathless tone. "Thanks. I'm, ah, embarrassed to admit you may have been right. The tree is enormous. The cabin isn't quite as big as I thought."

Without thinking, I reached out and plucked the pine needle from his face. His breath caught, and I pulled my hand back like I'd been shocked.

Maddox stood, brushing more pine needles from his jeans. "I usually am, and you're not the first guy to think something was bigger than it is." He shot me a wink.

I gave a shocked bark of laughter. "I promise some things *are* as big as I claim."

He rolled his eyes and pointed to a box on the floor. "I found some stuff lying around our back room. You can use whatever you want for lights and decorations."

Inside the box were five small boxes of new string lights, two boxes of silver and gold ball ornaments in various sizes, and three giant rolls of various wire-edged ribbon. Everything was clearly new, not something that had simply been "lying around."

I glanced up at him in surprise. "Are you serious?"

He shrugged and glanced toward the window, where snow had

begun to fall more heavily. "I should head back before this gets worse."

As if in direct challenge to his words, our phones both blared with an emergency warning. I pulled out my phone to read the details.

*Winter storm warning in effect. Expect blizzard conditions, high winds, and dangerous travel. Shelter in place and monitor local updates.*

I grinned at him and bounced my eyebrows. "Mother Nature says you should stay and help me wrangle the lights on this bad boy."

"Mother Nature can't fucking make up her mind. It's the storm that cried wolf."

We moved to the window together. Outside, what had been gentle snowfall just minutes ago had intensified dramatically. I could no longer make out the driveway past Maddox's truck as snow whipped across the landscape.

"Shit," Maddox muttered. His shoulder brushed mine, and neither of us moved away this time.

Suddenly, I worried he'd ignore the conditions and the warning in an effort to leave.

"Please stay," I urged, no longer joking. "Even if you know what you're doing out there, other people might not."

He sighed and pulled out his phone. "I need to check in with Maya, make sure she stays put."

While he texted his sister, I refreshed the weather app, watching the storm's progress with a mixture of concern and—if I was being completely honest with myself—a flutter of something like excitement or nerves.

Being snowed in with Maddox Sullivan hadn't been on my Christmas list, but I couldn't pretend I was disappointed.

"She's at Rosie's," he reported, pocketing his phone. "Bonnie closed the store about twenty minutes ago after Rosie picked Maya up to take her to the ranch. They're taking the weather alert seriously, and everyone's canceling plans."

"Speaking of cancellations," I said, remembering the text I'd gotten right before he'd arrived. "My third date canceled this morning. That's three for three. At this point, I've decided your sister's paying people to back out."

He rubbed his face with his hands. "Wouldn't put it past her, but I'm surprised about Reid. He loves ice fishing, and I think he wanted to make his ex jealous by being seen with you." He shrugged. "Did he say why?"

I shook my head. "Just that something had come up."

I looked around at the beautiful tree, the snow coming down heavily outside, and the stack of firewood ready to light in the fireplace. The cabin felt cozy, intimate—like a scene from one of those holiday movies I pretended not to love.

"You know," I said carefully, "we could film this. The tree decorating. We could light the fire, put license-approved holiday music on the Bluetooth speakers, and record it as the third date."

"With me as your date?" Maddox shot me a familiar look, one that smacked of annoyance and disapproval. "People are already getting the wrong idea."

He looked at me like he worried *I* was "people."

"You're right. Never mind," I said easily, pretending his reminder didn't sting.

I walked over to the bedroom and rifled through one of my bags to find my tripod.

When I returned to the living room, Maddox glared at me. "I said no."

"I heard you. Make yourself comfortable, but stay out of my fucking frame."

I continued setting up the shot, moving lamps around, lighting the newspaper under the stacked logs in the fireplace, and setting the tree and decorations within the frame. Though Maddox stood to the side, the weight of his stare was like a physical thing.

I went into the bedroom to pick out the right clothes from the Nordique collection, and my hands shook slightly as I pulled off my shirt, hyperaware that he was somewhere behind me. I stripped out of my own jeans and reached for the Nordique ones.

"What are you doing?" Maddox demanded, his voice noticeably gruffer.

The heat of his gaze seared my back as I pulled up the new jeans, but I didn't turn around. "Working."

"No sexy Nordique boxers?"

I turned, zipping the jeans and adjusting my junk to fit. "You don't find plain black briefs sexy?"

Maddox's eyes were dark and cheeks ruddy over his beard scruff. He swallowed hard before answering. "It's not the briefs I find sexy," he muttered before looking away.

His response shocked me. "I must've heard you wrong," I said, incredulous. "For a minute there, it sounded like you complimented me, Sullivan."

He looked up at the ceiling as if praying for patience. "Your sex appeal has never been in doubt."

"No, it's just everything else about me, right? Because I'm an asshole for selling a product for money... even though you do the same thing at the hardware store." I grabbed a soft Nordique henley and pulled it on, suddenly self-conscious of my body.

"It's not the same," Maddox insisted, closer now, though I hadn't heard him step into the room. "People need what we sell. We don't manipulate them into buying shit they don't need."

"No? There's an ad on the back of the bathroom stall door at the cafe offering free cinnamon-scented light bulbs with every purchase. 'Come on down to Sullivan Hardware for your holiday essentials!'"

"I don't do the advertisements," he said, cheeks darkening. "That's all Bonnie."

"How nice for you that you have other people handling your marketing so you don't need to dirty your hands with manipulation."

I stalked back toward the tree. Maddox didn't step away, and my arm brushed his chest as I passed. His sharp intake of breath sent a thrill through me.

"You make it sound like I have a damned marketing department. I don't," he said, losing his temper now. "Hell, maybe if I did, I wouldn't be dead broke and on the verge of losing the fucking store."

His words settled around us like shrapnel from a grenade blast. "Fuck!" he snapped, forking his fingers through his hair. "Can you just... forget I said that?"

I frowned. "You're having trouble with the store? It's popular as hell and the only place like it for miles and miles. You know, I have experience in marketing. I could help you—"

Maddox glared. "I said forget it."

"Fine." I moved to my phone and connected my wireless lapel mic to the Bluetooth before attaching it to my shirt.

Talking to Maddox Sullivan was like talking to the giant spruce in the corner. God forbid someone give the stubborn man advice, let alone help.

The fire had gone out, so I decided to film myself relighting it in case it provided an entertaining comedic relief moment in my probably boring Christmas-tree-decorating clip.

I knelt by the fireplace, fumbling with matches and kindling, very aware of Maddox watching from his corner with his arms crossed over his chest.

The first match went out immediately. The second barely caught before dying.

"That's not going to work," Maddox muttered.

"Feel free to take over," I chirped. "Unlike some people, I can admit when I need an assist."

He sucked in a breath through his nose and held it for a second, then marched over and squatted next to me. The heat from his body was immediate, his shoulder pressing against mine as he reached for the kindling. "Can't believe you don't know how to start a fire."

"I start fires all the time," I shot back. "I just do it on social media when I share shirtless vacation pics."

Maddox muttered under his breath and reached for some small sticks from a nearby copper bin. "It wasn't set right to begin with. Pay attention because I'm only showing you this once."

I rolled my eyes.

Maddox's gaze met mine with his usual intensity. "The first lesson in mountain survival is learning how to make a fire."

"Simmer down, big guy. This place has a furnace," I said, sitting back on my heels. But I didn't move away, staying close enough that our knees touched.

"And if the furnace goes out?"

"I feel confident the heat from your judgment would keep us both warm for a very long time."

Maddox flexed his jaw to hide a smile. "Watch and learn, city boy. First, newspaper or fire starter. Then small sticks, arranged like this—"

"Ahh, the teepee method," I said, leaning closer to watch what he was doing. My shoulder pressed more firmly against his, and neither of us shifted away. "I recall something about this from a YouTube short on survival skills."

"Lord help us if people are learning survival skills from click-bait shorts," he muttered. His breath was warm against my cheek as he arranged the kindling.

"As opposed to learning it from lecturing assholes? I could make an argument that—"

He cut me off. "Larger pieces on top, leaving space for air flow. Fire needs oxygen to—what are you doing?"

I looked up from where I'd pretended to take notes on my hand with an invisible pen. "Making a title note for my Instagram story. 'Mansplaining Fire: A Tutorial.' It's bound to be a hit with the ladies."

"Fuck off," Maddox muttered, elbowing me away from him. I teetered before falling on my ass.

I couldn't help but laugh. "No, seriously. Tell me more, Fire Whisperer."

"Humanity would be better off if you froze to death." But his voice lacked any real heat, and his eyes crinkled at the corners.

"I bet you a billion dollars that a clip of you making this fire will have at least a hundred women fanning themselves in the comments. No, make that a thousand women. Men, too, come to think of it." Although the idea of my male followers wanting Maddox made me feel a little gut twist.

"I'll take your billion-dollar bet," he said, grinning. "The commenters will be too busy roasting you for not knowing shit about fire building."

I shrugged. "Unfortunately, I don't have a billion dollars. But I'll bet you another date."

Maddox rolled his eyes. "Fine. We'll post that clip right now, and if it gets a thousand comments about *me* instead of your ineptitude, I'll..."

"Ice-skate with me tomorrow?"

"Can't skate. How about a holiday-themed date of my choosing?" he suggested.

I studied Maddox's face to see if he was playing me. "Your choice will be something stupid like snow shoveling."

His laughter was unexpected. "I actually have date game, Hayes. Admittedly rusty, but it exists."

"Prove it," I teased, enjoying both the warmth of the growing fire and the heat of our banter.

"What if I promise it'll be romantic? The kind of holidate your fans will lose their minds over."

I couldn't resist teasing him some more. "Deep down, you already know you're gonna lose. You said *it'll* be, not it *would* be," I said smugly.

"I'm not gonna lose. I'm just saying if I did, I'd make it the most romantic date you've ever been on. How about that?"

My heart leapt like the jumping flames in the fireplace next to me. For a moment, I let myself imagine it—Maddox Sullivan planning something special just for me. "Deal," I croaked.

I glanced over at the ornaments, suddenly anxious to get to work filming the tree decorating—if only it would change the tension in the room—when an idea came to me.

"In the meantime, you can help me string up these lights, generously donated by Sullivan Hardware store." I grabbed the box and pulled out one of the light sets. "What kind of lights are these anyway?"

Maddox seemed oblivious as he automatically began explaining what was great about those particular lights. His whole demeanor changed when he talked about something he was passionate about, his hands moving animatedly, eyes bright with enthusiasm. As we moved around the tree, preparing it for light-stringing, Maddox expounded on his knowledge of the different kinds of Christmas lights and why his store only carried the ones they carried.

"They're shatterproof, energy-efficient, and the wiring's reinforced. I tested them before I ordered a single box," he explained.

"Probably could have picked up cheaper ones at the dollar store," I said offhandedly, deliberately provoking him.

He glared at me from the other side of the wide tree. "Sure, if you want your place to burn down and your family harmed. Jesus, Hayes. The cheap ones don't just burn out. They overheat. The last thing I want is someone's house catching fire over a strand of faulty lights."

I spent a few moments arranging the lights in the branches before passing the rest of the string around to him. Every time our fingers brushed, I felt a spark that was hard to ignore. "What if I don't like all these twinkling colors? The fancy trees in California designer homes all have trees with white lights."

"Screw your fancy California trees," he said from the far side of the tree. "People around here like color. They like twinkling. They like some life in their holiday decorations."

After a minute, he sighed. "But if you want plain white lights, you can just change the selector here like this," he said, showing me the little green box at the end of the strand. "Easy peasy."

I bit my lip to hide my smile. "These are pretty cool. They have selectors for all kinds of options. What if I need more strands?"

"We have plenty at the store. You can connect them together."

"Are they expensive?" I asked, already knowing the answer because I'd seen the display in the window.

"No. More than the dollar store, but they're on sale right now with a buy two, get one offer. And it's more expensive to replace dead strands every year than to buy a good quality one from the jump."

"I'm not driving to Sullivan Hardware in this weather. Do you do online ordering or anything? Home delivery?"

He grumbled again. "I'll bring them out to you next time I'm out this way. It's fine."

"Answer the question, Sullivan. Do you offer online ordering?"

"Yes, okay? Jesus. SullivanHardwareLegacy dot com. But if I see an order from you, I'm ignoring it."

We continued working together on the lights on the tree, then moved to the decorations. Occasionally, our hands would brush, or I'd catch him watching me with an expression I couldn't quite read. Throughout the entire process, we gave each other hell about our placement choices, our complete lack of good taste, and any other thing we could think of to exchange good-natured insults over.

"That ornament's too heavy for that branch," Maddox pointed out, reaching around me to relocate it. His chest pressed against my back for a moment, his breath warm on my neck.

"You're just jealous because my side of the tree looks better," I managed, trying to ignore how my skin tingled where he'd touched me.

"Your side looks like a department store display. No soul."

"Better than your side looking like a five-year-old decorated it."

His soft laugh rumbled through me. Our teasing gradually gave way to something more comfortable. Away from prying eyes and local gossip, Maddox seemed to relax slightly, his responses becoming less guarded, his rare smiles less grudging. "Christmas trees are supposed to look like five-year-olds decorated them."

"Not in my family. We had professionals decorate them."

"Oh." Maddox turned off the camera since the tree was done. "What was it like for you, then? Holidays growing up in the Hayes household."

The question caught me off guard.

We settled on opposite ends of the sofa, the fire crackling between us and the colorful, twinkling tree. The storm howled outside, making the cabin feel like our own private world. I'd found a bottle of whiskey in the kitchen cabinet, and we were each nursing a small glass in between bites of cheese and crackers from a welcome pack I'd found in the fridge.

"Picture-perfect," I replied honestly. Something about the firelight and whiskey, the intimacy of being trapped together, made my usual deflections feel hollow. "Actually, that's a lie."

Maddox raised an eyebrow but waited silently. His patience unnerved me more than questions would have.

"They were... curated," I admitted. "Everything matched the color scheme my mother chose that year. Professional tree decorators and gift wrappers. Family photos in coordinating outfits, everyone smiling like we meant it. No messes. Nothing unexpected or unsanctioned." I traced the rim of my glass. "I made a paper chain for the tree when I was seven. My mother threw it away because it didn't match."

"Oof."

I shrugged. "My mother felt strongly that my father's insurance firm had an image to maintain. I guess we were extensions of that image. Nothing genuine allowed to spoil the aesthetic."

"I guess it led naturally into being a style influencer?"

The question hit closer to home than I wanted to admit. "Maybe. Maybe I wanted to control the image for once, instead of being controlled by it." I took a sip of whiskey, feeling the burn down my throat. "What about your family? Before..."

I trailed off, not sure how to reference the loss of his parents. The photograph I'd seen on the internet when I'd looked up the local news story had been devastating.

Maddox's eyes reflected the firelight as he gazed into his glass. "The opposite of yours. Chaotic. Loud. My dad insisted on cutting our own tree every year and making sure Maya and I knew how to use the axe and haul it ourselves. Mom baked enough cookies to feed half the town. The Sullivan Hardware Christmas Open House was an annual event—kind of still is, though smaller now."

"That sounds…" I searched for the right word. "Nice," I said lamely. "Really nice."

"It was." His voice softened with memory. "After the accident, Maya and I tried to keep as many traditions going as we could. For her sake, mostly. She was fourteen when it happened."

The weight of his responsibilities suddenly seemed so clear—not just the business but becoming a parent to his sister at a young age, preserving their family legacy while his own grief was still fresh.

"That can't have been easy," I said quietly.

He shrugged, a gesture that carried more history and grief than words could express. "You do what you have to."

Without thinking, I shifted closer on the couch. Not touching, but close enough to feel his warmth. "Is that why you're so resistant to my world? The content creation and 'manufacturing moments,' as you call it."

His gaze lifted to meet mine. "Maybe. After losing my parents, the difference between what's real and what's just for show became very clear. Connections matter. Time with loved ones. Everything else is just…" He waved his hand dismissively.

"Fluff," I finished for him.

"Your word, not mine," he said, but a slight smile curved his lips.

"Not all manufactured moments are meaningless, you know." I leaned forward slightly until our knees were almost touching. "Sometimes they're just… opportunities. Creating the right conditions for real things to happen."

*Like this*, I thought but didn't say. *Us, here, now.*

The fire popped loudly, sending a shower of sparks up the chimney. Outside, the wind howled, a counterpoint to the silence stretching between us.

"Yesterday," Maddox said suddenly, his voice low. "At the tree farm..."

My heart stuttered in my chest. "When you saved me from certain death by Christmas tree?"

"A bump on the head, maybe," he said with an eye roll but then grew serious again. "After, though. When we were in the snow..."

I swallowed, setting my glass down carefully. "Yeah?"

"Would you have..." He paused, seeming to search for words, which was unusual for someone usually so direct. "If I hadn't..."

Despite his incomplete question, I knew exactly what he was getting at. Would I have kissed him if he hadn't pulled away? If the cold hadn't interrupted us?

"Fuck yes," I said, the truth easier in firelight than it would have been in daylight. "Would you have let me?"

Maddox's eyes darkened, the gray shifting to something deeper. He set his glass down and shifted slightly closer on the sofa. "I'm still trying to figure that out," he admitted.

"Anything I can do to help you with the figuring?" I murmured, hardly daring to breathe.

His gaze dropped to my mouth, then back to my eyes. "You could stop looking at me like that, for starters."

"Like what?"

"Like you're imagining what I taste like."

"What if I am, though?" I challenged softly. "Not looking at you this way would be the opposite of helpful, wouldn't it? Inauthentic, really."

He huffed. "Makes it damn hard to think straight."

I licked my lips thoughtfully. "Maybe. But consider whether more *thinking* is really what you need."

Maddox tilted his head. "You saying I'm overthinking?"

I moved a few inches closer. Close enough now that I could

feel more body heat, see the slight tremor in his hands. "Your word," I teased, throwing back his comment. "Not mine."

"Shut up, Hayes," he murmured, but there was no heat in it.

I sucked in a breath and held it. "*Make me.*"

Maddox hesitated, conflict visible in his expression, and his eyes searched mine.

Apparently, he found what he was looking for.

A heartbeat later, he closed the distance between us, one hand came up to curve around the back of my neck, and his lips found mine.

The first touch was hesitant, almost questioning. His lips were softer than I'd imagined, warm and slightly chapped. When I responded, leaning into him with a small sound of approval, the kiss deepened, becoming something hungry and certain. His mouth was warm from the whiskey, his hand firm against my skin.

His fingers tangled in my hair, pulling slightly as he angled my head for better access. I gripped his shoulders, feeling the solid muscle beneath his flannel shirt, anchoring myself as the world went sideways.

I'd kissed plenty of men in my lifetime, but something about this felt different—as if we'd been building to this moment since our first meeting in the hardware store. All the banter, the tension, the resistance—it had led here, to this confluence of fire and snow and touch.

When we finally broke apart, both breathless, Maddox's eyes were wide and glazed. But just when I worried he might go back to overthinking, he lunged at me, kissing me more deeply this time. His weight pressed me back into the sofa cushions, one hand caressing my jaw while the other gripped my hip. The kiss was desperate, almost angry, like he was trying to prove something to himself or me.

I held him tighter, daring him to pull away. My fingers found the hem of his shirt, slipping underneath to touch warm skin. Maddox groaned into my mouth, and the sound vibrated through me, making me arch even closer.

The storm raged, piling snow against the windows, sealing us in our private world of firelight and heat. And I didn't waste a second thinking about angles or lighting or hashtags. I was simply present, every sense attuned to the man clutching me like I was something surprising and necessary.

There was no doubt in my mind Maddox would second-guess this later and go right back to overthinking, but I'd be damned if I didn't take as much of him as I could before he threw cold water on a fire this hot.

#SullivanSurrender  #ProductPlacement  #CityBoyMakeFire #FuckingFinallyWithTheLips #AThousandFanningWomen

**10**

# #THESTORMINSIDE

MADDOX

THE STORM HOWLED OUTSIDE like a living thing while something equally fierce raged inside me. Adrian's lips were insistent against mine, his body warm and solid beneath my hands as I pressed him deeper into the sofa cushions.

*What the fuck is wrong with me? Why can't I keep my mouth off his?*

Even as I thought this, my hand came up to grip his jaw and hold him in place, changing the angle of our kiss. His stubble rasped against my palm, a delicious friction that sent heat spiraling down to my groin.

Adrian made a sound—half whimper of surprise, half groan of pleasure—that vibrated against my lips. His fingers were hot against the skin of my back, and I shuddered. The way he touched me was nothing like I'd expected. Not calculated or performative, but hungry. *Desperate.*

"You've been driving me fucking crazy," he murmured against my neck, dragging his teeth across my skin.

"That makes two of us," I admitted, sliding my hand into his hair to tug his head back. As soon as his throat was exposed, I latched onto it with a deep suck. His pulse raced beneath my lips, proof that his polished exterior was hiding something wilder.

When my teeth grazed the sensitive spot where his neck met his shoulder, he cursed and arched against me, grinding his hard cock against mine. The friction was maddening, even through our clothes. I wanted more. More heat, more skin, more Adrian.

"Too much goddamned flannel," he complained, already working at the buttons of my shirt with fumbling fingers.

I should have stopped him. Should have remembered all the reasons this was a terrible idea—Adrian was temporary, he would leave, this was just another experience for him to collect and discard. But my body refused to listen to logic as his hands made short work of my shirt buttons.

"I never understood the lumberjack fantasy before, but fuck," Adrian said, his voice rougher than usual as he pushed the fabric from my shoulders. "I get it now."

"Yeah?" I asked, enjoying the strength of his reaction. "Something about this doing it for you?"

His fingers traced the contours of my chest, skimming over my nipples in a way that made my breath catch. "Yes," he said simply, and something in his tone cut through the haze of desire.

The word hit me strangely. Gave me an unexpected sense of pride or something. I quickly shook off the thought, not wanting this to be anything but physical. Nothing complicated. Nothing with expectations. That shit would only lead to disappointment when he was gone.

So instead of responding, I grabbed the hem of his ridiculous designer henley and yanked it upward with a grunted "Off."

Adrian complied with surprising eagerness, lifting his arms so

I could pull the shirt over his head. The firelight threw golden shadows across the planes of his chest and abdomen, highlighting muscles that were more defined than anyone had a right to have during cookie season.

"Like what you see?" he asked, turning it back around on me. There was a note of genuine curiosity in his voice, as if he truly cared what I thought of him.

I answered by lowering my head to his collarbone, tasting salt and expensive shower products. He gasped, hands moving to my shoulders, fingers digging in as I trailed my mouth down his chest. I scraped my teeth over his nipple, and the wobbly sound he made sent a surge of heat straight to my groin.

"Maddox," he breathed, fingers moving to grip my hair in a silent demand.

The sofa was too small, too constraining for what I wanted to do to him. I broke away, standing abruptly. Before he could protest, I grabbed his hand and pulled him up with me.

"Where—?" he started, but I cut him off with another kiss, walking him backward toward the hall.

We stumbled to his bedroom, unwilling to break contact, bumping into walls and doorframes. My hands found the button of his jeans, popping it open with more coordination than I expected in my current state. Adrian moaned into my mouth when my fingers brushed against his hard shaft through his boxer-briefs.

"These feel good. Maybe they're Nordique after all," I teased against his lips. "You wearing fancy pants for me, city boy?"

"I've thought about this, you know," he said, surprising me. "About your hands on me."

"Just my hands?" I asked gruffly before backing him against the wall and dropping to my knees.

The sound of my knees hitting the wooden floor echoed in the room despite the storm raging outside. Adrian stared down at me, eyes wide, lips parted in shock. This wasn't in our script. This wasn't sarcastic disapproval, and it sure as hell wasn't any kind of attempt at professionalism. This was me, on my knees, choosing vulnerability in a way I rarely allowed myself.

"Maddox," he whispered again, reverence and uncertainty mingling in his voice.

For a second, he looked breakable. Not fragile, but human in a way his curated persona never allowed.

I held his gaze as I hooked my fingers in the waistband of his jeans, tugging them down along with the black boxer-briefs. His cock sprang free, already hard and leaking, the tip glistening in the dim light filtering from the living room.

"You sure, Sullivan?" The roughness of his voice was something straight out of a dirty movie, the kind of sultry hero shit I'd secretly fantasized about when I was younger. His moment of insecurity turned teasing. "'Cause if you're not…"

"Shut the fuck up," I said, my voice rougher than I intended. "Unless you want me to stop."

And it was true. I wanted to take him apart piece by piece, to make him forget about cameras and content and curated perfection. I wanted to be the reason Adrian Hayes lost control.

And I wanted to see it happen in real time.

I wrapped my hand around the base of his cock, feeling it twitch in my grasp. Adrian's breath hitched, his head falling back against the wall with a soft thud. I took a moment to just look at him—flushed and wanting, coming undone before I'd even gotten my mouth on his cock.

I leaned forward and took him into my mouth.

"Fuck," he groaned, fingers sliding into my hair again. Not pushing or pulling, just holding on like he needed an anchor.

I worked him slowly at first, learning what made his breath catch, what made his thighs tremble. When I hollowed my cheeks and took him deeper, Adrian cursed.

His fingers tightened in my hair, the slight pain sending a jolt of pleasure down my spine. I hummed around him, and his hips jerked forward involuntarily.

"Fuck," he gasped, trying to hold still. "Sorry—"

I pulled off just long enough to look up at him. "I can take it," I said, my voice a challenge.

His pupils dilated further, leaving just a thin ring of blue around black. "You sure?"

In answer, I wrapped my lips around him again, taking him deeper than before, and then deeper still. His control slipped, his hips moving in small, careful thrusts. I gripped his thighs, encouraging him, letting him know it was okay to let go.

"Maddox," he chanted, like my name was the only word he remembered. "Fuck, I'm close. You should—"

I ignored his warning, redoubling my efforts. I wanted to taste his release, wanted to know what Adrian Hayes looked like when he came undone.

The wind and snow battering the windows felt like a soundtrack to the loss of control I felt the more I touched and tasted this man. Each gust that rattled the glass felt like it was rattling my resolve to keep him at arm's length.

The storm outside I could handle. But this one, the one in which I wanted to spend hours, days, *years* giving this man pleasure, terrified me.

His hands tightened in my hair even more, a wordless warning. I glanced up, meeting his eyes as he finally let go. The intimacy of that moment—his gaze locked with mine as his release overtook him—was almost too much to bear.

Afterward, I sat back on my heels, wiping my mouth with the

back of my hand. Adrian slid down the wall until he was sitting on the floor across from me, breathing hard, looking thoroughly debauched. His hair was in utter disarray, his eyes glassy, his lips and skin swollen and red from my lips and stubble.

He'd never been more gorgeous.

"That was, uh…" he began, then seemed to lose the words.

"Yeah," I agreed, not sure what else to say. The heat of the moment was fading, leaving an uncomfortable awareness in its wake.

And stark-raving terror.

*What had I just done? What did it mean? Why the fuck hadn't I kept my distance?*

Adrian reached for me, his hand cupping my cheek. "Your turn," he said with a soft smile that looked nothing like his Instagram grins.

I flinched. The tenderness in his touch terrified me more than the passion had.

This wasn't supposed to be tender. This wasn't *real*.

"I should head out." I pulled away, and his hand flopped into his lap. "The storm's easing up, and I need to get to the store in case anyone needs anything. It'll take time for me to shovel my truck out."

Confusion and hurt flashed across his face before he masked it with a fake-as-fuck smile. "Sure," he said, pushing himself up from the floor. "Whatever you want."

But what I wanted was the problem.

I wanted *him*—not just physically, but in ways that would hurt when he inevitably left. In ways I couldn't afford to indulge.

So I retreated behind the walls I'd built, blocking off the part of me that wanted to pull him close and never let go. It was easier that way. Safer.

Even if it felt like tearing something essential inside me.

Even if the walls only stayed up for mere moments before he tumbled them down again.

#TooMuchFlannel #LumberjackFantasyUnlocked #KneelingButNotSurrendering #PantsDownWallsUp #Ragrets

**11**

# #MISTLETOEAMBUSH

ADRIAN

WAKING up the morning after Maddox's extreme hot and cold routine was like waking up hungover... except without the benefit of a good drunk the night before.

Just when I'd thought he was willing to pull down his walls a little for me, he'd bolted like a scared mouse. I'd been left feeling a strangled mix of hollow and selfish.

I'd gotten mine, and he'd fucked right off without letting me reciprocate. Even if this thing between us had only been physical —and god knew I'd hoped for more than that—he should have at least let me even the score.

Instead, Maddox had texted before dawn to say most of town was still digging out, the roads weren't safe for anyone who didn't have a 4x4, and that I should stay put. He'd also helpfully included the details of where and when he'd be filming my fourth date.

What he *didn't* include was a single word about the night before... or an apology for his abrupt departure.

It was as if the whole thing had never happened.

I tried to keep myself as busy as I could, despite being

snowed in. I checked the stats on the video I'd posted of my tree-trimming "date" last night and found I was winning my bet with Maddox—the comments section was littered with sweating emojis and endless variations of "With a man that hot, honey, who needs to know how to build a fire?"—but the victory felt hollow. I couldn't imagine collecting on it, after everything.

Thankfully, the woods behind the cabin were perfect for shooting clips with my thoughts on Legacy, the holidays, Nordique's signature style, and anything else I could think of to riff on.

I kept my thoughts on flip-flopping lumberjacks to myself.

But after exhausting myself editing and scheduling posts all evening, I finally revisited the whiskey bottle from the night before and eventually fell into a fitful sleep that left me even more hungover for my date the next day.

At least this time, I could say I'd been good and drunk first.

The Legacy Christmas Market sprawled across the town square like something from a storybook—wooden artisan stalls draped with evergreen garlands, twinkling lights strung overhead in a canopy of stars, and the scent of cinnamon, pine, and roasted chestnuts perfuming the crisp evening air. Fresh snow from the storm blanketed the ground, crunching beneath boots and reflecting the rainbow of colored lights.

It was impossibly picturesque. Exactly the kind of aesthetic I'd fly across the country to capture. But I wasn't seeing any of it through my camera lens.

I was too busy watching Maddox pretend I didn't exist.

"So date number four is with Jamie Berg," he said, adjusting his camera settings while carefully avoiding eye contact. "He runs a coffee shop just up the street. Very photogenic, great smile. Locals love him."

"Sounds perfect," I replied, matching his professional tone even as my stomach knotted. "Where's he meeting us?"

"By Juni Dovetail's ornament stall in about twenty minutes. I figured we should get some establishing shots of the market first."

The awkwardness between us was as thick as the snow drifts on the side of the highway, and it was really pissing me off.

Maddox Sullivan was the king of acting like nothing had happened. Like he hadn't had his mouth on mine, his hands in my hair, my cock in his mouth. Like he hadn't shredded my composure, shattered me with pleasure, and then immediately rebuilt the walls between us, brick by goddamn brick.

I'd known he'd second-guess everything, but I hadn't expected him to ice me out completely.

And I hadn't expected it to hurt this much.

"You realize this is stupid, right?" I finally said, unable to maintain the charade. "We can't just pretend—"

"We have a job to do," Maddox cut me off, his voice tight. "Let's be professional and do it."

"Professional. Right." I couldn't keep the bitterness from my voice. "Is that what you call what happened the other night? Professional?"

His jaw clenched, a muscle jumping beneath the stubble I now knew felt deliciously rough against my skin. "That was a mistake," he said quietly. "The storm, the whiskey... it shouldn't have happened."

The words stung more than the frigid air.

"Funny," I said, struggling to keep my voice light. "You didn't seem to think it was a mistake when you had my cock in your mouth."

His eyes flashed dangerously. "Keep your voice down," he hissed, glancing around at the oblivious marketgoers.

"Or what?" I challenged, stepping closer. "Afraid the town

gossips will know you actually have feelings under that grumpy flannel exterior? That you're a flesh-and-blood man who—"

"I have a sister to look after. A business to run. A life here that will continue long after you've moved on to your next luxury sponsorship." His voice was low, almost desperate. "This isn't a game for me."

The raw honesty in his words doused my anger like cold water. He wasn't being cruel. He was afraid.

"Who said anything about a game?" I asked, softer now.

Before he could answer, a voice called out from behind us.

"Maddox! Adrian! There you are!"

We turned to see Maya hurrying toward us, cheeks flushed with cold and excitement. She was bundled in a red coat and matching hat, looking like a walking Christmas card.

"Hey, squirt," Maddox greeted, his tone instantly warmer. "Thought you were helping Mrs. Hernandez with her booth?"

"I am, but I came to tell you that Jamie can't make it. His truck was making a funny noise, and he had to take it to a shop in Billings." She delivered this news with suspicious cheerfulness.

Maddox's expression darkened. "Are you serious? That's four cancellations in a row."

"Total coincidence," Maya said, not even attempting to sound convincing. "Anyway, have you heard everyone talking about your most recent videos? They're all going nuts, but one of them is killing it. People can't get enough of you two!"

I couldn't disagree with her. My social media channels had been flooded with comments about how "perfect" the two of us were together and how "refreshingly homey" the tree-decorating date had been. It was even getting attention from other media outlets and potential sponsors. Vic was beside himself with excitement and already working his contacts to try and pin down future projects like this one.

It was harder for me to ignore the DMs in which various men told me in graphic detail what they imagined Maddox and I had been getting up to behind closed doors. If Maddox had seen any of that, he would've run me out of town by now, so maybe it was a good thing he didn't spend time on social media.

Maya tugged Maddox's coat sleeve. "Emerson said tree sales at the farm are already up since the tree-cutting video, and Bonnie told me just this morning that yesterday's online sales at the hardware store were double our usual! We're sold out of Christmas tree lights! Can you believe it?"

Maddox's jaw flexed, but he didn't respond. I had to admit I was secretly satisfied with the result of my casual mention of Sullivan Hardware and happy that I'd been able to help the store with my reach. But it would have been nice to hear Maddox acknowledge it.

His eyes flicked to me and away. "Maybe we can get Zach Jordan to stand in. He's a teacher at the high school, though, so he might not be allowed to do social media stuff."

Maya frowned at him. "Mr. Jordan's a terrible choice. Besides, he's still upset after *you* shot him down last Christmas."

I studied Maddox's face, suddenly very interested in this Zach Jordan guy. And also interested in a little bit of petty revenge. "How can we find him? Is he around today?"

Maya looked around quickly and shook her head. "Even if he is, you can hardly kiss a schoolteacher in public. Imagine what all the parents would say."

I couldn't help but laugh. "I don't need to kiss him. I only need him to walk around the Christmas Market with me and let your brother capture it on video." Then I glanced at Maddox before adding, "And maybe hold hands with the guy a little."

Maddox's jaw worked again.

Maya laughed. "You're so funny, Adrian. I mean, the Christmas

Market is great and all, but everyone knows we're really here tonight for the Mistletoe Ceremony, and if you're going to participate, you need someone you can ki—oh, I know!" Her face lit up like she'd just had a brilliant idea. "Maddox can be your stand-in again!"

"Maya," Maddox said in a warning tone.

She grinned like she hadn't heard him, proving that Maddox wasn't the only Sullivan who could block out reality. "Great! I knew you'd agree. Sounds perfect!"

After watching her dart off into the crowd, I couldn't help but ask, "Mistletoe Ceremony?"

"Ignore her," he grumbled. "It's a Legacy tradition. They hang a giant ball of mistletoe in the center of the square. Whenever they illuminate it, whoever's caught underneath shares the season's first mistletoe kiss." He gave me a hard look. "We won't be getting anywhere near that mistletoe."

"Oh, I don't know," I said, unable to resist needling him. "It sounds like perfect content for the video series. We should definitely capture it."

Maddox ran a hand through his hair, a gesture I now recognized as his go-to move when stressed. "Not together, we won't. We're being set up. And I don't appreciate it. We need to find you another date—"

"Or," I interrupted, watching his expression carefully, "we could stick with what's working and continue to watch our social media reach expand. You can't deny what we're doing is resonating."

He finally met my eyes and lowered his voice. "What we're 'doing' was a mistake."

"I'm not talking about that," I replied. His words made my chest ache, even as the memory of his touch sent heat coursing through me, and the one-two punch of it was really fucking annoying. "I'm talking about *content*. About the project. We work well together on camera. Why do you keep fighting this when it obviously helped boost sales at the store?"

He studied me for a long moment, and I fought the urge to fidget under his gaze. Finally, he sighed. "Fine. I'll stand in again. But we're steering clear of the mistletoe."

An hour later, we'd covered most of the market. Maddox had found Maya and convinced her to film us sampling mulled wine, admiring hand-carved ornaments, and chatting with local artisans —all while I modeled Nordique's caramel-colored alpaca scarf and a dark blue and cream sweater that someone had said matched my eyes almost perfectly. The cold had given my cheeks a natural flush that no filter could replicate, and the camera loved the contrast of luxury clothing against the festive market back-drop. And best of all, I'd gotten to stand next to Maddox Sullivan the entire time.

Despite our earlier tension, we'd fallen into an easy rhythm. Maddox's direction was subtle but effective, his eye for composi-tion turning ordinary moments into something magical. I found myself genuinely enjoying the experience—the warm spiced wine, the friendly vendors, the way snowflakes caught the colored lights above...

The company of the world's grumbliest but hottest videogra-pher, who made me laugh over and over with his dry, witty commentary once he forgot he wasn't supposed to be enjoying himself.

"Just one more shot by the tree," Maddox told Maya, gesturing toward the center of the square, where a massive pine towered, adorned with hundreds of ornaments and lights. "Then I think we're done here."

I told myself I wasn't disappointed. This was going to be ratings gold, and that was the most important thing to me.

At least, it always had been.

Maya agreed, but as we approached the tree, she stopped short and tilted her head. "Hang on, you guys. I want to grab a shot of you with Slingshot Mountain in the background. The lighting's *gorgeous* right now. It'll be the perfect thumbnail."

Maddox and I exchanged a shrug and obediently stopped.

Maya frowned at whatever she saw on the camera screen and made a shooing motion with her hand. "Take, like, two steps back? I don't want to get the Ringolds and the Hoffmans in the shot. A little more," she instructed. "Good. Now, just a bit to the right—"

Maddox bit out a curse under his breath and shot a glare at Maya. "I see what you're doing. Make it quick."

It took me a minute to realize what he was upset about, but then I looked up. There was a giant ball of mistletoe hanging above us.

Suddenly, the ball illuminated, shooting white lights in every direction like a wintery disco ball from hell.

"Gah!" I ducked my head into Maddox's chest to block out the glare.

"Oh. Gosh. Would you look at that?" Maya deadpanned. "What are the chances you'd be *right there* when it lit up?"

"Fucking Christ," Maddox muttered, close enough that only I could hear. "She planned this."

*Obviously.* What surprised me more were the satisfied looks I spotted on several other people, in addition to his sister.

"Looks like she wasn't alone," I whispered back. "The entire town is conspiring to get us together." In fact, it seemed like they'd latched on to the idea of #Maddrian harder than I'd initially thought.

"It's not funny," Maddox said petulantly.

I reached for his hand to keep him from bolting. "Actually, it's hilarious."

The crowd around us had grown, and I recognized several faces—Sadie from the Pinecone, Alex from Timber, and at least a dozen other Legacy residents who'd been following our "dates" on social media. Several people already had their phones out, no doubt streaming the moment to anyone around the world who wanted to share in this awkward moment with us.

Maya stood near the front, camera ready to capture whatever was about to happen.

Mrs. Hoffman's voice rang out. "Ladies and gentlemen! Welcome to the annual Legacy Christmas Market mistletoe lighting! As tradition dictates, whoever stands beneath the mistletoe when it illuminates must share a kiss, to ensure good luck and happiness in the coming year."

There was a smattering of applause and excited murmurs from the crowd. I glanced at Maddox, whose expression had shifted from annoyed to something closer to resignation.

I hesitated, feeling my smile fade. I enjoyed being with Maddox, undeniably. I enjoyed provoking him, too, probably to an unhealthy degree.

But I didn't want to force anything on him. I didn't want to make him uncomfortable. And I sure as hell didn't want him to kiss me because the Legacy matchmakers expected him to.

He'd had enough choices taken from him.

I tugged on the hand I still held. "Come on. We can leave. I'll take the blame—"

Maddox didn't budge. He looked at me—really looked at me—for what felt like the first time since the storm. A corner of his mouth lifted in a reluctant smile. "And disappoint your rabid followers?" he asked softly.

"For the love of Christmas," someone called out. "Just kiss already!"

"Kiss! Kiss! Kiss!" someone else started chanting, and others quickly joined in.

Maddox's eyes met mine again, and a silent conversation passed between us.

I recognized the look on his face now—the reluctant surrender, the moment he decided to stop fighting whatever was happening between us, if only temporarily.

"For the followers, then?" I offered, giving him the out he seemed to need.

"For the followers," he agreed quietly.

He stepped closer, one hand coming up to rest lightly on my hip underneath my coat. His touch, even through the remaining layers of clothing, sent electricity racing through me. I tilted my head slightly, heart hammering as he leaned in.

The kiss was gentle, almost tentative—nothing like the desperate hunger of our previous kisses. Just the soft press of his lips against mine, warm in the winter cold. It could have lasted only seconds, a perfunctory peck to assuage the press of the crowd. But Maddox leaned in a little more, deepening the kiss before catching himself and pulling back with the slightest hitch of breath.

With that little sound, I felt something inside me shift irrevocably.

When he stepped back, the crowd was cheering wildly. Mrs. Hoffman looked particularly smug, and Maya was bouncing up and down with excitement.

I barely registered any of it. I was too focused on the look in Maddox's eyes—a mixture of wonder and terror that probably mirrored my own.

My tongue snuck out in search of any remaining taste of him on my lips, breath still clouding between us in the cold air.

"There," he said, his voice rougher than usual. "Tradition upheld. It'll make for good content, right?"

"Right," I managed. "Tradition. Content."

But as we moved away from the mistletoe, accepting congratulations and good-natured teasing from the townsfolk, I knew this was a lie.

That kiss hadn't been for content or tradition or the crowd. It had been real—perhaps the most real moment I'd experienced since arriving in Legacy...

And I wanted more.

Not just physical contact, though god knew I wanted that, too. I wanted conversations by the fire, banter over breakfast, shared looks that didn't need words. I wanted Maddox—grumpy, authentic Maddox—in a way that terrified me.

I hadn't come to Legacy looking for connection. I'd come for my sponsor, for my career. For twelve staged dates with twelve different men. For a perfect holiday series.

But as I watched Maddox chatting with an elderly couple who'd stopped him to comment on his photos in the gallery, I realized with startling clarity that I didn't want twelve men. I wanted *one*.

Imperfect, unfairly gorgeous, maddeningly frustrating, genuinely good Maddox Sullivan was the only man I wanted.

Now, I just needed to figure out how to make Maddox forget about my followers, my "content farm," and his stupid Rule Three... and want me back.

#MistletoeMadness    #MoreThanContent    #KissMeAgain #ForTheLoveOfChristmas

**12**

# #JEALOUSYONICE

MADDOX

"IF YOU DON'T STOP pacing, you're going to wear a trench in my barn floor," Nate Lewis called out, amusement clear in his voice. "The horses are getting nervous."

I stopped mid-stride, shoving my hands into my pockets and trying to appear casual. "Sorry. Just, uh, planning camera placement around your ranch."

"Right," Nate drawled, the smirk on his face making it clear he didn't believe me for a second. "Nothing to do with that public kiss, then?"

My stomach clenched. Of course he'd seen the video. The entire town—possibly the entire internet—had seen the moment Adrian and I had kissed beneath the mistletoe last night at the holiday market. Maya had been particularly unbearable this morning, shoving her phone in my face to show me comment after comment about "relationship goals" and "Mistletoe Maddrian Magic."

The whole town watching us like some damn Hallmark movie made my skin crawl. Not because I was ashamed of Adrian, but because I wasn't. Because standing there under the mistletoe felt more right than anything had in years, and... I had no clue how to handle it.

"What were we supposed to do?" I muttered, the lie bitter on my tongue. "It's a Legacy tradition. Wrong place, wrong time."

Nate raised a skeptical eyebrow as he adjusted the harness on his massive Clydesdale. "Seemed like the right place, right time to me."

I didn't answer, just watched his steady, calloused hands as he worked.

Nate was tall, broad-shouldered, and muscular beneath his flannel shirt and worn jeans. He had the kind of rugged good looks that came from working outdoors, and he was talented in bed, too. We'd hooked up a few times over the years when pickings around town were slim and the winters too long.

Nate wasn't the relationship type, so I had no real fear he and Adrian would hit it off in a true love kind of way, but I knew from personal experience there was a high chance they might hit it off in a quick fuck, body-fluid-exchange kind of way.

And the thought of Nate's hands on Adrian made me wonder idly where the fuck I could get my hands on an industrial-sized bottle of antacids.

"Anyway," I continued, clearing my throat. "Thanks for agreeing to this. The sleigh ride will make for good footage, and so far, everyone else we've tried to enlist in the project has bailed."

"Happy to help," Nate replied, patting the horse's flank. "The guy's hot as fuck. Besides, Ladybug here loves showing off for cameras. Don't you, girl?" The massive horse nickered in response, nudging Nate's shoulder affectionately.

The sound of tires on gravel announced Adrian's arrival. I steeled myself, taking a deep breath as I stepped toward the barn door, but no matter how many times I saw him, the first glimpse always hit me like a sucker punch.

He emerged from his rental car looking like he'd stepped out of a luxury winter catalog—which, technically, he had. The Nordique charcoal wool peacoat fit his shoulders perfectly, and beneath it, he wore a forest green sweater that made his eyes look impossibly blue. A cream cashmere scarf was artfully arranged around his neck, and his cheeks were pink from the cold.

He'd styled his hair differently today—a little messier, a little more touchable. I wondered if he was trying to look more "authentic" for the rural setting or if he'd simply woken up late.

Maya had dropped me off earlier and taken my truck, which meant I'd be riding back with Adrian. I needed to get this ridiculous lust reaction under control before the two of us were alone on the long drive back to town.

"Morning," Adrian called, his breath visible in the crisp air. "Sorry I'm late. Got lost twice trying to find this place." His gaze moved past me to Nate, and something flashed in his eyes before his professional smile clicked into place. "You must be Nate. Thanks for doing this. Everyone's said great things about you."

Nate stepped forward, extending a hand. "Nate Lewis. Sleigh ride expert and, apparently, video date for hire." He shook Adrian's hand, holding it perhaps a second longer than necessary. "Been following your recent posts. Pretty impressive stuff."

Adrian's camera smile warmed and morphed into his genuine one. "Thanks. Maddox deserves the credit. He's definitely leveled up my content."

Nate's eyes flicked between us, a knowing expression on his face. "Yeah, I can see that. Chemistry like yours doesn't come along too often. And Maddox is no slouch in the kissing department, is he?"

Adrian's eyes widened, and he shot me a questioning look I didn't totally understand.

He couldn't be surprised Nate knew about our mistletoe kiss since the whole world had seen it by now. So was he surprised Nate and I had hooked up? Was he as irrationally pissed off at the idea as I'd been, imagining him with Nate?

I shouldn't have been so excited about this possibility.

I quickly looked away and cleared my throat. "We should get started. Daylight's best right now, and the forecast mentioned a chance of snow again later."

"Sure thing," Nate agreed easily. "Let me introduce you to the girls, Adrian." He led us toward where two magnificent Clydesdales stood waiting, already harnessed to a beautifully restored wooden sleigh. "This is Ladybug and June."

"They're gorgeous," Adrian said, approaching slowly with his hand extended. I could tell he was trying his best to be polite, but it was taking an effort. Was he scared of horses? If so, why hadn't he said something?

Nate nodded approvingly at his caution. "They're gentle giants, but it's always smart to respect their space. Here, like this—" He demonstrated the proper way to approach, and Adrian followed his lead, soon stroking Ladybug's nose while the horse leaned into his touch.

"She likes you." Nate's expression warmed as he watched Adrian interact with his "girl."

"Beginner's luck," Adrian replied with a smile that seemed forced. "I didn't grow up around animals, but I've always been intrigued by horses."

"You've got a natural touch," Nate approved, adjusting June's harness. "Most city folks are either too hesitant or too grabby. You've got the balance just right."

Something twisted in my gut as I watched them chat, Nate

offering interesting facts while Adrian began to relax and ask genuinely curious questions. They looked good together—both attractive men with easy charm and natural confidence. The sleigh ride date we'd planned suddenly seemed too romantic, too intimate for comfort.

And I realized I should have been filming all this friendly getting-to-know-you... but I couldn't force myself to turn the camera on.

Would the internet be calling for #TeamNatrian tomorrow? Would Nate be "filling in" for Adrian's next canceled date? Would the Legacy matchmakers turn their attention on someone else?

That would be a good thing, of course. Exactly what I'd wanted from the start. So why did my hands suddenly feel like lead weights?

"The sleigh is beautiful," Adrian commented, running his hand over the polished wood. "Is there a story behind it?"

"My grandfather built it," Nate explained with obvious pride. "I restored it myself a few years back. Each winter, we offer rides through the countryside. Best way to see Legacy in the snow."

"Well, I'm excited to give it a try," Adrian said. He shot me a quick glance like he'd forgotten I was there. "Maddox, you ready? Got the camera?"

"Yeah," I said gruffly, focusing on adjusting settings that didn't need adjusting. "Good to go whenever you two are."

"Perfect." Nate climbed up to take his position and held out a hand to Adrian. "Hop on up. There's fur blankets under the seat if you get cold."

I watched as Adrian settled beside Nate, something unexpected tightening my chest. They made an attractive pair framed against the winter landscape—Adrian with his model-perfect features and Nate with his rugged good looks.

"Coming, Sullivan?" Nate called, a knowing twinkle in his eye. "Or you planning to run alongside with that camera?"

"Give me a minute for a few establishing shots," I muttered before reluctantly climbing up to join them.

The sleigh was spacious enough for three, but I still found myself pressed against Adrian's side, his thigh warm against mine despite the layers between us.

The memory of that warmth—of his body against mine as we cut down a tree, of his skin under my hands while the storm raged outside, of his lips beneath the mistletoe last night—flashed through my mind with uncomfortable clarity.

I wondered if Adrian knew just how much the kiss last night had affected me. I'd almost lost my damned mind, dragged him into my arms, and indulged in something that would have humiliated me in front of the entire town—hell, the entire world—when he walked away.

Adrian Hayes was a threat to my equilibrium, my reputation... my fucking heart.

"All set?" Nate asked, gathering the reins.

"Yep," Adrian replied, pulling out his phone to capture a quick behind-the-scenes clip for his Instagram story.

"Yeah," I echoed grimly, hanging on to my self-control by the thinnest thread.

Nate clicked his tongue, and the horses moved forward, the sleigh gliding smoothly across the snow. The jingling of bells filled the air as we left the barn behind and headed toward the woodland trail, the winter landscape stretching out around us like a dream.

"Everyone always asks about the bells," Nate commented as we picked up speed. "They weren't originally for decoration. They served a practical purpose, warning other sleighs of your approach around blind corners."

"Really?" Adrian leaned forward, genuinely interested. "I never knew that."

"Lots of holiday traditions have practical origins," Nate continued. "Even mistletoe—" He shot me a wink. "Did you know it was considered a symbol of peace? Enemies would meet beneath it to declare a truce."

Adrian stretched his head from side to side as if trying to release tension. "Interesting timing for that particular history lesson."

Nate chuckled, acknowledging the point, and changed the subject. "This route has some of the best views in the county. We'll hit the river overlook in about ten minutes—perfect spot for those scenic shots you're after."

As Nate guided the horses along the trail, he kept up a steady stream of local history and stories about the land we were passing. Adrian seemed genuinely engaged, asking questions and laughing at Nate's jokes.

I focused on getting footage, trying to ignore the way their rapport made my teeth grind together.

"You know," Nate said casually after describing a particularly beautiful spot ahead, "I usually take couples on this route. It's considered the most romantic of our trails."

"Is that so?" Adrian replied politely.

"Absolutely. Something about the snow, the scenery, the closeness." Nate gestured around us. "Had three marriage proposals on this trail last winter alone."

I focused on adjusting my camera angle to avoid catching Adrian's reaction.

"No pressure, of course," Nate added with a chuckle.

"Well, Nate, I've enjoyed this date a lot so far, but considering we just met... Not sure a proposal's in the cards for us today."

Adrian's attempt at humor made Nate chuckle and my stomach twist uneasily.

"I figured," Nate said with a wink. "I was more wondering whether you and grumpy-ass over there wanted to pick up where you left off last night."

"Give it a rest," I bit out, turning the camera off. "You're starting to sound like my sister."

"Smart girl, Maya." Nate shrugged. "Have to say, after that kiss, I was pulling for #TeamMaddrian myself."

Heat crawled up my neck. I opened my mouth to tell Nate to back off again, but this time, Adrian beat me to it.

He let out a laugh that tinkled like the bells on the sleigh— high, clear, and just a bit brittle. "The kiss was staged, thanks in part to Maya and the other folks in Legacy. Maddox and I only went along with it because it made for good content. Which is the point of all of this, remember?" He smiled hard and didn't meet my eyes.

My skin flashed from hot to cold and then settled on clammy and unsettled.

Good content.

Right.

*Content.*

"I see." Nate nodded, guiding the horses around a bend in the trail. "It was Maya's fault that you two happened to be standing right there all cuddled up when the lights came on."

"We weren't cuddling! I was blinded—" Adrian protested.

"Knock it off, Nate," I muttered. "You heard the man."

Nate laughed. "Hey, I'm not the one you need to convince. It's a small town. Everyone's seen how you are with each other. Haven't you noticed that every potential date for Adrian mysteriously cancels at the last minute?"

Adrian's cheeks flushed, which was an unexpected reaction. "Maddox thinks it's a conspiracy."

Nate snorted. "There's actually a betting pool at Timber about when the two of you will—"

"Look at that view," I interrupted desperately. "Perfect shot of Slingshot Mountain coming up. We should stop here."

To my relief, Nate shut up and slowed the horses. "This is one of my favorite spots. This time of day, the sun hits it just right sometimes."

The sleigh came to a stop at a stunning overlook. Fresh snow blanketed the landscape, sparkling in the winter sunlight. The river winding below was partially frozen, creating a striking pattern of ice and dark water. Pine trees, heavily laden with snow, framed the mountains in the distance.

"It's breathtaking," Adrian said quietly.

"Take your time getting whatever shots you need," Nate suggested. "The horses could use a rest anyway."

I climbed down first, camera already in hand, surveying the scene for the best angles. Adrian followed, pulling out his phone to take a quick personal shot before we started the actual filming.

"Let's get some footage of you by that stand of pines," I directed, slipping into professional mode. "The light's hitting them perfectly right now."

Adrian nodded, moving toward the spot I'd indicated. I followed, stepping carefully through the snow, focusing on framing the shot rather than on the man in my viewfinder.

That was my mistake. Too focused on the camera settings, I didn't notice the patch of ice beneath the fresh snow until my boot knocked the tripod leg and began to slip. In an effort to protect the camera, my feet went out from under me, and I stumbled directly into Adrian's path as he lurched forward to keep me from falling.

"Maddox!" he cried as I crashed into his chest. My hands

cradled the camera as my nose buried itself in the soft scarf at the base of his throat.

For a moment, we stood frozen, my body pressed against his, his arms wrapped around my waist. His heart hammered through the thin skin of my cheek, matching the rapid beat of my own.

"You okay?" he asked, his voice rough and low.

I couldn't speak, couldn't move. His face was inches from mine, his breath warm against my cold skin. His eyes, wide with surprise, darkened as they fixed on mine. Something electric passed between us, a current that had nothing to do with the winter static in the air.

"Watch your step," Nate called from the sleigh, amusement clear in his voice. "Snow and ice are slippery."

His words broke the spell. I stepped back abruptly, nearly losing my balance again before steadying myself with the tripod legs.

"Sorry," I muttered, unable to meet Adrian's eyes. "Wasn't paying attention."

"'S'okay," Adrian replied, his voice still strangely tight. "Happens."

I busied myself checking that my camera hadn't been damaged, though I knew perfectly well it was fine. My heart was still racing, skin tingling where his hands had gripped me.

"We should, uh, get that shot before the light changes," I said, gesturing vaguely toward the pines.

"Right," Adrian agreed, moving back into position.

Something about the shot wasn't right. It took me a minute to figure it out.

*Fuck.*

"Nate!" I called. "You ready to shoot?"

Adrian's eyes widened as he realized neither one of us had

considered including Nate in the shot. It was supposed to be a date between the two of them after all.

The rancher came sauntering over. "Sure you need me? Seems like the two of you might create better content without a dusty ole rancher—"

"Shut the fuck up," I snapped. "Get in the shot, and let's get this knocked out."

We completed the shoot with a new tension between Adrian and me, both hyperaware of each other's movements. Nate seemed to enjoy every minute of it, occasionally offering suggestions for shots or angles, his knowing expression making it clear he saw right through our professional facade.

Since the two of them were supposed to be acting like they were on a date, I took several clips of them standing close together, gazing at the view, and even one with Adrian's arm threaded through Nate's. Every time Nate stood close to Adrian, I wanted to throw the sexy rancher clear off the nearest cliff.

"That's enough," I barked when Nate tugged Adrian closer with the tails of the Nordique scarf, pretending the same playful, flirty tone I'd suggested when framing the shot.

Adrian's cheeks darkened while Nate's head fell back in laughter.

"Alright, alright. The fun police are here, and they are not amused," Nate teased, shooting Adrian a wink. "I forgot to warn you never to poke a bear out here."

When we finally climbed back into the sleigh for the return journey, Adrian sat stiffly beside me, careful not to let our legs touch. I focused intently on reviewing the footage we'd captured, avoiding both his gaze and Nate's amused glances.

Nate, bless and damn him, filled the silence with more local history and stories about his horses, occasionally letting a huff of amusement slip out.

As we approached a particularly scenic stretch of the trail, Nate turned slightly. "Adrian, there's a barn dance at my place next weekend. Nothing fancy, just locals letting loose with some music and food. You should come."

I leaned forward and narrowed my eyes at Nate.

Before I could ask *Since when are you hosting a fucking barn dance?* Adrian replied. "Thanks. That sounds fun."

"Great," Nate said easily. "Looking forward to it. I'm not a bad dancer if the music's just right."

I kept my expression carefully neutral, though my grip on the camera tightened.

I had no idea what Nate was playing at. He'd been flirty with Adrian, but then he'd backed off long enough to tease us with the stupid #TeamMaddrian thing. Had he believed Adrian's explanation about the kiss being staged for content?

It shouldn't matter if Adrian attended a barn dance with Nate.

It shouldn't matter if they hit it off, if something developed between them.

After all, Adrian would be gone in less than two weeks, back to his perfect life in LA, while Nate would remain here—solid, dependable, part of the community. And apparently flirty as fuck.

So why did the thought of Adrian dancing with Nate, doing... other things with Nate, make me want to shove both of them off the sleigh bench?

No reason. No reason at all.

I dug into my pocket and pulled out two pieces of gum before shoving them into my mouth and concentrating on the sharp burst of flavor. *Get your head out of your ass and work, dumbass.*

When we arrived back at Nate's farm, the sky had darkened with approaching snow clouds. Nate busied himself with unhitching the horses while Adrian helped, listening attentively to instructions and seeming genuinely interested in the animals.

I hung back, packing up equipment in Adrian's rental and trying to maintain at least the illusion of professionalism.

"I wasn't kidding when I said you've got a natural touch," I heard Nate tell Adrian as they led June back to her stall. "Ever considered moving somewhere you could have horses of your own?"

Adrian's laugh floated back to me. "My condo association would have something to say about that. Besides, I'm not exactly the rural type."

Nate made a thoughtful noise. "You seem to be adapting pretty well to Legacy."

I forced myself to focus on the equipment, not on their conversation or the implications behind Nate's words.

Adrian wasn't *adapting* to Legacy; he was using it as a backdrop for his content, just like every other influencer who'd blown through here. Once he got what he needed, he'd be gone.

I was so absorbed in my thoughts that I didn't notice Nate approaching until he spoke directly beside me.

"Take that man to bed, Sullivan," he said casually. "And if the sex turns out to be as hot as it ought to be, then consider taking him into your heart, too. Since that's a thing some people seem to want."

My head snapped up. "What the fuck?"

Nate met my gaze steadily, his earlier teasing glint nowhere to be found. "You're not a dumbass, so stop acting like one." He glanced over to where Adrian was giving June a final pat. "I saw the way you look at him through the lens. Stop fighting what's obvious to everyone but you, Sullivan. Life's too short."

Before I could respond, he walked away, heading back to Adrian. I watched as he said something that made Adrian laugh, then suddenly freeze. After a moment, they shook hands, and

Adrian walked toward the passenger side of his rental, where I was already waiting.

"You mind driving?" he asked. "I'm not confident on snowy roads."

I grunted my agreement and began the drive back to town in awkward silence. Adrian stared out the passenger window at the darkening sky, occasionally checking his phone. I kept my eyes fixed on the road, hands clamped on the wheel.

"Thanks for driving," he said at length. "I had a near miss on a slick spot yesterday when I was heading to town. Glad not to be the one at the wheel, honestly."

The steering wheel creaked as my hands tightened further, imagining him in danger. Cold sweat prickled on my skin as memories of my parents' accident flashed through my mind like an old VCR tape worn thin in spots from being played too many times. "Anytime." I glanced at him. "I mean it. Anytime."

He nodded and swallowed. Silence descended again for several awkward minutes.

"So," Adrian said, breaking the silence. "Nate seems nice."

"Yeah," I agreed neutrally. *Don't fucking dance with him.* "Known him since high school. Good guy."

"He, uh, said something interesting to me before we left."

I tensed, keeping my expression carefully blank. "Ignore him. He's full of shit."

Adrian turned slightly in his seat to face me. "He told me Maya begged him to cancel on us."

That wasn't at all where I thought this conversation was going. "The fuck?" I reached for my phone, but Adrian caught my hand and held it.

"Stop. What are you going to say to her? She's a kid, Maddox."

I clenched my jaw. "A kid who shouldn't be playing with things she doesn't understand."

His thumb brushed across the top of my hand painfully lightly before he let go and shoved his hands into the pockets of his coat. "She doesn't want you to be alone. She cares about you."

My face heated with embarrassment. "I'm fine. Why does everyone think being alone is a bad thing?"

Adrian looked out the window on his side as we passed snowy fields and the ever-darkening sky. After a while, he murmured, "It gets old, don't you think?"

I glanced at him in surprise. "And you would know? I've seen your social media. You're never alone."

His lips tipped up in a hollow smile, but he kept his gaze trained out the window. "Social media tells a story, Maddox. Paints a pretty picture. A fantasy. Isn't that what you keep trying to tell me?"

I stared at him so hard he must've felt the heat of it because he turned toward me, his smile so obviously fake it made my stomach twist. "Nate must be a hell of a fuck, huh?" His smile faded. "He didn't just tell me about Maya's call when he pulled me aside. He mentioned you two had history."

Instead of continuing the drive to my place in town, I turned down the long, winding road leading to Adrian's rental cabin.

"What are you doing?" he asked, looking around at the vast expanse of snow. "How are you going to get home? I'm not *that* afraid of driving—"

"I'm coming home with you," I said. I kept my hands around the steering wheel to keep from reaching for his hand.

Adrian sighed. "I'm sorry. It's none of my business who you fucked. You don't owe me any explanations. Obviously."

"I know that."

"And I'm sorry he's gotten the wrong idea about us, if that messes things up for you. I did try to explain that it was all for content."

*Was that why he'd said those things?*

My hands were clenched so tightly around the wheel my fingers throbbed. "I heard you."

"Then why are you coming to my place? And did you happen to notice I didn't invite you?"

I struggled with what to say or whether to speak at all.

Part of me wanted to say that I cared about his feelings. About why he seemed to be hiding so much.

But I also didn't want to say anything. Wanted to lose myself in his body again and take what I needed from him as long as he was willing to give it.

Instead of either of those things, I gave him a sliver of my trust.

"My parents died," I said stupidly, telling him something he already knew. I swallowed the nerves climbing up my throat and continued. "Car accident on the mountain pass. They were, uh... coming back from a suppliers' convention in Billings. Black ice." I shook my head. "It was awful. I..."

Adrian's hand landed warm and solid on my leg and squeezed gently. "Fuck, Maddox. I'm so sorry."

I shook my head. "It's not... I don't..." I shook my head again. "I'm not still grieving them like that. Not like I was at first. I mean, I have good days and bad, but it's not about their death anymore. It's more... I worry about letting them down. With the store and with Maya. But also..."

I pulled in front of his rental and threw the vehicle into Park before rubbing my hands over my face and turning to meet his eyes. "Sometimes I feel like I'm doing what I 'should' do," I said, using air quotes, "and then my mom's voice is in my head telling me none of that stuff matters and to do what makes me happy."

Adrian reached over and ran his hand over my head and down into the hair at the base of my skull. "And then you loop yourself in circles wondering what the fuck happy even is," he said with a gentle smile.

"Yeah. That."

"I know what you mean. I feel like happy is a moving target. Some days, I think I'm happy doing what I do, traveling and meeting people all over the world, and then some days... some days, I wonder what the fuck I've gotten myself into. Some days, I loathe it."

Adrian's fingers toyed with the hair at my collar, sending goose bumps all over my skin. My eyes met his, and heat flooded my veins.

"What would make you happy *right now*?" My voice sounded whiskey-soaked and rough. At this point, I was barely keeping it together. I wanted him desperately.

His jaw flexed. "To stop imagining that rancher's hands on you."

"I don't want Nate's hands on me, Hayes," I admitted, not looking away from him.

Adrian's eyes moved to my mouth, and his nostrils flared. "If you come inside with me, you're staying."

I glanced back at him as I reached for the door handle. "Maybe this time, you'll do a better job of wearing me out."

#SleighBellsRing #FuckNate #ColdConfessions #YesPlease

13

# #HOTINSIDE

ADRIAN

THE MOMENT we stepped inside my rental cabin, the atmosphere shifted from charged to combustible. Snow from our boots melted into puddles on the hardwood floor, but neither of us moved to take off our coats. We stood there in the entryway, breathing hard, while unspoken words hung between us like a live wire, dangerous and electric.

"Hayes," Maddox said, my name rough on his tongue.

I reached for him, my hands fisting in the front of his flannel shirt. "If you're about to spout some nonsense about suddenly needing to get back to the store, fuck off," I grumbled before pressing my lips to his in a hard kiss.

The sound of air rushing in through his nose and the feel of his fingers sneaking under my coat to clutch at my hips turned me on even more than I already was.

"No," he said before quickly adding, "Not leaving. Not as long as you keep your hands on me. Your mouth on me."

The words were hot on my lips, mingled with the scent of melting snow and mountain air. Maddox tasted like cinnamon, and I remembered the flex of his jaw earlier as he'd chewed on a piece of gum angrily.

"You didn't like it when Nate touched me," I said, suddenly realizing the reason behind his bad mood. There was grumpy, and then there was standoffish. Maddox had been unusually quiet at Nate's place.

"No," Maddox agreed, his voice rumbling against my chest as he turned us and crowded me against the wall.

"That's rich, considering I'm not the one with a Nate fuck history," I snapped. My fingers brushed the warm skin above his collar and dipped underneath the edge of the fabric. The scent of him was intoxicating. Now that we were inside the heated space, I could smell his body, masculine and warm.

"Didn't mean anything," he said breathlessly before nipping at my chin. "He's not the relationship type."

I pulled away and forced him to meet my eyes. "And you are?"

Maddox's slate-colored eyes darkened as he glared at me. "Wasn't before."

The implication that things might have changed made my heart rate stutter. I opened my mouth to challenge him, to press him on whether he'd consider more than just a physical connection with me, but then I stopped.

How would that even work? What would it look like?

I couldn't answer those questions right now, and there was no way I'd waste minutes I could be enjoying his body with stupid, needy requests for reassurance and real feelings.

My stomach flipped as the words tumbled out. "Want you to fuck me."

Slate flinted and sparked. "Blowie didn't do the job the other day?"

The breaths came short and shallow in my chest. "Maddox... I want... I just..." I couldn't say it. Couldn't admit that I wanted him to take possession of me, even if it was temporary. "Yes."

Maddox's fingers tightened on my hips before letting go and moving up to my wrists. He pulled my hands away from his shirt and pinned them against the wall next to my head. Then he stepped even closer and ground his hard cock against mine. "You want me inside you, Adrian?"

His low, teasing voice was melted chocolate that seeped into all of the spaces between us and lay hot and sweet on my skin.

My eyes fell closed. All I could do was feel the tight grip of his fingers, the thick ridge of his cock, and the warm breath of his dirty promises on my cheek as he leaned in.

"You going to be my pretty boy?" he whispered. "Let me take off all those fancy clothes and lay you out just for me to see?"

My dick was painfully hard and trapped uncomfortably behind way too much fabric. "Stop fucking with me," I urged with about as much force as a cartoon feather floating above a sleeping cat.

Maddox's teeth grazed my earlobe as his voice snuck into my ear. "Promise me the real Adrian Hayes."

I opened my eyes in surprise.

He was watching me carefully as he leaned in to press soft kisses across my chin and cheek and lips. "Promise just for tonight," he urged. "No mask. No filters. Just you. The real you."

My heart thundered between us before I finally admitted the truth in a too-small voice. "What if I don't know who that is?"

His smile was soft and kind, unexpectedly warm and understanding. "Then be unsure. Authentically unsure."

The provoking asshole's words should have made my dick soft and my anger flare, but they didn't. It felt like an invitation instead of a challenge. An offer of a safe space. One I knew I could trust.

"I want *you* to wear *me* out," I admitted, watching carefully for his reaction.

He nodded, as if that was already understood. The heat in his eyes smoldered. "And?"

"And I don't want you to leave me in the middle of the night." There. Even though I'd already laid it down as a condition in the car, maybe saying it again would get the message across just how important it was to me. I didn't deal well with abandonment, and I needed him to understand that.

Maddox let go of one of my wrists and cupped the side of my face before pressing a long kiss to the side of my mouth. "I promise. No matter what happens, I will not leave until you tell me I can go."

"It's not like that," I grumbled, sneaking my free hand up the back of his shirt. "I just—"

"Get in the bedroom, Adrian."

I blinked at him as my stomach tightened. The sound of my name on his tongue when he normally would have called me *Hayes* did something to me.

"Or what?" I asked with a grin.

He pressed his lips hard against mine with a low grunt. "That fucking mouth, I swear to fuck."

I didn't remember getting from the wall to the bedroom, going from fully dressed to full-monty bare, or how the hell I ended up head-to-toe with Maddox in a sloppy sixty-nine. But I was very cognizant of how my orgasm was snatched away with one quick squeeze of his grip around my balls.

"Not yet," he warned.

"Not—? Are you fucking... what? *What*? Let me come. I need to come. I was almost fucking—oh fucking fuck!"

Maddox's slick finger breached my hole, but his other hand

still held my nuts in a vise grip. I clenched around him and sucked in a choking breath.

"Easy," he said on a chuckle, moving his finger across my gland and lighting me up impossibly more. "What's the rush, Hayes?"

I closed my eyes and fell back on the mattress, letting my knees fall open so he could do whatever the fuck he wanted to me.

"Your body is offensively fine," he said, like it was a disappointment. "Do you even consume alcohol? Preservatives of any kind? Jesus."

He released my sac and moved his hand up the lower plane of my belly, his rough fingers catching on my happy trail.

I opened my eyes and watched his face. "Good, clean living," I said, barely able to focus with his finger moving slowly in and out of me.

"Liar." He turned around while simultaneously piercing me with a second finger. This one went in easier.

"Where the fuck did you find lube?" I demanded, feeling light-headed from the lack of blood available in my brain.

His low chuckle made my skin prickle. "Top of the bedside table, you naughty boy. Right where anyone could see it." He leaned his head closer and nudged my cheek with his nose while his fingers began stretching me in earnest. "What were you up to last night, hm?"

"Had company," I teased.

His face froze before his jaw tightened. "Oh."

I grabbed the back of his head to keep him from pulling away. "I'm kidding, Jesus. I jacked off thinking of my grumpy videographer. What did you think?"

Maddox relaxed slightly. "I think you could get a hookup out here in two minutes, even though you're twenty minutes from town."

"I happen to have a hookup here. Didn't even take two

minutes. Just a blatant lie about not knowing how to drive in the snow."

His eyes widened. "Wait."

"I'm from Connecticut," I reminded him. "I took my driving test in a winter storm."

I suddenly realized I'd brought up the topic that had led to our discussion about his parents, and now it was my turn to freeze. "Shit, man. I'm sorry."

His eyebrows crinkled before he realized the connection I'd made. His smile was soft and easy. "It's okay. The wound isn't fresh. But I sure as shit don't want to talk about my parents when I'm getting ready to fuck you into this mattress."

I ran my fingertips across the stubble on his cheek and chin. "How about we stop talking entirely?"

Maddox's mouth crashed down on mine as his fingers pressed back inside me and thrust in deep, raking across the perfect spot as he pulled them back out again, leaving me suddenly empty and begging.

"We good to go bare, Adrian?" he murmured after another deep kiss. "I'm clear, and it's been a while."

Our eyes met. "Clear and on PrEP," I breathed. "Yes. Bare."

Within seconds, he was pressing into me, the slick, blunt head of his cock stretching me more than his fingers had.

"Fuck yes," I urged, pulling my knees up to give him easier access. "Don't go easy."

His nostrils flared as he looked up from where he'd been watching his cock disappear into my body. "Provoking shit," he grunted, flexing his hips and turning the stretch into a burn.

My fingers flexed on the bare skin of his hips, digging into the sides of his ass. "Still waiting for you to pull out and fuck off home," I teased through panting breaths.

Maddox's eyes narrowed, and his nostrils flared. "Said I wasn't leaving."

My body arched as he changed the angle and hit just the right spot where burn and bliss tangled together. "Ah, *fuck*!"

He thrust into me relentlessly until I was just on the brink of coming, and then he pulled out.

And shoved me onto my front before fucking into me again. And again. Shoving my knees up under me until my ass was in the air and my face was against the cool sheets.

All I could think, with my single remaining functioning brain cell, was that this was too good for me to ever give up. Maddox had said he wouldn't leave... but how the hell was *I* supposed to walk away when my time in Legacy was through?

#ICouldGetUsedToThis #FuckingFinally #FinallyFucking

## 14

# #STAYORGO

### MADDOX

THE HOT SQUEEZE of Adrian's body was a drugging lure, tempting me far off the path I'd sworn to take—the one that would keep me away from the temptation of him. Keep things professional.

Keep me fucking sane.

"Please."

His broken voice was catnip. I wanted to crack his impossibly perfect veneer wide open, learn every facet of the man I'd glimpsed beneath. Because that man—the real Adrian—was warm, and funny, and endlessly fascinating. And he'd crawled under my walls despite my best efforts to keep him out.

I gripped the back of his neck while I drove into him from behind. The taut muscles of his back and shoulders bunched as his large hands gripped the sheets.

Why did it feel so good? Why was *this* guy, of all the people I'd hooked up with over the years, the one who made me lose control?

He should have been nobody to me. Nothing. Quick as a blink, he'd be leaving Legacy, and I'd be a speck in his rearview mirror as he sped the hell away. Falling for him was a trap I knew to avoid.

But here I was.

I'd reached for the forbidden fruit hanging full and juicy from a high branch like I was new at this. Like I hadn't already learned my lesson. Like I didn't know what it felt like to be left behind... and to lose a part of myself in the process.

Adrian reached back and clutched my hand, pulling me out of my dark thoughts. He wove our fingers together and held tight, forcing me to focus on the present. "Gonna make me come, Maddie," he breathed. "Fuck, you feel good."

I moved our joined hands under his chest as I leaned down, pressing the front of my body along his hot back. My hips continued to roll, slower now, as I held him tight. My nose brushed the back of his ear.

"You going to come for me, pretty boy?" I murmured, smiling against my will at the joy I felt in hearing him lose control.

"Fucking asshole." He let out a gasp as I hit just the right spot. "Oh *god*. Right there."

With his face in the sheets, he moved his other hand to his cock and began stroking.

I focused on keeping him on the knife's edge. "Feel so fucking incredible. Tight. Hot. *Fuck*." I hadn't meant to say it out loud, to give him the satisfaction of knowing what he was doing to me, but I also couldn't be bothered censoring myself.

Being inside him was intoxicating. I wanted more, needed more. I didn't want it to end. Ever. And the idea that this could be my last time with him, *should* be my last time with him, made me even more desperate.

Adrian's fingers tightened around mine. He pressed our joined hands against the center of his chest and held them there, and I clenched my teeth against the conflicting feelings I was having.

Raw possession. *This man is mine.*

The pull of my impending orgasm. *It feels so fucking good.*

And the deceptive temptation to imagine these feelings could last. *It's just sex, Sullivan. Stop imagining more.*

But I couldn't stop. Because now that I had him, I imagined what it would be like to keep him. To slip back into his body whenever I wanted. To hear him break apart. To provoke him and tease him and accept him until his mask fell away for good.

"Come for me, dammit," I growled.

I needed this to be over. I needed to run. To get as far away from this temptation as possible. To reinforce my walls, build them deeper and higher, and keep these dangerous fantasies at bay.

I let go of his hand and moved my fingers to his hole, where I traced the edges of his sensitive rim, tugging the taut skin where our bodies connected.

That was all it took. His surprised cry vibrated from his body into my chest, setting off my own release and throwing all of my previous thoughts into the wind like scattered confetti shot from a cannon. I moved my hand back around to grasp his cock, and his warm release coated both of our fingers as I thrust deep inside of him one last time.

Adrian's body shuddered as he bit off murmured curses into the sheets. He was sweaty, rumpled, utterly undone, and there was nothing I wanted more than to gather him in my arms and hold him.

My throat *burned* I wanted that so much.

Still, I began mentally preparing my excuses.

"It's okay, you know," he said softly. "I won't hold you to your promise. You can go."

I hadn't even climbed off him yet, although I'd slipped out of him already as he'd shifted and straightened his legs. My damp chest was still pressed against his back.

"Not leaving," I said, annoyed that he thought so poorly of me.

Yes, I recognized the hypocrisy. But I'd be damned if I was going to give him the satisfaction of finding me that predictable.

The easy rumble of his laugh annoyed me even more. "Okay then. Stay."

"Don't need your permission," I said peevishly, shoving away from him against my gut-clenching need to stay as close to him as possible. "Need I remind you, you already invited me to stay? Ordered me to, even?"

He turned and glanced at me over his shoulder, his quirked-up lips finding amusement in something I couldn't identify. "Easy, tiger. You're very welcome to stay. I'd like you to. But don't do it because you promised. Don't do it for *me*. If you want to go, go."

His ass cheeks were ruddy from the hard fucking, and I couldn't resist the urge to make them even redder. So I slapped his ass, hard. "Shut the fuck up and get in the shower. You're covered in jizz."

Adrian's easy laugh followed me into the bathroom. I started the water and wet a cloth before reaching out to wash off the front of him while we waited for the water to warm.

"You taking care of me, Maddox?" he teased, allowing me full access without reaching for the cloth.

I focused on the tightening of his abs as I moved down his happy trail. His flaccid cock hung down his thigh, still plenty thick and sticky at the tip. I imagined kneeling down and taking it in my mouth.

"I'll take that as a no," he said.

I glanced up at him, blinking away my wayward thoughts. "'S'only right. After all, I'm the one who caused the mess." I shot him a wink that made him roll his eyes and let out another laugh.

"Mm, but maybe you're the one who needs taking care of," he suggested. "Ever consider that?"

Once we were under the spray, I closed my eyes and tried getting a hold of myself. But Adrian's easy acceptance of my presence, his casual intimacy, especially his recent words about taking care of me stirred up memories I'd buried. Memories of Michael leaving. The contrast between the two men was impossible to ignore.

*"I can't do this anymore, Maddox. The grief, the responsibility with Maya, the business. It's too much. I need a break. Hell, I deserve a break. It's a lot."*

"Hey," Adrian said softly, all traces of amusement gone from his voice. "What's happening right now? You look a million miles away."

I opened my eyes and saw his furrowed eyebrows, the sincerity and concern in his eyes. Adrian's large hands cupped my face, and he'd tilted my face toward his.

"Sorry," I said, clearing my throat. "Just remembered something I need to do at the store."

His face froze. "Yeah, fine. I understand."

I reached for his hips and pulled him closer. "That's not what I meant. Will you fucking stop? I'm not leaving. I told you."

*Even if I should.*

"And I told *you*—" he said hotly.

Instead of repeating the same conversation yet again, I leaned forward and took his mouth in a hard kiss. The slick flesh of his hips and ass fit my hands perfectly, and I slid a knee between his to widen his stance so I could reach down and fondle him while we kissed.

By the time we finished washing and dried off, we were both starving.

Adrian tossed me a pair of lounge pants and a hoodie while he pulled on a similar combo. "There are some prepared meals in the fridge. Can't promise they're any good, but let's see what we have."

We found a baked pasta dish and a bag of salad to go with it. As soon as Adrian slid the pasta into the oven, I realized I needed to at least edit enough of our day's shoot to get him something to post.

"Shit, let me get my laptop," I said. "I forgot you'd need to make a post tonight."

He watched me as I retrieved my gear bag and set up my laptop on the kitchen island. "I still have several of the other videos you've sent that I could post instead."

I shook my head and focused on the screen. "No, it's fine. I'll edit while we wait for the food."

Adrian moved around behind me to peer over my shoulder. "How's it looking?"

I caught the scent of his face lotion and realized that the only reason I could identify it was because I'd been with him when he'd stepped out of the shower. The memory of him with a towel wrapped around his waist, emphasizing his rounded ass, flooded my veins with heat. It annoyed me how distracting he was.

"Good," I grunted, not looking away from the screen. "Should edit together nicely."

Adrian leaned closer, ostensibly to get a better view of the laptop. His shoulder bumped mine as he pointed at the screen. "Can you rewind that part? I want to see how the lighting turned out at that overlook."

I clicked back, watching the footage of him and Nate standing by the overlook. In the frame, they looked good together—two attractive men against a winter wonderland backdrop. Exactly what we'd planned.

"Huh," Adrian murmured.

"What?"

"Nothing. It's just..." He shifted closer, studying the screen. I stopped breathing, if only to keep the scent of him from filling my nostrils. "Keep going. Let me see the rest."

I scrolled through more clips, growing increasingly unnerved as a pattern became obvious. Every shot of Adrian was perfectly framed, catching him in the best light, highlighting the way the winter air had flushed his cheeks. The shots of Nate, on the other hand, were... functional. Adequate. Like an afterthought.

*Shit.*

"Interesting," Adrian said, his voice carefully neutral.

"What's interesting?" I asked, though I already knew I was fucked.

"Well, either Nate's camera-shy, or..." He paused, letting the implication hang in the air. Then his voice turned teasing. "You seem to have a very specific idea of who the star of this date should be."

Heat crawled up my neck. "Of course I do. The point of the project is the sponsored content. You're the one wearing the Nordique pieces."

"Uh-huh." Adrian's mouth twitched like he was fighting a smile. "And in this shot here, where Nate's adjusting my scarf? You cut off his head entirely."

"Camera malfunction."

"Right. And this one where we're both supposed to be admiring the view? Somehow, the frame managed to capture me in perfect profile while Nate's mostly just... a flannel-covered shoulder."

I slammed the laptop shut harder than necessary. "You'll have what you need for the content. That's what matters."

"Maddox." Adrian's voice was soft, almost gentle. "Why didn't you get more footage of Nate?"

"I got plenty of footage of Nate," I said, and it was true. Footage of his boots, his elbows, the back of his head. Too much footage of Nate, if you asked me.

"Ahh, getting off on a technicality. I see." Adrian shifted to face me fully, those blue eyes sparkling with something that looked dangerously like affection. "You hardly got any shots of his face, Maddie."

My jaw clenched, but my insides melted at the soft shortening of my name. He'd done the same thing during sex, when his control had slipped.

"Maybe Nate's not as photogenic as he thinks," I argued, trying desperately to keep from admitting the truth.

Adrian's laugh was warm and delighted. "Holy shit! You were jealous."

"I was not—"

"You were!" He pointed an accusatory finger at me. "Grumpy, possessive Maddox Sullivan couldn't stand watching another man charm me, so you sabotaged his screen time."

"That's ridiculous," I said, standing up to put distance between us. But Adrian followed, crowding into my space with that infuriating grin.

"Is it? Because looking at this footage, someone might think you don't want to share me with anyone else."

"You're not mine to share," I snapped, then immediately regretted the words when hurt flickered across his face.

But the hurt disappeared as quickly as it had come, replaced by something calculating. "No? Then you won't mind if I call Nate about that barn dance. Maybe see if he wants to grab dinner one night before then."

My hands clenched into fists at my sides. "Do whatever you want."

"I will." Adrian pulled out his phone, thumb hovering over the screen. "He did say I had a natural touch with horses. Maybe he could teach me to *ride.*"

A growl escaped my throat before I could stop it.

Adrian's grin turned positively wicked. "Was that a no, Sullivan?"

"Fuck off, Hayes."

"Make me," he challenged, stepping close enough that I could feel the heat radiating from his body.

Needless to say, we burned the pasta. When we finally fell asleep after midnight, I was jelly-legged and dehydrated from all the rounds of sex we managed to have before our bodies simply couldn't do it anymore. Thankfully, we'd managed to find a pair of clean sheets, but that was about it. We'd pulled the duvet over us and passed out.

Stress dreams haunted me after a while, the way they did more and more lately. A myriad of images that didn't make sense but carried a sense of foreboding, or fear, or that horrible, overwhelming terror of missing something important.

"*Maddox.*" The voice sounded like my father's but also like Michael's. Or maybe it was Nate warning me off Adrian.

"*Maddox!*"

I wanted to respond, but my mouth was glued shut. Or maybe my lips were duct-taped. Maybe I'd been kidnapped. No, maybe Maya had been kidnapped. Was I trying to get to her? What if I couldn't get to her?

"*Baby, wake up.*"

A crushing sense of longing filled me, making my eyes smart with regret. For whatever reason, I wouldn't get to have that... that good, bright thing that was just on the horizon. Just out of reach.

"Dammit wake the fuck up you asshole!"

I blinked awake to the feel of Adrian's hands gripping my

shoulders. He loomed over me in the dark, hair wild and eyes glinting in the sliver of light from the hallway.

"Adrian? What's wrong?" My voice was sleep-graveled, and my brain was like a bucket of scattered LEGOs—more potential than structure. The parts were all there, but they didn't go together in any way that made sense.

"You tell me," he said, voice softening. He moved his fingers absently through my hair as his body relaxed. "You were having a nightmare."

He moved to lie next to me on his side, propping his head up on an arm.

I blew out a breath. "Sorry. Maybe I should have left after all so you could have gotten a decent night's sleep."

Adrian's mouth eased into a smile as he tilted his chin toward the bedroom door. "You could go now. Probably take the rental about an hour to warm up, but you're welcome to it. I've been meaning to do a post on the tourist shuttle to Slingshot Mountain anyway. I'll walk over to the store afterward and collect my keys."

I turned on my side to face him, grateful that he hadn't pressed me on the nightmares. There was something about him pulling back, choosing to lighten the mood and give me an out—literal and figurative—that made me want to do the opposite.

"Stress dreams, you know?" I began. "I've, ah... I've been stressed about work. About the store. It's part of the reason I took this job."

His smile faded. "Do you want to talk about it?"

"It's just hard trying to keep it all going on my own while trying to make it look like it's not that bad. I'm worried Maya will stay here instead of going off to school. That she won't have a choice financially or that she'll feel like she needs to stay and help. It burns me up inside. I don't want that for her."

What was it about the early morning or the middle of the night that made people confess shit they should keep to themselves?

Adrian reached over and ran his fingers through my hair again. My eyes drifted closed at the comforting touch.

"You want to give her a chance to escape because you couldn't?"

My eyes flashed open. "What? No! I love Legacy. I never wanted to leave."

"Oh," he said, shifting a little closer and moving his hand down to my shoulder and then further along my arm until his fingers twined with mine. "But you think she does?"

I blew out a breath. "I don't know. She doesn't have anything to compare Legacy to. I want her to have a chance to see what it's like to live just for herself. Not have to worry about me or the shop or anyone else."

Adrian toyed with my fingers as he gazed at me. His eyes were soft and understanding in a way that got under my skin. "What if she felt that way about you? What if she wanted you to leave? To, let's say, go to a fancy film school and leave Legacy behind for a while?"

*The documentary workshop in Denver.*

Adrian's lips quirked up in a knowing grin. "Ah ha! Hoist on his own petard."

"You don't strike me as the Shakespeare type," I muttered. I couldn't help but grin back.

"I'm not. But I dated a guy once who used that expression all the time." He pulled my hand up and kissed the back of it. "Maya may have mentioned the workshop you wanted to take."

I gritted my teeth, causing Adrian to huff out a laugh. "Relax. She only mentioned it in case there was any sponsorship bonus or other opportunities for you from Nordique. She specifically said you'd be too stubborn to ask but that she wished she could give you the workshop for Christmas."

Now it was my turn to scoff. "It's five grand. Hardly Christmas present money."

Adrian opened his mouth to speak, but I could tell he was getting ready to offer help again. Before he could, I clapped a hand over his mouth. "Don't."

His eyes widened. But then they narrowed.

I withdrew my hand and muttered an apology.

"What the fuck is your problem?" he asked, his voice lower and more gentle than I deserved. "All I'd have to do to earn you an extra five grand is post another video of the two of us kissing. Fully clothed. Only this time, it would have to be..."

My heart thundered, and my stomach clenched. I was almost afraid to ask. "Have to be...?"

His jaw ticked. "Never mind. I know you won't do it. And even if you did, you'd spend the money on the store."

He was right about both. I couldn't afford to have my friends and neighbors think I'd lost my heart to an outsider. That I'd once again allowed someone to love me and leave me. And even if I had the guts to accept what he was offering, the store had crushing debt that would take the money before it even hit my account.

Adrian pulled away, sat up, and put his feet on the ground until all I could see was the bare skin of his back in the shadows. "Maybe you should go, Maddox. You're due at the store in a couple hours anyway."

I wanted to reach for him. Put my hand firmly between his shoulder blades and feel the warm strength of him against my palm. But I didn't dare. The last time I'd reached for someone when I was vulnerable...

"After the accident," I started, the words scraping my throat raw. "When Maya was barely eating and the life insurance paperwork felt impossible and every breath had been a struggle..."

Adrian turned to look at me over his shoulder. "Go on."

I sucked in a breath. Fuck, this was hard. "I was dating someone. Guy named Michael. It was serious. At least, I thought it was. But then..."

Adrian turned back around to face me. I could tell by the tension in his body language he was already upset by what I was going to say.

"He... it was too much. My responsibilities. He hadn't signed up to be burdened with any of that." I shrugged. "So he left."

"How long after the accident?"

I met his eyes. They were dark like cut glass under water. Deceptively tempting.

I waved it off. "Does it matter?"

His voice was sharper than the cut glass. "How long after the accident, Maddie?"

My skin prickled with awareness, with the overwhelming feeling that someone cared, that he wanted to look out for me and protect me. That he would raze the earth to punish someone for causing me an injustice.

"Two weeks," I said, feeling impossibly, unexpectedly brittle.

Before he could offer me any comfort, before he could make it good or even attempt to, I moved back and climbed out of the bed, trying to stay calm while I collected and yanked on my clothes. "So you can see why I have to go, right?"

My voice was abnormally high and strange, like I was speaking through a cardboard tube.

Every molecule of my awareness was laser-targeted on his reaction, but I refused to let him see it.

Adrian was quiet for a long moment, and when he finally spoke, his voice was carefully controlled. "I do see. Self-preservation. Someone you trusted saw you as a burden rather than giving you support and love during the hardest fucking moments of your life. You don't want to risk that happening again." A pause. "Doesn't mean it doesn't suck ass to be on the receiving end of it."

The honesty in his voice—hurt but not accusatory—somehow made it worse.

I nodded at the floor, the numbness overtaking me a blessed relief. "Right. Good. Okay."

After shoving my phone into my pocket, I strode out of the room in search of his rental keys. My hands shook as I grabbed them and reached for the door.

There were no footsteps behind me.

*Damn.*

My eyes stung, probably in anticipation of the frigid cold outside.

*Motherfucker.*

I yanked the door open and was just about to break free of the hold he had over me when his voice called out from the bedroom.

"Just one thing, Sullivan. Remember that bet about our fire-building video getting a thousand thirsty comments? Well, the thing is... I *won*."

I closed my eyes, hand still on the door handle. Relief and disappointment warred in my chest—relief that this wasn't over, that I'd get to see him again. But disappointment, too, because some pathetic part of me had wanted him to fight harder to make me stay.

*Walk away, idiot. Get in the car and drive before you do something stupid like turn around and beg him to let you crawl back into his bed and into his body.*

His voice rang out again as his sleep-rumpled self appeared in the bedroom doorway. For a moment, hurt flashed across his features before his expression smoothed into something more controlled.

He lazily leaned against the jamb in his underwear. "Which means you owe me a date." He met my eyes, and molten lava slithered hotly through my veins. "A romantic one. An *authentic* one."

#NightmareToDream #ThousandThirstyComments #PayUp-Sullivan #Stay

## 15

# #SISTERLYADVICE
### ADRIAN

I stood outside Sullivan Hardware, debating whether to go in. The smart thing would've been to text Maddox to leave my keys in the rental so I could avoid another awkward encounter where I'd inevitably say something stupid about feelings or staying or any of the hundred other things Maddox clearly didn't want to hear.

But avoiding him felt like admitting defeat. And if there was one thing five years of building a social media career had taught me, it was that sometimes you had to push through the awkward to get what you wanted.

I still wanted, *needed*, this project to be successful. I definitely still wanted to spend time with Maddox. And, obviously, I wanted my damned rental car back.

The bell jingled as I pushed inside. Maya appeared from behind a tower of snow shovels, took one look at my face, and winced.

"Oof. That bad, huh?"

"I don't know what you're talking about," I said, attempting to project more confidence than I felt. "I just need my car keys."

Maya studied me with the kind of knowing look that was unsettling on someone who wasn't even eighteen. "He left two hours ago. But he took his own truck. He left your keys here and your car out back."

I leaned against the counter, suddenly exhausted. "He owes me a date."

Her face lit up. "Hell yeah. Finally!"

"Not like that. I made a bet with him about…" I suddenly realized it might be inappropriate to discuss thirsty comments with a minor. "Anyway, I won. He lost. So now he has to plan a romantic date for the two of us. For my social media."

Maya's eyes lit up. "Oh, this is perfect. He's going to have to actually put effort into being romantic."

"Knowing him, he'll probably try to wiggle out of it," I muttered.

"Oh no, he won't." Maya's expression turned calculating. "Maddox takes bets seriously. Always has. The question is…" She drummed her fingers on the counter. "What would actually be romantic to you?"

I blinked before narrowing my eyes. "If you're thinking about planning this for him, think again. It's not about what *I* think is romantic but about what *he* does."

"Listen, my brother's going to panic about this. He'll probably overthink the hell out of it and grumble about everything else being too cheesy." Maya leaned forward. "So what would actually make you happy? Like, forget what you think you're supposed to want. What would feel special to you?"

Before I could answer that, actually, dinner and a movie with Maddox sounded pretty nice to me, the bell jingled, and Mrs. Hoffman bustled in, shaking snow from her coat.

"Adrian! Perfect timing. I was just wondering how you're

settling in. This weather certainly takes some getting used to, doesn't it?"

"It's... definitely unpredictable," I admitted. "Takes some adjusting."

Maya caught Mrs. Hoffman's eye and made some kind of subtle gesture. Mrs. Hoffman's expression sharpened with interest.

"I imagine everything about Legacy is an adjustment for someone used to city life," Mrs. Hoffman continued, but now it felt like she was fishing for something. "What's been the biggest surprise for you? Good or bad?"

I thought about it. "Honestly? How quiet it is. Not just the noise level, but... I don't know how to explain it. In LA, I feel like I'm always on, even when I'm alone. Here, sometimes I catch myself just... being."

Maya and Mrs. Hoffman exchanged a meaningful look. Whatever it was they weren't saying, I felt like I was being managed silently, and I knew why.

I rolled my eyes. "Whatever the two of you are up to, give it a rest, okay? Maddox isn't interested in me like that."

Maya pursed her lips. "Maddox *says* he isn't interested. But those videos say something completely different."

Mrs. Hoffman nodded. "You two have such wonderful chemistry. And poor Maddox has been alone for far too long."

"Like I said, he's not interested," I repeated, shrugging as if I wasn't as bothered by it as I truly was. "And honestly, it's probably smart of him. It's not like he'd ever leave Legacy."

"Absolutely not!" Mrs. Hoffman insisted, while at the same time Maya said, "Why not?"

I didn't want to have this conversation. It was ridiculous. Maddox and I were... well, we were nothing. There wasn't a true path to happiness between us, so what was the point in talking about it?

"And I'm not made for small towns," I concluded, smiling in an attempt to lighten the conversation. "I'm made for mani-pedis, mimosa brunches, and same-day Amazon Prime shipping, which —by the way—you cannot get in Legacy, Montana. Had I known that—"

"Don't be ridiculous!" The vehemence in Mrs. Hoffman's voice made me jump. She stepped closer, her expression softening. "Do you hear yourself? Imagine if Maya had just described herself that way."

I firmed my jaw. "I would have been surprised, but I might have invited her to LA."

"Nonsense. You would have told her that people can change. That they can even compromise. You might have reminded her that there may be chapters in your life where you try new things. Maybe you think you aren't made for small towns because you've never lived in a small town." Her face softened. "Don't knock it till you try it."

"I have no need to try it," I said, memories of my own hometown hurling themselves at me unhelpfully. It hadn't been a small town like Legacy, but it had been small-minded and stifling.

The older woman eyed me. "Well, that's a shame because I think you'd love it here, and I damned well know we'd love to have you."

"She's right," Maya added. "You're pretty fun. And I like that you're different, too."

Her words surprised me. I didn't feel different. I felt like every other guy trying his best to make a living on social media while in constant struggle with his body image, personal relationships, and current state of relevancy. "Guys like me are a dime a dozen where I live," I huffed. "I'm hardly different."

Mrs. Hoffman pointed behind me at the wall of the hardware store, where a collection of framed photos hung in mismatched frames. One of them was of a younger Maddox Sullivan, bright-eyed and grinning with a man I assumed was his father. There was a lightness in his expression I rarely saw in him.

I remembered his nightmare, about the sheer amount of stress he was under. He was such a stubborn fucker he refused to let anyone help him.

Mrs. Hoffman noticed me staring at the photo of Maddox. "Something about you is different to *him*. You've got his antennae up unlike anything we've seen in years. Half of Legacy thinks you're the best thing that's happened to Maddox since... well, since before his parents died. And you make *him* different, too. Lighter. Like he remembers how to laugh."

It was surprising to hear her say that. He seemed so care-worn and tired to me. Sad. Lonely. Walled up and defensive. If there was any way I could make him laugh, make him feel lighter, I'd do it in a heartbeat.

If he'd let me.

Maya crossed her arms over her chest, nodding emphatically. "She's right. You should see him when he's editing your videos. He gets this little smile on his face, like he's seeing something no one else can see."

"Until he remembers he's supposed to be miserable and shuts down again," I murmured.

Mrs. Hoffman patted my arm sympathetically. "He's been hurt. Badly. Not just by that awful Michael person, but by life itself. When you've lost as much as he has, it becomes easier to push people away than risk losing them."

The bell jingled again, and Sadie from the Pinecone breezed in, her apron dusted with flour. "Maya, honey, do you have any of those small screws for cabinet hinges? I have a cabinet door that has it out for me—" She stopped short when she saw me. "Adrian! Hey! I was just telling Margie Peterson how much the breakfast crowd has been talking about you and Maddox. Ever since that video of the two of you bickering over breakfast went viral, we've been packed every morning with people hoping to catch a glimpse of you guys being adorable over coffee."

"They're having relationship troubles," Mrs. Hoffman informed her in a stage whisper.

"We're not in a—" I tried before Sadie cut me off.

"Oh no. What happened? Did someone say something stupid? Please tell me it wasn't Ned Harwick. That man has the social skills of a rusty nail."

"It was Maddox," Maya said bluntly. "Being an emotionally inaccessible disaster as usual."

"Typical." Sadie shook her head. "I swear, sometimes I want to shake him. Here he's got this gorgeous, successful man who's clearly crazy about him, and he's probably sabotaging it because he's scared."

I felt heat rise in my cheeks. "Who said I was crazy about him?"

All three women turned to stare at me with varying degrees of disbelief.

"Hey, I know!" I said with a giant fake smile. "Let's change the subject! Sadie, what's your favorite part about living in a small town? Mrs. Hoffman was trying to tell me it's possible to survive without delivery sushi, but I'm not sure I believe her."

Thankfully, they allowed me to shift the topic, each sharing their thoughts on sushi and delivery food in general.

"If we had delivery sushi, though," Sadie continued, "I might not have had a chance to try Hazel Marian's ginger and almond salad, which I'm now obsessed with. She and her wife made it for me one night after a long day at work. To die for."

Maya nodded eagerly. "Have you had Avery's chicken scallopini? She made it for Maddox for his birthday, and I craved it for like three months. No matter how many times I've tried to recreate it, it's never as good as when she makes it."

They exchanged a few more stories of home-cooked meals before Mrs. Hoffman asked me what my favorite was.

"No one cooks for me, so I'm not sure," I said, only realizing how pathetic that sounded after the words left my mouth.

Mrs. Hoffman's smile dropped a little. "What about meals your mom made when you were growing up? Or your dad?"

I cleared my throat. "My family never really had home-cooked meals. We had a chef who came in once a week and prepared things, or we ate at restaurants. It was always something I envied when I went to friends' houses for dinner."

Sadie's eyes went soft. "Well, maybe we'll have to surprise you with something before you leave. What's your favorite comfort food?"

I shifted uncomfortably under their collective attention. "I... honestly don't know. I've never really done comfort food." I felt like an idiot. Like I was missing out on some base human experience. "As an adult, food has always been about nutrition or presentation or whatever was trendy. I have to be careful about what I eat because of my job."

The silence that followed was profound.

"Never?" Sadie asked quietly.

I shrugged. "I'm used to it. It's not just my job. My parents were very focused on appearances. And the guys I've dated..." I trailed off.

How did I explain that most of my relationships had been as carefully curated as my Instagram feed?

"Comfort doesn't have to be food related. What about movies?" Maya asked suddenly. "When you need cheering up, what do you watch?"

"I don't really have a go-to." I paused, then admitted something that felt almost embarrassing. "I mostly watch whatever's trending for content ideas."

"Favorite Christmas movie?" she asked.

Before I could respond, the door opened again and Alex Marian walked in, looking harried.

"Maya, please tell me you have something that can fix a broken beer tap."

"O-rings and gaskets are right over there, plumbing section," Maya directed.

In hopes of getting the focus off me again, I asked, "Alex, what's your favorite Christmas movie?"

Alex paused, clearly confused by the nonsequitur. "Uh... *Die Hard*? What about you?"

"Never seen it," I admitted. "But I remember liking the Snoopy one."

The collective gasp at my response surprised me. I looked around at their shocked faces. "You guys don't like Snoopy?"

Alex stared at me like I'd just admitted to never having heard of Christmas. "You've never seen *Die Hard*?" He shook his head and wandered over to the plumbing section, throwing another comment over his shoulder. "It's true what they say about people from LA."

Maya laughed and called back to him, "You're from Napa. Don't go acting all local on us just yet. You've been here five minutes."

Mrs. Hoffman laughed and moved toward the display of little Christmas ornament hooks, grabbing a box of them.

Alex grinned and returned to the counter with the part he needed. "I've been here full-time for three years, and that's after a decade of summers in Legacy, little lady."

Mrs. Hoffman fell in line behind him but continued eyeing me. "So what are you filming next?"

"Oh, uh... Actually, I'm going to a holiday bonfire and s'mores tonight with, um..." I tried to remember the guy's name. "The fire chief? I can't remember his name."

Alex's head whipped around. "Oh my god, Maddox set you up with Kincaid after all? For real?" His nostrils flared, and he shook his head. "Good luck, I guess. He's the grumpiest human you've ever met. Makes Maddox look like a happy ray of sunshine in comparison."

I shrugged. "My business manager hooked me up with a small sponsorship to create fire safety content and just sent me the information this morning. He arranged it with the people at the search and rescue training program who are putting on the bonfire—"

"SERA," Maya supplied with a nod.

"Right," I agreed. "So we're going to film out there tonight." I'd hoped to ask Maddox to do the filming, but since he wasn't here, it would mean tracking him down elsewhere.

Alex headed toward the door, waving his hand over his shoulder. "Like I said, good luck. Chief Kincaid's an ass and ten times more stubborn than one. Enjoy!"

Mrs. Hoffman chuckled as he left. "Judd Kincaid's a nice man. And very professional. I've been to SERA's Holiday Bonfire a time or two. You'll have fun, I'm sure."

She didn't sound enthused, but I appreciated her sudden neutrality nonetheless.

"Well, if Maddox isn't around to handle the cameras, I might be back begging Maya here for a favor," I said, shooting the younger woman a smile.

Maya shook her head. "I'm sure Maddox will help." She met my eyes with a knowing look. "Although, after he stood me up last night, I'm not so sure."

My stomach dropped. "Stood you up?"

"Yeah, we were supposed to get started on the Christmas

cookie dough for the open house here at the store. I guess he found someone better to do."

She'd coughed a little bit on the "some*one*" part, but all of us had heard it. My face ignited.

"Um, well..." I shuffled backward toward the door until I remembered I still hadn't gotten my keys from her. "If you'll, ah, point me to those car keys, I'll get out of your hair."

After finishing Mrs. Hoffman's transaction and thanking her, Maya reached under the counter for my keys. As soon as she reached out to hand them to me, she pulled them back again.

"Did I mention Maddox only ran up to Meyers Creek this morning to deliver a very large online order? Four snowblowers and a generator. Apparently, the customer heard about us on social media." She raised an eyebrow. "In a video about menswear, if you can believe it. The influencer in the video made a casual mention of Sullivan's Hardware store being in business for four generations. Something about that spoke to the guy, so he canceled his big-box order and ordered from us instead."

My embarrassment from earlier turned into a flush of satisfaction. "Great."

"Adrian. The profit on that order alone covers our overhead for a month. Even if my brother will never say it outright... *thank you*."

I wasn't sure what to say, so I nodded awkwardly. "Yeah, good. No problem. Okay."

Maya finally handed over my keys, but her expression had grown serious. "You know, before you came here, Maddox was just... existing. Going through the motions. But with you? He's actually living again. *Feeling* something."

The weight of her words settled in my chest. "Maya—"

"I'm not asking you to save him or anything cheesy like that. I'm just saying... maybe think about what it would feel like to stop running toward the next perfect thing and start building something real."

I stared at her, this wise-beyond-her-years kid who saw too much and understood even more. "What if I don't know how?"

"Then maybe it's time to learn."

#TownConspiracy #HomeCooked #DieHardSnoopy #WorthTheRisk #OperationMaddrianIsAGo

**16**

## #LYINGSULLIVANS

MADDOX

I'D SPENT HALF the morning finishing edits on the video of Nate and Adrian, so I was in a shit mood by the time I spent the second half driving a big order up to Meyers Creek. The entire way there, I grumbled under my breath about how perfect Nate and Adrian had looked together on their sleigh ride... and about how Adrian had been right.

The footage was garbage. Because I'd been unprofessional as hell. Which was why it had taken me hours to cobble together decent videos for his social media accounts. Thankfully, there'd been a few shots of the two of us that I knew his fans would love. With any luck, they'd spend more time gossiping about those than noticing my shit composition on the rest.

The entire drive back to Legacy, I brainstormed about what kind of date to plan now that I'd lost the bet. Instead of bitching about it, I'd decided that I'd show him what it meant to date someone, small-town style. No dance clubs, no fancy martini bars, just simple things that showed you truly cared and wanted to make the other person feel seen.

Except... every time I thought of something to do with Adrian, he'd either already planned it as one of his "Twelve Dates of Christmas," or I began to second-guess myself and worry he'd think I was boring.

No way could I give him the date I truly thought he needed: a simple night at home, eating dinner on the couch. Downtime, where he could stop performing for a little while and simply *be*. He'd probably hate every second of it.

Some part of him must *love* performing, after all, since he'd made a career out of it. And he'd been around the globe experiencing all the excitement the world had to offer. A Friday night on the sofa would put him to sleep. It also wouldn't provide any footage he could turn into shiny content.

But then I'd remember Adrian's hollow smile when he'd said: *Social media tells a story, Maddox. Paints a pretty picture. A fantasy. Isn't that what you keep trying to tell me?*

He'd implied he was lonely. That his life wasn't the whirlwind party it appeared. Of course it wasn't; no one's would or could be. But was he truly lonely? Did he crave connection and companionship?

He'd begged me to stay.

And I'd still fucking left.

By the time I got back to the hardware store from my delivery to Meyers Creek, I'd twisted my thoughts into knots and was cursing him, myself, and anyone else I could think of. Why couldn't the man have picked someone else's charming small town for his winter fashion spread? Why'd he have to come here and interrupt my perfectly fine—

"Hey there, Maddox," Lennon Marian said as he came out of the store carrying a strap wrench and a pot of plumber's epoxy.

I glanced in surprise at the gruff rancher, barely stopping

before running him over. "Shit, sorry, Lennon. Wasn't watching where I was going."

He waved off the apology. "Glad I ran into you. Rosie said she already told Maya, but I wanted to be sure and invite you to Christmas at Marian Lodge. But just so you know, my family will *all* be there this year." He shrugged and shot an amused glance at me. "Don't say you weren't warned."

I laughed. "Thanks. I'd imagine we'll head that way like we always do. Appreciate the invite."

As I stood back to let him by, Lennon's amusement turned into a full grin. "And bring your boyfriend if you want."

I stared after him but he was down the street and into his dually before I had a chance to sputter out an answer.

When I turned back to the store, I caught Maya grinning at me.

"This your handiwork?" I asked, thumbing over my shoulder in Lennon's direction as I stepped inside. "Because you know telling people Adrian and I are a thing is a lie, and Sullivans don't lie."

Maya tapped her finger on her lips as if in thought. "That's funny, because my darling brother lied to me last night about where he was."

"Did not. I told you I'd be out late. And I was."

She tilted her head. "Late. Is that what we're calling sunrise? Huh. Maybe you're right." She turned back to the register and pretended to straighten a little stack of town maps on the counter. "You know what bothers me the most about this, Maddie?"

I could tell by her lack of eye contact she truly *was* bothered by whatever she was getting ready to say. I steadied myself and braced for it. "What?"

"You talk a big game about how *I* deserve to be loved. How I should give people a chance to change, a chance to do the right thing. You taught me that relationships make life richer and that I shouldn't let Mom and Dad's death scare me off of getting close to people."

I felt the arrow strike true and bury deep.

She took a deep breath and met my eyes. "If Sullivans don't lie, I wish you'd stop lying to yourself, Maddie. It's not just hurting *you* anymore."

Before I could say anything, the door jingled open, bringing a group of our local search and rescue experts in search of bonfire skewers for s'mores. They were joking around about the fire chief finally having a hot date and how they were planning to go out of their way to make sure the guy got laid.

Maya rolled her eyes and disappeared into the back room, so I shucked off my coat and took her place behind the register.

"So," I said, trying to make friendly small talk. "Chief Kincaid has a date? I'm guessing he and Alex Marian are finally going to admit they're not quite the adversaries they think they are?"

Gus blinked at me. "Kincaid and Alex?" He laughed. "Nah, man. Chief's thing is with someone from out of town. But I'll be sure and give him hell about Alex. Can you even imagine? He *hates* that guy."

They were checked out and halfway back to the firehouse before I realized the "out-of-towner" they'd meant.

I poked my head in the back room and found Maya leaning back in an old chair, scrolling on her phone. "Hey, you happen to know anything about this bonfire tonight?"

She glanced up at me. "Yeah, Adrian's going on a date with the fire chief. I thought he wanted you to film it, but maybe not." She shrugged and went back to scrolling.

"You talked to him about it? When?"

This time, Maya didn't bother looking up. "When he came to get his keys. Hey, did you know that man has never seen *Die Hard*? Did he grow up Amish or something?"

I blinked at her. It was true what they said about teenagers. They flashed from childish to mature-as-fuck and back again like a compass sitting next to a bag of magnets.

"He said he wanted me to film another date?" I prompted.

Maya pursed her lips. "Well, I asked if he did, but he got kind of... squirrelly. It's not one of his twelve fake dates, I don't think." She shrugged again.

*Not a fake date?*

I scowled. "Wait, are you sure it wasn't for the project?"

She sighed. "Look, all I know is that Chief Kincaid asked him out, and it's not part of the Nordique thing. The two of them are going to a bonfire and making s'mores together."

"And he *didn't* want me to film it?" I asked in surprise.

Maya waved a hand. "I don't know, Maddie. I guess if he didn't call you, he doesn't need you, right? None of your business since you've made it clear you don't have feelings for him." She finally looked up at me and met my eyes. "And Sullivans don't lie."

I groaned and dropped my face in my hands. "Fuck, Maya. I'm sorry I accused you of lying, okay? I'm just... I just... This guy. He's not sticking around. Everyone pushing me at someone who's just going to leave is frustrating as fuck."

Her eyes widened with every expletive. "What if he didn't?"

"He will," I insisted.

"What if he *shouldn't*?" she asked.

I opened my mouth to continue arguing, except... I realized she was right. He really shouldn't. He should leave the place that didn't love him back and consider settling in... someplace that would.

"I can't make that decision for him, Maya."

Her face softened. "Of course not. But you can at least show him he's wanted here. That we like him for who he is, not what he posts. And that there will be someone out there someday brave enough to love him. Maybe that's not here in Legacy, but who knows? Chief Kincaid seems like the kind of man who'd run into a fire for the person he loves."

"You're transparent as glass," I ground out. "You and the rest of the fucking town. Nate told me you tried to get him to cancel the sleigh date."

She pointed her finger at me. "Now, that *is* a lie! I told him to fake a butt injury so that he wasn't capable of sitting in the sleigh."

I rolled my eyes. "I love you. I'm sorry for not being a better role model."

She rolled her eyes right back, startling me with how much she reminded me of myself. "You're the best damned role model I could have asked for. Know why? Because you model being imperfect and trying your hardest anyway. And I love you for that."

Ned Harwick's voice broke the moment. "Ain't anyone back there give a shit about taking my money? I been calling out for an hour. Time's a wastin'. Chop, chop."

Maya clapped her hand over her mouth to cover a smile while I took a breath and tried to put on my customer service face. "Coming!"

It took twenty minutes to help him and the other customers in the store's checkout and another twenty to pull together the equipment I needed for the Hernandez family's photo shoot later that afternoon. By the time I glanced at my phone, I'd somehow missed a couple of hours of messages.

ADRIAN

Any chance you could help me again tonight?

Not like that. With a video camera.

Still sounded dirty. I meant… can you please take some video of me and another guy tonight?

Jesus. I'm incapable of making this sound normal. Pls call me.

I understand why you're ignoring my messages, but I promise I'm not soliciting you for a porno. Although…

No worries. Catch you another time.

I scrambled to text him back.

Was driving and then working. What time do you need me?

I didn't even bother to ask what it was for or whether it would make my schedule too tight after the photo shoot. Maya was right. I'd been lying to myself about not having feelings for Adrian Hayes, and I couldn't bring myself to be nonchalant about him going out with Judd Kincaid, no matter how innocent it may or may not be.

ADRIAN

You sure? I don't want it to be weird. And it's outside the scope I hired you for.

Instead of texting him back, I called. As soon as his voice came on the line, I felt the now-familiar prickle of relief and excitement.

"Hey," he said. "Judd said to be there around seven. I'd imagine it won't take more than an hour and a half, but I can't be sure."

"Yeah, I can do it." I tried to tamp down my curiosity, but it was a losing battle. "What's this for?"

"It's a thing with the fire chief."

"A date?" My mouth betrayed me. "Never mind. It's none of my—"

"Fire safety content," Adrian interrupted quickly. "My manager hooked me up with a side gig while I'm here. It's another sponsorship."

A rush of relief swept through me. "Not a date?"

"No, just... they want the two of us on camera together, but it doesn't have to look like a date or anything. The pay's good, so I can cover your rate. And, uh... I appreciate the help." He paused. "Actually, fuck it. I don't need the help for this one, Maddox. Honestly, I just want to see you again. There. I said it. Feel free to back out. I wouldn't blame you."

Something in my chest took flight at his admission. "I'm not backing out. I..." I closed my eyes and blew out a breath. "I want to see you again, too."

The beat of silence on the other end made me squirm. But when his warm, easy voice came back on the line, it was worth the wait.

"You know, if you ever want to see me, Sullivan, all you have to do is ask. I guarantee the answer will be yes."

Thankfully, no one was around to see the stupid grin on my face. "I'll pick you up at six thirty. And maybe if you're lucky... I'll pack a toothbrush."

I ended the call to the sound of his laughter. I could tell he didn't believe me, that he was just humoring me. But I couldn't deny how good it had felt waking up next to his solid presence after my nightmare.

Obviously, I was scared shitless. But Maya was right. Adrian Hayes deserved to be loved. And part of me wanted him to feel less alone.

To know that at least one person out there was beginning to care for him very much.

Maybe a little too much.

#FireSafetyMyAss  #ToothbrushPacking  #DieHardDeprived #ScaredShitless

## 17

# #WANTSMORE

## ADRIAN

THE SERA HOLIDAY Bonfire was exactly the kind of picture-perfect winter event that would make my followers weep with envy. Golden firelight danced against snow-laden pine boughs, rustic log benches were arranged in perfect Instagram-worthy circles, and the scent of woodsmoke and pine hung in the crisp evening air like nature's own aromatherapy.

I reveled in wearing my own coat this time—a thrift shop favorite in navy wool with subtle copper threading that would photograph beautifully against the flames—and pulled out my phone to capture some establishing shots. The marshmallow roasting stations looked like something out of a holiday movie, complete with vintage-style wire baskets and glass jars of graham crackers that caught the firelight like amber.

"Flame-proof content for a flame-proof evening," I murmured to myself. Vic had been thrilled about this fire safety sponsorship —apparently, there was huge money to be made in creating educational content that didn't feel educational. And after seeing

Fire Chief Judd Kincaid's rugged headshot on the Legacy Fire Department website, I'd understood why.

The man was built like a lumberjack who moonlighted as a male model. All broad shoulders and serious jaw, with the kind of competent authority that made people want to follow his instructions. Even the fire safety ones.

But as I panned my phone across the gathering crowd, looking for the best lighting, my chest tightened with a familiar anxiety.

Maddox wasn't here yet.

He'd asked me to grab a ride out here with someone else when a family portrait session had gone long. Now, I was second-guessing his explanation, wondering if he'd show up at all or if this afternoon's easy phone conversation had been another one of his emotional false starts.

Before I could spiral, the fire chief met my eyes with a quirked eyebrow. I nodded and began recording.

"Alright, folks!" His deep voice cut through the chatter. "Gather round for your mandatory fun safety briefing!"

Judd stepped up onto a makeshift platform—actually just a wide slice of tree stump—and the crowd naturally gravitated toward him. He was even more impressive in person, all six-foot-something of him wrapped in official-looking navy gear that somehow made fire safety seem sexy.

"Rule number one," he announced, his voice carrying easily across the clearing. "Don't wave flaming marshmallows in your friends' faces unless you want to meet me again—at the ER."

A ripple of laughter went through the crowd. I refocused on my phone screen, caught off guard by how naturally charming he was. There was something disarming about his gruff earnestness, the way he managed to make fire safety feel like friendly advice from your favorite uncle rather than a lecture.

"Rule number two: if your marshmallow catches fire, don't panic. Blow it out gently. Don't wave it around like you're conducting the Mormon Tabernacle Choir." He demonstrated with a skewer, his expression deadpan. "This isn't the Fourth of July."

More laughter from the audience. I noticed several people—mostly women, but a few men, too—watching him with obvious appreciation. A couple near me whispered something about him being "the one who's always showing up at Timber with random safety inspections," which only made me more curious. Why did he and Alex seem to have it out for each other?

"And rule number three," Judd continued, scanning the crowd with mock seriousness. "If anyone tries to convince you that s'mores taste better when you char the marshmallow to a crisp, they're lying. That's not rustic or old-school; that's just bad technique."

I was so focused on filming his surprisingly engaging safety talk that I didn't notice the familiar presence behind me until a low voice murmured directly in my ear.

"Don't fall for the chief. He'll have you filling out safety inspection paperwork before taking you to bed."

My skin prickled at Maddox's proximity, the warmth of his breath against my neck. I turned to find him standing close enough that I could smell his soap and see the amusement dancing in his eyes. He looked relaxed in a way I hadn't seen before—no tension in his shoulders, no guarded expression. Just easy confidence and a hint of a smile that made my stomach flip.

"Jealous, Sullivan?" I whispered back, not bothering to hide my grin.

"Of a guy who's more likely to have spare fire blankets in his bedside table than toys or lube? Hardly." But his eyes stayed on me rather than the chief, and something warm unfurled in my chest.

Chief Kincaid wrapped up his talk to enthusiastic applause,

and the crowd began dispersing toward the various activity stations. Maddox produced a thermos from his jacket pocket, unscrewing the cap to release the scent of cinnamon and something stronger.

"Spiked cider," he explained, offering it to me. "Family recipe. Maya suggested you might need a little warming from the inside out."

Instead of making an inappropriate comment about another way he could warm me from the inside out, I accepted the thermos gratefully, taking a sip of what turned out to be the most perfect combination of apple, spices, and just enough whiskey to do exactly as promised. "Your sister has excellent taste in beverages."

"She has excellent taste in general," he replied, settling beside me on one of the log benches positioned near the main fire pit. "Which is why she's been insufferable about you since day one."

The casual admission caught me off guard. "Insufferable how?"

"Constantly reminding me that I'm an idiot for not being nicer to you. For..." He gestured vaguely between us, then reached for the bag of marshmallows on the table nearby.

"For?" I asked, accepting a skewer from him.

Maddox hesitated before flashing an unexpected smile. "For not teaching you proper s'mores technique. Watch and learn, city boy. Watch and learn."

Before I could call him out for avoiding the question, he was already moving toward the fire, positioning his marshmallow at the perfect distance from the flames.

I fumbled for my phone, suddenly needing the familiar comfort of creating content, and walked closer to the fire.

"Okay, everyone," I said to the camera, finding my professional voice. "Fire safety lesson number one: maintain proper distance between marshmallow and flame. As demonstrated by—"

"That's close enough. Try not to set yourself on fire, Hayes," Maddox called, noting my position. His voice carried a familiar note of fond exasperation.

I zoomed in on his face, catching his concentrated expression as he rotated his marshmallow with practiced precision. "As demonstrated by local s'mores expert and fire-safety know-it-all Maddox Sullivan."

"Some of us grew up around actual fire," he replied without looking away from his marshmallow. "Instead of gas fireplaces activated by wall switches."

"Hey, those wall switches are very complicated. There's an on position and an off position. Sometimes there's even a timer." I moved closer and held my own skewer toward the flames, immediately catching it on fire. "Shit!"

"Language," Maddox chided, but I could hear him trying not to laugh. "And blow it out gently. Don't—"

I waved the flaming marshmallow frantically, trying to extinguish it and only succeeding in creating a sticky, charred mess. The laughter finally escaped him—a rich, genuine sound that made my chest tight with something I didn't want to examine too closely.

"What the hell is going on over here?" Judd asked, moving swiftly to remove the skewer from my hand and stick it in the empty tin can at his feet to starve it of oxygen. "Did you even listen to a word I said? Are you demonstrating what *not* to do?"

I held back my laughter while trying not to notice Maddox's eyes dancing in smug satisfaction. "Sorry, Chief. I got carried away."

He narrowed his eyes at me. "You're putting people at risk because you can't put your phone down."

Alex Marian stepped forward, grabbing Judd's arm and trying to pull him away. "Hey! He was just trying to film content like *you* asked him to. Take it easy on the guy. It's not his fault you're impossible to please."

The chief's eyes snapped to Alex's and narrowed, causing a fuck-ton more sparks than my flaming marshmallow ever had. "Not sure you're the one who should be giving safety advice, Fire-bug," he growled.

Maddox met my eye and tilted his head over to the side. The two of us slowly backed away to another spot around the fire before either of the other men noticed we'd left.

"Jesus," I murmured, glancing back at them. "Are they going to fight or fuck?"

Maddox watched the two of them sparring. "This has been going on for months. Maybe it's just the way they are."

"Okay, take two," I announced to the camera, grabbing another marshmallow. "This time with adult supervision."

Maddox stepped behind me, his arms coming around to guide my hands on the skewer. The position was intimate enough that several people around the fire exchanged knowing looks, but I found I didn't care.

Maddox didn't seem to care either. His chest was solid against my back, his hands warm over mine as he helped me position the marshmallow at the optimal distance from the flames.

"Patience," he murmured near my ear. "Let it toast slowly. The goal is golden brown, not nuclear meltdown."

"I don't do patience well," I admitted, very aware of how perfectly I fit against him.

"I've noticed." His voice was dry, but his hands stayed steady over mine. "Just focus on the marshmallow. Stop thinking about the camera. Just be here."

I tried to follow his advice, watching the white surface gradually turn golden under the gentle heat. There was something meditative about it, the simple focus required to rotate the skewer slowly and evenly. For once, I wasn't thinking about angles or lighting or how many likes this would get.

"There," Maddox said quietly, his breath warm against my temple. "Perfect."

I turned in his arms to show him the perfectly toasted marshmallow, suddenly aware of how close we were. His eyes had gone dark in the firelight, and for a moment, I thought he might kiss me right there in front of half of Legacy's population.

Instead, someone nearby called out, "Hey, lovebirds, you heating up marshmallows or each other?"

We stepped apart quickly, both of us flushing.

I cleared my throat and held up my golden marshmallow triumphantly. "Can't we do both?"

The group around the fire erupted in laughter and good-natured whistles. Maddox rolled his eyes but was fighting a smile as he helped me assemble my s'more with graham crackers and chocolate.

We found a quieter spot on a bench slightly removed from the main crowd, close enough to feel the fire's warmth but far enough away for something resembling privacy. I put my phone away and just enjoyed the moment—the taste of perfectly melted chocolate and marshmallow, the sound of laughter and conversation around us, the solid presence of Maddox beside me.

"These things can be kind of a lot," he said suddenly, his voice quiet. "Everyone watching everyone else's business. But with you here, it's... not bad."

I looked at him in surprise. This was the first time he'd admitted to enjoying my company without immediately following it up with reasons why it was a terrible idea.

"Careful, Sullivan," I said, keeping my tone light even as something warm bloomed in my chest. "You're starting to sound like someone who likes me."

"Maybe I do." He met my eyes, and I saw something vulnerable there, something real. "Maybe that's not the worst thing in the world."

We sat in comfortable silence for a moment, shoulders touching, watching the fire pop and crackle. I wanted to say something meaningful, something that would capture how good this felt— this easy intimacy, this sense of belonging somewhere, with someone. But the words felt too big, too dangerous.

Instead, I bumped his shoulder gently with mine. "Thanks for helping me not burn down Legacy on my first fire safety assignment."

"Don't thank me yet," he replied, gesturing toward where Chief Kincaid was approaching with what looked like official paperwork. "Pretty sure you're about to get a lecture on proper marshmallow technique."

But Chief Kincaid just wanted to make sure I had everything I needed for my content, to thank me for promoting fire safety to my followers, and to apologize for snapping at me earlier. He was professional and friendly, but I found myself comparing his straightforward charm to Maddox's more complex appeal. The chief was undeniably attractive, but he didn't make my pulse race or my stomach flip the way Maddox did with just a glance.

The three of us moved back to the fire, slipping into professional mode long enough to film a few more clips with the chief about bonfire and backyard fire pit safety, indoor fireplace safety, and proper fire-extinguishing techniques.

After Kincaid thanked me and moved on to check on other guests, I noticed Maddox helping a little girl who'd panicked and dropped her skewer in the dirt when the logs on the fire popped and crackled.

He crouched down to her level, handed her a fresh marsh-mallow to try again, and stood beside her with his hand on the stick covering hers.

Without really thinking about it, I turned my camera back on.

"I know it looks scary," Maddox said, patiently soothing the girl's fears in a gentle voice that made something squeeze tight in my chest. "But we've got this. See? As long as we hold on tight and don't let go."

"The best lesson from tonight's adventure," I whispered softly, watching Maddox laugh at something the little girl said, his whole face transforming with genuine warmth. "Even when you're scared, hold tight and don't let go."

I clicked off the recording immediately, my cheeks burning hotter than the bonfire. That definitely wouldn't be going in the final edit, but I couldn't bring myself to delete it either.

Some fires, I was learning, were worth the risk of getting burned.

#FireSafetyAndFlirtation   #BonfireBanter   #SmoreThan-Friends #HeatingUp

## 18

# # COMEHOME

MADDOX

THE BONFIRE WAS WINDING DOWN, families with small kids heading home first, leaving the adults to nurse their spiked ciders and debate whether Chief Kincaid and Alex Marian were going to murder each other or make out behind the equipment shed.

My money was on the latter, based on the heated looks they'd been exchanging all evening.

I watched Adrian pack up his gear, noting the easy way he moved now compared to his first day in Legacy. Less stilted, more natural. He'd stopped checking his appearance in his phone screen every five minutes but somehow managed to look more gorgeous than ever. The fire had left his cheeks flushed and his eyes bright, and when he caught me staring, his grin was huge.

"Good content tonight," he said, slinging his bag over his shoulder. "Though I'm pretty sure the real story was whatever was happening between those two." He jerked his head toward where Kincaid and Alex were still engaged in what looked like the world's most sexually charged argument about... fire code violations?

"Legacy's worst-kept secret," I agreed, grabbing my thermos and the bag of leftover s'mores supplies Maya had insisted I bring home. "They've been circling each other like wolves for months."

Adrian fell into step beside me as we headed toward the parking area. The snow had picked up, fat flakes drifting down to catch in his hair and on his shoulders. Without thinking, I reached over to brush them away, my fingers lingering longer than necessary against the soft wool of his coat.

"So," I said, my voice coming out rougher than intended. "About that toothbrush..."

His eyebrows shot up. "Did you actually—"

"No." I hesitated. When his face fell, I quickly added, "Come home with me, Hayes. I mean, if you want. No pressure. Just..." I shrugged, trying for casual and probably failing. "I didn't pack a toothbrush because I wanted to invite you to my place. Maya's spending the night with Rosie again."

The smile that spread across his face was worth every moment of terror at putting myself out there. "You know you can't just leave if we're at your place."

*Yeah. I'm very much aware.*

"Shut up and get in the truck," I muttered, fighting a grin of my own.

The ride back to town from the SERA campus went by quickly. Adrian asked a lot of questions about the Slingshot Emergency Rescue Academy and the people who worked there.

When I'd gotten held up at the Hernandezes' photo shoot, Adrian had snagged a ride to the bonfire with one of the SERA instructors, and I could barely get a word in while he gushed about how nice the guy was.

"Foster Blake's dating someone," I warned. "Just so you know. A doctor. He was there, too. Blond guy, attractive. Was probably looking at Foster like the man invented cheese."

I could feel the heat of Adrian's stare on the side of my face. "Damn. And here I was hoping Foster could rail me later tonight."

I glanced over at him in time to catch him rolling his eyes, but he was also grinning at me. "Why are you smiling?" I grumbled. "I was trying to be polite by letting you know he's not available."

"How's it possible for you to deny you're interested in me but also be possessive of me? It boggles my fucking mind. But even more mind-boggling is the fact that… I'm kinda here for it."

My stomach tightened. "I'm interested in you," I admitted gruffly.

His laughter rang out in the truck's dim cab. "No shit, Maddie. Fuck. Sometimes I wonder if this would all be easier on you if I got you drunk first so you could stop overthinking. But that's a little fucking creepy."

When I pulled into the parking spot behind the store and turned to him, the laughter was still in his eyes, and his cheeks were still dusky from the time outside. "Don't need to get drunk to want you."

His smile softened. "Good to know. Maybe I'm the one who needs a little liquid courage. Gotta admit, I'm kind of expecting you're going to boot me out in a couple of hours."

Rather than giving him a promise I might not be able to keep, I hopped out of the truck and came around to take his hand. "C'mon, Hayes. I have all the liquid courage you need upstairs."

"That sounded dirty," he murmured, leaning in to bump my shoulder as we approached the back stairs. "But maybe I'm just keyed up enough to think everything sounds dirty right now."

The apartment felt different with Adrian in it. Smaller, some-how, but also more alive. I watched him take it all in—the exposed brick walls, the leather couch Dad had insisted was an investment piece, the bookshelves Maya had organized by color despite my protests. His gaze lingered on the family photos scattered throughout the space, and I found myself seeing the place through his eyes.

It wasn't much. A small, two-bedroom apartment above a hardware store, furnished with a mix of our family stuff and impulse purchases from garage sales. But it was ours. Maya's personality was all over it, from the colorful "temperature" blanket she'd crocheted with the folks at the yarn shop to the "World's Okayest Brother" mug on the dish mat by the sink to the purple "Future Husky" hoodie thrown over the arm of the sofa.

"This is perfect," Adrian said quietly, stopping in front of a framed photo of all four of us taken the Christmas before the accident. We were wearing matching plaid shirts—Mom's idea—and grinning like idiots in front of the store's holiday display. "You all look so happy."

"We were," I said, moving to stand beside him. "Mom insisted on the matching shirts every year. Said it was good for the Christmas card, but really, she just liked having us all coordinated like some kind of lumberjack boy band."

Adrian's laugh was soft. "I love that. The coordinated chaos of it all." He moved to another photo—Maya's acceptance of an academic award at last year's end-of-the-year ceremony. "She must be so excited about college."

"Terrified is more like it," I said, running a hand through my hair. "She's never been anywhere but Legacy. Sometimes I worry —" I caught myself before I could spiral into my usual anxiety about whether I was doing right by her, whether I was holding her back.

"Worry about what?"

I gestured vaguely around the apartment. "This isn't exactly preparing her for the real world. She's never lived in a big city, never had to navigate anything more complicated than Founder's Row on market day."

Adrian was quiet for a moment, studying Maya's photo. "You know what I see when I look at this?"

"What?"

"A kid who's confident enough to dream big because someone's always believed in her. That doesn't happen by accident, Maddox."

The simple certainty in his voice hit me harder than any grand speech could have. I cleared my throat, suddenly needing to move, to do something with my hands.

"Wine?" I offered, heading toward the small kitchen. "I've got a bottle of red that's supposedly decent. Gift from a customer who was grateful I carried the specific type of valve he needed for his old radiators."

"The glamorous life of a hardware store owner," Adrian teased, following me. But when I glanced back, his expression was warm, not mocking.

As I pulled down glasses and uncorked the wine, Adrian continued his gentle exploration. I watched from the corner of my eye as he noticed the box labeled "Mom's Christmas Stuff" tucked under the bench by the window, the stack of Maya's report cards held down by a paperweight shaped like a tiny hammer.

"Maddox," he said suddenly, his voice careful. "Can I ask you something?"

"Shoot."

"After your parents died, how did you manage it all? I mean, financially? Running the store, taking care of Maya..."

I paused, the wine bottle halfway to the glass. It wasn't a question I'd expected, and definitely not one I was comfortable answering. But something about the way he asked—not prying, just genuinely curious—made me tell the truth.

"I sold the house," I said finally, focusing on pouring the wine so I wouldn't have to meet his eyes. "The one we grew up in. It was too big, too many memories. Maya begged for a fresh start anyway. I think she felt like we were living in a cemetery.”

“And you?”

“I didn't mind it, but I was willing to do whatever would ease her grief.” I handed him his glass, our fingers brushing briefly. “With the money we got, I was able to pay off my parents’ debts, make this apartment livable, and put aside a little bit for Maya's college fund, too. And no, I *won't* put that money toward the business, no matter how badly we need it,” I added, just in case Adrian wanted to make any of the same arguments Maya had made when I'd told her about the money. “It's for her future. Our parents would have wanted it that way.”

Adrian set down his wine without taking a sip. “That's… god, Maddox. That's incredible.” He stepped closer, his eyes intent. “You gave up your childhood home to secure her future. That's huge.”

I shrugged, uncomfortable with the praise. “She's all the family I've got left. Anyone would—”

“Not everyone would,” Adrian interrupted gently. “Trust me on that.”

Something in his tone made me look at him more closely. There was a shadow in his expression, a hint of old hurt that made me want to pull him closer and demand names of whoever had failed to take care of him the way he deserved.

Instead, I reached up to touch his face, my thumb brushing across his cheekbone. “Talk to me,” I said gently, afraid of asking too much, too soon. “Tell me more about your family. You started to tell me the other night, but somehow, we got to talking about mine instead.”

He shrugged and smiled. “That might have been deliberate.”

“I figured. And I'm not falling for it a second time.” I nodded at the sofa and handed him back his glass of wine. As he passed the window, he glanced out at the square again.

"It's weird how quiet it gets here at night."

I watched him carefully. "You say that like it's a bad thing."

Adrian huffed a breath, not quite a laugh. "No. It's just... quiet feels different here. Not like in LA. There, it's more like... loneliness in a crowd. Here, it's—" He paused, brow furrowing. "It's full. Like the quiet means something."

I reached for his hand and pulled him toward the sofa. "That's the pine trees and generational trauma talking."

He smiled faintly. "Maybe."

A beat passed as we settled on the couch, bodies angled toward the dark fireplace. I reached for the remote and clicked it, watching the gas logs roar to life.

Adrian gasped and let out a choked laugh around the wine he'd just sipped. "J'accuse! You made fun of me for wall switches! How dare!"

I shrugged and grinned. "Maya had one condition on moving out of the house. She wanted a fireplace. Chief Kincaid and I had words about my options, and then he reminded me I could use the store's wholesale discount for it."

"Cheater," he murmured before taking another sip of wine.

"I prefer the term dream-fulfiller."

Adrian stared into the flames for a few minutes as the silence settled around us. "I used to think bonfires were trashy," he said after a minute. "Like, suburban dad energy. Oversized hoodies, red Solo cups, that sort of thing."

"And now?" I asked, eyes on him.

"Now I think I maybe missed something important." He tilted the glass in his hands, watching as the light sparkled off the burgundy wine. "We never had stuff like that growing up. No bonfires. No cocoa stands or community potlucks or town parades.

We had... galas. Brunches. Pressed napkins and catered shrimp towers."

I made a sound of encouragement.

Adrian shifted until his back was against the arm of the sofa and he was facing me. "I know I sound like an asshole, complaining about the fancy shit—"

"You don't," I said, voice low.

Adrian inhaled through his nose. "It's just... I don't know. I'm not saying I was neglected. I wasn't. Not in a way that counts. I had everything. Clothes, school, skiing in Stowe, and summers on the Cape. I just—" He shook his head, eyes flicking to the fire again. "My dad said I could absolutely be gay; I just needed to do it in private if I wanted to have a decent career. My mom once told me I'd never get anywhere with 'that tooth.' So I got braces for a third time. At sixteen. Even though the orthodontist tried telling them it wasn't easy to twist a tooth that was otherwise perfectly aligned."

He pointed to the crooked canine I already low-key had a crush on and tried for a laugh, but it came out too thin. "Isn't that fucked-up? That these stupid things bother me? Like... I didn't have it that bad. Nobody hit me, or screamed at me, or... or left."

I didn't speak, but my heart felt like it was being shredded. I reached my hand out and slipped it into his and squeezed.

"I've told myself for years it wasn't that bad," Adrian whispered. "Because it wasn't. I just don't... remember being anyone's favorite. Ever."

Adrian's admission was devastating because I imagined they represented an all-too-common experience. The fact that Adrian had experienced it made me want to fly to Connecticut and hunt down his fucking parents.

I set my glass down and shifted closer. My voice was rough around the edges when I spoke. "That's a wound no one allows you to claim," I told him softly. "And it breaks my fucking heart, Adrian."

Adrian's throat worked as he tried to swallow.

"You deserved more than being the good-looking accessory in a Christmas card," I continued. "You deserved to be loud and messy and loved anyway. You deserved someone who looked at you and thought, 'That one's mine.'"

Adrian blinked hard.

I squeezed his hand and cupped his cheek before leaning forward to press a kiss to his lips. Gentle. Solid. *Real.*

"You're still trying to be so good for everyone," I murmured, pulling back only enough to meet his eyes. "You're perfect just as you are, Adrian. Messy and real. Crooked tooth, weird oat milk fixation, and all."

He sniffled and grinned, reaching out to poke me between the ribs. "Jackass. Sadie doesn't think my oat milk fixation is weird. She said lots of her customers have been using that creamer since she started buying it for me."

I caressed his cheek with my thumb again before moving my thumb to lift his upper lip, exposing his crooked canine. "Do you know that the first time we met, I kind of, sort of had a thing for this tooth?"

"Liar."

"It's true. I thought it made you perfectly imperfect. I would imagine if you were able to fix it, you wouldn't look like yourself anymore. You'd look like all the other pretty boys on socials. Boring."

"Keep lying," he teased, though his voice sounded rough. "I like it."

I tilted his chin until he met my eyes. "Anyone who makes you feel small for wanting to be loved, to be chosen—they're the broken ones. Not you."

Adrian's voice was hoarse when it came. "Stop saying nice shit, or I won't leave before morning."

I grinned. "Not letting you leave before morning. Did I mention I also get a wholesale discount on chains?"

The air between us shifted, the gentle intimacy of the conversation bleeding into something more charged. Adrian's gaze dropped to my mouth, and I felt that familiar pull, the gravity that seemed to exist between us.

"Adrian," I said, my voice rougher than I intended.

"Yeah?"

Instead of answering with words, I closed the distance between us, capturing his mouth with mine. This kiss was different from the desperate hunger we'd shared before—slower, more deliberate. Like we had all the time in the world to explore each other, to learn the taste and texture of want without the fear of interruption.

Adrian's hands fisted in my flannel, pulling me closer as he deepened the kiss. I could taste the lingering sweetness of marshmallow on his tongue, could feel the wine-warm heat of his mouth against mine. When we finally broke apart, both breathing hard, his eyes were dark with desire.

"Bedroom?" I asked, the word coming out somewhere between a question and a plea.

"God, yes."

My bedroom was as simple as the rest of the apartment—a queen bed with a quilt Maya had given me for Christmas the year before, a dresser that had belonged to my grandfather, windows that looked out over Founder's Row and the square. Nothing fancy, nothing designed to impress. Just the space where I slept and read and tried not to think too hard about the future.

But with Adrian in it, the room felt transformed. He moved to the window first, looking out at the snow-covered street below.

"I can see the gallery from here," he said softly. "And the café. It's like having the whole town as your backyard."

"Sometimes it feels more like a fishbowl," I admitted, moving to stand behind him. "Everyone knows everyone's business. Everyone has opinions about how you should live your life."

"Is that why you've been so resistant? To this?" He leaned back against my chest, and I wrapped my arms around him instinctively.

"Partly." I pressed my face into his hair, breathing in the scent of him—expensive shampoo and woodsmoke and something that was purely Adrian. "Small towns have long memories. If I let myself care about you and you leave..."

"Everyone will know," he finished quietly.

"Everyone will know I was stupid enough to fall for someone whose whole life is about leaving."

Adrian turned in my arms, his expression serious. "What if I told you I'm not sure I want to leave?"

My heart stuttered, hope and terror warring in my chest. I swallowed hard. "What if... what if I told you that scares me more than you leaving?"

"Why?"

"Because wanting you to stay feels selfish as hell. You've got this whole life, this career, this world that's bigger than Legacy could ever be. What right do I have to ask you to give that up?"

Adrian's hands came up to frame my face, his thumbs stroking across my cheekbones. "What if you weren't asking? What if I wanted to give it up? What if I wanted something solid and real instead of shallow and empty?"

Before I could answer—before I could find words for the storm of emotions his question unleashed—he kissed me again. This time, there was desperation in it, a need that went beyond physical desire. It was the kiss of someone trying to say with his body what his words couldn't quite capture.

I kissed him back with everything I had, pouring years of loneliness and want and careful distance into the connection between us. My hands found the hem of his sweater, tugging it up and over his head. He was beautiful in the lamplight, all lean muscle and smooth skin, and I took a moment just to look at him.

"You're staring," he said, but there was no self-consciousness in it. Just warm amusement.

"Can you blame me?"

Adrian responded by reaching for my flannel, working the buttons open with steady fingers. When his hands spread across my chest, I had to close my eyes against the intensity of it—not just the physical sensation, but the emotional weight of being seen, being touched, being wanted.

"Maddox," he whispered, my name carrying words unspoken.

We moved to the bed slowly, taking time to explore and relish. This wasn't the desperate fucking of our first time or the hungry reclamation of the cabin. This was something else entirely—a conversation conducted in touches and sighs, in the press of skin against skin and the soft sounds of pleasure.

Adrian lay back against the quilt, legs parted, eyes wide and dark with want but also trust. Trust I didn't take lightly.

I took my time prepping him—tracing every line of him, coaxing him open with slow fingers and slick warmth. Teasing and tantalizing until he couldn't remember his own fucking name.

I didn't rush it. Didn't want to. There was something sacred about it, the way Adrian's body gave way to mine inch by inch, the way he gasped when I curved my finger just right, when I kissed the inside of his thigh like it was something meant to be tasted, savored.

"You always this thorough?" he asked, voice wrecked and teasing.

"Only when it matters," I murmured, twisting my wrist just enough to make him shudder.

His breathy whimper made my cock leak and my balls tighten. I felt like I was halfway there just from edging him. "Jesus fuck. You're gonna make me come just watching you," I admitted in a low growl.

By the time I was ready to press inside his body, he was soft and flushed and ready for me—his breath shaky, his hands clenching the sheets, his whole body humming with need.

I paused, one hand on his hip, the other cupping his jaw. "Tell me you're okay."

"Better than okay," he said, eyes searching mine. "Just... don't stop touching me."

Never planned to.

When I finally moved inside him, both of us slick with sweat and shaking with need, it felt like coming home. Not to a place but to a person.

"Stay," I whispered against Adrian's neck as he moved beneath me, his hands gripping my shoulders like I was his anchor. "Stay with me."

"I'm here," he gasped, misunderstanding. "I'm not going anywhere."

I meant more than just tonight, and I think he knew it. The words hung between us as we moved together, building toward something that felt too big for my small apartment, too real for the careful distance I'd been trying to maintain.

When Adrian cried out my name as he came, arching beneath me with an abandon that stole my breath, I followed him over the edge with an intensity that left me shaking. We collapsed together in a tangle of limbs and racing hearts, both too overwhelmed to speak.

Later, as he dozed against my chest, I stared at the ceiling and tried to process what had happened. Not just the sex—though that had been incredible—but the shift in what this was between us. The way he'd looked at me, confided in me, responded to me. Like I was something precious and trustworthy instead of convenient and fleeting.

His phone buzzed from somewhere in the pile of discarded clothes, probably another message from his manager or a notification about his social media. But he didn't move to check it, just burrowed deeper against my side with a soft sigh.

I'd planned to keep my distance, to enjoy whatever this was while it lasted without getting attached. But right now, with Adrian Hayes sleeping in my bed, wearing nothing but my old flannel sheets and the scent of our lovemaking, I realized I'd failed spectacularly.

I was already attached. Already imagining mornings that started with his sleep-warm body against mine, evenings that ended with his laughter filling my quiet apartment.

Already dreading the day he'd realize Legacy and I weren't enough for him.

The snow continued to fall outside my windows, the flakes randomly catching the sparse moonlight. In a few hours, the town would wake up to another perfect winter morning, and Adrian would probably remember all the reasons why staying was impossible.

But for now, he was here. Real and warm and *mine*, even if it was only temporary.

I tightened my arms around him and tried not to think about tomorrow.

#ToothCrush #DiscountChains #ComeInside #Mine

19

# #DEALSORFEELZ

## ADRIAN

I woke up in stages—first to the sensation of warmth, then to the soft rasp of the world's scratchiest sheets against my skin, and finally to the realization that it was Maddox Sullivan's chest hair tickling my cheek in the most perfect way imaginable.

Snow fell steadily outside the bedroom window, muffling the sounds of Legacy waking up. The only noise was the distant hum of the hardware store's ancient heating system and Maddox's steady breathing beneath my ear. His arm was wrapped around my waist, holding me against him like I might disappear if he loosened his grip.

I didn't want to move. Didn't want to break whatever spell had been cast over this small apartment above Sullivan Hardware, where mismatched furniture somehow felt more welcoming than any five-star hotel I'd ever stayed in. Where the scent of cedar soap and coffee and something indefinably Maddox made me feel safer than I could remember feeling in years.

This was what I'd been missing in my life. Not just the sex—though Christ, that had been incredible—but this. The quiet intimacy of shared space. The weight of another person's arm around me, keeping me tethered to something real.

It had been seven days since the first time I'd shared this bed with him. Seven days since the night he'd invited me into his home and into his life.

In that time, we'd filmed four more dates for the project—including ice skating with Fannin (Maddox's least favorite date), cookie making (Maya's favorite), the barn dance at Nate's place (my favorite because he'd been possessive as fuck), and Sullivan Hardware's Holiday Open House just last night, where I'd been volun-told to play Santa for the kids in full beard and padding (which made it Maddox's favorite).

Almost every night, we ended up together at his place or mine.

Maya was insufferably smug these days, but I'd overheard Maddox reminding her several times that this was only temporary.

*Only temporary.*

While the words were true—if I stuck to my original plan, I'd be leaving in just three days—the reminder had stung every time. With each passing day, I felt more and more at home in this quirky little town and with this warm, down-to-earth family.

Maddox stirred, his hand moving to brush across my cheek. "Morning, Santa," he murmured, his voice rough with sleep.

I tilted my head to look at him. His dark hair was standing up at odd angles, and there was a crease from the pillow across his left cheek. He looked rumpled and warm and completely open. Not a wall in sight.

"Morning," I whispered back, not wanting to break the spell of quiet that surrounded us.

He leaned down to press a soft kiss to the top of my head, and I felt myself melt into even more of a ridiculous puddle than I already was.

"Coffee?" he asked, shifting to sit up.

"Only if you promise not to judge my inability to function before I get it down."

"Wouldn't dream of it, city boy. This isn't my first morning serving at the pleasure of Adrian Hayes's caffeine addiction."

Twenty minutes later, we were in his small kitchen, moving around each other with surprising ease. He handed me a mug that read "Duct Tape Saves Lives," while he claimed one that said "I survived driving school. As the teacher."

"Is that yours, or was it your parents'?" I asked, accepting the perfectly brewed coffee with gratitude.

"Mine. I will forever carry the scars from teaching my sister how to drive." Maddox moved to the small stove, already reaching for eggs from the refrigerator. "We finally have some time for me to make you breakfast instead of grabbing something at the Pinecone."

"You going to cook for me, Sullivan?"

"Only if you like eggs," he said with a wink. "Fair warning: I'm about to show off."

I leaned against the counter, content to watch him work. True to his word, he flipped the eggs with unnecessary flair, sending them spinning in the air before catching them perfectly in the pan.

"The man has hidden talents," I accused, grinning into my coffee.

"Years of practice. Dad used to do the same thing every Sunday morning." His smile softened at the memory. "Maya always insisted he was going to drop them on the floor eventually, but he never did."

I moved to the toaster, determined to contribute something to our breakfast. "Well, prepare to be equally impressed by my toast-making skills."

"This should be good," Maddox said, not even trying to hide his amusement. "Do you remember what Chief Kincaid taught you last week about fire safety? Do you need me to pull up the footage?"

Five minutes later, the smoke alarm was going off, and I was staring at two pieces of what could generously be called charcoal.

"Nailed it," I announced, waving a dish towel at the alarm until it stopped shrieking.

Maddox's laughter filled the small kitchen. "You're a disaster, Hayes."

"A very sexy disaster," I corrected, moving to wrap my arms around his waist from behind. "Besides, now you get to rescue me with your superior bread-toasting abilities."

"My hero complex thanks you for the opportunity," he said, leaning back against me.

For a moment, I let myself imagine this being routine. Waking up tangled together every morning. Burning toast while he made perfect eggs. Fighting over who got the last of the coffee. It felt so natural, so right, that the wanting of it was almost painful.

I'd never had anything like this. But I'd dreamed about it for a very long time.

The fantasy was interrupted by the sharp buzz of my phone from the bedroom. I ignored it, pressing my face into the space between Maddox's shoulder blades and breathing in the scent of his skin.

The phone buzzed again. Then again.

"You should probably get that," Maddox said gently. It wasn't the first time he'd pointed out messages I'd tried my best to ignore. I'd been blowing off many of my responsibilities, including updates from Vic, for days now. Reality had no place here in my winter fantasyland.

"It can wait." But even as I said it, it buzzed again. And again.

My phone only went off like that for emergencies or career opportunities. Given that I was three thousand miles from any emergencies, it had to be the latter.

The thought made my stomach clench.

"Go," Maddox said, turning in my arms to kiss my forehead. "I'll rescue the toast situation. But first—" He gestured toward the kitchen window, where a large box truck had just pulled up. "Looks like we've got an unexpected delivery downstairs. Give me ten minutes?"

I nodded, watching him grab his phone and disappear down the stairs. As soon as he was gone, I padded to the bedroom and picked up my phone with the same enthusiasm I'd have for handling a live snake.

Seven missed calls from Vic. Twelve text messages. And one email marked "URGENT" from Nordique's marketing director.

My hands were shaking as I opened Vic's most recent text:

> **VIC**
>
> CALL ME NOW. This is it, babe. This is everything we've been working for.

I hit his number before I could talk myself out of it.

"Adrian! Jesus, I thought you'd fallen off a mountain or something." Vic's voice was practically vibrating with excitement. "Tell me you're sitting down."

"I'm standing. Just tell me."

"Nordique wants to lock you in for a year-long exclusive deal. Global campaigns, resort partnerships, the works. But that's not even the big news."

I sank onto the edge of the bed, Maddox's scent still clinging to the rumpled sheets. "What's the big news?"

"The Solenne Collection wants you as their global brand ambassador. Permanent position, Adrian. Not a campaign—a career. Luxury hotels worldwide, first-class everything, unlimited travel budget. They're calling it 'Elevated Wandering,' and they want your face on it."

The words hit me like a physical blow. This was it. This was everything I'd worked for, everything I'd built my entire adult life around. Global recognition. Financial security. The kind of career that most influencers could only dream of.

"They want an answer by Friday," Vic continued. "Which gives us time to negotiate terms, but Adrian... this is life-changing money. This is a legacy-building opportunity. You'd be everywhere."

*Everywhere.*

I looked around Maddox's small bedroom—at the quilt his sister had picked out for him, at the photo of his parents on the nightstand, at the view of Founder's Row covered in fresh snow and the few eager holiday shoppers already wandering along the shoveled sidewalks. This quiet, simple life that had somehow started to feel more real than anything I'd experienced in years.

"Adrian? You still there?"

"Yeah," I managed. "I'm here."

"This is what we worked so hard for," Vic said, his voice softer now. "All those years of grinding, of building your platform, of proving yourself. This is why we did it."

I didn't love his easy use of the term "we." Yes, he'd worked hard to procure many of my gigs, but I'd been the one to miss a connecting flight to Paris during a torrential rainstorm in Amsterdam, try to find an urgent care in Puerto Vallarta when I was sick with the flu, and get hit on by an aggressive hotel manager in Miami. All while *#KeepingItReal*.

The truth was, this job was a lot. Traveling all the time was exhausting. Social media followers were fickle. And platform algorithms were constantly changing.

But this *was* my job. Vic was right. I'd worked damned hard to be successful at it. And now, I'd finally gotten the recognition I'd wanted.

"Thanks, Vic," I said, meaning it. "I... I'll get back to you. I'm not sure what, ah... direction I want to go in."

After I hung up on his squawked response, I walked slowly through Maddox's apartment, seeing it with new eyes. Everything here told a story—a small collection of hand-carved animals his grandfather had made him lined up on a shelf, one with a broken ear that someone had lovingly glued back together. A photo of Maddox holding a much younger Maya at what looked like a fall festival, cotton candy in her hand, both of them grinning at the camera. A stack of books on wilderness photography next to a collection of Maya's honor roll certificates and something that looked like a little pot of lip balm imprinted with "LHS Band" on the cap.

A life in Legacy wasn't what I'd imagined for myself. It wasn't glamorous or globe-spanning or always Instagram-worthy. But I liked who I was here. I liked the man who bragged about his eggs and worked two jobs just to keep his own dream alive. I liked feeling wanted for something other than my follower count or my ability to make luxury brands look aspirational.

I picked up a small wooden horse from the little animal collection, turning it over in my hands. It was imperfect—the proportions slightly off, one leg shorter than the others—but it had been made with love. You could see it in every careful detail, every smoothed curve.

A banded stack of envelopes on Maddox's desk caught my eye, the paper inside the top one a light red. A note on the outside in his careful handwriting read, "To be paid Jan 1." I almost picked it up—almost gave in to the curiosity—but stopped myself. Whatever it was, it wasn't mine to know. Not yet. Maybe not ever.

The sound of boots on the stairs announced Maddox's return. I quickly set down the horse and moved back to the kitchen, where he appeared a few minutes later with the scent of winter air and the familiar sawdust smell of the hardware store wafting in alongside him.

"Another shipment of Christmas lights," he announced, moving to wash his hands at the sink while talking to me over his shoulder. "Thanks to you, that makes three more reorders we've gone through since the videos you posted decorating the tree. Even Kev Petersen bought another set, and he already has enough lights on his house to attract visitors from outer space. Also, Maya called and begged me to bring you to the 'impromptu' snowball fight that always happens around this time at the ballfields. She said, and I quote, 'It'll make for prime reels. Tell Adrian.' What do you say? You up for getting your ass kicked and your fancy clothes messed up?"

I watched Maddox at the sink, noting the careful way he cleaned each finger, the competence in his movements. Everything about him was so solid, so rooted. The exact opposite of my carefully curated nomadic existence.

"Yeah, sure. Sounds good."

"You've got that look," he said, drying his hands and turning to face me.

"What look?"

"The one you get when you're thinking hard about something." Maddox moved closer, concern flickering in his eyes. "Everything okay?"

I could tell him. *Should* tell him. About the call, about the opportunity, about the choice I suddenly faced. But looking at him —hair still mussed from sleep, flannel shirt soft from years of washing, eyes warm with affection—I couldn't bring myself to shatter this perfect morning with the weight of reality. With the confirmation that what was holding him back was possibly imminent.

Instead, I kissed him. Soft and sweet and desperate, pouring all my conflicted feelings into the connection between us. He responded immediately, his hands coming up to frame my face, and for a moment, the outside world ceased to exist.

"Toast trauma," I said when we broke apart, forcing lightness into my voice. "The usual."

"Right." His smile was skeptical but fond. "Let me guess—you burned it on purpose so I'd pity-feed you again."

"Obviously. Gotta stay on brand." I managed a grin that felt only slightly forced. "Can't let you think I'm actually competent at anything domestic."

"Ah, weaponized incompetence," he murmured, pulling me close again. "My love language."

I let myself sink into his embrace, memorizing the feel of his arms around me, the steady beat of his heart against my chest. In a few days, I'd have to make a decision that would change everything. But not right now. Right now, I could pretend that the only choice I had to make was what to have for lunch.

"So," I said, pulling back enough to meet his eyes. "What's the plan for Date Ten?"

I kept waiting for him to mention the romantic date he owed me after losing our bet, but he hadn't brought it up all week, and I found myself reluctant to remind him. Was the pressure of planning it too much? Was Maddox hoping I'd forget about it? Did it make our "temporary" thing feel too real?

"Snowball fight and stolen kisses," he replied, interrupting my wayward thoughts. "Maybe some hot chocolate afterward if you haven't already drowned in the stuff. You in?"

"I'm all in," I said and meant it with every fiber of my being.

He grinned, the expression transforming his face from merely handsome to absolutely devastating. "Good. Because Maya's been planning our defeat since yesterday. She has strategies, Adrian. Actual battle plans."

"Bring it on," I laughed. "I'll have you know I was the reigning snowball champion of my prep school. Three years running."

"Prep school snowball fights don't count. This is mountain warfare, city boy. You're not ready."

As he pulled me toward the bedroom to get dressed, I caught sight of my phone on the nightstand. Before I could second-guess myself, I grabbed it and fired off a quick text to Vic:

> Not no. Just… give me some time.

His response was immediate.

VIC
> How much time?

I looked at Maddox, who was now digging through his dresser for what appeared to be thermal underwear, muttering something about Maya's ruthless approach to winter combat. He caught me watching and winked, completely unaware that my entire future was balanced on a knife's edge.

> You said we have until Friday, right? I'll let you know by then.

I turned off my phone and tossed it onto the bed. Whatever happened, whatever choice I ultimately made, I needed this. One perfect snowball fight. One afternoon of stolen kisses and hot chocolate.

One day to pretend the only thing that mattered was the way Maddox Sullivan looked at me like I was something precious and worth keeping.

Outside, the snow continued to fall, blanketing Legacy in pristine white.

And for now, that was enough.

#ToastTrauma  #SolenneOrSullivan  #StayOrGo  #OneMoreSnowDay

**20**

# #SNOWMUCHTOHOPEFOR

## MADDOX

THE LEGACY COMMUNITY Ball Park looked like it had been taken over by an elite alpine warfare regiment. If the regiment had been run by five-year-olds with a sugar kink.

The SERA team had transformed the place into what could only be described as organized chaos—thermoses of hot cocoa and bags of leftover marshmallows and candy canes were lined up on picnic tables like soldiers, hastily built snow forts lay scattered across the field, and the sound of laughter echoed off the mountain beyond us.

I stood at the edge of the parking lot, camera bag slung over my shoulder, taking in the scene. Foster Blake, his boyfriend, Tommy, and a couple of the SERA guys were already locked in a heated battle with some of the high school kids, while Rosie Marian directed traffic like a tiny, bossy general in a purple parka.

And there, right in the middle of it all, was Adrian Hayes.

He was wearing what he claimed was the latest craze in winter hats—a "Nordique Chasseur with ultra-luxe earflap detailing" that would have made anyone else look like a cross between Sherlock Holmes and Kyle from *South Park* but somehow just made Adrian look hotter.

He shrieked with laughter as someone nailed him square in the ribs with a perfectly aimed snowball, and something inside my chest loosened, a knot I hadn't even realized was there unraveling as I watched him stumble backward, arms windmilling dramatically before he toppled into a snowbank. His hat popped off and he laughed again, clear and bright.

God help me, but I could see it. All of it. Family holidays with Maya rolling her eyes at our ridiculous snowball fights. Lazy Sunday mornings with Adrian wrapped in one of my old flannels, complaining about the coffee while secretly loving every minute of it. Hot cocoa by the fire after days like this, his cold feet pressed against my calves under a blanket.

A life that felt full instead of just functional.

"Maddox!" Maya's voice cut through my daydreaming. "Get your ass over here! We're picking teams, and I refuse to be stuck with Adrian. He's already proven he can't throw for shit."

"I heard that!" Adrian called from where he was attempting to extract his hat from the snowbank and jam it back on his head. "And for the record, that was a tactical retreat!"

"Your tactical retreat looked a lot like getting your fancy ass handed to you," Maya shot back, grinning wickedly.

I made my way across the field, dodging stray snowballs and trying not to smile too obviously at the banter flying between them. They'd developed an easy sibling-like relationship over the past week, all affectionate insults and shared conspiratorial looks. It made that distracting wanting in my chest grow even stronger.

"Alright, alright," I announced, setting down my camera bag and pulling out the equipment. "Before anyone gets seriously injured, let me get some footage. This is supposed to be content, remember?"

"Buzzkill," Rosie muttered, but she was already posing dramatically with a snowball cocked and ready to throw.

I spent the next twenty minutes capturing what had to be some of the most genuine content Adrian had ever been part of. No careful poses or strategic lighting—just pure, unfiltered fun. Adrian getting absolutely demolished by a fourteen-year-old's surprise attack. Maya building a snow fortress that would make military engineers weep with pride. Foster and his boyfriend Tommy engaging in what could only be described as indecent snowball warfare.

"Teams!" Maya announced once I'd gotten enough establishing shots. "Maddox, you're with me, Rosie, Robyn, and Foster. Adrian gets Alex, Tommy, Jasper, and..." She scanned the group. "Marco, if he ever shows up from that emergency call."

"This seems deeply unfair," Adrian protested, brushing snow off his absurdly expensive jacket. "I'm being discriminated against for my obvious athletic superiority."

"Your what now?" I couldn't help asking.

"I told you I was a three-time prep school snowball champion," he said with mock dignity. "Remember? I'll have you know these hands are weapons of mass winter destruction."

The laughter that escaped me was unexpected, and I saw Adrian's expression soften as he caught it. There was something in his eyes—warm and pleased and just a little sad—that made my chest tighten.

"Weapons of mass destruction," Rosie repeated flatly. "Right. This'll be good."

What followed was thirty minutes of the most ridiculous winter combat I'd ever witnessed. Adrian turned out to be surprisingly scrappy, diving behind snow forts and pop-up attacking with gleeful abandon. His form was terrible, his aim was questionable, and his hat was downright ridiculous, but his enthusiasm more than made up for it.

The best moment came when Foster managed to nail Adrian right between the shoulder blades with a perfectly packed snowball. Instead of just stumbling, Adrian threw himself forward with the drama of a Shakespearean actor, arms spread wide as he collapsed face-first into the snow.

"I'm hit!" he cried, voice muffled by the snow. "Tell my followers... tell them I died as I lived... extremely photogenic!"

I was laughing so hard I nearly dropped my camera. This ridiculous, dramatic, beautiful man was lying spread-eagle in a snowbank, making death rattles for the entertainment of a bunch of small-town locals, and I was completely gone for him.

"You're supposed to be filming this!" Maya scolded, but she was laughing too hard to sound serious.

"Can't film when I'm busy watching Adrian's Oscar-worthy death scene," I managed, wiping tears from my eyes.

Adrian lifted his head just enough to shoot me a snow-covered grin. "Did I mention I was also in the drama club?"

"Of course you were," I said, offering him a hand up. When he took it, his fingers lingered against mine just long enough to send heat shooting up my arm despite the cold.

"You okay?" I asked softly, brushing snow from his cheek.

"Better than okay," he replied, and something in his voice made me want to pull him closer, crowd him against the nearest tree, and kiss him until neither of us could think straight.

Instead, I settled for letting my hand rest on his waist a beat longer than necessary, my thumb brushing against the strip of skin where his jacket had ridden up.

"Ugh, gross," Maya announced from across the field. "Get a room!"

"We're literally standing in a public park," Adrian called back.

"Then get a tent!"

After the snowball war ended in what could generously be called a draw—mostly because everyone was too cold and too covered in snow to keep accurate score—Maya suggested we build a snowman.

"You go ahead," I said. "I'm way too cold. These hands are begging for hot chocolate."

Adrian held up his own hands, showing his damp gloves. His hat was missing—probably buried in a snowbank, thanks to his dramatic performance. "These hands are begging for something too," he said in a low voice. He bounced his eyebrows at me and opened and closed his fingers as if trying to grab me.

His gloves were trashed. I reached out to grab them and began pulling them off. "Give me these. You can wear mine. They're nice and warm."

Adrian looked at me with heart eyes, but before he could say anything, Maya shuddered dramatically. "Ew! I changed my mind about matchmaking the two of you. You're super cringe."

I began laughing again—that helpless laughter that seemed to happen more and more around Adrian. When I caught him watching me with another soft smile, my heart did something complicated in my chest.

"What?" I asked.

"Nothing," he said, but he was already pulling out his phone. "Just... you should smile like that more."

He showed me the photo he'd captured—me mid-laugh, covered in snow, completely relaxed in a way I hadn't seen myself in years.

"You look free," Adrian said quietly.

The words hit me harder than they should have.

*Free.*

When was the last time I'd felt free? Not just from responsibility or obligation, but free to want something for myself? Free to imagine a future that included more than just surviving day to day?

"C'mere," I said, grabbing his hand and towing him toward my truck.

We sat on the tailgate, legs swinging, sharing a thermos of cocoa that was spiked with enough peppermint schnapps to warm us from the inside out. The rest of the group was focused on building the world's gayest snowman, their laughter carrying across the field.

"Today was good," I said, my knee bumping against Adrian's. "Really good."

"Yeah?"

"Yeah." I turned to look at him, noting the way the cold had flushed his cheeks, how his hair was sticking up at odd angles from his hat. He was beautiful, but more than that, he was *here*. Present and real and mine...

At least for now.

"You're good for me, Adrian. This... whatever this is between us. I want it."

Something flickered across his face—pleasure, but also something that looked almost like pain.

"You okay?" I asked, reaching out to touch his cheek.

"Just tired," he said, but his smile didn't quite reach his eyes. "Too much hot chocolate, not enough sleep."

It was true we hadn't gotten much sleep last night. Every time we drifted off, one of us would shift and wake the other, and then wandering hands would turn into another heated encounter until the sheets were on the floor and our breath fogged the windows by my bed. It was like we were caught in an unspoken race against time, trying to wring every last drop of happiness from the moments we spent together.

But whatever was troubling Adrian now seemed like something more. Something different.

Before I could question him further, Maya called us back over to help with some finishing touches on our snow sculpture, and the rest of the afternoon passed in a blur of laughter and stolen touches.

Later, we separated only long enough to shower and change before I dropped Maya off at a friend's and picked Adrian up for his eleventh date, this one for a drinks tasting at Timber.

Alex Marian had come up with several options, including a whiskey flight, several wine flights, and a holiday-themed cocktail flight. The plan was for us to walk over to Timber and for Adrian to come back to my place afterward so neither of us had to drive after drinking.

When he got in the truck, I was shocked to see him wearing one of my flannel shirts.

"Speechless," he said with a chuckle. "Who knew all it took to get you to stop grumbling was to steal the shirt off your back."

The wash-worn flannel was a plaid mix of red, green, and cream. He'd rolled up the sleeves, exposing strong forearms sprinkled with golden-blond hair. "You look…" I swallowed. "Holy fuck. Can we go inside for a minute?"

His eyes danced in the dashboard lights. "We can't be late for the tasting. Alex said he was mixing up something special for me."

"I'll mix something special for you," I teased as I leaned forward and grabbed the back of his head, pulling him in for a hard kiss across the center console. When I finally let him go, I kept him close and leaned our foreheads together. "Not that I don't want to eat you in that shirt, but I thought you were supposed to wear Nordique stuff."

"You might not like this answer," Adrian warned, pulling on his seatbelt. "But one of Nordique's marketing campaigns is about 'elevating the everyday,' meaning you can use a few of their statement pieces to make your regular shit look better."

"Regular shit," I repeated, not offended in the least since I didn't give a single fuck about fashion. "Nice."

His grin showed he knew exactly how little I cared. "For instance, I'm wearing a Skog henley under your flannel in the perfect Glacier Milk colorway. I'm also sporting Vinter Denim, and when you see how these jeans hug my ass, you're suddenly going to care very much about my elevated assets."

I snuck an appreciative glance at him, noticing a few thin leather bands snapped around one wrist, as well as a coordinated leather thong around his throat with a silver pendant hanging just at the dip between his collarbones.

My own jeans were suddenly too snug, so I shifted in my seat uncomfortably. "Oh."

The warmth of his laughter made me close my eyes and breathe him in. "You okay over there, Sullivan?"

"No," I admitted. "In fact, I can go ahead and say I appreciate your elevated assets now. But I have to admit I'd appreciate them more if you were buck naked and Nordique was nowhere in sight."

I kissed him hard again before finally shifting the truck into gear and backing out of the driveway. Despite having a reversing camera, I turned and did it the old-school way with my arm behind his seat and my head turned close to his.

I could smell the fancy cologne scent of him, only this time it was mixed with my own laundry detergent, which made me wonder what my bed smelled like now that he'd slept in it with me.

My voice sounded strangely rough when I spoke. "We make this short and sweet, yes? Try a few drinks and head back to my place? I promise to let you have as many drinks as you want after that."

The edge of Adrian's lips curled up. "You gonna get me drunk, Maddie?"

"If that's what it takes to get you into bed," I teased. "I'm not above a few dirty tricks."

I reached out to crank the blower higher because our combined body heat was already fogging up the windows. Outside, the last tinges of dusk turned the snowbanks lining the road a glowing pink as my tires crunched down the road to town, and Billie Holiday's voice on the radio sang "I've Got My Love to Keep Me Warm."

"My, my, how you've changed," Adrian joked. "Aren't you the same man who insisted he wasn't interested in anything I had to offer?"

I sucked in a breath before letting it out slowly. "I may have been... reluctant to admit that I was into you at first."

His bark of laughter made me jump. "Hoo boy. You are a riot, Sullivan. Reluctant to admit you were into me? You don't say."

"Alright, alright. Keep your pants on," I grumbled around a smile. "I told you I had reasons."

"Mmhm."

I turned to look at him and saw him smiling out the passenger window. After reaching across the console for his hand, I said, "I don't actually want you to keep your pants on."

Adrian let out another laugh through his nose before turning to catch my eye. "Duly noted."

I brushed my thumb across his knuckles. "I *am* into you, you know."

"Yeah?" His grin was big and easy. The man was so damned comfortable to be around, it was like being with myself, only better. "What made you change your mind about admitting it?"

My eyes returned to the road ahead. "I decided to give myself a Christmas present." I shrugged. "Even though you're only here for this project, I thought I might allow myself to enjoy my time with you while it lasts. Stop worrying so much about the future."

"Even though the town's still planning our wedding?" Adrian joked. "Because I've got to tell you, your sister's probably already booked the venue."

I winced. "Yeah, I'm sorry about that. The town is invested in seeing me happy, after everything with my folks. And Maya... I think she feels guilty leaving me alone next year. Maybe she thinks if I'm with someone, it'll be easier. I'm sorry she's dragging you into it."

Adrian's fingers moved into the back of my hair, causing my skin to prickle. "Maddox, I've known all along what I was getting into with the Legacy matchmakers. You laid it out for me on day one, remember? Right before you gave me all your rules." He grinned and added softly, "And I knew what I was getting into with *you*, too. In case you hadn't noticed, I've been into you since the day we met. You're the one who was so dead set against giving things a chance."

Thankfully, we'd pulled into my spot behind the hardware store, so I quickly threw the truck into Park and turned to take his face in my hands so I could give him another kiss.

"You sure you don't want to run upstairs for a few minutes before we head to Timber?"

Adrian's mouth tasted like toothpaste. I wanted to kiss him until there was no trace of it left and all that remained was the flavor of me.

He pushed me away with a laugh and a hand to the chest. "Some of us have to *work* for a living, Sullivan. You wouldn't know a thing about that, would you?"

Considering he'd borne the brunt of most of my hectic schedule this past week with holiday portrait sessions and long hours at the store, I knew he was only teasing.

"Right, because standing around looking pretty while other people take your picture is so much harder than actual manual labor. Tell me, Hayes, do you get hazard pay for the risk of breaking a nail?"

We exchanged barbs the entire walk down Founder's Row to Timber. Despite the teasing, I held Adrian's hand in mine and kept him as close as I could without tripping him.

Because I was incredibly aware that after tonight, there was only one official date remaining until Adrian Hayes was gone for good.

#BoyfriendShirt #StopTheClock #MoreThanSnowIsFalling

21

# #ELEGANTLYHAMMERED

ADRIAN

T IMBER LOOKED like a holiday fever dream designed by someone with impeccable taste and a secret obsession with rainbow Christmas lights.

Traditional evergreen garlands wound around the bar's rustic beams, but interspersed with them were strands of subtle rainbow bulbs that cast everything in a warm, welcoming glow. The effect was both festive and unmistakably queer-friendly—a perfect representation of Legacy's unexpectedly progressive heart.

"This place looks incredible," I murmured to Maddox as we shed our coats. The bar was about half-full, couples and small groups scattered around intimate tables, everyone speaking animatedly, as if energized by the season.

Although, to be fair, they could have been energized by the drink specials, too.

Alex appeared beside us like he'd been waiting by the door. "Adrian! Maddox! Perfect timing." His smile was bright, but I caught an edge of nervous energy underneath. "I've got three flights set up for you—the cocktails, the wines, and the whiskies, paired with some small bites I thought would photograph well."

"You didn't have to go to all this trouble," I said, though I was already mentally cataloging the best way to capture everything. The man had clearly put serious effort into this, and I wanted to get him as much publicity as possible.

"Are you kidding? This is a great opportunity for Timber. Plus..." Alex grinned. "I've been dying to show off these holiday cocktail recipes I've been working on. Fair warning, though—they're stronger than they taste."

Maddox was already scoping out camera angles, his professional eye assessing the lighting. "This'll work great. The ambiance is perfect for the cozy winter vibe Adrian's fans have been enjoying."

The fact that Maddox had paid enough attention to my posts to know how they were being received made something warm inside of me. I was proud of my work, of the platform I'd built, and I was even prouder of the work we'd done together.

I watched Maddox work, noting how much more relaxed he seemed in public now. No more careful distance between us, no more worried glances to see who might be watching. When he caught me staring and winked, my stomach did that familiar flip that I was beginning to associate with being completely gone for this man.

"Alright, let's get you started," Alex said, leading us to a table near the fireplace, where he'd arranged three beautiful flights. Each one was artfully presented with appropriate glassware and small cards describing the offerings. It was the kind of setup that would make my followers weep with envy.

As Maddox adjusted his camera equipment, I found myself distracted by the way his dark sweater stretched across his shoulders. *My* dark sweater, actually. Before hopping out of the truck, he'd sheepishly asked if I wanted him to wear a Nordique piece since I was wearing his shirt. I'd whipped one out of the overnight bag I'd packed.

There hadn't been a chance in hell of me saying no.

The combination of my clothes on his body and his shoulders stretching the Borealis Noir sweater more than mine ever would was doing things to my concentration that had nothing to do with alcohol.

"You're staring again," he murmured without looking up from his camera.

"Can you blame me? You look very... competent right now."

"Competent?" He raised an eyebrow, fighting a smile. "That's the sexiest compliment I've ever received."

"Is that so? Because I could go on—" I began, giving him a heated look.

Alex cleared his throat pointedly. "Should I leave you two alone with the alcohol, or...?"

"Shit, fuck," I said quickly, trying not to notice Maddox's knowing smirk. "Sorry. We're ready."

"I'm just watching the hard worker in action," Maddox said, batting his eyelashes like an asshole.

Before I could formulate a snarky response, the front door opened with enough force to rattle the windows. Chief Judd Kincaid strode in like he owned the place, tablet in hand and an expression that could curdle milk on his handsome face.

The change in Alex was immediate and dramatic. His shoulders tensed, his smile disappeared, and I swear the temperature in our corner of the bar dropped lower than the outside temp.

"Oh, for the love of fucking Christ," Alex muttered under his breath.

"Someone grab the popcorn," Maddox murmured under his breath. "Shit's about to get complicated."

"By complicated, you mean Kincaid's about to make my night a living hell with another ridiculous inspection to make sure Timber's living up to his impossible standards," Alex said, not bothering to lower his voice as Judd approached the bar.

I watched the fire chief work his way toward us, noting how his presence seemed to part crowds like the Red Sea. He was objectively attractive in a rugged, authority-figure way that probably made half the town weak in the knees, but something about the way he moved—purposeful and slightly aggressive—made me understand Alex's hostility.

"Evening, Firebug," Judd called, his deep voice carrying easily across the bar. "Hope you're not burning anything down, with all of these poor innocent townsfolk trying to enjoy the holiday season."

Alex inhaled sharply through his nose. "You know what? I actually expected you tonight, Kincaid. It's been a whole week since your last inspection," he shot back. "Figured you were due for another power trip."

The tension between them was so thick you could cut it with a knife. I glanced at Maddox, who was watching the exchange with barely concealed amusement.

"This happens often?" I whispered.

"About twice a month," he replied. "They've been dancing around each other like angry cats since summer."

Judd had reached the bar now and was making a show of examining the holiday decorations with his flashlight. "These lights properly secured? Electrical cords in good condition? You know what happens when bars get careless with their wiring."

"The lights are fine. The cords are fine. *Everything* is fine," Alex said through gritted teeth. "It was one time, Kincaid. And nothing fucking happened."

The chief tilted his head at Alex and pretended to be confused.

"I'm sorry, you didn't just suggest lighting something on fire thanks to your carelessness was 'nothing,' did you?"

Alex closed his eyes. His jaw ticked. He took a breath before opening his eyes and plastering on a fake smile. "What can I do for you, Chief Kincaid? Would you like a holiday cocktail? It's on me. I'd love to help you celebrate the season with a *sedative*."

"Thanks for your kind offer, but I have to decline. I have a hot date tonight with my—"

"Great, have fun," Alex snapped, cheeks crimson. "Good night."

I watched, fascinated, as Alex moved away and began aggressively mixing cocktails. His movements were sharp and precise, but there was definitely more alcohol going into each drink than the recipes probably called for. When he set the first flight in front of me, the glasses were notably fuller than they should have been.

The fire chief watched him go, murmuring, "My book and a frozen pizza," too softly for Alex to hear.

After a beat, his shoulders fell, and he turned to leave.

Maddox's voice was low, his breath hot against my ear. "See what I mean? You could charge money for this shit."

Before I could say anything, Alex returned, his voice overly bright. "Let's start with the holiday cocktails! This first one is my take on a cranberry Moscow mule—cranberry juice, ginger beer, and vodka with fresh mint and lime."

I took a sip and immediately felt the burn. Alex wasn't kidding about these being stronger than they tasted. The cranberry masked most of the alcohol, but there was definitely a generous pour of vodka in there.

"Wow," I managed, reaching for Maddox's hand as the warmth spread through my chest. "That's... potent."

"Good thing we're walking home," Maddox said, already

reaching for his own glass. His fingers lingered against mine when he took it, and I felt that familiar spark of electricity.

As we moved through the flight—a spiced pear whiskey sour that tasted like Christmas in a glass, followed by a pomegranate champagne cocktail that was dangerously easy to drink—I found myself relaxing in ways that had nothing to do with the alcohol. This felt natural, easy. Like something we'd done a hundred times before.

"You know," I said, leaning closer to Maddox to supposedly check the camera angle, "this flannel smells like you."

"That's because it's mine," he replied, but his voice had gone rough around the edges.

"I know." I let my fingers trail along the collar, ostensibly adjusting it for the camera. "I like wearing your clothes."

His eyes darkened. "Yeah?"

"Makes me feel like I belong to someone," I murmured.

With alcohol comfortably zinging through my system, the words slipped out before I could stop them, honest and raw and completely unfiltered. Maddox's breath caught, and for a moment, I thought he might kiss me right there in front of everyone.

Instead, he reached up to brush a strand of hair from my forehead. "Good," he said simply, and the single word settled in my chest.

Alex reappeared with fresh shots in his hands. "Who's ready for some Christmas Courage? I know I am."

"Christmas Courage?" I asked, accepting the glass.

"My own creation. Whiskey, honey, cinnamon, and poor life choices." Alex raised his glass in a toast. "To welcoming new people and seeing the backs of others. Cheers!"

We clinked glasses, and I threw back the shot, immediately feeling the burn all the way down to my toes. The whiskey was smooth but potent, and combined with the cocktails I'd already consumed, it left me feeling warm and loose-limbed and increasingly fixated on the way Maddox's hands looked wrapped around his glass.

"You know," I said, leaning into Maddox's space, "your hands are really nice."

"My hands?" He looked down at them with amusement.

"Mmhmm. Strong. Competent."

"Competent again, huh?" Maddox leaned closer.

"Yeah. I like watching them work." I reached out to trace one of his fingers, marveling at the calluses from years of manual labor. "I like how they feel on me, too."

Maddox's breath hitched. "Adrian…"

"What? I'm just making conversation." I grinned at him, suddenly feeling bold and reckless and completely unconcerned with who might be watching. "Perfectly innocent conversation about your perfectly innocent hands."

"There's nothing innocent about the way you're looking at me right now," he said, his voice dropping to that gravelly tone that made my knees weak.

"Yeah? How am I looking at you?" I demanded, letting my own voice go deep with want.

Alex appeared beside us again, this time with the wine flight. "Okay, kids, let's try to get through this tasting before you scandalize my other customers."

But even the wine—a selection of local vintages paired with artisanal chocolates and cheese—couldn't distract me from the way Maddox kept finding excuses to touch me. Adjusting my collar for the camera. Brushing crumbs from my lip. Letting his hand linger on my thigh while explaining the tasting notes for the video.

Each touch sent heat shooting through me, and by the time we reached the whiskey flight, I was having trouble concentrating on anything except the way his lips moved when he spoke.

"This one's a local rye," Alex explained, setting down amber glasses. "Distilled just outside town. Very smooth, with notes of vanilla and oak."

Even though by now, everything had taken on a slightly blurry quality, I dutifully took a sip and made appreciative noises for the camera, but what I was really appreciating was the way Maddox's eyes had gone dark and heavy-lidded. He was watching my mouth like he wanted to devour it, and the knowledge sent liquid heat pooling in my belly.

"Very smooth," I agreed, licking my lips slowly. "I like things that go down easy."

Maddox nearly choked on his whiskey. "Jesus, Adrian."

"What? I'm talking about the alcohol." I batted my eyelashes at him. "What did you think I was talking about?"

The look he gave me was affectionate and warm, which made me restless and hot as fuck.

Maddox leaned closer. I closed my eyes in anticipation of the kiss, but it never came. Instead, his voice slid into my ear. "Baby, we need to go. You're elegantly hammered."

I licked my lips in search of the taste of him, but instead, all I found was cab sav. "Mm. Will you let me taste you at home?"

His eyes heated, and when his words came out, they were soft like I wasn't the only drunk here. "You may taste any and every part of me as much as you want. I promise. Let's get out of here."

Maddox and I gathered our things with the exaggerated care of people who were definitely too drunk to be trusted with expensive equipment. I kept getting distracted by the way his jeans hugged his ass when he bent over to pack up the camera and had to grip the edge of the table to steady myself.

"You okay there?" he asked, straightening up to find me staring.

"I'm great," I said honestly. "Better than great. I'm fantastic. Except you're moving too slow."

"I'm not the one standing and staring at people's asses," he said with a smirk.

I stepped closer, close enough to smell his cologne mixed with whiskey and the faint scent of sawdust that always clung to his clothes. "If you could see your ass right now, you might understand."

His eyes went molten. "Start walking, Hayes."

The walk back to Maddox's place was an exercise in self-control that we both failed spectacularly. We kept nipping at and teasing each other before I finally pulled him into the doorway of Sullivan Hardware and kissed him like the world was ending. He tasted like whiskey and honey and something that was purely Maddox, and I couldn't get enough.

"Adrian," he groaned against my mouth, his hands fisting in my jacket. "People can see us."

"Don't care," I mumbled, nipping at his lower lip. "Let them see. Let them all know you're mine."

That seemed to break the last of his resistance. He spun us around, pressing me against the door, and kissed me with a hunger that made my knees buckle. His hands were everywhere—my hair, my face, sliding under my jacket to find warm skin.

"We need to get upstairs," he said raggedly, pulling back just enough to speak. "Before our next video goes viral for the wrong reasons."

We stumbled the rest of the way around to the back entrance, stopping twice more for heated kisses against lampposts and storefronts. By the time we made it up the stairs to his door, my lips were swollen, and my hair was a mess, and I was pretty sure my jeans were going to leave permanent marks from how tight they'd gotten.

Maddox fumbled with his keys, cursing under his breath as his hands shook. I pressed against his back, unable to keep from touching him, my hands sliding around his waist to feel the warm muscle of his stomach through his shirt.

"You're not helping," he said, but he leaned back into me anyway.

"I'm not trying to help," I murmured against his neck. "I'm trying to get in your fucking pants."

The lock finally gave way, and we practically fell through the door, hands already reaching for each other before it had even closed behind us.

"Bedroom," Maddox said, but his voice lacked conviction as I pressed him against the nearest wall and kissed a line down his throat. "We should... God, Adrian..."

"Bedroom sounds good," I agreed but made no move to stop what I was doing. "Eventually."

His laugh was breathless and rough. "We're not getting naked in the living room where my sister could see us."

"She's out tonight," I reminded him, and kissed him until neither of us could remember what room we were in to begin with.

#DrunkOnYou #ChristmasCourage #AngryFirebug #Merrily-Unfiltered

**22**

# #ONEDGE

MADDOX

ADRIAN WAS RED-FACED AND HAPPY. His eyes were whiskey-bright and a little glassy as he glanced over his shoulder at me on his way to my bedroom. "First one to get naked wins."

The curve of his ass in those ridiculous Nordique pants derailed every coherent thought in my brain. I'd meant to let him get a head start, maybe even leave him guessing for a beat.

But when he glanced back at me with those flushed cheeks and dark-lashed eyes, I was done for.

"You're killing me in those fucking jeans," I growled, stalking him toward the bedroom. "Wiggling that little influencer ass like you don't know what it does to me."

"That right?" Adrian asked, breathless and grinning. "You like the Vinter Denim? I'll let corporate know."

"You do that." I slid my finger through a belt loop and yanked him close. "Did you know you lean into me every time we film? And your pupils blow wide when I touch your wrist?"

His lips parted, but no words came.

I dipped my head to his neck and kissed a slow line just beneath his ear. "I feel your eyes on me every time we're together."

Adrian whimpered and grabbed at my shirt. "Fine. Maybe I'm a little obsessed."

"You don't know obsessed," I murmured, kissing him harder this time.

"Tell me," he breathed as I moved my mouth down to suck on his Adam's apple, the late-day stubble prickling my tongue.

I pushed him down onto the bed, crawling over him slowly. Not rough. Not hurried. Just deliberate. I wanted to savor this. Wanted to see him get twitchy with need.

"Driving me fucking nuts," I grumbled.

He arched up to kiss me again, but I shook my head with a wicked smile.

"Nuh-uh," I said, slipping my hand beneath his shirt and brushing my fingers over his stomach. "You've been turning me on all fucking night. I'm not letting either one of us come that fast, Hayes."

He made a strangled noise and collapsed back against the mattress. His cock pressed hard against the inside of my thigh. "Maddox…"

"You want it bad, don't you?" I whispered, dragging my mouth down his neck, licking that perfect spot just above his collarbone. "Bet I could make you come just from touching you, teasing you."

"Try me," he dared.

I chuckled, biting gently at the edge of his jaw. "Careful. I love a challenge."

I took my time stripping him down. Every button undone with slow fingers. Every inch of skin exposed kissed, tasted, teased. When he was finally naked and squirming under me, I knelt between his legs and just looked at him.

"You're ridiculous," I muttered, palming his thighs. "How are you this fucking pretty?"

"I moisturize," he gasped through a grin, trying to grind up into my hand. His eyes were still glassy and nose bright from my own stubble. "You need tips, mountain man? I hear jizz is good for the skin. You should try it. Like, right now."

"Sassy." I pushed him back down with a rumble of laughter. "You trying to get me to hurry up? 'S not gonna work."

I kissed the inside of his thigh, just shy of where he was hard and aching. He whimpered.

"Tell me what you want, Adrian," I said, brushing my lips closer, deliberately not touching.

"You *know* what I want."

"Mm," I teased. "But I like hearing you say it."

"Maddox," he said again, softer now, voice trembling. "Please."

That did it. I groaned and leaned in, licking a long, slow stripe up the underside of his cock. He moaned like I'd knocked the wind out of him.

"You taste so fucking good," I said, wrapping my hand around the base and watching his hips twitch. "Every time you open that pretty mouth to sass me, I just wanna shut you up with my—"

"Maddox."

He didn't have to finish the sentence. I dropped my mouth over him and went slowly. Letting him feel it. Letting him fall apart in my hands.

I sucked his shaft before moving down to pull his balls into my mouth one by one. My tongue pressed a hard stripe across his taint before moving up to suck him down again.

By the time he was panting and flushed, begging me to let him come in a voice that was making my cock leak in sticky lines along his thigh, I pulled back just enough to whisper, "Turn over for me."

He obeyed instantly, presenting himself with a breathless little gasp when I kissed between his shoulder blades.

"God, look at you," I said, running my hands over his hips. "You're shaking."

"You're fucking evil."

"No," I growled, slicking my fingers and moving between his muscular cheeks to his tight hole. "I'm careful. I'm going to take my time wrecking you."

Adrian whimpered as I worked him open slowly, fingers curling down just right to make him gasp.

"Look at you. Always so polished and tidy," I whispered, mouth at his ear. "Always put together. But not right now. Not with my fingers inside you and your cock still dripping with my saliva."

He whimpered again, pushing back against my hand.

"Imagine if your followers could see you now, Adrian Hayes," I gritted out, jaw clenched. "All those people leaving little comments, wishing they could see the two of us behind closed doors. Bet there are dozens of guys sliding in your DMs, too, aren't there? They'd kill to take my place."

Adrian shook his head wildly as I stroked him. "D-don't care. Don't want them. Don't want anyone else."

"That's fucking right," I said, low and fierce. "Nobody else gets to see you like this because right now, you're mine. Dirty and beautiful and perfect... and *all fucking mine*."

The noise Adrian made deep in his throat and chest was wrecked and broken.

When I finally pushed into him, slow and deep, it was my turn to groan. My eyes rolled back as I felt the tight heat of his body squeezing me.

"Fuck, you feel so good, baby," I whispered, making sure I was fully seated before bending over him, skin to skin. "So fucking good."

Our bodies were warm and damp from sweat as I rolled my hips and pressed in deeper. Adrian grabbed one of my hands and threaded our fingers together, squeezing tight. "Promise me, Maddie," he gritted out.

In that moment, I would have promised him anything. Anything at all. "Promise you what, baby?" I asked before pressing a kiss against his hot cheek.

"Promise you won't let me go."

His words shocked me, but before I could answer him, he was coming, his body arching back and his hand in mine closing in a fist as the sound of his broken cry rang out.

The sound of his orgasm was enough to make mine slam into me and take my breath away. The hot clench of his body around mine, the combined scents of sweat, jizz, and the faded remnants of whiskey on his breath, and the feel of his tight fist still holding mine all mixed together to make my head spin.

As the two of us faded quickly into sleep, all I could think about was the breathy plea in his voice right before he came.

*Promise you won't let me go.*

"Never," I breathed into his damp hair before pressing a kiss into his skin. "Not on your fucking life."

Because Adrian Hayes was it for me, and I finally knew exactly how to show him I meant it.

#WhiskeyKisses #BeautifulAndPerfectAndMine #VinterDenimFTW #NeverLettingGo

23

# #WHYNOTBOTH

ADRIAN

I WAS SITTING on the couch in my rental cabin, staring at my phone like it might spontaneously combust, when a knock at the door made me jump. I'd been avoiding Vic's increasingly frantic calls for two days now, and the weight of the Solenne Collection decision was sitting on my chest like a boulder.

Through the window, I saw a man in a SERA jacket standing on the porch, snow dusting his shoulders. I recognized him—Dr. Tommy Marian, Foster's boyfriend. The one who'd been laughing as he pelted Maya with perfectly aimed snowballs, while somehow managing to look like he'd stepped out of a medical drama.

"Adrian?" he called through the door. "It's Tommy Marian. We met the other day."

I opened the door, immediately hit by a blast of cold air and Tommy's easy smile. Up close, he was even more striking—the kind of wholesome, all-American handsome that probably made patients feel better just by walking into the room.

"Hey," I said, stepping back to let him in. "Is there another epic snow battle on the horizon? Am I being drafted?"

He laughed. "Not today, but you're on my list for next time." He stepped inside, shaking snow from his jacket, and held up a thermos. "I'm here to deliver you some cocoa my mom said you liked and to issue an invitation. We're having Christmas at the lodge— the whole extended Marian clan, plus anyone we've adopted along the way. Once my mother heard about you possibly being alone on Christmas, that was it. She said you're part of the family, whether you like it or not. I'm afraid now it's a command performance."

The words hit me harder than they should have. *Part of the family.* I'd heard similar phrases my whole life, but they'd always felt hollow, obligatory. This felt different. Real.

"That's really nice of her," I managed. "I'd love to come, assuming I'm still in town."

Tommy tilted his head, something shifting in his expression. "Assuming?"

I shrugged, trying for casual. "You know how it is with work. Things come up."

"Everything okay?" The question was gentle, with that particular tone medical professionals seemed to master—genuinely concerned but not pushy.

I found myself hesitating. I hadn't talked to anyone about the Solenne offer except Vic. But there was something about Tommy's presence that made me want to unload the weight I'd been carrying.

"You want to stick around for a coffee or maybe some of that cocoa?" I asked. "I could use some advice."

He didn't answer but handed me the thermos and immediately moved to the hooks by the door to remove his coat. When he returned to the kitchen, he took two mugs from the coffee station and poured us each a cup.

"What's going on?" he asked.

"It's kind of a work situation," I admitted, curling my hands around my mug. The cocoa was still hot, and the warmth was comforting. "Got offered this huge opportunity, but the timing is... complicated."

Tommy settled his ass against the counter and crossed his arms, giving me his full attention. "I happen to have recent relevant experience about this. Tell me more."

"It's a global brand ambassador position," I found myself saying. "Everything I've worked toward for the past five years. Financial security, international recognition, the works. My business manager's been calling nonstop because they need an answer by Friday."

"Sounds like a dream opportunity," Tommy said carefully. "What's making it complicated?"

I ran a hand through my hair, surprised by how much I wanted to tell him. "It would mean leaving Legacy. Like, immediately. Flying to Paris next week for the launch campaign, then living out of hotels for the next year while I travel the world creating content for the brand."

"Mmhm." His face softened in understanding. "And there's something here you'd be leaving behind."

"Someone," I corrected quietly, even though I could tell by the look on his face he knew. "Maddox and I... I don't know what we are exactly, but it's the most real thing I've felt in years. And Maya, and this whole town that's somehow started to feel like home." I laughed, but it came out shaky. "I know that sounds crazy. I've been here for what, less than three weeks?"

"It doesn't sound crazy at all," Tommy said gently. "Sometimes you just know when something fits."

"But this opportunity..." I gestured at my phone. "It's every-thing I thought I wanted. My manager keeps saying this is what we worked so hard for, and he's not wrong."

Tommy was quiet for a moment, and I could see him weighing his words. "Is this what *you* worked so hard for, or what your *manager* worked so hard for?" His voice was careful, nonjudgmental. "Because sometimes those things aren't the same."

The question hit me like a punch to the gut. I opened my mouth to say of course it was what I wanted, but the words wouldn't come.

"I had a similar choice just a few months ago," Tommy continued when I didn't answer. "Stay in New York, following a career track that looked perfect on paper, or try something differ-ent, something unexpected. I struggled with the idea that I was giving up everything *I'd* worked so hard for, so I know exactly how you feel."

"What did you do?"

"I came here on my way to my 'something different' and found something even more different... but so fucking perfect." His smile was soft, certain. "Best decision I ever made, even though it scared the hell out of me at the time."

I stared at him, something loosening in my chest. "Do you ever regret it?"

"Never. But I realized something important—I'd been making 'smart' decisions that were making me miserable. Following a preconceived script for what my life should look like instead of asking what would actually make me happy and allowing that idea of what a happy life looked like to change."

We sat in comfortable silence for a moment, sipping our drinks as snow continued to fall outside the window.

I thought about waking up in Maddox's bed, about Maya's

laughter, about feeling like I belonged somewhere for the first time in my adult life.

Tommy let out a soft laugh. "Isn't it wild how many of us work hard to fulfill the dreams of an ignorant teenager?"

I glanced at him over the edge of my mug. "How do you mean?"

"I was fourteen when I decided to become a doctor. I researched the hell out of it and came up with a dream and a path to achieve that dream. Then I ticked off all the boxes on the path until I had it all in the palm of my hand." He shrugged. "What I had was a fourteen-year-old's idea of a happy life instead of an *actual* happy life, you know?"

"Yeah," I said softly.

I thought back to the day I'd left home. How I'd been bound and determined to prove I could succeed on my own. My idea of happiness had been making lots of money and doing it my own way. Not by joining the family business and being the cookie-cutter Perfect Son my parents wanted, but by impressing people with my own... *something*. My own special sauce. My own talent. My own achievement.

And now, here I was. Successful because I was a pretty man who was good at standing next to pretty things in pretty clothes.

The sound of my snort was unexpected, causing Tommy's head to snap up. "What?"

I started to laugh. "I just realized I was so fucking determined to succeed without my parents, I ended up building a career based on the same fake persona bullshit that they raised me with. Talk about irony."

His forehead crinkled with confusion. "Fake? You don't come off as fake on social media. Are you just *that* good at it?"

I shrugged because I couldn't stop laughing. It was either that or cry.

Tommy frowned again and came around the island, reaching for my elbow to pull me over to the sofa. We dropped down into the soft cushions before he turned to face me. "Was the story about the one-footed duck made up?"

My laughter stopped with an aborted kind of hiccup. "The one in Melbourne? No, that duck only had one foot. He was born that way. Cute little fucker. You saw that?"

He nodded. "And when you posted the link to the donation site for the duck rescue place, was that made up?"

"'Course not. Jesus. I learned about the group from a woman on the plane next to me. She and a bunch of volunteers go out—"

"Not the point," Tommy said with a patient smile. "The point is, you met someone with a cause that pinged something in you, and you used your platform to make a real, authentic impact. To do some good."

I blinked at him.

"So tell me about the most fake post you ever made," he said, settling back into the cushions.

I thought back to all of the many posts I'd made and the various sponsorship clients I'd had. "The rave review of Destina Suites on the Jersey Shore," I muttered. "Although I was careful not to actually say I liked it. I pointed out the things that were good about it and tried to make it sound better than it was without actually misleading people."

He lifted his eyebrows. "So you were honest? Real?"

I rolled my eyes. "And then there was the time when I posted about loving Crete while secretly battling a disgusting bout of food poisoning. I hate Crete. Will definitely never go back there despite the hidden nude beaches. And the cats. I liked the cats."

He smiled. "Did you post about the cats? I might need to look those posts up."

"Of course. I posted more about the stray cats than I did about the travel insurance company I was there to promote, although they didn't know that. I kind of used the cats as the content to explain that without the insurance, I wouldn't be able to enjoy the cats as much. Not true. I still would have enjoyed them plenty."

His laughter was warm and easy. "Bet that insurance company didn't cover a nice banana bag at a local med spa. Would have fixed you right up. Hydration. Electrolyte replacement."

"How'd you know Foster was the one?" I blurted.

Tommy blinked at the change in topic, but his answer was immediate. "Because as soon as I met him, I knew I wanted to orbit around him like the neediest little planet lucky enough to bask in the warmth of his sun. Somehow, I knew the minute I stepped out of that light... I'd live in a kind of darkness for the rest of my life."

Yes. *That.* That was exactly how I felt with Maddox.

"It doesn't make sense," I murmured.

Tommy's smile was kind and understanding. "Nope. Is it supposed to? I'm not sure. Does it matter? Does it change anything about who you want to be with?"

"No. But I just met this guy. And he lives..." I gestured out at the frozen tundra beyond the window. Before I could make a snarky statement, I noticed movement in the distance. I stood up and walked closer to the window. "Is that a *moose*?"

Tommy joined me at the window. "Nah. Those are elk. See the other ones just off to the right? They're probably coming down from the mountain, looking for easier pickings. They do that in winter. We've seen a bunch at SERA recently."

I watched as the small herd moved across the empty landscape between my cabin and the forested base of the mountain. "Holy fuck," I breathed.

He chuckled as he moved back to the sofa and reached for his coffee again. "Legacy never fails to impress, no matter what time of year it is."

I couldn't keep my eyes off the elk. "You must be used to the weather."

"Only because I lived in New York for a while. But I grew up in California. The Bay Area. I'll take Legacy's sunshine and snow over San Francisco's fog or New York's gray winters any day."

"I bet the summers are beautiful," I said wistfully.

Tommy hesitated. "Adrian, I've seen the way you look at Maddox, and I've seen how this town has embraced you. Maya talks about you like you're already family. That's not something you find everywhere."

I finally peeled my eyes away from the view. "I know that. I do. But I have to work. I can't just—"

"Work doesn't have to end just because you change zip codes," Tommy interrupted gently. "You've got a platform, skills, connections. Those don't disappear if you're not physically in LA."

I blinked at him. "You... you don't think it would be stupid to be based so far away from a big city or a hub airport? My job requires traveling, like all the time."

"I think you could make anything work if you wanted it badly enough." Tommy stood, moving to the kitchen to place his mug in the sink. "But more importantly, you deserve to be happy. Really, genuinely happy. Not just successful or impressive or whatever other people think you should be."

He paused in the process of reaching for his coat. "You know what my mom said when she asked me to invite you to Christmas?"

I shook my head.

"She said, 'Adrian belongs here now. Make sure he knows it.'" Tommy's smile was certain and warm. "So I'm telling you—you belong here, Adrian. Not because of your job or because of

Maddox, but because you've chosen to see this place and these people as home. And we want you here."

After he left, I sat in the silence of the cabin, his words echoing in my head. If I deserved to be happy, what did that look like? When was I happiest?

The answer was easy. Every morning I woke up in Maddox's arms. Every time I shared a joke with Maya. Every moment I felt like I was part of something bigger than my carefully curated—but definitely isolated—online presence.

Coming to Montana had felt like a detour from my "normal" life.

But what if it wasn't a detour? What if it was the destination I was meant to find all along?

I picked up my phone and, for the first time in days, didn't feel the familiar dread. Instead, I felt something that might have been hope.

Maybe Tommy was right. Maybe the biggest risk wasn't taking a chance on love. It was playing it safe and missing out on everything that could make me truly happy.

I scrolled to Vic's contact and took a deep breath. It was time to stop following someone else's script and start writing my own story.

#FollowYourHeart   #DoctorsOrders   #WriteYourOwnScript #ElkMoose

**24**

# #COMFORTFOODANDFEELINGS

MADDOX

I STARED at the ingredients spread across my kitchen counter like I was preparing for surgery rather than cooking dinner. Mom's handwritten lasagna recipe—faded ink on a card stained with years of use—sat propped against the flour canister, her careful script a reminder of all the family dinners I was trying to recreate.

The nerves jangling in my stomach were ridiculous. I'd made this lasagna dozens of times. It wasn't complicated.

But tonight felt different. Tonight, I was trying to impress someone I truly cared about, and the stakes felt impossibly high.

My phone buzzed on the counter.

ADRIAN

What exactly does one wear to a Maddox Sullivan date?

I grinned despite my nerves, typing back quickly.

Just dress comfortably.

ADRIAN

Define "comfortably."

If I recall correctly, you once told me my fashion sense was 'I just wandered off the cover of Lumberjack Quarterly' so I'm not sure I'm the person to ask.

The pause before his response felt endless.

ADRIAN

While that is true, and BTW I stand by my assessment, I still need to know what to wear tonight!

Anything's fine. Surprise me.

ADRIAN

Will you at least tell me where we're going on this date so I can make an informed decision? What if I show up naked?

That would definitely be surprising considering your sensitivity to cold and tonight's expected low temps, but I can't say I'd be upset about it.

I set the phone aside and tried to focus on browning the meat, but it was hard now that I had a certain image in my head.

"You'd better save the leftovers," Maya said, coming up behind me and peering over my shoulder. "Because that smells amazing."

"You're welcome to stay and join us," I said. "The point of the date is a comfortable night in. Having annoying siblings around is part of that experience sometimes."

Her grunt of annoyance was expected and only made me smile more. "I have my own date to go on, thank you very much."

I spun around and pinned her with a glare. "With whom? And why am I just finding out about this?"

Maya's face lit up with her laugh. "Oh, that's rich. Your

boyfriend gets to sleep over, and I'm not even allowed to go to dinner and a movie with someone?"

"You didn't answer the question. Also, you're seventeen."

She rolled her eyes. "For six more weeks. And it's Tomás. We're going to see *The Frostbite Directive*."

"That sounds ridiculous," I muttered, turning back to the meat sizzling in the pan. "But if it's just Tomás, that's fine."

He was a good kid who worked part-time for Lennon at the ranch. He and Maya had been friends forever.

"I'll remember you said that," she singsonged as she danced toward the door, grabbing her coat from the hook before flitting out into the darkened night.

I was too distracted by my nerves to do more than throw her a wave over my shoulder and tell her to make good choices.

When was the last time I'd been this nervous about anything? When was the last time someone's opinion had mattered this much?

The truth was, I'd never tried to impress anyone the way I wanted to impress Adrian.

With Michael, things had been easy from the start—we'd fallen into a comfortable routine without much effort. And if I were being totally honest, we'd fallen out of our relationship the same way.

This was different. More important. I wanted Adrian to see a side of me I didn't show most people. I wanted him to know he was worth any amount of time and effort. I wanted to show him without words how I felt about him.

Which was a tall order, even for my mom's amazing lasagna.

I finished the sauce and drained the noodles before assembling the lasagna and sliding it into the oven. After making the salad and opening a bottle of red wine to breathe, I glanced at my handiwork. In addition to the fairy lights I'd strung around the windows, candles flickered on every surface that wouldn't consti-tute a fire hazard, and I'd even dragged out Mom's good dishes—the ones we only used for special occasions.

The coffee table was set with mismatched napkins, and the quilt Adrian had admired the first time he'd been here was now folded neatly over the back of the couch, ready for snuggling later. I'd even cued up *Die Hard* on the television so I could educate him on the finest Christmas movie ever made.

Everything was perfect... or as perfect as I could make it in a small apartment above a hardware store.

So why did I feel like I was about to jump out of my skin?

A knock at the door interrupted my spiraling anxiety. I wiped my hands on a dish towel, took a deep breath, and opened the door to find Adrian Hayes in matching flannel pajama pants and top sticking out from under my old hardware store hoodie.

He was also wearing slippers. Actual slippers.

His hair was artfully mussed, like he'd run his fingers through it just enough to look effortlessly attractive, and his cheeks were pink from the cold. He looked comfortable and relaxed and abso-lutely fucking gorgeous.

"Perfect," I said aloud, unable to keep the grin off my face.

Adrian raised an eyebrow. "You have to be kidding. No restau-rant's going to allow me in pajamas. I'm only wearing this to prove a point. You need to tell me what to wear. I brought options."

"Who said anything about a restaurant?" I stepped aside to let him in, catching the scent of his cologne mixed with the crisp winter air.

He stopped just inside the door, taking in the fairy lights and candles and the smell of garlic and herbs wafting from the kitchen. Something soft crossed his face, surprise giving way to something warmer.

"Maddox," he said quietly. "This is..."

"Dinner," I finished, suddenly self-conscious. "I hope you're hungry."

"Starving," he replied, but he was looking at me instead of toward the kitchen, and the heat in his eyes had nothing to do with food.

I led him to the small dining table near the living room windows, where the fairy lights cast everything in a warm golden glow. Adrian sat down carefully, running his finger over the edge of his plate.

"These are beautiful," he said.

"They were my mom's. She only brought them out for special occasions." I paused, realizing what I'd just admitted. "I mean—"

"This is a special occasion," Adrian said simply, meeting my eyes. "Our first real date."

I met his eyes. "You wanted the Maddox Sullivan experience, right? Well, for you, tonight, that means home-cooked comfort food. A movie you haven't seen—but definitely need to. And absolutely no cameras in sight you need to perform for."

His smile was radiant. "A night in just for us?"

"That's the deal. What do you think?"

"I think you need to lose more bets because this sounds amazing."

But as I served the lasagna—layers of meat and cheese and pasta that had taken me three hours to perfect—I knew we were both aware that tonight was more than the settling of a debt.

This was me trying to show Adrian what I could offer. Not fancy restaurants or expensive wines, but something made with my own hands, in my own home. Something made with care... for the man I already cared about more than was probably wise.

Adrian took his first bite and closed his eyes, a soft sound of pleasure escaping him.

"Fuck," he breathed. "Maddox, this is incredible."

"My mom's recipe, too," I said, warmth spreading through my chest at his reaction. "She'd be very impressed to hear I made it on my own and it isn't terrible."

"Did she cook a lot?" he prompted with a smile.

"Oh yeah." I nodded. "Ours was the house where everyone congregated, hoping to get asked to stay for dinner."

"God, I had a friend like that," Adrian remembered with a laugh. "Jack Klingman. One of his dads made the most amazing burgers and homemade fries. Every Friday night, we'd all hang out at Jack's after shooting hoops in hopes they'd ask us to stay."

"Yeah?" I smiled softly. "It's great that you had that experience. It was rare to find a family with two dads around here when I was young... which is maybe surprising, given what a queer haven Legacy's become in recent years."

"It was pretty great," Adrian confirmed. "I liked his dads better than the burgers, honestly. Seeing them together made me feel for the first time that being attracted to other guys was a totally normal thing to do."

I watched him carefully. "And what did your parents think about Jack's dads?"

He shrugged. "They politely ignored them. The Klingman family didn't have much money, which meant they were irrelevant. Why spend time with people who can't do anything for the business or your reputation?"

I reached over and covered his hand with mine. "Do you remember the first date we had, the one at the Marian Lodge, when you went over to meet those girls and their family?"

He crinkled his forehead, remembering. "The family from Virginia? Yeah."

"I overheard them outside, when they first saw you. One of the girls said you changed her life. You posted something about burnout. And then another time, you posted about your parents. Something about family complications."

Adrian's fingers tangled with mine as he held on. "Yeah. That was last Christmas. It kind of sucked. My parents made a big deal of inviting me back to Connecticut for the holidays. I canceled a trip to Puerto Vallarta with some friends in LA and flew back. It was nice, at first. My mom gushed over how popular I was online. My dad asked me questions about social media and how it worked being an online influencer. It was... pretty fucking validating."

"And then?"

"And then Dad asked if I could put him in touch with the CEO of one of my sponsors, which just so happened to be a Fortune 500 company." His bitter laugh broke my heart. "He thought that my little ten-thousand-dollar sponsorship, in which I posted about their trendy sparkling water, would somehow translate into his being able to sell the company insurance. Enough to level up his damned company. What a moron."

I moved closer and covered our hands with my other hand, pulling them up to kiss the back of his. "What did you tell him?"

"The truth. That the CEO of Summit Beverages didn't know who I was, and even if he did, I wouldn't jeopardize my relationship with them by bringing in my dad to sell them insurance." He shrugged. "And perhaps unsurprisingly, when a couple of friends invited them over for Christmas lunch, they accepted. Hayes, party of two, not three."

I shoved his chair back from the table and climbed onto his lap, wrapping my arms around him and holding him in the tightest hug possible. "I hate them," I grumbled in his ear. "Hate them so fucking much."

"Thank you," Adrian whispered. He was quiet for a moment, just holding me as tightly as I held him. "No one's ever cooked for me before," he said finally, his voice muffled in the side of my neck. "You have no idea how much this means to me."

The admission hit me harder than it should have. I thought of all the meals I'd shared over the years—family dinners around our old kitchen table, holiday spreads that took all day to prepare, the easy comfort of home-cooked food made with love.

The idea that Adrian had never experienced that made something protective and tender rise in my chest.

"If I have my way," I said, the words coming out before I could stop them, "this is the first of many."

Adrian pulled back and met my eyes. There was something soft and sweet in his expression. "Yeah?"

"Yeah." I meant it. More than I'd meant anything in a long time.

"Then maybe get off me and let me enjoy it before it gets cold," he teased. But he pulled my face close to give me a long kiss before he let me go.

We ate in comfortable companionship after that, occasionally commenting on the food or the snow falling outside the windows. Adrian asked about the holiday traditions I'd grown up with. I found myself talking more than usual, sharing stories I hadn't told anyone in years.

"She used to make this every Christmas Eve," I said, serving him a second helping without asking if he wanted it. "The whole house would smell like garlic and herbs for hours. Maya and I would sneak down to steal tastes while it was cooling."

"Did you get caught?"

"Every time. Mom would act all stern and shoo us away, but she'd always cut us tiny pieces anyway." I smiled at the memory. "She said the best part of cooking for people was watching them enjoy it."

Adrian was looking at me with that soft expression again, the one that made my chest tight. "She sounds wonderful."

"She was." I cleared my throat, suddenly emotional. "She would have liked you."

"You think so?"

"I know so. I think she'd've had a weakness for smart-ass city boys with good hearts."

Adrian's laugh was warm and delighted. "How do you know I have a good heart?"

"Because you've been putting up with my grumpy ass for weeks," I said, reaching across the table to brush my thumb across his knuckles. "And because of the way you talk to Maya. The way you've thrown yourself into this town, even though I know it's not your usual type of place."

"I think I've changed my mind about what my type of place is," Adrian said quietly.

My heart rate kicked up. "Yeah?"

"Yeah." His fingers turned under mine, palm to palm. "I like it here. More than I expected to."

The weight of that admission settled between us, carrying implications neither of us was quite ready to voice. Instead, I squeezed his hand and stood to clear the dishes.

"Leave those," Adrian protested. "Let me do them."

"Absolutely not. You're the guest. Besides, I have a very important cultural education to provide." I gestured toward the living room, where my sweet man was getting ready to have his *Die Hard* cherry popped hard.

I'd arranged pillows and blankets on the couch, creating a cozy nest that was definitely more intimate than necessary for movie watching.

Adrian groaned dramatically. "If you make me watch *It's a*

*Wonderful Life*, I'm not going to be in the mood for sex. We'll have to find a pair of twin beds and be all 1930s and shit."

"I promise you'll want to fuck after this."

He narrowed his eyes at me. "If it's *Home Alone* or anything where the Santa gets progressively fatter, I'm out."

"Stop flapping your jaws and trust me."

"I don't love *Elf*, but I do love Zooey Deschanel singing," he said, as if reluctantly offering me options.

"I don't need your concessions, asshole," I said, yanking him down beside me. "I just need you to take a breath and let this happen. Okay? Tonight's date is my plan. *Mine*. Understand? You'll watch this and you'll like it."

"So bossy," Adrian complained. But as he tumbled down beside me, he sucked in a breath of excitement. "Wait. Are we watching what I think we're watching?"

"Zip it," I said, reaching for the remote.

He grinned at me and mimed zipping his lips before leaning in and making a production about kissing me without opening his mouth.

I shoved him off with a laugh. "You're so weird. Stop and pay attention."

The movie started, but I found myself more interested in watching Adrian's reactions than the familiar action on-screen. He made sarcastic comments during the exposition, laughed at the one-liners, and gradually relaxed until his head was resting on my shoulder and his hand was splayed across my chest.

"Okay," he admitted during the scene where McClane writes his message on the dead terrorist's shirt, "this is actually pretty entertaining."

"Just wait until the ending. 'Now I have a machine gun. Ho ho ho.'"

"You're such a dork," Adrian said fondly, turning to press a kiss to my neck that sent heat shooting down my spine.

"*Your* dork," I replied without thinking.

Adrian went very still against me. "Are you?"

The question hung in the air between us, loaded with meaning. I could deflect, make a joke, pretend I hadn't just claimed him in the most casual way possible. But looking down at him—hair mussed from the pillows, eyes soft with something that looked deceptively like affection—I found I didn't want to take it back.

"If you want me to be," I said quietly.

Instead of answering with words, Adrian shifted until he was straddling my lap, his hands cupping my face as he kissed me slow and deep. He tasted like red wine and possibility, and when he pulled back to rest his forehead against mine, we were both breathing hard.

"I want you to be," he whispered.

The rest of the movie played forgotten in the background as we kissed on my couch, hands roaming over familiar territory that somehow felt new in this context. This wasn't desperate fucking driven by lust and alcohol. This was softer. More tender. Like we had all the time in the world.

Like we were marking the beginning of forever, instead of counting down to the end of temporary.

When we finally made it to the bedroom, Adrian was wearing my old Sullivan Hardware hoodie and nothing else, and I was pretty sure I'd never seen anything more beautiful in my life.

I woke up before dawn to the sound of snow hitting the windows and the warm weight of Adrian's body against mine. His hair stuck up on one side, and there was a small purple hickey under his ear, but he looked perfect. Peaceful in a way I'd never seen him when he was awake and performing for the world.

I slipped out of bed carefully, not wanting to wake him, and padded to the kitchen to start the coffee. The apartment was quiet and warm, fairy lights still twinkling in the windows, the lingering scent of garlic and herbs mixing with the smell of snow and contentment.

As the coffee brewed, I found myself thinking about the evening before. The way Adrian's face had lit up when he'd seen the dinner I'd prepared. The soft sound he'd made when he'd tasted my mother's lasagna. The casual intimacy of watching a movie together with his head on my shoulder like we'd been doing it for years.

I poured coffee into two mugs—making sure his had just the right amount of oat creamer in it—and carried them back to the bedroom. Adrian was starting to stir, making soft sleepy sounds that made my chest tight with affection.

"Morning," I murmured, setting his coffee on the nightstand and leaning down to brush a light kiss across his temple.

He made a pleased humming sound, eyes still closed. "Coffee?"

"Of course."

"You're perfect," he mumbled, finally opening those blue eyes to blink at me sleepily. "What time is it?"

"Early. I need to open the store, but you should sleep in."

"Mm. Don't wanna. I'll come with you."

The casual way he said it—like accompanying me to work was the most natural thing in the world—made something flutter in my chest. "You don't have to."

"Want to," he insisted, sitting up and reaching for his coffee. "Besides, someone needs to make sure you're not being too grumpy to the customers."

An hour later, I was beginning to think bringing Adrian to the hardware store had been a mistake. Not because he was causing problems, but because watching him interact with my world was doing dangerous things to my heart.

He'd come downstairs wearing another one of my old Sullivan Hardware hoodies—a gray one with the faded logo that I'd had since high school—and carrying his coffee in the hardware store mug like he belonged there. His hair was still sleep-mussed despite his attempts to tame it, and he had the relaxed, satisfied look of a man who'd been thoroughly loved the night before.

Bonnie had greeted him warmly, and the two had immediately gotten into a long conversation about the Christmas window display while I sorted stock... albeit a little more distractedly than usual.

"Morning, Bonnie! Morning, Maddox!" Mrs. Hoffman called as she bustled in, shaking snow from her coat. She stopped short when she saw Adrian behind the counter, organizing receipts with the focused attention he usually reserved for creating content.

"Morning, Mrs. Hoffman," I replied. "What can we help you with today?"

But she was staring at Adrian, taking in the hoodie and the mug and the casual way he was moving around the space behind the register. A knowing smile spread across her face.

"Well, well," she murmured. "Isn't this domestic?"

Adrian looked up from the receipts, cheeks flushing slightly. "Morning, Mrs. Hoffman. How are you?"

"Much better now that I've seen this," she replied cheerfully. "You look very... settled, dear."

I felt heat creep up my neck. "Did you need something specific?"

"Light bulbs for my porch fixture. But I'm in no hurry." She settled in to browse, clearly planning to observe our interaction for as long as possible.

It seemed Mrs. Hoffman got busy on her gossip group chat while she browsed because over the next hour, a steady stream of locals filtered through the store. Each one took note of Adrian's presence, his obvious comfort in the space, and the way he chatted easily with customers about everything from the weather to local holiday events, and each one also seemed to give me an indulgent smile that might have been the Legacy equivalent of "I told you so, Maddox." I found I didn't care.

Adrian helped old Mr. Peterson find the right-size gasket for his plumbing repair, listened patiently as Sadie explained her ongoing war with her temperamental coffee machine, and even managed to sell three sets of Christmas lights to tourists who'd wandered in looking for directions to tonight's Starlight Spectacular ski event.

"You're good at this," I said during a brief lull, watching him rearrange a display of gift cards.

"It's not hard," he replied, glancing up with a smile. "Not this part, anyway, where I'm just interacting with customers and rearranging things. People just want to feel heard. And most of them are buying things they actually need, not just things they want to show off."

The simple observation hit me harder than it should have. Adrian understood the difference between necessity and luxury, between authentic connection and performance. He got what Sullivan Hardware represented—four generations of serving the community, of being the place people came when they needed solutions rather than status symbols.

"Hey, Maddie!" Maya's voice preceded her through the back door. "Did you see the— Oh." She stopped short, taking in the scene: Adrian in my hoodie, organizing inventory like he worked here, me watching him with what was probably an embarrass-ingly besotted expression.

"Morning to you, too, squirt," I said, trying for casual and prob-ably failing spectacularly.

"Adrian's helping out," Maya observed, her grin widening. "How... helpful of him."

"I volunteered," Adrian said, completely unbothered by her knowing look. "Figured someone should make sure your brother doesn't scare off all the customers with his sparkling personality."

"Good thinking. He can be pretty terrifying when he wants to be."

Bonnie hurried out of the back room, where she'd been running our sales reports, and shoved her laptop in my face. "Maddox Sullivan, look at these numbers!"

I glanced at the screen, and my eyebrows rose.

I knew sales were better than usual, of course, but I hadn't taken the time to analyze just how much. Online sales were up nearly 300 percent from this time last year, with orders coming in from all over the country. Christmas light sets, winter gear, even specialty hardware items that had been gathering dust for months.

"This is all from the videos," I said, moving over to grab Adrian and pull him closer so he could see. "I told you people were ordering from us because of your posts."

Adrian shrugged, but I caught the pleased flush on his cheeks. "Good products sell themselves. I just helped people find you."

It was more than that, though. Looking at the sales data, reading the customer notes that mentioned seeing us on social media, I realized what Adrian had done wasn't just promotion. He'd told our story. He'd shown people what Sullivan Hardware meant to Legacy, what it meant to have a family business that cared about quality and service and community.

He'd made us matter to people we'd never met.

More than that, he'd shown me what a difference online reach —the kind of reach I could make with my own videography— could make to our bottom line.

"The profits from this quarter alone will cover Maya's first-year tuition," I said quietly, the truth of these numbers finally sinking in.

"Really?" Maya's eyes went wide. "Like, all of it?"

I nodded. The weight I'd been carrying for years—the constant worry about money, about Maya's future, about keeping the store afloat—had lifted so suddenly I felt dizzy.

"Thank you," I said to Adrian, meaning it more than I'd ever meant anything. "I don't know how to—"

"Don't," he interrupted gruffly. "You don't owe me anything. This is what good partnerships look like."

*Partnerships.* The word settled in my chest like a promise.

As the morning wore on, I found myself stealing glances at Adrian as he moved around the store. The way he remembered customers' names after meeting them once. The patience he showed with Kin Nay when she couldn't decide between two different types of weather stripping. The genuine interest he took in learning about products he'd never have use for back in LA.

It felt like family. Like the kind of chosen family I'd never thought I'd have again after losing my parents.

As the lunch crowd started to thin out and people began heading home for afternoon naps or holiday preparations, I found myself standing apart from Maya and Adrian, who were discussing the relative merits of different sandwich toppings with the seriousness of professional food critics.

Adrian was laughing at something Maya had said, his whole face lit up with genuine affection. In my old hoodie and worn jeans, one errant strand of hair still stubbornly sticking in the wrong direction from earlier, he looked like he'd always belonged here. Like *this* was his natural habitat instead of luxury hotel suites and fancy events.

If this were real—if it could stay like this—I'd be the happiest damn man alive.

"Earth to Maddox," Maya called, snapping me out of my reverie. "Did you even hear what I said?"

"Sorry, what?"

She handed me Adrian's phone. "Pick out whatever you want from the Pinecone, and he'll call in an order for lunch."

I glanced up, instinctively searching for Adrian, but saw he was being yanked down the plumbing aisle by Marty Kovach, who was in the middle of a basement renovation.

"What are we getting?" I mumbled as I scrolled through Sadie's menu of specialty sandwiches. "Pastrami or the grilled chicken wrap?"

Before I could make my decision, a text notification popped up.

> VIC
>
> Stop fucking ignoring me!

Another popped up and quickly replaced it.

> VIC
>
> Do not turn down the offer of a lifetime because of your dick.

I blinked at the screen. And then I did something I'd never done before, ever. Not even when Maya was going through a tough time and wouldn't talk to me about her feelings.

I snooped.

I didn't intend to. I clicked the message notification on instinct and was taken to Adrian's text conversation. I clicked out almost immediately... but not before seeing the details of Adrian's job offer from Solenne, which Vic had recounted in an angry message an hour ago.

*Luxury resorts*, Vic reminded him. *Jaw-dropping locations. Santorini, Paris, the Maldives, the freaking Alps. Celebrity sightings, Adrian! High-end shoots. This is the deal of your fucking lifetime. What the fuck more do you want out of life?*

It was an offer that would make anyone's head spin, but especially Adrian's. Getting an offer like this was the entire reason he'd come to Legacy. And if he accepted it, he'd be traveling around the world full-time.

*What the fuck more do you want out of life?*

I felt the blood drain from my extremities and nearly lost my grip on the phone before handing it back to Maya. "I have to go," I said in a shaky voice.

Then I ran out of the store as fast as I possibly could.

#YourDork #FallingFast #OhShit

# 25

# # WILDGEESE

## ADRIAN

I RETURNED from helping Marty Kovach untangle his basement plumbing nightmare to find Maya standing behind the register, looking like someone had just told her Santa wasn't real.

"Where's Maddox?" I asked, glancing around the store. The rush had died down, leaving a young mother browsing the seasonal clearance section with a baby strapped to her chest and an older guy debating the merits of different snow shovels with Bonnie. "Did he call in the lunch order?"

Maya looked at me in confusion. "No. I don't know where he went. He just... left? He looked spooked."

As she handed my phone back, I noticed new messages from Vic marked as read. The blood drained from my face as I scrolled through them.

VIC

Stop fucking ignoring me!

Do not turn down the offer of a lifetime because of your dick.

> Another offer like Solenne will not come around if word gets out you declined it.

"Fuck," I breathed. "He saw texts from my business manager about my job offer."

Maya's eyes widened. "What job offer?"

"Global brand ambassador for the Solenne Collection. Travel the world, live in luxury resorts, basically everything I've worked toward for the past five years." The words tasted like ash in my mouth. "Everything that would take me as far away from Legacy as possible."

"Oh my god," she breathed. "You're actually leaving?"

"No!" The answer exploded out of me. "I told Vic no yesterday. But I don't know if Maddox scrolled up far enough to see that."

Maya's face crumpled. "So he thinks you're leaving?"

"How could he?" I sank onto the stool behind the counter. "If he honestly thinks, after everything we've talked about, that I'd just leave without so much as discussing it with him... he must still think the worst of me. That I'm a fancy city boy with a temporary life, always moving on to the next perfect thing."

"He doesn't," Maya said firmly. "I'm positive Maddox doesn't think that about you anymore."

"How do you know?" I demanded. "He's spent weeks reminding me—and you—that this was temporary. That I'd leave eventually."

Maya bit her lip like she wanted to argue but couldn't.

"Even if he thought I wanted the job, why the fuck would he just *leave*? Was this his way of protecting himself?" I tried calling Maddox's number, but it went straight to voicemail. In deference to Maya, I tried to keep from biting out a curse. "That... *jerk*. Why couldn't he have at least talked to me?"

Maya grabbed my wrist. "Adrian, stop. You don't know what he's thinking. Maybe something came up—"

"And he couldn't throw an explanation over his shoulder on the way out?" I laughed, but it came out hollow. "Classic Maddox Sullivan. The moment things get complicated, he freaks out and starts building his walls as high and as thick as he can."

Maya's face dropped because she knew I was right.

I tried texting him.

> We need to talk. The job offer isn't what you think.

> Please call me back.

> Maddox. Please. Just give me five minutes.

After a minute, I finally got a response.

MADDOX

Meet me at the Starlight Spectacular tonight at 7pm.

I stared at the phone, trying to decide if I felt relief or dread.

> Are you mad at me?

MADDOX

Furious. And annoyed. Disappointed. And hurt.

My hands shook as I started to type another message, but I couldn't go through with it. I was too scared to push him over text and risk him changing his mind about meeting me.

> I'm so fucking sorry I didn't tell you. I said
> no. I hope you saw that. You don't need to
> respond. Just… I'll see you tonight.

When I looked up, Maya was still looking at me with a pitiful expression on her face. I pulled her into a side hug.

"He's going to meet me at the ski thing tonight."

Her face softened in relief. "Good. Then you can clear the air."

I didn't mention that if he'd truly wanted to talk things through, he would have chosen a less public venue. It was never a good sign when a man you were dating wanted to have The Talk in a public place.

I kept that thought to myself.

"I should go find him," I said instead. "It's silly to wait until tonight if he's out there right now, hurt and thinking the worst. Right?"

Before Maya could respond, the bell jingled, and Mrs. Hoffman bustled in, shaking snow from her coat. Her usually bright demeanor seemed forced, almost frantic.

"Adrian! Just the man I came to see! I need a huge favor."

I blinked at her. "What kind of favor?"

"Emergency, ah... catering situation. The Hendersons were supposed to provide desserts for the rec center's holiday potluck tonight, but their oven just died." Mrs. Hoffman clasped her hands together in supplication. "I know it's last minute, but could you help me run some supplies over to Avery? She's agreed to whip something up at her place, but I need someone with a car to transport everything since she said the baby is down for a nap and her wife is caught up on a work call."

"Actually, I'm a little busy. I was going to—" I began.

"Please?" Mrs. Hoffman begged.

I sighed. "I... sure, I guess." It was probably good to give

Maddox a chance to cool off before we talked. "What do you need me to do?"

"Just drive me to pick up ingredients, then help carry everything to Hazel and Avery's place. Should only take an hour." She and Maya exchanged a look. "Or possibly two. Depending."

Maya nodded encouragingly. "Go ahead. I'll find Maddox and see where his head is."

The next few hours passed in a blur of grocery runs and kitchen prep. Halfway through our first grocery shop, Mrs. Hoffman remembered an important appointment of her own, so she left me with an extensive list.

And when I got to Avery and Hazel's place, it wasn't the quick drop-off I'd been promised. They drew me into the kitchen, sat me down with a cup of coffee, and chatted about their baby's first Christmas and various bits of town gossip for another hour. It felt rude to leave when Hazel kept getting work calls and Avery needed someone to keep an eye on the oven timer while she checked on the baby.

Every few minutes, I'd pull out my phone to see if there were any messages from Maddox or Maya.

Nothing.

"You're going to join us at the lodge for Christmas, right?" Hazel smiled as I eventually helped her arrange cookies on decorative platters. "Tommy said he passed along the invitation, and we'd love to have you."

"I, ah..." I tried to figure out how to tell her I wasn't sure of much of anything right now, especially how long I would be staying in Legacy. "I'd like to, but I don't know."

Hazel's smile dimmed. "This have something to do with your grumpy videographer?"

Before I could answer, her phone buzzed. She glanced at it, then suddenly straightened. "Oh! Dang. I just remembered Avery and I promised to help Rosie with something at the ranch. Right this very minute. No time to lose. Adrian, is there any chance you can deliver the cookies to the rec center for us? I can text the Hendersons to meet you there."

"Oh. Well, I—"

Avery looked at her wife like she'd grown a second head. "But Hazel, we—"

"Thanks so much!" Hazel was already grabbing her coat and Avery's and shoving a blanket over the baby on Avery's shoulder. "You're a lifesaver!"

And then they were gone, leaving me alone with three dozen sugar cookies and a growing sense that something weird was happening.

My phone rang, making me jump. But it wasn't Maddox—it was Alex from Timber.

I needed another meddling Marian like a hole in the head.

"Adrian!" Alex said before I could express that. "Thank god you answered. I need backup. Legacy's asshole fire chief just called in another 'random inspection,' and I'm about to lose my fucking mind. Can you come keep me company while he's here and help me not commit homicide?"

"Alex, I really can't. I'm kind of in the middle of—"

"Please? I'll owe you forever. Plus, we have a pizza special today that'll make you forget I owe you one. Pretty please?"

I groaned. "Fine. Give me twenty minutes to deliver these cookies to the rec center, wherever that is."

By the time I'd finished making small talk with the Hendersons and got to Timber, the sun was starting to set. The bar was packed with tourists and locals clearly enjoying the blazing fire and the festive Friday night mood.

"Adrian!" Alex greeted with a bright smile as I slid onto an empty stool. "You made it!"

"I did." I glanced around the bar. "Where's the fire chief?"

"Oh. Right. It was a, um... false alarm," Alex replied, looking sheepish. "Oops. We got our wires crossed."

I raised an eyebrow. "And you didn't think to call back and tell me?"

"Well, I figured if you were already on your way, you might as well stay for some whiskey." He handed me a spiked hot cocoa. "Drink up."

As I sat at the bar sipping my drink, I found myself venting about the morning's events. Alex listened with the patience of a professional bartender, occasionally making sympathetic noises or refilling my mug.

"He said he's furious and disappointed and hurt," I said in a small voice. Just thinking about it made my stomach hurt. "But then he ran off like he immediately assumed the worst, and he hasn't texted me all afternoon."

"So let me get this straight," Alex said when I'd finished. "You turned down your dream job to stay here with Maddox."

"Correct." I took another sip of cocoa.

"But you didn't tell Maddox about the offer *or* turning it down, so he was blindsided when he saw your phone."

"I... I suppose that's one interpretation," I admitted reluctantly. To be fair, I was kind of building up to such a big discussion. Maddox was a little bit like a small animal on the side of the road. One false move and he'd either dart under the tires or disappear into the woods. Either way, I'd lose him.

"And now *you're* assuming the worst of *him*—that he's given up on you without giving you a chance to explain."

I narrowed my eyes. "You're making it sound like I was partly to blame for the miscommunication and that I'm the one jumping to conclusions like an asshole."

He lifted an eyebrow.

"Alex, I texted him asking what was up, begging for a chance to explain, and he put me off till tonight. We were literally in the middle of ordering lunch together when he raced out without a word." I took another sip of the hot drink. "I appreciate his need to cool off before talking, but I've been on edge all day worrying about it."

Alex shot me a look that somehow seemed all-knowing. "It's going to be okay," he said firmly.

I pushed to my feet. "What do you mean? Do you know something?"

He nodded. "I do. And I have a question for you. Have you told Maddox how you feel? Like, specifically?"

I dropped back down. "I've told him I want him. That I... that I have..." I tried to think of the exact words I'd said.

Was *I want you to be my dork* not specific enough?

Alex must have read the truth on my face because his expression turned distinctly amused. "Have you said the words 'I love you, I want to stay here, I choose you over everything else'?"

The question hit me like a slap. "Not exactly."

How could I admit the L-word to *Maddox* when I'd only gotten used to the idea myself? Wasn't it too soon?

"Uh-huh." Alex leaned against the bar. "You know what's not complicated? Telling someone you love them. Everything else is just noise."

"But..."

"And if you love him, Adrian," Alex said softly, "then trust him."

Before I could respond, Tommy Marian appeared beside us like he'd materialized out of thin air.

"Adrian! Perfect. I need you to—"

I shook my head. "No. I'm sorry. No more wild goose chases. If someone needs cookies or a ride or to be saved from a rogue fire inspection, you're gonna need to find someone else. I have to find Maddox. I have to get to—"

"Slingshot Mountain?" Tommy finished. His smile was suspiciously bright. "Good, 'cause I'm here to drive you. To make sure you get there safely."

I frowned. "I can drive myself," I said stupidly.

Alex shook his head. "You're upset, and you've been drinking. You should go with Tommy. Foster kitted out his truck with every winter safety feature known to man."

"It's true." Tommy's cheeks turned pink. "Don't mess with a Wyoming sheriff when it comes to road safety. Apparently."

"I'll be okay," I insisted.

The two of them exchanged a look before Alex said. "What if you need a friend there to drive you home?"

My stomach twisted. "What, like after a breakup? Are you trying to make me cry? Jesus, Alex. Fuck."

He held up his hands, wincing. "That's not what I mean."

Tommy shoved Alex away. "What my insensitive cousin meant was, if you *happen* to meet up with someone else and want to ride home with them, it'd be more convenient if you didn't have your own car. Besides, parking's tight on Starlight Spectacular night."

This made sense, I supposed, but something was definitely off. Mrs. Hoffman's emergency baking situation, Hazel and Avery's sudden departure, Alex's fire-inspection-that-wasn't, and now SERA's medical team lead acting as my chauffeur? I had no clue what was happening, but I also didn't have it in me to protest any further.

"Fine," I sighed. "But I'm probably not staying for the whole thing. I'm not in a festive mood." Especially if my meeting with Maddox didn't go well.

Tommy eyed me carefully. "That's too bad. I thought tonight was supposed to be your twelfth date of Christmas?"

"I thought so, too," I muttered. But I couldn't imagine wanting to film this.

The drive to Slingshot Mountain took twenty minutes on winding roads that were slick with fresh snow. Tommy kept up a steady stream of conversation the whole drive about the Starlight Spectacular—how volunteers spent the whole day tricking out the slope with thousands of colored lights, how magical it looked when it all came together—but I found myself tuning him out as we climbed higher. I was way too anxious to embrace the magic.

When we reached the base of the mountain, though, I was surprised by just how much activity there was, even though the main event didn't start for another hour. Tommy had mentioned a team of volunteers, but there were dozens and dozens of people scattered across the mountain, working with what looked like an elaborate lighting setup.

Way more elaborate than I'd expected, even knowing what a big deal this event was for the town.

"Wow," I said, stepping out of Tommy's truck. "This is really something."

"Yeah, there's a reason why people come from all over to see this. But somehow, I think tonight's Starlight Spectacular will be extra spectacular." Tommy grinned as he shoved a motley collection of hat, scarf, and gloves at me. "Come on, Foster's coordinating from the base lodge. Maybe he knows where your date is."

As we made our way through the crowd, I started recognizing faces. Mrs. Hoffman was there, along with Sadie and Hazel. Even Chief Kincaid was helping string lights, working alongside several firefighters I didn't recognize.

Maya appeared at my elbow, slightly out of breath like she'd been running.

"Adrian! There you are. We've been looking everywhere for you."

"We?"

She gestured vaguely at the crowd. "I mean, ah... *me*. And... well, anyway, come on! You need to check out the view from over there."

I looked around as Maya towed me toward the base lodge, noting the way people kept glancing in my direction and then quickly looking away. The way conversations seemed to stop when I got too close.

"Maya," I said carefully, "what's going on?"

Her eyes went wide with manufactured innocence. "What do you mean? It's just folks getting ready for the Starlight Spectacular. Happens every year."

"Uh-huh. And where is your brother?"

"Maddox? Oh, around here somewhere. Probably helping with the technical stuff. You know how he is with equipment."

The sun had almost completely set now, and the first strings of lights were beginning to flicker on across the slope. But instead of the random twinkling pattern I'd expected from videos of previous years' events, the lights seemed to be forming shapes.

*Letters.*

My heart stopped.

"Maya," I whispered, "what the hell is happening right now?"

She followed my gaze to the mountain, where more and more lights were coming online. The message was becoming clearer with each passing second, spelled out in massive letters across the entire ski slope:

*#TeamMaddrian*

*#RealLifeRomance*

And a final row of lights, almost blinding in their all-caps glory.

*ADRIAN STAY*

"Oh," Maya said with obviously fake surprise. "Would you look at that."

For a split second, I thought this was a poorly timed prank Maya and some of the townspeople had perpetrated. Some new level of matchmaking, maybe.

But then the shadowy figure of a man walked out on the slope. I immediately knew it was Maddox, just from the way he carried himself. But even if I hadn't, I'd have recognized that he was wearing my charcoal wool peacoat, indigo-blue scarf, and the Nordique Chasseur hat with "ultra-luxe earflap" detailing that Maddox had proclaimed "ultra-ridiculous."

"Oh my god," I whispered.

Then Maddox made a slight motion with his hand, and a string of tiny white fairy lights lit up on the front of the coat, spelling out another message.

*I love you.*

I sucked in a breath. *Holy shit.*

He held out his arms to the side so the message was clear to see. And then he shouted.

"Adrian Hayes, I don't need you to stay in Legacy. I need you to stay with me." He brought a hand to his chest and banged a fist over the letter *I*. "I need you here. With me. In my heart. Always. No matter where you go or what you do. This heart is your home now. Do you understand?"

His voice broke before he could say more, but I'd already launched myself toward the slope, barely aware of Maya's delighted, relieved laughter behind me.

Unfortunately, I spent most of my time at sea level, which meant I was heaving from lack of oxygen after running only halfway up the mountain. Thankfully, Maddox had run down to meet me, somehow not falling and turning into a human snowball on the way.

When he finally got to me, I lunged into his arms, knocking him over and shooting fresh powder everywhere.

"I love you, too," I gasped before kissing him. His lips and tongue were warm and sweet. Familiar and exciting at the same time.

Maddox's hands moved up and down my back. When he'd gotten his fill of kisses, he pulled back. "Do you get what I'm trying to tell you, baby? I don't want you to give up your dream for me. I want to be part of it."

"You're the whole dream," I confessed breathlessly. "The entire thing. I'm not giving it up. I finally found it, and I'm not letting it go."

Maddox bit off one of his gloves and pushed damp hair back from my eyes, shoving it under the cap and then caressing the side of my face. The way he looked at me, with raw affection and the banked embers of need, made me even more breathless.

"We can figure it out. Travel together. You know, I happen to know how to work a video camera. I can help with your job. I *want* to."

My heart was hammering in my chest as I grinned down at him. "Yeah? And where would you stay? Solenne would only provide one hotel room…"

His eyes danced in the shifting light from the fairy lights mashed between us. "I guess I'd have to bunk with you, wouldn't I?"

"And what if I didn't want to travel anymore?" I asked softly. "What if I wanted to stay here and work on building out Sullivan Hardware's online presence so that you can have more time for your photography, and I could come home to your mom's lasagna more often?"

"Then that's what we'll do." He tugged on a lock of my hair. "I don't care what our happy ever after looks like, as long as it has you in it."

I leaned down and kissed him again, but it only took half a second before I realized there were catcalls and shouting all around us.

"Fuck," I cried, shoving off him. "I was about to make out with you in front of the entire town."

I reached down to help him to his feet, then began dusting the snow off his chest.

He shot me a teasing grin. "Copping a cheap feel instead?" he teased.

"I'm not stupid," I said with a wink. "Gotta take my moments any way I can."

Maddox looked around us before pulling his glove back on and reaching for my hand. "I think our moment was captured by more than the town," he murmured.

Sure enough, cell phones were raised over people's heads, filming every moment as Maddox and I made our way down the slope. But Maddox didn't seem unhappy about it. If anything, he seemed... satisfied.

"You realize you're going to be immortalized wearing earflaps, right?" I tugged at the edge of the hat. "And I can't believe this coat even fits you." I pushed the scarf aside and spotted a vintage cable-knit Nordique sweater beneath. "Wait, is that...?" My words trailed off as I realized the effort he'd gone to... and why.

"My dad's old sweater." Maddox nodded, his expression relaxed and happy. "I figured there was no better time to pull it out. If I was going to create a viral moment, why not make your sponsor happy?"

"But... this was our moment," I protested. "It was about us."

"It was. It *is*. But it doesn't have to be one or the other," he said softly. He pulled me to a stop beside him, wrapping his arms around my waist. "That's what I was trying to tell you with this." He waved a hand to indicate the mountain, the crowds of smiling tourists and townsfolk, and the two of us. "I know I said a lot of shit about your work when you first came to Legacy—"

"You said the content I created was manufactured moments. And you were right," I admitted. "About some of it, anyway."

"But not all. You do a lot of good, too, baby. You make people feel seen and understood. You bring light and joy to their lives. You sure as fuck did for me." His eyes glowed with love and adoration. "I don't want you to feel like you have to choose between me and your work. I care about your career, too. We can build something together that works for both of us."

I grabbed him by the lapels and kissed him again because I couldn't help it. I was pretty sure the crowd erupted in cheers and applause, but I was too giddy and lost in the moment to care one way or another.

When we finally reached the bottom of the slope, Maya launched herself at both of us, nearly knocking us over again.

"I can't believe we pulled this off!" she cried, bouncing between us. "Your plan rocked, Maddie. Mrs. Hoffman organized the ways to keep Adrian distracted—which was easy, since we already had a group text going from when we canceled all your dates. Foster helped with the lighting crew. Alex handled logistics. Tommy managed transportation—"

"Maya," Maddox interrupted with a laugh. "Breathe."

"And Chief Kincaid!" she continued, ignoring him completely. "He actually volunteered to help with the electrical setup. Said something about making sure nobody burned down the mountain with all those lights."

I glanced around, finally understanding the scope of what had happened. "You planned all this?" I demanded. "You, the man who was determined not to let Legacy matchmake for him, got the entire town involved?"

"Not the *entire* town," Maddox said modestly. "Just... most of it."

Mrs. Hoffman appeared beside us, eyes bright with tears. "Oh, this is better than any Christmas movie I've ever seen!" She pulled out her phone. "I got the whole thing on video. Wait 'til I show the girls at book club!"

Before I could process what was happening, we were surrounded by well-wishers and congratulations. Sadie pressed thermoses of spiked hot chocolate into our hands. Nate slapped Maddox on the back and teased him about "finally growing a pair." Even Chief Kincaid nodded approvingly from across the group, though I noticed he was standing suspiciously close to where Alex, who must've left Timber right after me, was distributing hot drinks.

"How did you come up with this?" I asked as the crowd gradually dispersed to watch the *actual* Starlight Spectacular begin.

"When I saw those texts this morning, I was angry," Maddox admitted. "Hurt, too. I really wish you'd told me about the job offer."

"I should have. I *would* have. But I was scared if I said anything, I'd pop this happy bubble we've been in," I confessed. "It's been a long time since I let myself want something this much."

"Same," Maddox whispered.

"But I need you to know I never would have taken that job without talking to you. You do know that, right?" My gaze searched his.

Maddox frowned. "Of course. Adrian, your manager was giving you shit about *not* taking the job offer. And I know you're half in love with Legacy. You shine here. More than that, I know *you*. I know that's not the kind of man you are." He caught my jaw in one gloved palm. "I just figured if Vic was reminding you of all the reasons you should leave, the least I could do was remind you of the reasons you should stay."

I looked around at the sight—the lights on the slopes set off by snowy trees along the edges, smiling faces and cloudy breaths from nearby laughter, the colorful mix of hats and parkas—before meeting Maddox's eyes. "There are a lot of things worth staying in Legacy for. But the most important one is you." I took a deep breath and repeated the words Alex had given me earlier, words I'd felt in my heart for a week but hadn't been brave enough to speak aloud. "I love you. I want to stay here. I choose you over everything else."

"Fuck, Adrian," Maddox growled.

"Thank you for doing all this," I said, my eyes burning a little. "I've never... I've never had anyone go to so much effort for me. I've never been picked like this before. It..." My throat was too full to continue, so Maddox pulled me in close and tucked my face into his soft scarf.

"You deserve to be picked, Adrian Hayes," he murmured against my ear. "You deserve someone who'll fight for you instead of running away and putting up walls to protect himself. Someone who'll choose you publicly, loudly, without hesitation. And I will pick you every damn time. I promise you."

I kissed him fiercely, sealing our connection, and let myself relax into his embrace as the lights across the mountain began their traditional twinkling pattern, thousands of tiny stars dancing across the slope in synchronized waves.

Despite being surrounded by all of Legacy and their cell phones, all I could see was the man beside me, snowflakes catching in his dark hair, his eyes warm with love and certainty.

"So," I said at length, trying for casual and failing spectacularly. "What happens now?"

"Now?" Maddox pulled me closer, his voice rough with emotion. "Now we go home. Maya's spending the night at Rosie's, which means I have you all to myself. I'm going to make you my grandmother's hot chocolate, we're going to sit by the fire, and you're going to tell me all about how we're going to make this work."

"And if I don't have all the answers yet?"

His smile was soft and certain. "Then we'll figure it out together. That's what partners do."

*Partners.* The word settled in my chest like a promise.

As we made our way to Maddox's truck, my phone buzzed with notification after notification. I didn't bother looking. I knew the videos of our mountain declaration were probably already spreading across social media, hashtag #Maddrian trending alongside #LegacyMontana and #RealLifeRomance.

"Your followers are probably losing their minds," Maddox observed, nodding at the phone buzzing in my pocket.

"Let them." I shrugged. "I've got more important things to focus on."

Three hours later, we were curled up on Maddox's couch, the fire crackling softly while snow continued to fall outside. I was wearing his old flannel shirt and nothing else, completely content to let him trace lazy patterns across my bare thigh while we talked about the future.

"Vic texted again while you were cleaning up in the bathroom," I said, taking a sip of the promised hot chocolate. It was perfect—rich and warming, with just a hint of cayenne heat. "Turns out rejecting Solenne didn't shut out other opportunities the way he expected after all."

"Oh?"

"Three different companies want to partner with me on 'authentic travel experiences.' One of them specifically mentioned that they'd love to feature small-town American destinations." I grinned at his surprised expression. "Apparently, authentic is very *in* right now."

Maddox rolled his eyes, just as I'd known he would.

"And I may have mentioned that I happen to know an incredibly talented videographer who specializes in capturing real moments." I shifted to straddle his lap, loving the way his hands immediately moved to my hips and bare ass. "Someone who could help me tell better stories."

Maddox's eyes darkened. "Is that so?"

"Mmhmm. Guy's got great hands, too. Very... skilled."

"Adrian," he growled, but he was fighting a smile.

"What? I'm talking about your camera work. Your technical abilities." I leaned down to press a kiss to his neck. "Your incredibly professional... equipment handling."

"You're impossible."

"You love it."

"I love you," he corrected, and the simple certainty in his voice made my heart stutter.

"Good," I murmured against his lips. "Because you're stuck with me now. I've got a lease to break, a life to relocate, and a very important job interview to ace."

"Interview?"

I pulled back to meet his eyes. "Sullivan Hardware needs a marketing manager. Someone to handle their online presence, coordinate with influencers, maybe even expand into content creation. I hear the benefits package includes access to the owner's bed."

Maddox's laugh was warm and delighted. "The position might be available. But I should warn you—the boss can be pretty demanding."

"I can handle demanding."

"And I've heard he's grumpy. Very, very grumpy."

"I specialize in grumpy mountain men, actually. It's my niche."

He kissed me then, soft and deep and full of promise. When we broke apart, his forehead rested against mine.

"Are you sure about this?" he asked quietly. "Really sure? Because once you're here, really here, I'm not letting you go."

I thought about the life I was leaving behind—the constant travel, the carefully curated loneliness, the hollow pursuit of likes and follows. Then I thought about waking up in this man's arms every morning, about Maya's laughter, about being part of something as lasting as the nearby mountain.

"I've never been more sure of anything in my life," I said. "Legacy isn't just where I want to be, Maddox. It's *who* I want to be. The best version of myself. The version that belongs to someone and somewhere."

"To me," he said fiercely. "You belong to *me*."

"And you belong to me."

"Always."

Outside, the snow continued to fall, cloaking everything in untouched white. Inside, wrapped in Maddox's arms with the fire warming our skin and love warming our hearts, I finally understood what home felt like.

It felt like forever.

It felt like family.

It felt like the truest, realest, most authentic thing I'd ever experienced in my perfectly curated life.

And for the first time in longer than I could remember, I couldn't wait to see what tomorrow would bring.

#TheRealMaddrian #Stay #ILY #FinallyHome

# EPILOGUE: #ADRIANHAYESSTAYS
## MADDOX - ONE YEAR LATER

THE HISS of the espresso machine in our new coffee corner made me smile as I adjusted the display of Nordique jackets for the third time that morning. A year ago, I'd have laughed at the idea of merchandising eight-hundred-dollar parkas. Now? I wanted every detail of this grand opening to be right.

"Stop fussing," Adrian called from behind the hot chocolate station. "They were perfect twenty minutes ago."

"They were *good* twenty minutes ago," I corrected. "They definitely were not *perfect*."

Maya didn't look up from her livestream. "He's been like this all week," she informed our followers. "Yesterday, he reorganized the socket wrenches because they weren't 'visually compelling.'"

"I'm standing right here," I muttered.

"You were supposed to hear that." Her voice was full of affection—and pride. Home for winter break from UW, she'd slotted back into the rhythm of our little family effortlessly, balancing sass and strategy like a pro. Her "Sullivan Saturday" series had doubled our followers and made her a surprisingly effective brand ambassador, a thing I wouldn't have even known existed a year ago.

"Maddox," Adrian said gently. "Baby. You're stress-organizing again."

I set down the headlamp I hadn't realized I'd picked up and walked over to him, wrapping my arms around his waist. He leaned back against me without missing a beat.

"I'm not nervous," I lied into his Sullivan Hardware hoodie, one of the new ones with the updated logo.

He snorted. "You've been up since five."

"I just want today to go well. This—" I gestured around us. "—this is everything we've worked for."

"And it's already amazing," he said, turning to face me. "Look."

I did as he asked, taking in the space we'd created together. The original Sullivan Hardware section maintained its authentic, old-school charm—the same wooden floors my grandfather had installed, the vintage cash register that still worked perfectly, the wall of family photos documenting four generations of Sullivans serving Legacy. But now, it flowed seamlessly into the expanded section next door, where modern outdoor gear and apparel were displayed alongside curated selections of local artisan goods, hiking maps, and guidebooks to Montana's wilderness areas.

The coffee corner anchored the space with mismatched vintage chairs we'd found at estate sales, local artwork on the walls, and fairy lights strung overhead that cast everything in a warm, welcoming glow. It felt like an extension of our home—authentic and comfortable, but elevated.

Most importantly, it felt like us. Like the life we'd built together.

"See that?" Adrian pointed to a framed photo hanging near the register—one of dozens that now decorated the store, documenting our travels over the past year.

The photos ranged from one of us grinning at the camera from the edge of a cliff in Norway, the Northern Lights painting the sky behind us in impossible shades of green and purple, to one from our trip to Japan in the spring, surrounded by cherry blossoms.

But the photo he was pointing to, the one that always stopped me in my tracks, hung just above the espresso machine. Adrian stood in an Italian olive grove surrounded by ancient trees heavy with fruit, late-afternoon sunlight filtering through the leaves to create dappled patterns across his face and shoulders. He was laughing at something I'd said—probably some stupid joke about olives or Italian pronunciation—and the joy on his face was so vivid, so carefree, that it had taken my breath away when I'd captured it.

The photo had gone massively viral when he'd posted it last summer on his newly named Instagram, @AdrianHayesStays. It had been shared by travel accounts and lifestyle blogs around the world. But for me, it represented something else entirely: the moment I'd realized I was no longer just falling in love with Adrian Hayes but had fallen completely, irrevocably, and *permanently*.

"That one's still my favorite," I murmured.

"I know," Adrian said softly. "You stop and stare at it every time you walk past."

"Can you blame me? You look…"

"Extremely photogenic?" he suggested with a grin.

"Happy," I finished. "Really, genuinely happy. Like you finally found what you were looking for."

His expression softened. "I did. I found you. Found this." He gestured around the store. "Found home."

Before I could kiss him properly—because that look in his eyes demanded he be kissed—Maya cleared her throat loudly.

"As much as I love watching you two be disgustingly cute," she announced, "we have actual work to do. Adrian, the delivery truck just pulled up with the last of the catered food. Maddox, Mrs. Hoffman is here early, and she's already critiquing your menorah display."

"Shit," I muttered, reluctantly releasing Adrian. "I better go deal with that before she reorganizes them again."

"I'll handle the food delivery," Adrian said, pressing a quick kiss to my lips. "Try not to let Mrs. Hoffman give you an anxiety attack before our guests arrive."

As he headed toward the back door, I couldn't help but appreciate the view. A year of regular hiking and outdoor activities, in addition to lifting and hauling deliveries to the store, had added even more definition to his already impressive physique, and the way those jeans hugged his ass was a work of art.

He caught me staring and winked over his shoulder, making me grin like a teenager.

"Ew, gross," Maya commented. "At least pretend to have some dignity."

"Never," I replied cheerfully, heading toward the front of the store where Mrs. Hoffman was indeed examining my menorah display with the intensity of a museum curator.

The next hour passed in a blur of final preparations and the arrival of more friends and family. After greeting everyone for a solid hour, I finally grabbed a cup of my grandmother's hot cocoa and joined Foster and Tommy by the window display.

"This place looks incredible," Foster said, looking around with obvious approval. "You two have really created something special here."

"Thanks," I replied, feeling that familiar flush of pride. "It's been a team effort."

"Speaking of team efforts," Tommy added with a knowing grin, "has anyone seen Chief Kincaid? He said he needed to do a 'routine safety inspection' before the opening."

Maya snorted. "He's in the back room with Alex. Has been for the past twenty minutes. Very thorough inspection, apparently."

Foster and Tommy exchanged amused glances. "You think they realize the only fire danger around here is the sparks flying between the two of them?"

I chuckled, but then I spotted Adrian talking to several people across the room, and my attention caught on him as it usually did.

Watching him discuss the merits of different hiking boots with a family from Colorado, I felt a familiar surge of pride and love. He wasn't Adrian Hayes the brand; he was just *Adrian*, sharing something he cared about with people who appreciated it.

"You're staring again," Maya murmured with her phone held out to capture candid shots of the crowd.

"Can you blame me?" I asked, not bothering to deny it.

"Not really. He does look pretty good in Sullivan Hardware merchandise." She paused her filming to give me a more serious look. "You know, this time last year, I was worried what would happen to you when I left for school. Worried you'd fall into a pattern of working too much and not taking care of yourself."

"And?"

"And I'm really glad I was wrong. Well, you're still a workaholic —both of you are—but you look... lighter. Happier. Like you remember how to have fun again, too." Her smile turned mischievous. "Plus, our online sales have tripled since Adrian took over the marketing strategy, so clearly, this partnership is working out."

"Clearly," I agreed, laughing. "Though I hope you know this partnership includes you. You've worked your ass off helping Adrian build out our online presence."

Her involvement was a topic of constant check-ins, times Adrian or I—or both—reminded her to make time for fun.

Maya's smile was indulgent. "I can tell what you're thinking. I promise I have a life outside of work and school. You've met my friends and seen our Thursday night game nights."

"As long as you're happy," I said, still worrying despite her admonishment.

"I'm happier than I ever imagined. I love what we're doing here, and it makes me proud. I wish Mom and Dad were around to see it."

"Me too. But I agree. They'd be proud of us."

She poked me in the side. "They'd tease you for your social media stardom."

I rolled my eyes. "It's all Adrian. He's impossible not to obsess over. I, of all people, understand why his fans are his fans."

"Please. Half our female followers are here for your grumpy mountain man aesthetic, and the other half are here for the relationship goals content with the two of you."

She wasn't wrong. Adrian's documentation of our life together —both the travel adventures and the quiet domestic moments— had resonated with people in ways I still didn't fully understand. He didn't share everything, of course. Not even most things. He was often too busy enjoying our life to think of making it content. But when he did post photos of us drinking coffee in the morning or assembling furniture for the store expansion, or candid shots of me working on a photography project, they consistently got thousands of likes and hundreds of comments.

"I still don't get why people care so much about our normal, everyday stuff," I admitted. "But I'm happy the income has enabled us to do this expansion."

"They care because it's real," Maya said simply. "In a world full of fake relationships and manufactured content, you two are genuinely happy together. People can tell the difference."

Before I could respond, a commotion near the back of the

store caught my attention. Through the crowd, I spotted Judd Kincaid emerging from the storage room looking slightly rumpled, followed by Alex, whose hair was suspiciously messed up and whose lips looked recently kissed.

"Safety inspection complete!" Kincaid announced to no one in particular, his usual stern expression somewhat undermined by the fact that his shirt was partially untucked.

"Everything... er... passed," Alex added, his cheeks slightly flushed. "After a very... thorough evaluation."

Maya snorted. "Subtle as a brick to the face, those two."

The crowd had grown substantially, with people spilling out of the store and gathering on the sidewalk despite the cold. Adrian had set up the outdoor speakers to play a mix of holiday music, creating a festive atmosphere that drew even more curious passersby.

Maya, Adrian, and I continued to mingle and thank people for coming, stopping to shake hands and accept congratulations from people I'd known my whole life and tourists who'd become customers over the past year. Watching Adrian charm everyone made me strangely proud. Proud to see him so relaxed and comfortable in his own skin, proud of the people of Legacy who'd adopted him even faster than I had, and proud of the open communication we'd established that had allowed us to trust each other.

That trust had allowed me to believe him when he'd stated only a few months ago that he wanted to cut back on travel and focus on building out the store. And because of that trust, he'd believed me when I'd reluctantly admitted to enjoying sharing our lives online.

When everyone was finally gone, including Maya, who I assumed had already gone up to bed, Adrian turned the lock on the door and grinned at me. "Congratulations, Mr. Sullivan. I'd consider that a huge success."

I moved forward and pulled him into my arms. "Same. And we have you to thank. I can't imagine ever doing something this incredible if it hadn't been for your vision."

Adrian's eyes crinkled as he smiled at me. "Sweet talker. Keep going."

I leaned in and kissed him. "How'bout I keep going upstairs in bed. Preferably while you're getting naked."

Adrian's hand moved into the hair at the back of my neck, and he pulled me in for a long kiss. "Not quite yet. First, I need you to find me a three-eighths-inch galvanized hex nut with a locking flange." He pulled back and made a shooing motion toward the nuts-and-bolts aisle.

I blinked at him. "A what?"

"You heard me. Go. The sooner I get my nut, the sooner you can get yours," he said with a wink.

I narrowed my eyes at him but started walking backward toward the necessary aisle. "Since when do you know what a galvanized hex nut with a locking flange is?"

He lifted his eyebrows. "Since I began running a hardware store, that's when. Stop being an ass."

I blew out a huff of air and grumbled as I went to grab what he needed. "What's this for?"

"A permanent solution to an issue I've been having."

"An issue with what?" I called over my shoulder, already scanning the bins out of habit.

He didn't answer.

I crouched down and pulled open the drawer labeled *3/8" Galv Hex Nut—Lock Flange*. Inside, nestled among the dull silver hardware, was a small velvet ring box.

My heart stuttered.

I stared at it for a beat too long before reaching in and picking it up. When I turned around, Adrian was standing a few feet away, suddenly looking less smug and more... terrified.

"I, um—" He cleared his throat. "You once said the secret to making s'mores was to hold on tight and not let go, even when you're scared. And, ah... that's what I want. For us." He swallowed. "Shit. This sounded much better in my head."

I couldn't speak, not even to chuckle at his loss of composure.

Adrian took a shaky breath and stepped closer. "Maddox Sullivan, will you marry me? And keep holding on? Even when it's hard. Even when you're scared. Even when I'm being a dramatic, overaccessorized pain in your ass."

I looked down at the ring box, then back up at him, grinning like a fool.

"Glad you mentioned that last part," I managed, my voice thick. "But yeah. Yeah, I'll marry you. I told you I'd pick you every time, Adrian Hayes."

He exhaled a laugh that cracked into a relieved sob, and when I grabbed him, the ring box bounced to the floor and clattered on the old hardwoods, forgotten for the moment. Because I was kissing my fiancé in the damn nuts-and-bolts aisle—and there wasn't a single part of my life I didn't want to hold on to.

Especially him.

"I love you so fucking much," he said, voice rough against my throat. "I can't believe I get to have this. Have you, and Maya, and... our family here. Just... everything. I'm so fucking happy."

"I love you, too," I agreed, turning his face to kiss his lips before meeting his eyes. "And I will be your family for the rest of our lives. Nothing would make me happier than to share my life with you forever."

Adrian pushed me up against the wall of tiny hardware draw-ers, kissing me deeply and shoving his thigh between mine. When he finally pulled back, his eyes carried the promise of a heat I was desperate to kindle. I just needed to get him upstairs and into our bedroom first.

"C'mon, you promised me a nut," I said, straightening up and adjusting myself.

His face broke into a teasing grin. "I gave you one, jackass. And you dropped it on the floor."

*Shit, the ring.*

I scrambled down to the floor in search of the velvet box. By the time I found it and opened it, Adrian had moved next to me and squatted down on one knee to watch my reaction.

Inside was a black band with an inlay of dark wood. "Holy fuck," I breathed. "It's gorgeous."

"It's tungsten inlaid with old-growth heart pine." He tipped my chin up until I met his eyes. "Taken from one of the planks we had to remove from the shop floor during the expansion. This wood has seen a hundred winters, a thousand boots, and a lifetime's worth of memories of the man I fell in love with. I figured it was an important part of our next chapter."

I was speechless. It didn't surprise me that he'd recognized how important my family's legacy was to me, but I was still bowled over by his thoughtful gesture.

"I don't know what to say," I croaked.

"I just need you to say yes when the officiant asks you a ques-tion one day very soon."

I nodded like a bobblehead as he pulled the ring out of the box and slipped it on my finger. I let out a choked "I love you" again and tackled him to the ground, kissing and hugging him like I'd gone a little bit loopy.

Adrian yanked me up from the floor and began to tug me past

the window displays, through the back room, and up to our apartment.

Outside, snow had begun to fall yet again, covering Legacy in new snow that sparkled under the streetlights. As he pulled me to the bedroom, I realized I had never been happier to be exactly where I was.

"How is it possible to be this happy?" I murmured.

His smile was soft and warm and full of promise, but before he could say anything, he stopped and stared at the small, wrapped present on the end of our neatly made bed.

"What's this?" he asked, turning toward me.

I shrugged, but he could tell from my expression I knew exactly what it was. "Guess you should open it."

"Santa came early, hm?" Adrian picked it up and turned it around, investigating it before beginning to pull apart the wrapping paper.

"At least someone got to come," I teased. "Because I still have plans for you."

Inside was a new framed photo for our wall. A large print of the shot Maya had gotten on our very first date, the one where I had a dot of whipped cream on my nose and Adrian had reached over to wipe it off. The chemistry in that one shot had been enough to catapult us into sudden stardom.

Engraved in the wooden frame at the bottom were the words #FuckRuleThreeForever.

Adrian's eyes filled as he grinned at me. "This is better than my ring. Better than the documentary workshop in Denver Maya and I got you for your birthday. I really need to up my game."

I shook my head and laughed, gently removing the photo and setting it on the nearby dresser. "Baby, if we start keeping score now, we're in trouble."

"I'm going to buy you a house," he insisted.

I reached for the bottom of his hoodie and pulled it up and off him. I couldn't resist staring at my ring as I moved my hands up over his head.

"How about you get me a second one of these rings so I can give it to my boyfriend?" I suggested.

"You mean your *fiancé*," he corrected, lowering his voice until it made the hairs prickle on my scalp.

"My fiancé," I agreed, looking into the blue eyes I adored. "My partner. My love. My home. My favorite holidate."

He snorted, though his eyes were still misty as he caught my hand and pressed a kiss just over my ring. "*Only* holidate."

"Forever-holidate," I whispered, overwhelmed by the certainty in his voice, the solid weight of the ring on my finger, the man in my arms who'd chosen to stay.

Outside, snow continued to fall on Legacy, but inside our little apartment above the business we were building together, everything was warm and right and exactly where it should be.

Adrian's hands found the hem of my shirt, his touch gentle but insistent. "Do you want to come to bed with me, fiancé?"

"I do," I said, and I let him pull me toward our future.

#OneYearLater  #NewDreams  #NutsNBolts  #SullivanHayes #Home

*Want to read more stories set in Legacy? Check out the Made Marian Legacy series here → https://readerlinks.com/l/4975912*

*If you'd like to see a (very) NSFW illustration of how Adrian and Maddox passed the time while snowed in, sign up for my newsletter here → https://readerlinks.com/l/4976327*

*OR if you want to pass on the artwork but still want access to all my freebies, bonus stories and more, you can click here → http://readerlinks. com/l/1444217*

# A LETTER FROM LUCY

Dear Reader,

Thank you for reading *Hashtag Holidate*!

Last year when all of the exciting holiday stories came out, I realized I was missing out on the excitement of writing and releasing a holiday story. I haven't written a holiday-themed novel in four years! It was time to dive back into the spirit of the season.

I knew I wanted my holiday story to be light and fun, but I also wanted it to be a little Hallmark-y, meaning small-town vibes and maybe a fish-out-of water set-up with one of the main characters arriving from out of town.

The decision to set *Hashtag Holiday* in Legacy, Montana, was an easy one. I've been enjoying writing the Made Marian Legacy series in this fictional town, and I knew I wanted to continue fleshing out the town in this holiday novel while also keeping this story as a standalone. I hope you enjoy reading it as much as I enjoyed pulling it together. Maddox and Adrian ended up capturing my attention for longer than I anticipated, and this book became an easy favorite.

Be sure to sign up for my newsletter to get bonus content, sales announcements, and more, including discounts on the next releases! If you're ready for more stories set in Legacy, be sure to check out the Made Marian Legacy series here → https://reader links.com/l/4932758

You can also follow me on your favorite retailer site to be notified of new releases, and look for me on Facebook for sneak peeks of upcoming stories. You can also join me right now on Patreon for exclusive content and behind-the-scenes glimpses.

Please take a moment to write a review of *Hashtag Holidate*. Reviews can make all the difference in helping a book show up in searches.

Feel free to stop by www.LucyLennox.com and drop me a line or visit me on social media. To see inspiration photographs for all my novels, visit my Pinterest boards. The Pinterest board for Hashtag Holidate can be found here → https://www.pinterest.com/lucy_len nox/hashtag-holidate/

Finally, I have a fantastic reader group on Facebook. Join us for exclusive content, early cover reveals, hot pics, and a whole lotta fun. Lucy's Lair can be found here.

Happy reading!
Lucy

# ABOUT LUCY LENNOX

Lucy Lennox is the USA Today bestselling author of over fifty gay romance titles including the GoodReads Hall of Fame winner Wilde Love. Born and raised in the southeast USA, she is finally putting good use to that English Lit degree she earned before the turn of the century.

Lucy enjoys naps, pizza, and procrastinating. She stays up way too late each night reading romance because it's simply the best.

For more information and to stay updated about future releases, sales and audio news and to grab some free and bonus reads, please sign up for Lucy's author <u>newsletter</u> on her website at <u>Lucy-Lennox.com</u> or to stay in the know, join her exciting reader group, <u>Lucy's Lair</u> on Facebook.

facebook.com/lucylennoxmm

instagram.com/lucylennoxmm

amazon.com/Lucy-Lennox/e/B01N0I0YPT

bookbub.com/authors/lucy-lennox

patreon.com/lucylennox

pinterest.com/lucy_lennox

# ALSO BY LUCY LENNOX

Find me online → https://www.lucylennox.com/links/

Read my books:

Made Marian Series

Forever Wilde Series

Aster Valley Series

The Billionaire Brotherhood Series

Made Marian Legacy Series

After Oscar Series (with Molly Maddox)

Twist of Fate Series (with Sloane Kennedy)

Licking Thicket Series (with May Archer)

Champion Security Series (with May Archer)

Honeybridge Series (with May Archer)

Find a complete list of my stand alone romances and novellas at www.LucyLennox.com along with audio samples, freebies, suggested reading order, and more!